One-Hit Wonder

LISA JEWELL

PENGUIN BOOKS

PENGUIN BOOKS

Penguin Books Ltd, 80 Strand, London WC2R 0RL, England
Penguin Putnam Inc., 375 Hudson Street, New York, New York 10014, USA
Penguin Books Australia Ltd, Ringwood, Victoria, Australia
Penguin Books Canada Ltd, 10 Alcorn Avenue, Toronto, Ontario, Canada M4V 3B2
Penguin Books India (P) Ltd, 11, Community Centre,
Panchsheel Park, New Delhi – 110 017, India
Penguin Books (NZ) Ltd, Cnr Rosedale and Airborne Roads,
Albany, Auckland, New Zealand
Penguin Books (South Africa) (Pty) Ltd, 24 Sturdee Avenue,
Rosebank 2196, South Africa

Penguin Books Ltd, Registered Offices: Harmondsworth, Middlesex, England

First published by Penguin 2001

1

Set in 12.5/14.75 Monotype Garamond
Typeset by Rowland Phototypesetting Ltd, Bury St Edmunds, Suffolk
Printed in England by Clays Ltd, St Ives plc

To my mother, Kay, and my father, Anthony,
with deepest love

Ana Wills

12 Main Street

Great Torrington

Devon

EX38 2AE

12th September 1999

Dearest Ana,

I never expected to have a sister. I was eleven years old when you came along and thought that the world revolved around me. Everyone expected me to be so jealous of you but I loved you from the first moment I set eyes on you. You were so tiny and weak in that incubator and I thought that I would die if anything happened to you. I'd just started my periods at the time and I remember thinking how I could have been your mother. When you came home I wanted you all to myself. I thought you were mine. I didn't let Mum get near you. You were so precious and perfect, like a tiny little doll – almost like you were custom-made for my small arms. And you were such a good little girl. So obedient, always happy to tag along with me and run errands for me. You even gave me my name – Bee. I'd always hated Belinda, and then one day you were calling after me and you called out Bee and it stuck. I've been Bee since that day and I can't imagine a time when I was called anything else.

You probably don't remember much about the few years we lived together in Main Street. But I do. I remember everything. And you and I were very close. After Dad left I felt like I was all alone in the world. And then when Mum remarried I felt completely abandoned. Until you came along. You were my little sister and I loved you. I'll never forget your face when I left, the tears running down your cheeks and the way you insisted I take your rabbit, William. Do you remember him? I've still got him, you know. He sleeps beside me, on my

I

pillow. I always used to think he brought me good luck, but I'm not so sure any more . . .

You were four years old when I left and you thought I was abandoning you. I want to explain to you now why I had to leave. Life with Mum was unbearable, obviously, but it wasn't just that. There was so much I wanted to do with my life and none of it was in Devon – it was all in London. But, if I'm to be completely honest with you – and I may as well be, now – I've nothing to lose – the main reason I left was because I was jealous of you. For having Bill. Your very own father. And even when you were tiny you looked just like him and there was this huge bond between you. I had no one. Only Mum and . . . well, you know.

I wanted to be with my father. So I left and went to live with Dad in London, and as much as it broke my heart to leave you behind, it was the best decision I ever made. I loved my father so much, Ana, and I'm in pain thinking about how you must be feeling now, without Bill. He was a wonderful, kind and gracious man. He was gentle and quiet, like you, and I can't tell you how sorry I am for you. I also want you to know that it does get better. The pain does go away. Eventually. It really does. I won't be at the funeral, Ana. It's all too complicated, as I'm sure you're aware, but I want you to know that I'll be thinking about you every single second on Thursday.

I think about you often, Ana. I don't know what you're doing now or who you're with or anything. But I often wish you were here. I should have written before, I know that. We should have kept our bond, but circumstance and Mum and all that stupid ephemeral stuff seems to have got in the way of us being what we used to be – sisters. I'd love it if you came to visit, Ana – came to stay with me. I'm living in a beautiful flat in Belsize Park (that's posh, by the way!) and I've got a cat and a motorbike. I think you'd love London. You were always such a shy little thing. So nervous. Sometimes you need to take yourself out of a familiar situation and throw yourself into the unknown to get to know yourself properly, to find out who you really are. God – listen to me – I'm acting like time stood still after the last time I saw you, like you're still thirteen! You're probably living in New York or trekking through the Himalayas or something right now. But somehow, Ana, I can't quite imagine it . . .

It's hard to imagine at your age, but one day you'll be thirty-six years old – it'll happen before you know it. You won't have any youth left to look forward to – it'll all be behind you and you'll wonder where the hell it went. Don't waste it, please. I've realized that I was never meant to be middle-aged. Every night, when I stand in the bathroom brushing my teeth, I look in the mirror and I cry, because it's the end of another day. It's like a little death, every day. Music doesn't move me any more. Kind words and good friends and happy days don't move me. The thought of the future doesn't move me. There's no magic left in anything. What I'm trying to say is this – youth is so fleeting – now's the time to take risks. Did you keep up your music lessons? The guitar? And singing? You must be so brilliant by now – it wouldn't surprise me if you were a hundred times more talented than me. Well, it wouldn't surprise me if anyone was more talented than me, but that's a different story!

I've changed a lot, Ana, since we last met. I've learned guitar! And I've grown up a lot. I'm not that ambitious, greedy, hard-nosed girl I used to be. Things have happened over the years. Terrible things. Things that change a person beyond recognition. Things that I could never tell anyone about. And I'm humbler now and hopefully I'm nicer, too. God, I'm rambling. Sorry. All I'm trying to say is that I'd love to spend some time with you. Here, in London. I know you probably feel like you don't owe me anything, and you don't. I've been a terrible sister to you – selfish, self-serving, thoughtless. But I've always loved you, and nothing would make me happier than to spend some time with you now. Show you my world and the new, improved Bee. I'd love to see London through your eyes – it might reawaken the magic within me . . . And to get to know you. Yes – mostly, I want to get to know you.

I don't expect to hear from you again. But nothing would make me happier. I want this very much.

3

My thoughts will be with you tomorrow. Please say a prayer for Bill from me.

Your ever-loving sister.

Bee xxxx

Prologue

Bee hissed under her breath at the sack-of-potatoes cab driver sitting there in all his Rothman-breathed, greasy-haired splendour while she hoisted boxes and boxes of stuff from the back of his estate car. Then she turned to hit Mr Arif, the corpulent and slimy property agent who was grinning at her from the front step, with one of her sweetest smiles – when what she actually wanted to do was put his repellent testicles into a Corby Trouser Press and squeeze them till they popped.

It was one of those days. Wild and woolly. The sky was an intense blue and full of overfed clouds being dragged across the sun by an insistent wind, and it was bitterly, almost sadistically, cold.

Mr Arif sucked in his gut to let her squeeze past in the doorway and smiled at her, lasciviously. Bee nearly gagged on the smell of his liberally applied aftershave.

'Maybe, Mr Arif,' she began sweetly, 'it would be easier if you waited for me in the flat.'

'Oh yes, Miss Bearhorn, of course. I will await you. Upstairs.' He backed away, grinning at her as if she was the answer to all his prayers. And in a way, she was. She'd phoned him that morning, asked to see a selection of flats, looked at this one off Baker Street just an hour after their phone conversation, told him she'd take it, gone back to his office, filled in some paperwork, given him cash for three months' rent in advance and was now moving in a mere four hours after first contacting him. He'd probably never had to do so little for his commission.

It really was a bloody miserable flat but with the meter running on the minicab and John threatening to do something unmentionable in his cat box at any minute, time to find the perfect flat hadn't been a luxury available to her. And, besides, she quite liked the anonymity of the area around Baker Street. The blandness of it. There was no 'scene' in Baker Street, no vibe, just streets of blank-faced mansion blocks full of foreigners and retired people. In her current state of mind, Bee wasn't ready to fall in love with a neighbourhood again. And, anyway, this was only going to be temporary, just six months to get her life back together, make some money, and then she might even buy a place somewhere.

An elderly lady with intricately curled silver hair and a tartan-jacketed Dachshund was waiting outside the lift as Bee made her way up with John in his carrier. She smiled at Bee as she pulled open the metal grille and then down at John.

'Well, well, well,' she said, addressing the cat, 'you're a very handsome young man, aren't you?'

Bee smiled at her warmly. Any friend of John's was a friend of hers.

'What a beautiful creature,' the woman said, 'what d'you call him?'

'John.'

'John? Goodness. That's an unusual name for a cat. What type is he?'

Bee stuck a finger between the bars of John's carrier and played with the fluff on his chest. 'He's an English Blue. And he's the best boy in the world. Aren't you, my little angel?' John rubbed himself against her finger, purring loudly.

'And who's this?' Bee asked, addressing the small, bizarrely shaped dog sitting at the old lady's feet. She didn't really want to know but thought it only polite, having discussed her own pet in such detail.

'This is dearest Freddie – named after Freddie Mercury, you know?'

'Really!' exclaimed Bee. 'And, why – er – Freddie Mercury?'

'He loves Queen, would you believe? He can howl his way through the whole of "Bohemian Rhapsody".' She chuckled and eyed her pet affectionately.

Well, thought Bee, you never could tell about people, you really couldn't.

'So, dear. Are you moving in today?'

Bee nodded and smiled. 'Number twenty-seven.'

'Oh good,' said the old lady, 'then we shall be neighbours. I'm at twenty-nine. And it's about time we had a new young person about the place. There's too many old people in this block. It's depressing.'

Bee laughed. 'I wouldn't call myself young.'

'Well, dear – when you get to my age, just about everybody seems young. Alone, are we?'

'I beg your pardon.'

'Are you moving in alone?'

''Fraid so.'

'Oh well. A beautiful young thing like you, I shouldn't imagine you'll be alone for long.' She squeezed Bee's arm with one tiny, crêpey hand and shuffled into the lift. 'Anyway. I'd better get on. It was charming to meet you. My name is Amy, by the way. Amy Tilly-Loubelle.'

'Bee,' said Bee, feeling for once like her name wasn't quite so whimsical, 'Bee Bearhorn.'

'Well – nice to have met you, Bee – and John. See you around.'

Bee smiled to herself at the old lady's closing blast of modern lingo and then the lift creaked and clanked and began its snail's-pace journey back down to the lobby. She walked down the corridor towards number twenty-seven – her new flat.

Mr Arif was sitting on the sofa, going through some paperwork, but stood up abruptly and let his papers fall to the floor when he saw her walk in.

'Oh, no no no no, madam. No no no.' He was crossing his hands in front of his chest and shaking his head, quite violently. 'This is simply not allowed. This animal. It must go. Now.' He pointed at John as if he were a sewer rat.

'But – he's my cat.'

'Madam. I do not care if he is the cat of the Queen. No animals, of any description, allowed in any of my properties. It must go – now.'

'But he's an indoor cat. He's never been outdoors. He's fully house-trained, he's quiet and he doesn't even moult and . . .'

'Madam. I have no interest in the personal character-

8

istics of your animal. All I know is this — it must leave. Now.'

Bee wanted to cry. She wanted to hit Mr Arif. Really hard. In fact, the way she was feeling right now, after the events of last night, she'd really quite like to kill him. With her bare hands. Put her hands around his big squishy neck and squeeze and squeeze and squeeze until he went purple and his eyes started bulging and then . . .

'Miss Bearhorn. Please. Remove this animal. I cannot give you the keys until this animal is gone.'

He's not an animal, she wanted to scream, he's a human being. Bee could feel her temper building, a pounding in her temples, a painful lump in the back of her throat. She took a deep breath.

'Please. Mr Arif.' She perched herself on the edge of the sofa. 'I need time to think. I need . . .'

'Madam. There is no time to think. These keys remain in my pocket until I can no longer see your animal.'

Bee lost her battle to control her anger. 'OK. OK, fine!' She leapt to her feet and grabbed John's carrier by its handle. 'Fine. Forget it then. Forget this flat. I don't like it anyway. I want my money back. Take me to your office and give me my money back.'

Mr Arif smiled at her indulgently. 'May I draw some points to your attention at this moment, most charming Miss Bearhorn. First of all, the contract is signed and your money is on its way to the bank. It is too late for any form of cancellation. And second of all, are you really wanting to take away all of your possessions when you have just this minute carried them up here? Possibly it would be easier to leave your animal with a friend or family?'

Bee looked around her at the piles of boxes and decided that although she'd be more than happy to sacrifice every penny of the cash she'd given Mr Arif in exchange for a place where John would be welcome, she really couldn't stomach the thought of lugging this stuff all the way back downstairs, with Mr Arif watching her with his smug little raisin-eyes, and then having to find another letting agency and look at another flat and go through this rigmarole all over again. So she took a deep breath and decided to lie.

'OK,' she said, 'no problem, Mr Arif. None at all. You're absolutely right. I'll just make a call and find an alternative home for my – er – animal.'

She pulled her mobile phone from her bag and dialled in a made-up number.

'Hi!' she said breezily, to an unavailable tone, 'it's Bee. Are you around? Cool. I need you to do me a favour. Can I leave John with you? I don't know. For a while. Three months at least. Really? You don't mind? God – thank you. That's brilliant. You're a star. I'll be round in about ten minutes. OK. See you then.'

'All is sorted out?'

'Yes,' she beamed, tucking her mobile phone back into her handbag, 'all is sorted out.'

Outside the block, she agreed to meet Mr Arif at his office later to pick up the keys and then watched his huge arse swinging its way back down the street towards his offices in Chiltern Street. She gave his receding back the finger and stuck out her tongue. 'Fucking tossy wankhead arseknob shitbag *cunt*,' she murmured under her breath, before leaning towards the cab driver, who was waiting impatiently for her to unload her last few boxes and pay her fare.

'Hi!' she beamed, switching on the charm, 'there's been a slight change of plan. I need you to drive around the block a bit with my cat.'

'You what?' The fat cab driver looked at her in horror.

'You heard me,' she hissed, 'just take the cat and drive around a bit. I'll meet you back here in half an hour.'

The driver's expression softened when Bee forced three tenners into his sweaty hand. 'There'll be more where that came from when you bring him back. OK?'

'Whatever,' he shrugged, folding up his copy of the *Racing Post*. 'Whatever.'

She slipped John's box on to the passenger seat and tickled him under the chin. 'You be a good boy,' she whispered into his ear, 'I'll see you in half an hour. Be good.' And then she closed the door and felt tears tickling the back of her throat as she watched the car pull away and her beloved cat disappearing into the early evening London traffic.

She sighed and made her way to a Starbucks, where she sat for a few moments sipping an Earl Grey tea and taking stock of what had happened in the last twenty-four hours. Her life, as she knew it, was over. And all she had to show for it was as much as she could fit into the back of an Astra estate. She had no idea why she'd left her flat, no idea what she was doing moving into this one. It was just a gut reaction, really, to what had happened last night. And in a strange way it felt sort of . . . preordained.

After ten minutes she picked up her bag and headed for Mr Arif's office. He looked thrilled to see her *sans* cat and handed over the keys with what seemed to be unbridled joy.

'And may I wish you many, many, *many* years of contentment in your beautiful new home, most charming Miss Bearhorn. I am sure you will be most happy there.'

Bee took the keys and headed wearily for Bickenhall Mansions, thinking that that was very unlikely indeed.

I

August 2000

Ana's train finally arrived in London, an hour after it was due. She stepped from the train while it was still moving and strode out into the sunshine with relief. The train she'd got on at Exeter, the train on which she'd got a seat, the train in which she'd been perfectly happy, had broken down just outside Bristol. They'd had to walk a quarter of a mile then, to the next station, and the next train had already been full when it arrived, so she'd had to stand the whole way from Bristol to London, with her feet trapped between three very large pieces of somebody else's luggage, while the wind whistled through a stuck window, making tangles of her hair.

Ana sometimes wondered if she was cursed. And then she'd wonder, more seriously, if Bee had got all the good luck in her family and left none for her. If that had been Bee sitting on the train just now, everyone would have fallen over themselves to come to her rescue. That was no exaggeration – men and women alike. If Bee had had to get off a train and trudge for a quarter of a mile through the countryside in a heatwave, someone would have offered to carry her bags. Actually, someone would probably have offered to charter a helicopter for her. But really and truly, the thing about Bee was that she wouldn't have been on a defective train in the first place – she'd have been on a train that worked. That was the bottom line.

Ana stood briefly in the middle of the concourse at Paddington, while she considered her next move. The midday sun fell in glittering columns through the glass roof, casting a hot chequerboard on to the marble floor. People walked unnaturally fast, as if they'd been put on the wrong setting. Everyone knew where they were going, what they were doing. Except her. She felt like she'd been sucked into the centre of a huge, swirling vortex. There was a line of sweat rolling down between her breasts.

Ana had no idea how she was going to find Bee's flat. She'd never been to London before and had no mental map to work from. She knew it was divided into north, south, east and west and that a river ran through it. She knew that Bee's flat was somewhere near the centre, somewhere in the vicinity of Oxford Street. But that was as far as her knowledge went. She needed an *A–Z*.

She spotted a W. H. Smith's and walked self-consciously across the marble on her new-born-foal legs. That was the thing with being nearly six foot tall: you ended up looking like one of those fashion illustrations – and it was all very well to look like a fashion illustration if you were just a drawing, but it didn't look nearly so good when you were an actual human being. It looked plain freakish. Ana had suddenly sort of *stretched* when she was twelve, quite dramatically. It had been like a special effect in a horror film – you could almost hear the muscles twanging and the bones creaking as her skinny little girl's body shot up six inches in the space of a year, leaving her with the lankiest, knobbliest limbs ever seen in Devon. People kept telling her that she'd 'fill out' – but she never did. Instead she developed a special way of holding herself, her shoulders hunched forward, her head bowed, curtain-like hair swinging forward to cover her face and a way of dressing – muted colours and flat shoes – in an effort to disguise her height.

Ana looked around her as she walked and realized that women in London looked like newsreaders, or TV presenters, like the sort of women you only ever normally saw on the telly. Their hair was all shiny and dyed interesting shades of blonde and mahogany. They wore tight trousers and strappy dresses and shoes with heels. They had full make-up and all-over tans. Their handbags matched their shoes, their nails were all the same length. They smelled expensive. Even the younger women, the ones in their teens and early twenties, looked somehow *finished*. There were women of all colours and all nationalities, and they all looked fantastically glamorous.

And there were breasts absolutely everywhere – hoisted high in balcony bras, tamed and contoured under tight tops in T-shirt bras, firm and unfettered inside tiny dresses. And nearly all paired up with minuscule bottoms and tiny, taut waists. My God, thought Ana, was having a fabulous pair of breasts a prerequisite in this city? Did they hand them out at Oxford Circus? Ana peered down at the contents of her Lycra top and felt a burn of inadequacy. And then she caught sight of her reflection in the front window of Smith's. Her long, black hair was dirty and tangled, and because she'd left home in such a hurry, the clothes she was wearing had come straight off her bedroom floor – faded black jeans, khaki Lycra top with white deodorant patches under the arms, nubby old black cardi she'd had since she was a teenager and scuffed brown Hush Puppies – the only pair of shoes she owned, because it was next to impossible to get decent shoes in a size eight.

She thought of her mother's parting words to her as she saw her off at the door that morning: 'If you get any spare time at all while you're in London, go shopping, for God's sake, get yourself some decent clothes. You look like a –' she'd searched around for a sufficiently disparaging description, her face crumpled with the effort '– you look like a . . . *dirty lesbian.*'

Her mother might have had a point, Ana conceded. Maybe she should make more of an effort with her appearance. She looked around the concourse and became aware that the only person who seemed to have made less of an effort to look good than she had was a guy sitting cross-legged against the wall with a sandy-coloured dog and a cardboard sign that said 'I Nead Money. Thank You.'

The man who served her in Smith's didn't make any eye contact with Ana, didn't really acknowledge her in any way. In Bideford, in her nearest branch of Smith's, there would have been an attempt at conversation, some inane commentary, a smile. In Bideford Ana would have been expected to give a little of herself back to the assistant, whether she liked it or not, just so as not to be thought rude. She found the lack of interaction pleasantly refreshing.

The Underground map on the back of her newly acquired *A-Z* informed her that it was only two stops to

Baker Street Tube station on the Circle line, and that she wouldn't have to change lines, which came as a great relief to her. She sat, sweating damply on an almost empty Tube for what seemed like only a few seconds and then found her way easily to Bickenhall Street, a short road filled with faintly menacing red brick apartment blocks, seven storeys high.

Bickenhall Mansions came as a complete shock to her. When she'd looked at Bee's address for the first time this morning and seen the word 'mansion', she'd thought, without surprise, that Bee must have been living in some great detached pile of a building, with security gates and a driveway. But these were just flats. She felt all her other expectations about Bee's lifestyle – housekeepers, health spas and charity do's – drop down a notch or two, proportionately.

She perched herself on the stairs in front of the block and nibbled her fingernails nervously, watching the world go by. Tourists; business people; girls in trendy trouser suits; couriers on huge motorbikes. Not an old person in sight. Not like Bideford, where the OAPs outnumbered the youthful by three to one.

'Miss Wills.' She jumped as someone loomed into view and boomed at her. A large hand with fat knuckles and a big gold ring was thrust towards her. She shook it. It was a bit clammy and felt like a squidged-up shammy leather.

'Hello,' she said, getting to her feet and picking up her bag. 'Mr Arif?'

'Well, which other people do you know who might know you by your name in the middle of the street, young lady?'

He laughed, a pantomime laugh, amused by his own humour, and let them into the building. He was quite short and quite wide and had a very large behind. The fabric of his trousers was silky and thin and Ana could clearly see the outline of a pair of unappetizingly small briefs digging into his fleshy buttocks.

He was highly aromatic, and as the doors closed on the coffin-sized lift, Ana was enveloped in a rich and pungent cloud of perfume. The lift clunked loudly as it finally hit the third floor, and Mr Arif pulled open the brass grille to let Ana out. He gestured expansively at front doors as they walked down a broad, dimly lit corridor that smelled faintly of gravy and old mops.

'These, all my flats – all short term – but all fully rented – 365 days a year. Here. Here and here. Famous London Stage Actress, here. Here – a lord. There – an MP.'

Ana didn't really have any idea what he was talking about but she nodded politely anyway.

Mr Arif slipped a key from a very large bunch into the lock of flat number twenty-seven, swung open the door and flicked on the light switch.

'Here all day with the police and such and who knows what on the day that we found her. A bad day. A very bad day. Four days she'd been here. In this heat. You can still smell it.' He twitched his nostrils and his large moustache quivered. 'Breathe in deep like so, and the stench – it is still there.' He jabbed at his throat with the side of his hand to demonstrate exactly where the stench was and began heaving open grimy sash windows at the other end of the room, holding a monogrammed handkerchief over his mouth.

'How is this, that a woman as beautiful' – he pointed at a framed poster of Bee on the wall – 'could be dead and nobody be knowing this thing? How is it that I, her landlord, come to be the one to be finding her? *I* am not her friend. *I* am not her lover. *I* am not her family. I am her landlord. This – this is not right.'

He shook his head from side to side for a good twenty seconds, allowing time for the not-rightness of the situation to be fully absorbed, his body language implicitly informing her that in his culture this sort of thing would not be allowed to happen. Ana gently placed her bag on the floor, and stared in wonder at the photo of Bee on the wall, realizing with a jolt that she'd almost forgotten what her sister looked like.

'So.' He clapped his hands together and then rubbed them, his flesh squishing together like bread dough. 'The cleaners are arriving at nine o'clock tomorrow morning. By this time all extraneous matter to be removed. I have famous Royal Ballerina moving in on Saturday morning. All has to be perfect. Your beautiful sister has not left you a very great task. Your beautiful sister has not very many possessions.' He laughed again, that pantomime laugh, and then stopped abruptly. 'Here is the inventory. You will be needing this so you are not taking away the property of the – er – property. Unfortunately, Madam, I am not able to leave you with a key, but if you are needing to go outside, the porter knows you are here and will allow you to move freely. And now I leave.' And he did, shaking her once more briskly and damply by the hand and clip-clopping away down the long corridor in two-tone slip-on shoes.

Ana pulled the door closed behind her and breathed a sigh of relief. She turned and flicked the security lock on the front door and then she stood for a moment or two and stared around her.

So. This was Bee's flat. It wasn't what she'd imagined. She'd imagined brightly painted walls and huge scarlet sofas, Warhol-type prints of Bee on the walls, lava lamps, mirror balls and lots of generally eclectic, groovy, colourful funkiness. She'd imagined that Bee's flat would be an extension of her and her outrageous personality. But mainly, when she'd thought of Bee's flat, she'd imagined it full of people. And, more specifically, she'd imagined it with Bee in it – her red lips parting every few seconds to uncover those big white teeth; her smile carving dimples into her cheeks; her black bobbed hair swinging glossily back and forth. Talking too much. Smoking too much. Laughing like a drain. Being the centre of attention.

Alive.

What surrounded her, instead, was the somewhat dreary, beigey, dusty flat of an elderly, widowed gentleman. The walls were papered with a faded but expensive-looking embossed floral design. The furniture was reproduction in dark mahogany and teak. In one corner stood an ornate birdcage filled with junk. The net curtains were yellowing.

She began slowly to walk around. The flat was huge. The ceilings were at least ten foot tall, the rooms extremely large. But in spite of so much space it still seemed oppressive. The buzz of city life floated in through the open windows but was somehow muted, as if the volume had been turned right down.

Nailed to the wall of the hallway was a gold disc in a heavy glass frame. Ana squinted to read the inscription:

'GROOVIN' FOR LONDON' BY BEE BEARHORN.
ELECTROGRAM RECORDS © 1985
PRESENTED TO BEE BEARHORN IN RECOGNITION OF SALES OF
750,000 DISCS

A door on Ana's right was open, revealing the bathroom. The suite was a pale, minty green with heavy Deco taps of chrome. The floor was grey linoleum, the window dimpled and opaque, surrounding a cobwebbed windmill vent creaking slowly round and round, as if someone had only just left the room. Ana shivered.

Further down the hallway was a closed door with a large cartoon bumble bee pinned on to it. It had a bubble, attached by a wire, coming from its mouth that said 'Bzzzzzzz'. Bee's bedroom.

Ana put her hands to the door and felt chilled suddenly, almost as if Bee's body would still be lying there on her bed where she'd been found three weeks ago, as if the floor would be littered with pills and capsules, the room buzzing with flies. She pushed the door open slowly, her breathing suspended momentarily. The curtains in the room were closed but for a tiny gap of an inch or two letting in a bright slice of daylight that fell across the huge double bed and the wooden floor, dividing the room in two. Shapes loomed out of the overcast shadows at Ana, and there was an odd smell in the room. She put her hand over her mouth and nose and glanced around the room again before reaching around the corner of the door and feeling for a light switch.

21

She hit the switch, looked around the room and then released a blood-curdling yell when she saw a small woman with a black bob and red lipstick standing in the corner of the room.

It was a cardboard cut-out. Of Bee. Ana put her hand to her galloping heart and slumped against a wall with relief. It was a stupid life-size cardboard cut-out, a promotional thing for 'Groovin' for London'. She remembered seeing one in Woolworths back in 1985 when she was only ten years old and the single had just come out, and wishing that she could have one to take home with her. Bee was wearing a black-leather minidress with a huge silver belt draped around her waist and big platform shoes. She had her arms folded across her waist and one finger touching her mouth, and was staring at the camera as if she'd just shagged it. She looked quite ridiculous, and Ana couldn't help thinking that Bee was probably the only person she knew (apart from her mother) who would have felt comfortable sleeping in the same room as a giant great cardboard cut-out of themselves.

Ana thought back to that afternoon in Woolworths all those years ago, when she'd first seen the cut-out and had realized, probably for the first time, just exactly how famous her sister actually was. She'd blushed when she'd seen it and looked around her to see if anyone had noticed, and she'd had to bite her lip to stop herself shouting out to anyone who'd listen, 'That's my sister – *that's my sister!*'

1985 was one of the most exciting years of Ana's life – the year that Bee had become famous. She'd signed a huge record deal at the start of the year and was marketed heavily as the British answer to Madonna, but nobody could have been prepared for the ensuing phenomenon. 'Groovin' for London', a virulently catchy dance song, went straight into the charts at number one and stayed there for five weeks, and suddenly Bee's face was everywhere. For over a year Ana basked in Bee's reflected glory. She was the most popular girl at school. Even the older kids knew exactly who she was. She was Bee Bearhorn's sister. Like – how cool was that? When Bee's second single failed to make an impact on the charts four months later, Ana's status as Most Interesting Person in School started to look a bit shaky. And when her third single was released and greeted with critical derision – the general consensus was that it was the most abysmal record of the year – barely grazed the top fifty and then disappeared without trace, Bee Bearhorn came to be seen as just another naff one-hit wonder of the Eighties and Ana's relationship to her became more of a hindrance than a social advantage. The crueller girls at her school used the disastrous – and very public – disintegration of Bee's career as fuel to bully Ana, and for the rest of her schooldays Ana was commonly known as One-Hit Wonder Wills.

The bedroom Ana now found herself in was vast. It had two large sash windows and an enormous double bed, which had been stripped of all its clothing except for a large piece of what looked like cashmere in electric pink, folded at the foot of the bed. A lime-green feather boa was draped across the bed head and the windows were framed with multicoloured fairy lights. The floorboards were painted sky blue. This was much more the sort of room Ana had expected Bee to have been living in. Ironic that it should be the room in which she died.

Ana touched the naked mattress first, gently, with her fingertips, before sitting down on it. The bed was soft and saggy and made an odd twanging sound as she sat. She picked up the soft, pink cashmere blanket and brought it to her nose. It smelled a bit musty, with undertones of some grapefruity, appley perfume.

And there, perched on a pillow and much to Ana's surprise, sat William. He was older and more threadbare than Ana remembered him, but it was definitely him – a small, knitted rabbit in blue dungarees, clutching a carrot between his front paws. She'd given him to Bee when she'd told her she was leaving home, age fifteen. Ana had been only four at the time, but she remembered the moment vividly, remembered Bee's lacy, fingerless Madonna gloves and the smell of Anaïs Anaïs when Bee had held her in her arms and told her not to say a word to their mother. She remembered Bee trying to give him back to her, saying, 'I can't take William, he's your favourite,' and herself forcing him back into Bee's hands, as serious as anything. 'No, Be-Be, you have William. I've got Mummy.'

Ana picked him up and looked at him in wonder. Bee had kept William. For twenty years. And not only had she kept him, but she'd kept him on her pillow. Where she slept. He'd been there when she died. He'd seen it all.

'Here, William,' Ana whispered into his velvet-lined ear, 'tell me – whatever happened to Bee Bearhorn?'

2

Although Bee was her half-sister, Ana tended to think of her as more of a sixteenth-sister, or a sixty-fourth-sister, or even, to put it decimally, a nought-point-nought-nought-nought-one-per-cent-sister. Other times she felt as if Bee was a dream, someone that Ana had made up.

In the age of the disintegration of the traditional family unit, Ana's family had somehow managed to be even more complicated and unconventional than most. Ana's mother Gay married Gregor Bearhorn in 1963 and had a baby, Belinda. Gregor gave into his long-repressed but ultimately uncontrollable homosexual urges and left Gay in 1971. Gay was married again, to Bill, a retired headmaster twenty-two years her senior, in 1974. A second daughter, Anabella – or Ana as she would later wish to be known – was born in 1975 (Anabella and Belinda – Ana occasionally thought that her mother would rather have given birth to a pair of Bijon Frises) and Bee left home four years later to join her father Gregor in London. He died in 1988. And so did Bill, in 1999.

As convoluted as this state of affairs had become, it had all started off in a fairly straightforward manner. Ana's mother, a budding actress, had met Gregor, the burly young director at her local theatre, when she was twenty-two. They married, they honeymooned on the Amalfi coast, they drove a racing green Morgan, they had raucous parties and they lived in a cosy state of mild, middle-class bohemia. And then Gay got pregnant and everything started to go wrong.

Gay suffered six long months of terrible post-natal depression, brought about mainly by the physical horror of what pregnancy and childbirth had done to her previously immaculate little body, the shock of her sudden lack of independence and the abrupt end to her dreams of being a famous stage actress. Gay failed to bond with her first-born and became neurotic, bitter and miserable. Consequently, Bee became a rebel, and her husband finally emerged from the closet and ran away to London to pursue his career and a young man called Joe.

Even in their small Devon town, nobody had been particularly surprised by the news. The colourful, neckerchief-wearing giant of a man had always been suspected of being a little bit *that way inclined*. But Gay had been so distressed that she hadn't left the house for a month and had dressed entirely in black for the rest of the year. She married Bill three years later, for reasons of practicality and companionship rather than romance, who'd known her since she was a child. Ana was born nine months later, when Gay was thirty-six and Bill was fifty-eight and the late-in-life arrival was the talk of the village.

Bill was eighty-two when he'd died of a heart attack ten months ago – a good innings in most people's books, but tragically young as far as Ana was concerned. She missed him so much that bits of her ached.

Gay maintained that she missed him, too. Every now and then her kohl-lined eyes would fill with tears and she'd look pensively into the distance and whisper her late husband's name desperately, under her breath. 'Bill,' she'd breathe, and then abruptly busy herself with something else. She'd been robbed – *robbed* – of the finest man in all the world. Her Bill. Her wonderful, kind, loving Bill, who'd put her on a pedestal and denied her nothing – which was quite funny really, Ana thought, given the fact that she'd been a complete bitch to him while he'd been alive.

Gay had never really got over the departure of her glamorous, talented and gruffly handsome first husband and had always seen Bill very much as a consolation prize. But as wonderful and unusual as Bill might have been, he was still just a man, and had loved his beautiful Gay to the point of spoiling her, shell-shocked until the end that he'd ever managed to persuade a woman like her to marry a 'wrinkly old beanpole' like him.

Bill wasn't alone in his adoration of his wife. Everyone in Torrington loved Gay Wills. Ruddy-cheeked gentlemen who remembered Gay as a young girl, the town beauty who looked like Elizabeth Taylor, with her hand-span waist, gleaming black hair and violet eyes. Before she'd become agoraphobic she'd been a familiar sight in Great Torrington, spinning around the town on her old black pushbike, a basket full of flowers draped artfully across the handlebars, embroidered skirt flapping about in the breeze, rising tantalizingly to mid-thigh every now and then. She was a woman who knew exactly the effect she had on men and played it up to the max – she was only happy if there was at least one person miserably in love with her. She was charm personified. A bit scatty – yes.

A bit odd sometimes – undeniably. But such a beautiful, charming, engaging woman. Really. An angel. A delight. To everyone.

Except her children.

'Really, Anabella,' she would often sigh in exasperation, 'how a girl as unattractive as you could possibly have come from my body, I have no idea. That's the risk one takes when one mixes one's genes with a man's, I suppose. You never know *what's* going to emerge.'

Gay didn't say things like this intentionally to upset Ana – she genuinely didn't see that there was anything wrong with what she was saying. As far as she was concerned, it was just a statement of fact. Gay was far too wrapped up in the Wonderful World of Gay Wills to realize the implications or consequences of her comments. She had much more important things to worry about than her daughter's feelings – things like picking leaves off the lawn in their back garden by hand, one by one, or embroidering cushions with Turner landscapes, or obsessively counting every last calorie she consumed in a day to ensure that her intake never exceeded 1,500.

As well as her basic agoraphobia, which had set in shortly after Gregor's funeral in 1988, Gay seemed to develop a new neurosis every day and now refused to answer the phone, answer the doorbell unless she was expecting a visit, eat red meat, drink tap water, take off her shoes except to go to bed, touch anyone she didn't know, allow any animals in the house, use the Hoover, the dishwasher, the microwave or the tumble-drier (though she did still use the washing-machine) or comb her hair with anything other than the old horsehair brush that used to belong to her grandmother and smelled disgusting. She also had some strange little rituals, like having to walk across the living room with the same amount of footsteps each time, having to water the houseplants in exactly the same order every day and wearing the same seven cardigans in weekly rotation; and the slightest interruption to any of these practices could send her over the edge into a momentary hysteria.

Ana had moved back home last year, shortly after Bill's funeral, and she'd soon become accustomed to these 'quirks' in her mother's behaviour, mainly because they really didn't impinge on her very much. She wasn't expected to do anything more than let Gay get on with it and not disturb her more than necessary. All Gay asked from Ana was that she drive into Bideford once a week to do the big shop, that she pick up odds and ends from town occasionally and that she answer the telephone when it rang. As long as Ana did this, then Gay really couldn't have cared less about her, about what she was up to, what she was thinking, who she was seeing or where her life was going. She'd sometimes look startled to see Ana in the house, almost as if she'd forgotten that she lived there, and Ana couldn't really blame her for this as she herself often wondered whether or not she actually existed . . .

Ana's memories of Bee were all very fuzzy and imbued with a kind of Technicolored, high-octane aura of dimples-hair-and-boobs, turning-a-drama-into-a-crisis, look-at-me-look-at-me-type behaviour. When Bee was a teenager, she was all fingerless gloves, pink hair, cigarettes and boys. After she left home and moved to London she was all studied cool, avant-garde make-up and raw, gauche ambition. And from the day she became famous, in 1985, she was all rush-rush-rush, coffee-fag-coffee, this-flight-that-interview-the-other-TV-show, excuse-me-do-I-know-you-oh-you're-my-mother-I-thought-I-recognized-you-and-who-is-this-strange-skinny-tall-person-oh-yes-that's-right-you're-my-sister disregard.

Ana's feelings towards Bee had always been enormously ambivalent. On the one hand she found her quite fascinating. Bee was a mesmerizing person who could make your day complete by smiling at you. When Bee was in a room, nobody else existed. She was captivatingly beautiful and could be extremely amusing if the mood took her. But on the other hand, Ana had always found Bee frustratingly shallow and occasionally downright cruel. Her nickname for Ana when she was a child was 'the Twiglet', a reference to her knobbly knees and bony arms, and after her sudden growth-spurt at twelve, Bee started calling her 'the Towering Twiglet'. Some people might think that was cute – funny, even – Gay certainly appeared to, and Bee thought it was *hysterical*. But not Ana. Ana spent her whole life trying not to draw attention to her height, and it took just one 'Towering Twiglet' comment from Bee for Ana to feel a complete freak.

Bee had always refused to come home to Devon after she'd left, not even for Christmas or birthdays, claiming that the mere thought of the place brought her close to a panic attack, while Gay, conversely, had a fervent hatred for London, which had been brewing and bubbling ever since Gregor had left her for the temptations of the big city. She talked of London disparagingly, as if it were some great brassy harlot with badly dyed hair and a whiff of fish about it.

So, as some kind of desperate compromise, Ana and her family would traipse all the way to Bath or Bristol to meet Bee for rushed meetings in smoky bars, when the conversation would be invariably tense and occasionally fractious, particularly at their very last meeting, in the summer of '88. Ana hadn't known at the time that it was going to be the last time she saw her sister, and maybe if she had, she'd have appreciated the experience a little more than she did. Because within three weeks, Gregor was dead, and Gay and Bee had fallen out completely and irretrievably.

3

July 1988

The Catacomb was a Goth club in the centre of Bristol. Gay, Bill and Ana were here in the middle of the day – which was strange in itself, as it was a venue quite obviously not designed to be seen during daylight hours. Ana could imagine that at night the purple velvet pinned to the walls, the towering candelabras full of molten church candles and the fluorescent rubber bats stuck to the ceiling might have made for quite an eerie atmosphere. At two in the afternoon, however, the place looked scabby and naff.

'Hi, Bill.' Bee stretched on to her tiptoes and kissed Bill on the cheek, leaving a streak of oxblood lipstick on his cheek.

'Hello there, Belinda – and don't you look marvellous?' He held her hands and appraised her. She was wearing a skin-tight Lycra panelled dress that came almost up to her crotch, towering Vivienne Westwood platforms fastened with ribbons, and her sleek hair was greased back off her face. She looked like one of the girls in the 'Addicted to Love' video.

'Thank you,' she smiled, giving him a little curtsey, 'and you're looking rather lovely yourself, if you don't mind me saying.'

Bill scoffed pleasurably.

'*Twiglet!*' Bee exclaimed, noticing Ana skulking behind her father. 'How's my skinny-minny?'

Ana smiled reluctantly and leaned down to kiss her big sister. 'I'm all right,' she murmured, feeling a blush forming on her face and shoving her hands into the pockets of the sensible twill skirt her mother had bought her from Long Tall Sally.

'Jesus, you are getting *so tall*,' she said, appraising Ana at arm's length. 'You'll never find a boyfriend now, you know – men *hate* tall girls – they make them feel inadequate.' She winked, to let Ana know that she was only joking, but it was too late – her words had already left a brand on Ana's fragile soul. 'Mum,' she said, turning to Gay, who was waiting impatiently in line, wearing her new green suit, 'how are you?'

Gay offered up her cheek for Bee to kiss. 'Tired,' she said, 'exhausted. The traffic. Terrible. And this heat.' She flapped at her face with her hand, and Bill immediately strode off to find a chair for her.

Gay sat down primly on the chair that Bill had brought her and looked round the club with undisguised disgust. 'And *what*,' she began disdainfully, 'could you possibly be doing in a place like this?'

'Oh – don't start, Mum. Please. I've had a bad week. Can't we just have a nice time for once? This place belongs to a friend, OK? A very kind, very wonderful friend who has also lost someone to AIDS, who is about the only person who can make me smile at the moment and who I happen to be staying with tonight.

'Bill,' she said turning to her stepfather and clapping her

hands together, 'let me get you a drink. What would you like?'

'Oh – just a soft drink for me, Belinda. I'm driving. A lemonade or something.'

'Twiglet?'

Ana looked at her and shrugged. 'I don't mind,' she said, forcing a smile, 'anything.'

'Er, right – OK.' Bee grimaced at her sideways and Ana felt herself die a little inside. She never knew what to say to Bee. That was the trouble. She was always worried she was going to say something stupid or embarrassing. So she usually ended up saying nothing at all – which was just as bad, because then Bee just thought she was an illiterate cretin. And Bee was so beautiful, thought Ana. Look at her. Those huge eyes, framed by thick lashes. And her tiny little nose. Ana would have quite happily killed for that nose. Sometimes she'd play around in the mirror at home, trying to see what she'd look like with a little nose like Bee's. She'd already decided she was going to get a part-time job the moment she turned fifteen and she was going to save up every penny and have a nose job. And when she did, she'd take in a picture of Bee and tell the surgeon, 'I want *that* nose.'

And her breasts. Round and creamy, tucked into her tight Lycra dress. Why? thought Ana, staring at them with a gut-churning envy, *why*? Same mother. Same gene pool. Same chances of being petite and big-bosomed and pretty. But no, she thought, looking resentfully at her father, I get to look like Bill Wills.

Bee handed Ana a can of Coke with a straw in it and smiled at her. Ana smiled back tightly.

'How's your father?' Gay asked, in a tone of voice that suggested she was secretly hoping that Bee would say he was dead.

Bee sighed and leaned back against the chipped black bar. 'Bad,' she said, 'very bad. He's been talking about the hospice.'

'Hospice?'

'Yes. The place in St John's Wood. You know.'

Gay nodded sagely and pursed her lips.

Ana took a slurp of her Coke and wondered what a hospice was.

'So, Twiglet,' said Bee, changing the subject and turning towards her, 'what've you been up to?'

Ana shrugged. 'Nothing much,' she said, 'you know, just school and stuff.'

'How are the guitar lessons going?' Bee mimed strumming a guitar.

'Good,' said Ana, relaxing a little now that they were discussing her favourite thing in the world, 'I just mastered the bar chord.'

Bee looked at her blankly and Ana felt a small stab of disappointment. She'd been hoping that Bee would have been impressed by her achievement – Bee was supposed to be the famous pop star – but she couldn't play an instrument to save her life. 'Cool,' said Bee, pulling open a packet of Camels and offering one to Bill, before slipping one out and lighting it. 'And boys,' she said, winking at Ana, 'tell me about boys.'

Oh God. Ana hated it when Bee did this – this teasing thing. A blush started percolating in her chest and rose steadily and hotly to her cheeks. 'There's nothing to tell,' she managed to stutter.

'Oh, come on now' – Bee exhaled a cloud of smoke – 'you're . . . what are you now? Thirteen? Fourteen?'

'Thirteen,' muttered Ana, 'I'm thirteen.'

'Thirteen years old. You must be – you know – getting all hormonal about now. No? Getting a bit restless in the old *downstairs* department?'

Ana's flush went up a few ratchets and she looked at her father desperately to rescue her from this humiliation, but he just smiled at her benignly as if to say, 'Isn't she a hoot?'

'Oh my God – look at the colour of you!' shrieked Bee, 'there must be something going on. Who is he? Go on – you can tell me –'

'No one,' muttered Ana hotly, 'there's no one.'

Bee grinned wickedly, licked her finger and rested it against Ana's cheek. 'Szzzzz,' she hissed, and tossed her head back to laugh.

Ana pushed her hand away and grimaced at her. And then Bee turned to talk to Gay, her interaction with Ana officially over. That's all it ever consisted of – a brief moment of humiliation before going back to more grown-up matters. Ana watched her as she chatted with Gay and Bill, about Gregor, about what she was going to do when he'd passed away, about her career, and she noticed that Bee seemed different somehow. There were circles under her eyes, her hair needed a trim, there was a small outbreak of spots around her mouth, and her body, although as lithe and firm and trim as ever, was sort of *tired*-looking – her shoulders slumped, her spine curved. And she was thinner. And she looked . . . older. Much much older. Everything about her seemed forced, unnatural, like she was putting on a show.

Ana felt suddenly overcome by a desire to ask her how she was – *how are you, Bee?* – but she knew there was no way she'd ever ask her. Bee would just look at her like she was insane and say something to make her feel ridiculous for ever having considered her state of mind.

The guy washing glasses behind the bar, whose peroxide hair was interwoven with little purple tufts and who was wearing black lipstick and had a metal spike growing out of his eyebrow, handed Bee a cocktail. She picked it up, and as she brought it to her lips Ana noticed her hands shaking. Maybe she was having a nervous breakdown, she pondered. Ana had just found out about nervous breakdowns – everyone else seemed to be having them, particularly Americans. Or maybe she was on drugs. That made your hands shake, didn't it? And it made your skin bad and made you lose weight and gave you circles under your eyes. Ana watched her sister, mesmerized. Was it possible, she thought, that Bee was a drug addict? It wouldn't surprise her. There'd been one time, a couple of years ago, when they'd been to see Bee in Swindon and she'd smoked marijuana – *in front of them*! Ana had thought it was just a funny-looking cigarette at first, and then she'd noticed that it smelled really weird, and then her mother had said, 'Belinda – I hope that's not *marijuana* you're smoking,' and Bee had said 'Don't be stupid, it's just a herbal cigarette,' and Gay had said 'Do you think I was born yesterday – I was alive in the Sixties, you know – I know about these things.' Bee had just raised an eyebrow at her and handed the 'cigarette' on to some bloke who was wearing a dress. And they said, didn't they, that smoking pot could lead on to other things – harder drugs – like *heroin*. A shiver ran down Ana's spine as she pictured Bee lying on a concrete floor in a windowless council flat, sticking a syringe into her arm. Ana might live in a sleepy, middle-class Devon town, she mused, but she'd seen *Made In Britain*. She knew a bit about how the world worked . . .

The conversation between Bee and Gay was becoming predictably fractious, and Ana pulled herself from her day-dreams.

They were talking about this 'hospice' that Gregor was apparently going to be staying in. Ana presumed it was a kind of hospital. Bee had finished her cocktail and banged the empty glass down on the bar in response to something Gay had just said. 'It's all about you, you, you, isn't it, mum? My father is *dying*, for fuck's sake.'

'Yes,' sniffed Gay, 'and whose fault is that? Hmm?'

Bee pulled another cigarette from the packet and began pointing it at Gay like a fencing foil before sticking it in her mouth and allowing Bill to light it for her. 'You make me sick. D'you know that?'

Ana gulped. It didn't matter how many times this happened, it always got to her. And it didn't matter how many times this happened, she always expected the next time to be different. She'd day-dream for weeks in advance about these meetings. This time, she'd think to herself, Mum will be in a really good mood and she won't start in on Bee, and we'll all get on really well, and me and Bee will talk. And this time I'll make Bee laugh and tell her funny stories about school and show her how well I can play guitar, and she'll tell me stories, too, about famous pop stars and *Top of the Pops* and first-class flights to New York. And this time we'll all go out for lunch somewhere, and I'll have a glass of wine and we'll have fun, and when we get into the car to go home we'll all hug Bee and she'll look really sad to see us go. And this time Bee will say, 'Why don't I come home next time? Why don't I come and stay at Main Street? And then we can have a proper time together and take Tommy for a walk and wear sloppy socks and cook together.' And then, thought Ana, maybe I won't feel so lonely any more . . .

'Look – can we just change the subject, Mum. I really can't take your shit at the moment.'

'Oh yes, of course. It must be terribly hard for you having to cope with all your father's money and his enormous house . . .'

'It's not a house – it's a flat.'

'. . . and having nothing to do all day long. You wait – one day you'll be my age, then you'll understand what it's like to have a hard life. Imagine – surviving on a *teacher's pension*.' She spat out the words and flicked a spiteful look at Bill. 'Imagine not being able to go shopping for designer clothes whenever you feel like it. Imagine being *me*, Belinda . . .'

'Oh *God*.' Bee slapped her forehead in frustration. 'Bill,' she beseeched, 'how do you put up with this? *Why* do you put up with this? Run away,' she teased, 'run away now . . .'

Bill smiled at her impotently and scratched the back of his neck. Ana stared at Bee desperately, drinking her Coke, trying to send her telepathic messages that she was on her side and wishing more than anything that Bee and her mother could be friends so that she could actually enjoy these rare, precious afternoons with the glamorous big sister she barely knew.

'You look terrible. Your skin. Have you been taking your make-up off at night?'

'Yes, Mum, I've been taking my make-up off at night. I'm just stressed, that's all.'

'That dress. I can almost see your breakfast. Don't you ever think about the impression you give people, Belinda? I mean – I'm your mother. I know you're a good girl. But other people. Well – they might just get the – wrong idea.'

'Oh. Great. Now my mother is telling me that I look like a hooker. Jesus.' She stubbed out her cigarette and turned to face the spiky-eyebrowed man behind the bar. 'Can I have another one, Tarquin?' She slid her empty glass towards him. 'Thanks, sweetie.'

'And you drink far too much, Belinda. *Far* too much. Do you know what all that alcohol will do to your skin by the time you're my age? It'll suck you dry – desiccate you – you'll look haggard by the time you're thirty. You'll look like Katie Dewar's mother – believe me.'

And so it went, on and on and on. Bee's hair gel was going to kill the shine, her shoes would damage her spine, if she lost any more weight she'd get osteoporosis. Her posture was terrible and as for the 'horrible London accent' she was developing . . .

They left the Catacomb two hours later, having managed a few bursts of civilized conversation, particularly when

Bee's friend who owned the club had dropped by to say hello. Gay had been charm personified when Jon, a tall man with dyed black hair, pointy little sideburns, tight black jeans and a leather jacket with fringed sleeves, had introduced himself. For a while the conversation had been lively and friendly and Ana had sat on her bar stool, sipping her Coke and basking in it. But then Jon had left and the atmosphere had turned sour within moments.

Bee walked with them to the car park where they'd left the car. As they walked, every single man they passed looked at Bee. Every single one. Young, old, black, white, thin and fat. Proper, head-turning, walking-into-lamp-posts looking. Ana watched in awe as her sister kept walking, completely unfazed by the amount of attention she was getting, her bum still swaying from side to side, a cigarette burning nonchalantly between the fingers of her right hand. Ana just couldn't imagine ever, ever, ever being on the receiving end of so much undisguised male desire. What power Bee had. What must it be like?

The atmosphere was one of distinct relief as Bill unlocked the doors of his car and everyone said goodbye and pretended that the last three hours hadn't actually been a social form of water torture.

'Maybe next time,' said Bee, grinding her cigarette out on the concrete of the car park, 'we can try to be a little bit more pleasant to each other. I'm exhausted right now, Mum. I'm looking after Dad round the clock. I'd really like it if we could just all try to, you know, get along.'

'Yes, well,' began Gay, lowering herself, with Bill's help, into the passenger seat, 'maybe if you didn't insist on dragging us out to these godforsaken towns and making us sit around in these awful *places* with all these strange people, it would be a little easier for me to relax.'

Bee's face softened for a second, and she leaned into the passenger window. 'Maybe,' she sighed, 'maybe you're right. Maybe next time I'll come to Exeter. How about that? And you can choose where to go. We could have tea at Dingle's. What d'you say?' She smiled wryly.

'Hmm,' said Gay, 'we'll see. And for God's sake, stand up straight, will you? Standing there with your bum sticking out in the air like a *baboon*. With all your bits showing, no doubt, in that dress.'

Bee smiled defeatedly but with a certain amount of amusement and straightened herself out. 'Bye, Mum, bye, Bill,' she said, patting the side of the car. 'Have a safe journey. I'll be in touch soon. I promise.' She peered into the back window and gurned at Ana. 'Ta-ta, Twiglet,' she said, 'say hi to your boyfriend.'

And then, as Bill carefully manoeuvred the car out of the parking space and headed towards the exit, Bee turned around and sauntered away from them. Ana twisted in her seat to wave at her through the back window. Bee waved back enthusiastically, grinning her big, toothy grin. But as the car disappeared into the exit tunnel and Bee thought she was out of view, Ana saw her drop her hand, break off her smile and let her shoulders slump forward before turning and heading slowly towards the lifts.

And Ana's last ever glimpse of her sister was of a beautiful woman in an Azzedine Alaïa dress, standing against a stark concrete backdrop in a dank Bristol multi-storey car park, who looked like life had knocked all the stuffing out of her.

Three weeks later Gay travelled down to London for Gregor's funeral, leaving Ana and Bill at home with a very firm 'Don't be ridiculous – the place will be overflowing with homosexuals – why on earth would *you* want to come?' She booked herself into Claridges, bought herself a new dress from Jaeger and had a hat specially made. She booked a minicab, packed an overnight case, filled the fridge with enough meals for about a week, made a complete fuss about leaving and then came back ten hours later, in tears so hysterical that mascara almost dripped from the end of her nose.

Bee, apparently, had kicked her out of the crematorium, during the service. Physically. Using her hands – she'd shown them the muted bruising on her upper arms. And in front of everyone. Called her a bitch. Said she never wanted to see her ever again. Or Bill and Ana for that matter. Said she was disowning her family. Said she hated all of them, that she was ashamed of them.

There was no Bee, Gay had said, when a tearful Ana asked if she could call her. Bee, she said, no longer existed. There never had been a Bee. And Ana had numbly, obediently, put Bee in a box marked 'vague memories from my past' – and left her there.

Ana had occasionally wondered about her sister, looked for her blunt black bob and red-lipsticked mouth in the celebrity pictures in her mother's trashy magazines. Gay had invited Bee to Bill's funeral and Ana had stood at his graveside, her grief tempered by a sense of trepidation that at any moment her mysterious sister might appear from behind a tree. But she hadn't come and Ana had chalked it up as yet another disappointing moment in her life. Bee did send Ana a card, however, with a photograph of a lily on the front. It didn't say much – just 'My thoughts are with you, all love, Bee.' It was nice, but it was coolly polite, and Ana had meant to write back to say thank you and how are you and what've you been up to, but the bond between the two sisters was so slight and so flimsy that she'd just never got around to it. Ana always thought that she'd meet up with Bee again, one day, maybe go up to London for a weekend, hang out together. The age gap between them would have been less of an issue as Ana hit her twenties, and she was sure that Bee would have calmed down a bit, maybe got a proper job, maybe married, maybe even had a child or two. She imagined Bee meeting her at the station awash with perfume and Gucci, taking her to be pampered at a health spa and then to dinner at a posh restaurant run by Gordon Ramsay or that other chef bloke with the curly hair and the double-barrelled surname, and maybe taking her out to Bond Street the following day and insisting on buying her something disgustingly expensive from a designer clothes shop. It would have been a pleasant weekend, and Ana would have enjoyed the diversion, but when it came to an end the two women would have hugged and smiled kindly but sadly at each other, because they'd both know there was no friendship to be had, no bond to be formed, and that they'd probably not bother seeing each other again. Because, really, they'd have nothing in common.

But now even that sad little scenario was impossible.

Because Bee had made the ultimate dramatic exit. She'd gone and died. At the age of thirty-six.

The police had paid a visit nearly three weeks ago to Gay's handsome Devon townhouse. Bee's body had been found on Tuesday afternoon by a Mr Whitman, the building's porter, who'd let himself into the flat after a bad smell had been reported by the neighbours. He'd called Bee's landlord, who'd called the police. Apparently she'd been wearing a silk dressing-gown and a diamond necklace.

The police had been unable to find a contact number for Gay at first, but after two days they'd finally managed to get through to Bee's solicitor, who'd given it to them. Bee's body had been formally identified by a Mrs Tilly-Loubelle, the next-door neighbour, who claimed to be on 'quite friendly terms' with her. Her body had been taken to St Mary's Hospital, somewhere in central London, and was currently subject to an investigative autopsy, the results of which would not be made available for a few weeks.

'How come it took so long for anyone to find her body?' Ana had asked.

Gay had sniffed and shrugged. 'It's unthinkable, Ana-bella. That's London for you, though. A heartless, uncaring city. It happens all the time. It doesn't surprise me in the slightest.'

'But *four days*, mum. And over a weekend, too. Bee always had so many friends, she always had so many people around her. I don't understand.' There'd been a moment's silence while Ana arranged the words of her next question in her head.

'Did she – did she kill herself? D'you think?'

'Of course not,' Gay had snapped.

'So then – what happened?'

'That,' her mother replied abruptly, 'remains to be seen.' Gay had sniffed again and nodded sadly. And Ana had looked at her, at her tiny, pretty, doll-like little mother, with her tumble-down hair and her over-kohled eyes, a snotty tissue scrunched up between her bony old-lady fingers and, suddenly, for possibly the first time in her life, felt desperately sorry for her. She'd had such dreams for her life and it had come to this. Being trapped by her own insecurities and neuroses in this house, with two husbands dead and buried and the only thing in life she'd always been able to rely on, her good looks, rapidly letting her down. Her life was one big disappointment and the only light that had shone upon her dashed dreams had been the memory of her exotic eldest daughter. And now she was gone, too. Gay suddenly looked very small and very old, and for one bizarre moment Ana was overcome by a desire to hold her. She put out a tentative hand and brushed it against the satin of Gay's blouse.

But as her fingers made contact with the fabric she felt her mother's body tense up and Gay's bony hand leapt from her lap to slap Ana's hand away, so hard it stung. She turned and eyed Ana angrily.

'It should have been *you*!' she spat. 'You should be dead. Not her. Not my Belinda. She had everything to live for – looks, money, personality, talent. And you have nothing. You – you sit in your room all day with your big, dangly body and your lank hair and you play your horrible music and pick your spots and bite your nails. You've got no

46

friends and no boyfriend, no job, nothing. There is no point to you. You are pointless, Anabella – pointless. And yet – you're alive! You're alive and Belinda's dead! Ha! Something's gone wrong – something's gone wrong – up there,' – she pointed at the ceiling – 'with Him. Up there. He's made a mistake. That's what is it. Why else would he take away everyone – Gregor, Bill, Belinda – and leave you? Why would he leave you, Anabella?

'God,' she said, addressing the ceiling, her voice quavering like the Shakespearean actress she'd always dreamed of being, 'God – you have fucked up. You have fucked up . . .' She held out her hands in exasperation as she boomed at the Creator, and then pulled herself from the sofa and stalked from the room, stifling a sob as she went.

Ana had overlooked this tirade – it was nothing new – and instead she'd concocted filmic, romantic vignettes of Bee, draped all over a well-lit bed, her pale, bloodless arms trailing on to the floor, her green eyes staring glassily at the ceiling, a puddle of pills next to the bed. She'd prodded at her subconscious for some emotion, a sense of grief, but it wasn't there. She'd felt shocked, but not sad.

It was ludicrous, Bee being dead. People like Bee didn't die. Glamorous, beautiful, successful, rich, popular people didn't take a load of drugs and die alone and not get found until four days later. That was what happened to sad losers, to people with nothing and no one, to people like Ana, in fact. How could Bee be dead? Why would a woman who had everything throw it all away? It made no sense at all.

Ana spent the rest of the evening going through all the possible explanations in her head, trying to give her sister's death some sort of structure, but it wasn't until a couple of hours later, lying in bed listening to the unnerving sounds of her mother downstairs being her mother and coping with her grief in ways at which Ana could only guess, that a sense of loss finally hit her.

She was never going to see Bee again.

She may not have seen Bee for the last twelve years, but she'd always sat on the emotional nest-egg of the knowledge that she could if she wanted to. That she could go to the train station, buy a ticket to London and *see Bee*. Whenever she wanted. But she never had wanted to. And although Bee was practically a stranger to Ana, she was still her sibling, the only person in the whole world who could ever have possibly understood the things that Ana went through living with her mother, and now she was gone and Ana was totally alone.

It took a long time for Ana to get to sleep that night and when she finally did, her dreams were sad and hollow.

4

When Ana came down for breakfast that morning, her mother had been standing at the foot of the stairs with a letter in one hand and a bowl of cereal in the other.

'Now,' she began, as if the conversation had already been going for some time, 'sit down. Eat this. And hurry up. I've got plans for you – things for you to do.' Ana had felt a nervous nausea rising in her gut. She hadn't seen her mother this animated in months.

As she munched, she heard her mother upstairs, banging and clanking about in what sounded like the attic. Ana could hear her mother talking to herself as well, and then moments later she came clattering down the stairs. Her hair was all dusty and extra tousled. She was smiling. *And* it was a Thursday and she was wearing her Wednesday cardigan. Something very, very strange was going on.

'The last time I used this was 1963. For my honeymoon.' She got a faraway, wistful look in her eye and then plonked a suitcase on the breakfast table, right in front of Ana. It was small. And musty-smelling. And it was fashioned from a woolly tartan fabric in bright red and bottle green. It was disgusting. 'Anyway, Anabella,' Gay said, whisking the cereal bowl away from under Ana's nose and dropping it noisily in the sink, 'there's no time for sitting around today. You've got things to do.' She said this as a parent might tell a child that they had sweeties in their handbag.

'Mum. D'you mind telling me what the hell you're going on about?'

'I received a letter this morning' – Gay tossed it on the table in front of her – 'a letter from Bee's landlord. Her lease has just expired, and if her possessions are not removed by tomorrow morning, he intends to dispose of them. So. There's a train in just over an hour. Mr Arif will meet you outside her flat at one-thirty. He says you can stay in the flat overnight. I've organized for a removals company to bring her things back. They'll be there at nine-thirty tomorrow morning. I've spoken to that Mr Arnott Brown person, Bee's solicitor thingy – well, I thought since you were going to be there, you may as well kill all these birds with one stone – and he'll be expecting you at midday tomorrow. Here's his address. Your return train is at four-thirty and you'll be back here by about seven tomorrow evening. Here's some money –' she dropped a comically large bundle of notes onto the table – 'and here's the address.'

Ana scanned the letter briefly, looked at the pile of strange, inexplicable things in front of her and then at her mother. This was utterly ridiculous. How could her mother expect her just to wake up one morning, pack a suitcase and go to London, of all places? On her own. She'd get lost. She'd never find Bee's flat in the whole of London. She'd end up in Brixton or Toxteth or something and get mugged. Someone would steal all her money and her suitcase, and she'd be wandering the streets of London with only the clothes on her back. And people would laugh at her. All those cool, hard-nosed London types. Ana's heart started to race under her pyjamas. This was madness.

She strode into the living room and addressed her mother's back. 'But why can't we get the removal men to pack away Bee's things?' she'd asked desperately, knowing already that it was futile.

'I am not allowing a bunch of grubby, overweight buffoons to go rifling through my darling dead daughter's personal things with their big, dirty fingers. How could you even consider such a thing. I mean – her *lingerie*, for God's sake, and all her female bits and pieces. Absolutely not. Go and pack. Immediately.'

So Ana had. And here she was. In London. On her own. And she hadn't got lost and she hadn't been mugged and, in fact, she was feeling almost excited to be here.

Ana called downstairs to the porter, who locked up for her and gave her directions to the nearest supermarket. She bought herself a chicken mayonnaise sandwich and a can of Coke and asked the Indian guy stacking shelves for some cardboard boxes. He gave her a huge flattened stack of them and she bought herself a roll of parcel tape and lugged everything back to Bickenhall Mansions.

It was dazzlingly bright out in the street, but back in the overcast gloom of Bee's flat, it may as well have been a late November afternoon. Ana picked up Mr Arif's inventory and leafed through it while she nibbled on her sandwich.

1x	Black plastic ladle w/green handle	*slight melting on handle*
1x	White plastic toilet brush in stand	*good condition*
1x	Three-seater sofa upholstered in 'Normandy Rose' design fabric	*slight fraying around legs, small burn on left arm*

It went on in this tedious, painstaking manner for twelve pages. Ana sighed and put it down.

She looked around the flat for a moment, threw away the crusts of her chicken sandwich, gulped down her Coke, and then began the peculiar task of sifting through the debris of her enigmatic older sister's life. She started in the bathroom, figuring that the least of the work would need to be done in there. She made up a small cardboard box and began placing Bee's things in it, very slowly, item by item, making a mental inventory of her own as she went, hoping that by piecing together all these disparate, insignificant bits and pieces, somehow, miraculously, a fully rounded picture would emerge and she would come to know her sister and why she died.

1x	box of Tampax Super	*4 left*
1x	transparent plastic Oral B toothbrush	*very good condition*
1x	interspace toothbrush	*green*
1x	tube smoker's toothpaste	*squeezed in middle*
1x	bottle Listerine mouthwash	*nearly full*
1x	Boots own-brand dental floss	*open*
1x	*OK* magazine – Patsy Palmer on cover	*dated 7 January '00*
1x	*Hello* magazine – Ronan Keating on cover	*dated 8 June '00*
1x	large chrome ashtray	*full*

3x	houseplants	*dead*
1x	box matches	*Pizza Express*
1x	box matches	*Vasco and Piero's Pavilion*
1x	box matches	*Titanic Bar and Grill*
1x	box pessaries (for thrush)	*half full*
1x	pessary applicator	
1x	tube Canesten	*used*
1x	Jolene Crème Bleach	
1x	box mixed fabric plasters	*half empty*

Ana failed to find any clues to her sister's state of mind amongst these objects – all they told her was that Bee was a woman who liked to read trashy magazines on the toilet, signifying prolonged, possibly masculine-style bowel movements (which Ana found quite disturbing, as she'd never really thought of Bee – in much the same way as the Queen and Claudia Schiffer – as the going-to-the-toilet type), and that she was very conscious of oral hygiene, although not so concerned, it would appear, with other aspects of her physical health – as indicated by the presence of a full ashtray on the side of the bath. She was not green-fingered, and suffered from thrush, unwanted facial hair and somewhat heavy periods. She was also, it seemed, not a big believer in rinsing out the bath after use, as demonstrated by a small cluster of curly black hairs clinging to the grimy tidemark that ringed the bath.

Ana stared at them for a while. Bee's pubes. Bits of Bee. A sudden and painful reminder of why Ana was there. Bee was dead. Her sister was dead. And nobody could tell her why. All the evidence pointed to suicide but, for whatever reasons, a tragic accident seemed somehow the more palatable option. When Bee went to bed that Friday night, had it occurred to her that she wouldn't wake up the next morning? When she brushed her teeth that night, had she known that she'd never see her reflection again? Had she moved around the flat before she went to her bedroom, saying goodbye to things because she knew she was going, or was it just another Friday night, a late night, too much to drink, staggering around trying to get ready for bed, reaching for the sleeping pills when she couldn't get off, grabbing the painkillers when her hangover kicked in, not thinking what she was doing?

Maybe she was here now, a soul in limbo, watching Ana packing away her things and wondering what the fuck she was doing. Ana often had this really strange thought when famous people died untimely deaths – the thought that they didn't *know* that they were dead, that no one had told them. She imagined Diana on that Sunday morning in 1997, coming down for breakfast and reading the headlines, switching on the TV and seeing pictures of the mangled Mercedes in the underpass, the photos of Henri Paul, the CCTV of her and Dodi leaving the Paris Ritz and thinking no, no, no and . . . Ana sighed and got to her feet. She really was a very morbid, very weird person sometimes. And she really did think all sorts of peculiar thoughts.

She moved to the kitchen, and into a second box, or in some cases, into the bin, went the following:

1x	copy of *How to Eat* by Nigella Lawson	*pristine, untouched, signed with a handwritten inscription saying 'To my best friend, who sometimes needs reminding, with love from Lol'*
1x	glass bowl of lemons	*green fur in places*
2x	chrome cocktail shakers – one small, one large	*sticky residue at bottom of both*
1x	bottle of Jose Cuervo	*nearly empty*
1x	bottle of triple sec	*nearly empty*
1x	bottle of Absolut vodka	*nearly full*
1x	bottle of Bombay Sapphire gin	*unopened*
1x	bottle of Tabasco sauce	*half full*
1x	bottle of Worcester sauce	*two-thirds full*
1x	bottle of tonic water	*unopened*
1x	bottle of soda water	*nearly empty*
1x	packet Coco Pops	*half full*
1x	jar silverskin onions	*two left*
1x	jar cornichons	*five left*
1x	book called *101 Classic Cocktails*	*dog-eared – stained*
1x	box Twinings Earl Grey teabags	*twelve left*
1x	jar brown sugar	*very hard*
1x	espresso machine	*a bit dirty*
1x	blue ceramic jar of real coffee	*type unknown*
1x	loaf of unsliced brown bread	*very hard*
1x	pink 'lip'-shaped ceramic ashtray	*full*

In Fridge

4x	bottles champagne	*various brands*
1x	jar cornichons	*unopened*
1x	jar mixed nuts	*unopened*
1x	packet Sainsbury's Normandy butter	*half-used*
12x	bottles nail polish	*various brands and colours*
1x	large box of Charbonnel et Walker chocolates	*only two missing*
1x	tub Tesco's brand cottage cheese	*with garlic and chives*
3x	litre cartons Libby's tomato juice	*green fur round spout of one*

In Freezer

1x	2kg bag Party Ice	*open*
1x	large rump steak	
1x	Tesco's brand strawberry shortcake ice-cream	*one scoop missing*
1x	bottle of Jose Cuervo	*unopened*

Bee, it seemed, had liked to drink. These bottles and shakers didn't look the type that sat around waiting for special occasions or important guests. They appeared to have been in everyday usage. Ana thought back to the fancy green, blue and pink things in odd-shaped glasses sporting parasols and sticky cherries that Bee used to drink when she and her parents went to see her all those years ago. She wondered briefly whether Bee might have had a drinking problem, whether that might have had something to do with her death. But, thought Ana, ideas going off in her head like fireworks, surely someone with a drinking problem wouldn't go to all the effort of making cocktails every time they wanted a drink. No, thought Ana, Bee just liked a drink; she didn't have a drink *problem*.

Ana headed towards the living room and stopped on the way to open a small door set into the corridor wall. It was an airing cupboard, which contained, in addition to the traditional piles of folded towels and bedsheets, a used ashtray, a dirty mug and a black evening jacket. The label inside the jacket read 'Vivienne Westwood'. It was heavy with sequins and smelled of strong perfume. She examined the label. It was a size ten. She searched it for pockets and found a small one located in the lining. Inside the pocket was a ring – a silver ring set with three large diamonds. Ana took it to the window in the living room and held it to the light. The sunlight glittered and gleamed off the stones, and the metal had a sheen about it that suggested something more valuable than silver – platinum, or white gold. She slipped the ring on to her finger and thought for a moment how ridiculous it looked on her skinny, scuffed fingers with their bitten, uneven nails, but she kept it there anyway, enjoying the heaviness of it and the way it caught the light.

The living room really was shockingly bare. There was no sense of 'living' about it at all. No ornaments, no lamps, no mirrors, no paintings on the walls – just lots of ugly furniture, and books and records piled up around the place in a way that suggested they had been put there temporarily and never been moved. A motley crew of assorted soft toys and animals sat staring at Ana from the mantelpiece and, resting against the wall at the furthest side of the room, she caught sight of something quite heartbreaking – two of the saddest-looking guitars she'd ever seen, one acoustic, one electric, both broken, both missing strings, both covered in a fine layer of dust. For Ana this was equivalent to finding two abused, abandoned puppies in a cardboard box. How could people be so cruel? She picked up the acoustic. It was – had been – a beautiful instrument. There was a hole gouged out of the back panel and a massive chip in the head. It looked like it had taken a few beatings. She managed to extract a few discordant chords from the poor, unloved creature and then stroked it gently before wrapping it up in a pair of bath towels and nesting it gently into a cardboard box.

Ana wondered when Bee had learned to play guitar. Who'd taught her? Had she been any good? A person had to get pretty low to treat their guitars like that, Ana thought sadly to herself.

Glancing around the room she decided to abandon her mental inventory – she was losing hope of finding anything even vaguely enlightening in this dump. She was throwing things rapidly into the boxes now, slowing down only to leaf through Bee's CDs, books and videos and coming quickly to the astounding realization that Bee had pretty good taste. And not just the sort of good taste you could buy by the pound, the sort of stuff that Sunday supplements told you to enjoy, but intelligent good taste, wide-ranging, eclectic, thoughtful and, most surprisingly, unpretentious. Her music collection contained everything from David Bowie to Barry Manilow, the Candyskins to the Cocteau Twins, Paul Westerberg to the Pretenders and Janis Joplin to Janet Jackson. Her videos ranged from *Mary Poppins* to Bill Hicks and from *Gregory's Girl* to –

Ana was hugely impressed to note – *LA Confidential*, her favourite film of the last few years. Amongst her dog-eared and well-thumbed books were titles by writers as diverse as Noam Chomsky, Stephen King and Roald Dahl and biographies of people from wildly disparate walks of life like Alan Clark, Siouxsie and the Banshees and Adolf Hitler.

Ana had always thought disparagingly and, she supposed, superciliously, of Bee as a woman with bubblegum tastes in popular culture, and felt slightly ashamed and saddened to find so many similarities between her own tastes and those of her sister.

She looked at her watch and was surprised to see that it was nearly eight o'clock. The day was beginning to fade away and Ana had been so absorbed by what she was doing that she'd hardly noticed the time passing. It was dinner-time and her stomach was rumbling slightly, the chicken mayonnaise sandwich now a distant memory. She headed for the kitchen and pulled open Bee's fridge. The interior light cast a glow over the darkened room and gave the solitary items within a spot-lit Hollywood quality. A bottle of Perrier Jouet and the box of chocolates smiled seductively at her, Mae West-style. Why not? thought Ana. Why not? She plucked them from the fridge, pulled a glass from a cupboard and headed back towards the bedroom.

It was nearly dark in there now and Ana felt a little spooked. This building was full of strange noises, bangs and creaks and clunks, and the sounds of city life floating through the windows were angry and disturbing compared to the clean silence of Torrington on a Friday night. Ana found the switch for the fairy lights that framed the windows and flicked them on. On the other side of the room was an old table-lamp covered with a claret chiffon throw. She switched that on, too, and then looked around her. She shivered. It was lonely and empty and cold in here. It was spooky. Music: that's what this room needed.

She retrieved a CD from next door – Blondie's *Greatest Hits* – and put it in the tiny CD-player next to Bee's bed. And as the first bars of 'Heart of Glass' filled the room and music pulsed through her feet she felt herself being lifted out of herself and into the body of someone much more interesting. Some groovy, bohemian woman who lived alone in a Baker Street apartment. Some decadent, beautiful creature who drank champagne on her own and ate expensive Belgian truffles with wild abandon. She popped the champagne, poured out a glass and helped herself to a pistachio truffle. The fridge-cold crust of the chocolate shattered and the creamy centre got stuck to her teeth. The ice-cold champagne bubbles fizzed over her tongue and down her throat. She found herself smiling.

She danced across the room in time with Blondie and pulled open Bee's wardrobe, knowing even before she did that the essence of Bee would be contained behind those doors. Bee was all image and no substance, and her image was mainly about her clothes.

But even Ana's greatest imaginings couldn't have prepared her for the magical, fairy-tale dressing-up box that was Bee's wardrobe. Sequins. Satin. Silk. Beads. Crystals. Frogging. Fur. Chiffon. Organza. Golds. Scarlets. Purples. Paisley. Polkadots. All arranged in a colour spectrum from black, through ink blue, purple and oxblood red to palest pink, faded lime and snowy white, all glittering and gleaming. In the bottom of the wardrobe sat Bee's shoes, all with towering heels, all bearing the expensive, wooden horns that wealthy men with loads of handmade shoes from Jermyn Street use. Hanging from the doors were feather boas and scarves and diamante belts, tasselled shawls and furry things – and handbags, dozens of them. What use would one woman have for so many bags? Tiny ones, vast ones, chainmail, Lurex, marabou, embroidered, patent leather, floppy-patchworked suede.

Ana pulled on a pair of grape-coloured crushed-velvet gloves that covered her elbows, and admired them in the muted light. Very elegant. She knocked back the rest of her champagne and poured herself another glass, holding the stem genteelly between velvet fingertips. She threw a boa around her neck, a particularly fat one in deepest red, and twirled it round herself a couple of times. She headed for the full-length mirror at the other side of the room and ponced about a bit with her champagne and her hair, when Bee's dressing-table suddenly caught her eye.

Here was a dressing-table designed for the delight of six-year-old girls everywhere. It was piled high with cosmetics – not just smeared tubes of liquid foundation and manky old mascaras, but proper old 1930s-style cosmetics. Powder puffs and compacts, wooden hairbrushes, resin sets with trays and pots, jars of glitter, false eyelashes, eyelash curlers, brightly coloured powders, rows of silver-cased lipsticks. Expensive-looking bottles of perfume – Vivienne Westwood, Thierry Mugler, Jean Paul Gaultier. Even Bee's tissues were kept in an engraved box and her cotton wool popped out of a shiny metal dispenser, ball by ball.

Ana sat down and switched on the – almost predictable – light bulbs that framed the mirror and examined her reflection in the harsh light: terrible – she looked appalling, and her skin was particularly pallid next to the rich redness of the feather boa. She began examining the pots and jars, picking them up, reading the labels, sniffing them, sticking her fingers in them, putting them down again. And then her eye was caught again by a box on a shelf next to the dressing-table – a huge wooden box. She lifted the heavy lid and gasped at the contents: piles and piles of jewellery. Costume jewellery. Heavy, glittery, antique, most of it. Bits of Deco mother-of-pearl. Garnets. Amethysts. Aquamarine. Diamanté. Huge earrings. She picked out a pair of delicate Victorian crystal drops and looped them through the holes in her ears. And then her eye moved to a semicircle of glittering diamonds – a tiara, a bloody tiara. Only Bee, she thought, only Bee could own a bloody tiara . . . She really was the ultimate princess, and the tiara just proved it. But it *was* gorgeous, Ana thought, picking it up and examining it – filigree and spilling over with hundreds of tiny little diamonds. She couldn't help herself. She tucked it into her hair and felt something happening to her the moment she looked in the mirror. Something like vanity, like pleasure, like excitement. Sod it, she thought, downing her second glass of champagne and pouring herself a third, I'm going to be a princess, too.

She walked to the CD-player, turned it up full-blast so that 'Atomic' filled the room to the exclusion of any other noises, and headed for Bee's wardrobe.

Half an hour later, Ana was transformed. Her lips were red, her eyes were lashed, her hair was big and she was wearing a floor-length fuchsia dress in duchesse satin with a fake fur stole. And she was literally dripping with diamonds, from the top of her head to her lobes to her wrists.

She eyed herself in the full-length mirror and burst into fits of hysterical laughter. She looked ridiculous. She'd been trying for the Madonna-in-the-'Material-Girl'-video look but had ended up looking like Lily Savage on Oscar night. And the dress had quite obviously been designed for someone with breasts, as it gaped open sadly at the top, revealing Ana's razor-sharp collarbones and little else. But Ana didn't care now, she was having fun. She was pissed. For the first time in ages she was actually enjoying herself. For the first time in nearly a year, since the morning her father had collapsed while gardening for his precious Gay. For the first time since she'd watched his coffin, custom-made for his gangling frame, being lowered into the ground. For the first time since she'd moved back into her mother's house ten months ago and left Hugh, her job, her flat and her life in Exeter behind her.

Ana toasted herself in the mirror with her fourth – or was it her fifth? – glass of champagne and leapt in the air with a whoop of excitement when 'Union City Blues', her favourite Blondie song, came on. She slid across the room in her socked feet (she hadn't even attempted to squeeze her feet into any of Bee's ludicrously small shoes) and sang into the empty champagne bottle, in a tribute to Tom Cruise in *Risky Business*. She twirled her stole around and flicked her hair. She strutted and sang her heart out. She hadn't realized until that moment how long it had been since she'd last sung out loud and how much she'd missed it. And then, as the closing bars faded away and she took her final bow, breathless and euphoric and full of adrenaline, the room fell silent and the doorbell rang.

5

Ana panicked. A million thoughts landed in her head at once. Mr Arif? Police? Drug-crazed rapist with chainsaw? Can't open door. Tiara. Lipstick. Silly hair. Pink dress. Pissed. Very pissed. Shit. Fuck. What to do? What to do?

She ripped off the tiara and threw down the stole and tucked her bouffant hair behind her ears in an attempt to tame it, then tip-toed across the hall and towards the front door in her socked feet, barely allowing herself to breathe. She put her eye to the spy-hole and peered out into the corridor, thinking immediately of that weird Oasis video as the fish-eyed view came into focus. And *there* was a surreal image if Ana had ever seen one: a tiny, over-rouged old lady with strangely curled white hair under a hairnet, wearing a pink, fluffy dressing-gown with matching slippers and clutching a small sausage dog wearing a pink knitted vest to her bosom. She was looking extremely concerned, in that way that only vulnerable and lonely old people can. Ana picked up her cardi from where it lay on the sofa, threw it on over her dress and made her way back to the front door.

'Just coming,' she called, flattening her hair down again and wiping off her lipstick with the back of her hand, 'just coming.'

'Oh,' said the old lady, recoiling slightly as the door opened and putting one tiny, crêpey hand to her chest.

'Hello,' said Ana, attempting to smile normally but failing quite miserably judging by the worried look on the old lady's face.

'I was just, er, locking up, about to go to bed and I heard all sorts of noise coming from in here. Is everything all right?'

'Oh yes. Fine. I'm sorry if I disturbed you, I was just – er – listening to some music, you know.'

'I'm Amy Tilly-Loubelle. I live next door. And you are?'

'I'm Ana,' she extended a hand and offered it to the neighbour, who flinched slightly.

'Moving in, are we?' she asked, her pale blue eyes fluttering nervously around the hallway behind her.

'No. Moving out. My sister used to live here and I've come up to . . .'

Suddenly Mrs Tilly-Loubelle's face lit up, and her demeanour changed entirely. 'Oh, so *you're* the famous Ana,' she said, clapping her hands together with delight and making her little dog start. 'Bee used to talk about you all the time.' Her face dropped again and she rested a hand on Ana's arm. 'I'm so terribly, terribly, un*speak*ably sorry about the dreadful thing that happened to your sister. I feel so completely responsible – you see, I live next door and I didn't notice and . . .'

But Ana wasn't listening. She was still reeling from the 'Bee used to talk about you all the time' comment.

'Erm, I was just about to open another bottle of champagne,' Ana found herself saying, much to her own surprise. 'Would you like to have a glass with me?'

Mrs Tilly-Loubelle's face lit up and she grinned naughtily. 'How delightful. I'd love to, dear.'

Ana was incredibly grateful to the old lady for not mentioning her bizarre appearance, but then she wasn't really in a position to say anything, Ana supposed, given the matching pink dressing-gown, slippers and dog-vest ensemble.

She let Amy in and locked the door behind her.

'Oh, she was a lovely girl,' said Amy, sipping enthusiastically at her second glass of champagne. 'From the minute I set eyes on her I thought – there's a girl after my own heart. She reminded me so much of myself at the same age, so stylish and well turned-out. Always had her nails done, her hair was always just so. And so unconventional.'

'Did you see her often?'

'No,' she shook her head, 'not as often as I'd have liked. We shared a pot of tea from time to time. She always took a very kind interest in my well-being. But young people, they have their own lives to live, don't they? We've had our turn.' She chuckled and then became sad again. 'It's just so, so tragic that her turn was cut short. It never occurs to you, when you get to my age. I'd left her all sorts of things in my will, you know, bits and pieces she'd admired in my apartment – and I was going to ask her to look after dear Freddie, here.' She pointed at the long dog slumbering beside her on the sofa. 'Just presumed I'd pop off first. You don't think of young people going first.'

'Have you – do you have any idea what happened here on that last night?' Ana asked. 'Did she have anyone . . . here? With her?'

Amy shook her head. 'I heard her going out at about nine o'clock, just as I was getting ready for bed. I recognize the click of her door, you see. And then I went to bed, put in my earplugs and that was the last I knew until the next morning. I'm a very heavy sleeper, you see. Once I've conked out, nothing can wake me.'

'And what happened the next day? Did anything seem strange?'

'Goodness,' Mrs Tilly-Loubelle chuckled, 'have you ever thought of joining the police force?'

'Sorry. It's just that we – me and my mother – we don't really know very much. Only what they told us on the phone, and . . .'

'Where is your mother, by the way? Is she not here with you?'

Ana shook her head. 'No,' she said, 'my mother's agora-phobic. She can't leave the house, so she sent me.'

Amy clutched her heart with her hand. 'Oh, how simply awful,' she gasped. 'Imagine – not being able to leave your own home. It would be like being a prisoner. I'm so sorry, Ana – that's simply dreadful. But to answer your question, no. Nothing seemed strange the next day. Bee wasn't around, but then she was away most weekends. There didn't seem to be anything unusual about that.'

'Where did she go? At the weekends?'

Amy looked surprised and smiled quizzically at her. 'Why – to see you, of course!'

'*Me?*'

'Yes. To stay with you. In Devon.'

'In Devon?'

'That's right, dear.'

'And Bee told you that? Bee told you she spent week-ends with me in Devon?'

'Absolutely. She told me about your lovely little flat overlooking the sea and the two of you playing your guitars and going for walks together. She needed to escape, that's what she used to say, get away from all the hustle and bustle. She said that the air in Devon was like medicine for her soul.'

Ana tried to smile through her confusion. 'And how often did she, er, come and see me?'

'Well, nearly every weekend, wouldn't you say? That's why nothing seemed out of the ordinary when I didn't see her or hear her on that terrible, terrible weekend.' Her pale-blue eyes filled with tears then, and she quickly fished a handkerchief out of her sleeve, burying her pretty, rouged old face into the cotton, her tiny shoulders trembling. 'Oh, Ana – I feel so terrible. To think. All weekend I was there, next door. All weekend, just pottering around, getting on with things. In and out to the shops. Making phone calls. Watching the television. And all that time your beautiful sister, that angelic, unique woman who had everything ahead of her, was lying there' – she indicated the bedroom with her now-pink eyes – 'dead. All alone. *All alone.* I think it's the most tragic thing that's ever happened to me and I've lost a lot of people in my time. But I will never, ever get over losing your sister. Do you understand? Some people die – but others are taken. And that girl was taken.'

'You don't think it was suicide?'

Amy shook her head vehemently. 'No. Absolutely not. There is no way that girl would take her own life.'

69

'So what d'you think happened?'

'An accident. A terrible, tragic accident. That's what I think. She would never have killed herself. She had too much to live for.'

'Like what?' Ana was still reeling from Bee's inexplicable lies about how she spent her weekends. She was half-expecting the old lady to tell her that Bee had had six children or something.

'Well,' Mrs Tilly-Loubelle began, looking affronted by the question, 'you, for a start. She adored you. I hope you realize that.'

Ana opened her mouth to say something and then shut it again. The words to express her confusion didn't seem to exist.

'And John,' Amy continued.

'John. Who was John?'

'Her cat. A beautiful cat.'

A cat. Called John? 'And where is he now, this – er – John?'

Amy shrugged. 'Someone must have taken him away, I suppose. The RSPCA. A friend. I have no idea. I was hoping he'd gone to you. Gone to Devon.'

Ana shook her head. 'No. He's not in Devon.'

It fell silent for a while as Ana and Amy sipped champagne and stared at the carpet. 'Did Bee have any special friends, any boyfriends, or anything that you knew about?'

Amy screwed up her face and then nodded. 'She had a couple of friends who used to visit occasionally. I haven't seen them in a while, though. In fact, I'd say she had no visitors at all in the last couple of months.'

'What did they look like?'

'A black girl – very pretty. And a large man. A handsome man.'

'Bee's boyfriend?'

'No. More's the pity. No, he was just a friend, that's what Bee told me. A very old friend. And she never mentioned any other men. I often wondered if she was perhaps a lesbian.'

Ana choked as her champagne went down the wrong pipe. 'I beg your pardon?' she spluttered.

'Your sister. I often wondered if she was gay. She had that Radclyffe Hall look about her, like one of those old-fashioned lesbians. Very glamorous but with quite a hard edge, if you see what I mean.'

'And did you – did you think she was?'

She shrugged. 'Never saw men coming up here, never saw women either. Maybe she was asexual. Anyway – what other people get up to is their business. I try not to pay too much attention. What about you?'

Ana started, thinking surely she couldn't be asking her if she was a lesbian.

'Do you have a boyfriend?'

Ana thought of Hugh – was a boyfriend still a boyfriend when you hadn't seen him for six months? – and shook her head.

'And you're back to Devon tomorrow, are you?'

She nodded.

'Well – you should get yourself out tonight, see what you can find. There are some very beautiful young men in this city, you know.'

'Really?'

'Oh yes. I see them all the time. Every day. Everywhere I look. Beautiful young men and so well-dressed these days. Men seem to be paying much more attention to their grooming and their appearance, more like they used to in my day. Still – I must stop talking like this. I'll get myself all excited, and there's nothing much an old woman like me can do about it when they get themselves into that state.' She winked at Ana and Ana nearly fainted.

'Anyway,' Amy said, picking up her snoring dog and rearranging her fluffy gown, 'it's been very nice to meet you, Ana, but it's way past my bedtime, and if I don't get myself off now I shall fall asleep here on the sofa and you'll be stuck with me! But thank you so much for inviting me in. People don't tend to do that in London these days, you know. They don't invite you in. I think they're all too scared you'll never leave.' She laughed, sadly. 'And I'm sorry we had to meet under such dreadful circumstances. Your sister was a true original, Ana. A one-off. I miss her very much.'

Ana led Amy towards the front door, wishing that she wouldn't leave, but knowing that she had to. 'Can I ask you one more question?' she began with one hand on the door, 'about Bee?'

'Certainly.'

'You know – you know on the Tuesday? You know when you had to go to the hospital and – you know – identify her. Well, what, er . . . what did she look like? I mean – did she look peaceful, or . . . ?'

Amy put a hand on Ana's arm and smiled at her. 'Ana,' she said, her blue eyes twinkling, 'she was smiling. I swear on Freddie's life. Bee was smiling. She looked tired, but she looked beautiful and she was smiling. She didn't look like a woman ravaged by life and disappointment, a woman so unimpressed by all the world had to offer that she decided to take her own life. She looked like a small girl who'd just been told a wondrous bedtime story and drifted into a sweet, untainted slumber.'

'Thank you –' Ana smiled with a strange sense of relief – 'thank you very much.'

And then Amy Tilly-Loubelle gave Ana's arm one more squeeze, before letting herself into her flat next door, and fastening about twelve different locks and chains against the world.

Ana flopped on to the sofa, poured herself yet another glass of champagne and forced her pissed mind to try to make sense of everything she'd just discovered:

A Bee was away most weekends and lied about where she was going
B She generally had no visitors to her flat
C She had a cat called John whose whereabouts were unknown
D She'd gone out at nine o'clock on the night she died
E There was a vague possibility that she might have been a lesbian

Ana got to her feet and marched back into Bee's bedroom. It was now nine-thirty. She wasn't going to bed until she'd discovered something significant. She threw things desperately into cardboard boxes, reading them for clues, but they told Ana very little other than that her sister was a woman who looked after her clothes, her skin and her hair much better than she looked after her health or her home, that she dressed in a bold and theatrical style and appeared to have shunned entirely the casual/sporty look so fashionable for the past few years. She didn't even own a pair of trainers.

It appeared that Bee smoked, ate, drank, read and watched TV in bed. It was likely that she spent most of her time in this room, evidenced by her tentative attempts to 'decorate' it with colourful chiffon throws/fairy lights, etc. And it was possible, by the sound of it and by the look of it, that towards the end of her life, Bee spent rather too much time in this room . . .

However, Ana did manage to uncover a couple of slightly more interesting things:

1x crash helmet
1x suitcase with Virgin Atlantic tag, unopened but still full
1x small silk-covered notepad

It seemed that Bee either owned a motorbike or knew someone who did and knew them well enough to have her own helmet. One of the five keys from the bunch she'd found in Bee's handbag might well belong to a bike, but Ana wouldn't recognize an ignition key for a motorbike if it poked her in the eye.

She fiddled with a catnip mouse she'd found under the sofa and wondered about this cat called John. Where was he? Who had him?

And then she opened the little notepad and angled it

towards the light. There was writing on only the front page and this is what it said:

A Song for Zander

When I think of you now
I can think of anything
Any place and any life and any happy ending
I can think of sunshine
Think of joy
I can think of summer
Think of you, my boy
One day when our time is up
We'll meet
On a beach
And I'll hold your hand, my boy
We'll run on the sand, my boy
And you'll understand, my boy
That I loved you more
Than my words can

And there it stopped. Whether the last line was complete or not, Ana couldn't tell, although she was buggered if she could find a word rhyming with 'more' to close it. 'Implore'? 'Stand for'? No, thought Ana, those last two lines needed rewriting completely. But the rest of the song – well, it was quite good. Well, it certainly wasn't bad as such. It suggested a rhythm. Probably quite a soulful sound, building to a crescendo that had yet to be written. Ana started working out chords in her head, absent-mindedly strumming on strings made out of thin air. She found a pen and started jotting down music.

Ana's mind had left the building.

This often happened to her when she started composing a song in her head. She just forgot where she was entirely. A high-pitched police siren outside brought her back to reality and she jumped slightly, feeling almost surprised to find herself sitting cross-legged on Bee's bedroom floor in a full-length evening dress with a cardi and socks. She looked at Bee's song again. Who was Zander? A boyfriend? A secret lover? Maybe a married man?

In a flash of inspiration she picked up Bee's address book and flicked to the back page. Zoe B . . . Zoe L . . . Zach . . . No Zander. And then she pulled the suitcase towards her. It was a huge holdall-style bag in black leather. It looked battered but expensive. Ana slowly unzipped it and peeled it open.

The first thing that got her was the smell – a rank, mouldy, stale smell. She pulled a duty-free carrier bag from the top and immediately found the culprit – a white bikini that had been packed away wet and left to fester and was now green and brown with mould. She scrunched the bag up tightly and threw it to the other side of the room. And then she began pulling items from the bag, one by one: pink sarongs, orange sarongs, chiffon sarongs, silk sarongs, swimsuits, bikinis, beaded thong sandals, flowery flip-flops. Sun cream, malaria pills, mosquito repellent. There were things packaged in brittle brown paper, too – ethnic-looking bowls and textiles and boxes that smelled of cinnamon and asafoetida. There were brass horses with tiny bells attached and elaborate pieces of jewellery, saris and tunics and baggy trousers in all sorts of vivid colours and luxurious fabrics. And there, underneath, as if any more evidence was needed, was a *Rough Guide to Goa*.

My God, thought Ana, staring in amazement at the exotic, aromatic bazaar that was now spread out around her, Bee went to India. Ana herself had been planning to go to India a couple of years ago, before her father died. She and Hugh were going to pack in their jobs and go together. They'd saved for it and everything. But the thought of Bee in India was every bit as unthinkable to Ana as the thought of Bee on the toilet. And, in fact, the two were inextricably linked. She just couldn't imagine it – Princess Bee amongst all that poverty and dirt and human suffering, Princess Bee with a dodgy gut having to poo in dirty toilets, Princess Bee eating rice with her fingers and wiping her bum with her hand. But then again, thought Ana, Princess Bee probably stayed at all the top hotels and went everywhere by cab. Princess Bee probably hardly even noticed she was in India. But as she flicked through the Rough Guide, examining Bee's little pencil marks and notes, it became apparent that she hadn't done it in high style at all. Two- and three-star hotels were marked, local restaurants and off-the-beaten track attractions.

Ana put the book down and dropped her head into her hands. Who was this Bee person she was coming to know? This person who lived in a scruffy, ill-furnished flat, who had no friends, who rode a motorbike, who had a cat, who had great taste in music and who could play guitar? This person who dressed like a glamourpuss but lived like a student, who disappeared away somewhere every weekend, who befriended lonely old ladies and who went to India and stayed in hotels with dodgy plumbing? This Bee was beginning to sound scarily like someone that Ana could have been friends with. She rubbed her face, sighed a big sigh and carried on unpacking.

More ethnic artefacts, a John Updike novel, a mosquito net, an evening dress, embroidered slippers, and there, at the bottom – jackpot! – a tiny silver camera with a half-used film in it. Photographs. There were no photographs anywhere in this flat, except for some framed ones of Gregor on the walls. She would have to get this developed, as soon as possible.

Ana yawned. The champagne was catching up with her now and she was starting to feel almost hung over. She stretched and got to her feet, pulled open her horrible tartan suitcase and began placing objects in it. The camera, the notebook, the catnip mouse. The address book and the keys. She pulled off the jewellery she was wearing and put that in there, too. And some of the lovely Indian clothing from the suitcase. And the black sequinned jacket. And the rest of the chocolates. And the Blondie CD. And William, the knitted rabbit.

And then she threw everything else back into Bee's suitcase, zipped it up and took it to the front door along with the rest of the boxes she'd spent all day packing up. It was getting late now and time for bed. Ana was exhausted. She took one last look around the bedroom, checking that she hadn't left anything. Something underneath the bed was casting a shadow. She got down on her hands and knees and stretched out flat, trying to reach the shadowy shape. She got a purchase on it, pulled it out and looked at it: a cigar box. She blew some dust off the top and opened it up – and gulped. Money, lots and lots of money. She picked it out of the box, note by note, with trembling hands. She'd never seen so much money before in her life. She emptied the notes on to the floor and started counting them up: £7,350. Her breath caught: *£7,350* – in cash – just sitting there. Belonging to no one, unwanted, unaccounted for. She should keep a hold of this, she thought, she really should. It wouldn't be safe to put it in the removal van tomorrow. No, she thought, popping the cigar box into her tartan suitcase, she should *definitely* keep a hold of this. She fastened the clasps on her case and felt her heart racing under her top, almost as if she was doing something wrong.

As she passed through the hall she caught sight of a packet of Bee's Camels sitting on top of one of the boxes. Ana had never smoked in her life. It was strange in a way because everyone she went to college with had smoked, Hugh had smoked, her father had smoked, but Ana had never been even slightly tempted. She wasn't anti-smoking in any way and the smell of it didn't bother her like it did some people. But now (and maybe it was the effect of wearing a Vivienne Westwood evening dress and drinking champagne for the best part of four hours), it seemed like the right thing to do. Nothing was normal today. It had been one of the oddest days of her life, in fact, and for some reason that she couldn't quite put her finger on, she found herself taking a book of matches out of one of the boxes, picking up the cigarettes and heading towards the window. She heaved it open and stood where she imagined Bee would have stood, with an ashtray where she'd found it on the windowsill to her right. After a day of city noises, drills, horns and traffic, it was now silent, and the night air was still warm. Ana breathed it in greedily, tasting the alien flavours of car fumes and hot tarmac. The street below was empty, the lights in the mansion block opposite all switched off. There was nothing to look at but the very urbanity of it, the very fact of her location – London W1, Bee's flat – and her aloneness lent the view a certain spine-tingling magic. She dragged the match through the phosphorous strip and watched with pleasure as a flame came to life. Then she arranged a cigarette in her mouth, self-consciously, before lighting the tip of it.

She inhaled.

It was disgusting.

She inhaled again.

It was still disgusting.

She smoked the whole thing.

Ana's thoughts started to meander, and as she smoked she tried to imagine Bee's last few months in this flat. She turned to face the front door and, as if it were a movie playing in her head, she saw Bee walk into the room. She was wearing tailored men's trousers, low slung, with a powder-blue satin bustier that pushed her bosom up towards her throat, which glittered with a diamond collar. As she walked through the room she kicked off a pair of towering baby-blue suede platforms and lit a cigarette. She headed towards the window and came to stand right next to Ana. Close up, Ana could see that her skin was the matt white of foundation – she looked immaculate, like a doll. There were wide diamond cuffs around her narrow wrists, and her nails were oxblood red. She tipped ash into the street below and blew smoke from her lungs like a Twenties movie star, with an exaggerated puff of her full, lipsticked mouth. She sighed and rubbed the soles of her bare feet against the backs of her legs. Her toenails were red, too.

Ana couldn't take her eyes off her. She was captivatingly beautiful, but it was a different kind of beauty from the boisterous, loud-mouthed, high-octane beauty of a young girl bursting at the seams with joy and youth and energy that she used to have. It was a more composed beauty, cold, unattainable – completely asexual.

She watched Bee grind down the last half-inch of her cigarette, head towards the kitchen and fix herself a Bloody Mary – five drops of Tabasco, three shakes of Worcester, a big squeeze of fresh lemon – and then run herself a bath. She watched her take her drink into the bedroom and then sit at her dressing-table for a few minutes, staring blankly at her reflection, before sighing again and reaching for the cotton wool to remove her face. She tied back her glossy black hair with an elastic band, slipped out of her clothes, hung them up and then took her drink and her Camels to the bathroom, where she let the door shut behind her . . .

Ana stubbed out the end of the cigarette and took in one last lungful of the balmy night air before pulling down the window and switching off the lights. She considered having a shower, washing the day's grime off her thin, hungry body, but she was too tired, so she slipped out of Bee's dress, pulled on a T-shirt and pyjama bottoms, brushed her teeth and walked into the bedroom. And then she stopped in her tracks as a gust of cool air stroked her cheek and images of her sister's dead body lying festering on her big empty bed, alone and unaccounted for, flashed frighteningly through her mind. Is this what it was like? Is this what it was like for Bee at the end? An empty flat, too much to drink, sleeping pills – a preoccupation with her fading youth? She must have had friends – she must have had someone she could have talked to? A boyfriend? A lover? It just wasn't possible that someone like Bee could have died like an unloved pensioner, alone and with no one to notice she'd gone.

Ana shuddered, took one last look at the empty, ominous bed, switched off the light and made her way back to the living room, where she eventually fell asleep on the sofa, under Bee's pink cashmere blanket which still smelled of her Vivienne Westwood perfume.

6

At nine-fifteen the following morning, Ana's deep sleep was rudely disturbed by a team of four Romanian women, three half-naked men from Newcastle and Mr Arif, all arriving at the same time. She had barely detached herself from her dreams, and acknowledged the existence of a hideous hangover when she found herself peering through the spy-hole into the enlarged eyeball of a grinning Mr Arif. And there they were, standing behind him. Dozens of them.

'Good morning, Miss Wills! And tell me. How are my fine ladies here to clean my flat when there are also here these three large gentlemen?' He pulled his monogrammed hanky from his pocket, wiped his brow and gestured dismissively at the bare-chested men behind him.

As he walked into the flat the four women dutifully piled in behind him, clutching buckets, mops and carrying cases full of cleaning products.

'Well, maybe,' began Ana, tugging self-consciously at her pyjamas, 'the ladies could start in the kitchen and bathroom and these gentlemen can begin removing these things – you are . . . you are here to remove things, aren't you?' she asked, thinking suddenly how embarrassing it would be if they weren't and they were actually journalists or something. The three nodded. 'Good, excellent. And maybe while you're all doing that, I could – er – get dressed?'

'Yes, yes, yes, of course, Miss Wills. Of course. Ladies' – he turned to the somewhat sad-looking women behind him, all in their twenties but with the demeanour and hairstyles of women in their forties – 'follow me, if you please.'

Ana scuttled into the bedroom and closed the door behind her. This was horrible. After the intimacy she'd experienced last night while she was here alone, the presence of so many strangers was deeply upsetting – and so final. The moment that last box was heaved into the big white van out there, she would have to leave, and she would never be allowed to return. Because it wouldn't be Bee's flat any more. It would be the flat of some Prima Ballerina. And, quite to her own surprise, Ana wanted to stay here. Not for ever or anything, but she wanted another night, at least, just to breathe in the atmosphere and get to know her sister.

But instead, she would be sitting on a train, all alone, hurtling back to Great Torrington and her bedroom. And, more depressingly, to her mother. Ana sighed and moved towards the window. Down on the street below, one of the burly, bare-chested removals men was already hoisting a box into the back of the van. Ana recognized it as the one into which she'd packed Bee's shoes and felt suddenly and horribly sad.

It didn't take long to load up Bee's paltry possessions, and by ten-thirty Ana was waving off Bez, Al and Geoff and watching Bee's life trundle down Bickenhall Street towards Devon. She had an appointment with Bee's solicitor at twelve, so she returned to the flat to bid farewell.

Mr Arif was also preparing to leave, slotting paperwork

into the inside sleeve of a maroon leather attaché case and whistling under his breath. 'So, Madam,' he said, smiling widely at her now that he was convinced that everything was under control, that the flat was being cleaned and that his Prima Ballerina could happily move in the next morning, 'now it is all over. Your sister is in boxes and your task is complete. To where are you going now?'

Ana shrugged. 'Well – I've got to see Bee's solicitor first, sort out her financial affairs, that sort of thing. Then I'm going home. I guess.'

'And home is?'

'Home is Devon.'

'Ah yes! The beautiful English countryside. You are very lucky. Very lucky girl. Maybe if your lovely sister here had stayed in the beautiful English countryside, instead of living here in this cesspool city, then this bad thing here would never have happened?' He laughed, uproariously, and highly inappropriately, but it suddenly struck Ana that here was a man who may have been with Bee recently, may have had conversations with her while she was living and breathing – and possibly contemplating dying.

'Mr Arif,' she began, 'I, er, didn't see my sister very much in the last few years. Twelve years, in fact. I just wondered if you'd spoken to her recently or anything. You know – how she'd seemed?'

'Seemed?' questioned Mr Arif, his hooded eyes springing open momentarily in surprise, 'seemed?' He clicked closed his attaché case and adjusted the cuffs of his shirt. 'Madam – I find this question very peculiar. If you are asking me how she seemed, all I can say is that she seemed like a very beautiful, very charming tenant who paid her rent on time and who died on her bed and left herself for me to find. Now. I have many urgent appointments and I will have to be leaving you. I thank you for your efficiency and I wish you a safe and pleasant journey home, Miss Wills.'

He turned to leave but Ana had one last thought. 'The cat, Mr Arif . . . ?'

'I beg your pardon?'

'Bee's cat. What happened to him?'

'Ah. The animal. Naughty Miss Bearhorn deceived me for many months with her animal. But her deception was uncovered and now her animal resides with a friend.'

'Friend? Which friend?'

'Oh my goodness, Miss Wills. You cannot expect me to be knowing all this minutiae of my tenants. A friend. That is all I know. Now I leave.'

And then he left, the only sign that he'd ever been there the dense fug of aftershave lingering in the living room.

7

Bee's solicitor worked from a very small office in a very large office block in Holborn and he looked like neither a solicitor nor someone who would be called Mr Arnott Brown. He was wearing a T-shirt for a start. It wasn't exactly a Megadeth T-shirt, or anything – it was just plain and red – but it was still a T-shirt. ('I do apologize for my appearance, Miss Wills,' he'd said when he greeted her at the lift, 'we've just introduced a Dress-Down Friday policy. I can't say I'm awfully comfortable with it, myself.') And he looked extraordinarily young. The sun streaming through his office window sat on his smooth pink skin and clearly picked out the sparse, almost prepubescent tufts of hair poking from his chin. He wore a wedding band and on his desk sat photographs of an equally young-looking wife and a pair of photogenic toddlers.

He was very shy and appeared to be having trouble maintaining eye contact with Ana through his spectacles. 'Yes,' he was saying, almost in a whisper, 'your sister kept her financial affairs very much in order. Well, perhaps not your sister, exactly. I've always had the feeling that she'd have kept all of her money under her mattress if it had been up to her. But she had a good accountant and everything is as it should be. No debts, no tax bills, no overdrafts. Unfortunately she didn't make a will. It was something I'd been trying to persuade her to do for a long time, but she thought it was a, aaah, silly idea. So. All her assets will go to her next of kin who I believe is her, aaah, mother.' He looked up from his paperwork and directly into Ana's eyes until she nodded, and then he looked abruptly away again.

'Yes,' said Ana, 'she is, but she's agoraphobic, you see, she can't leave the house, so I'm here on her behalf.'

'I see. I see.' He began leafing through his paperwork again and pulling out various sheets. 'Yes – Bee inherited a very large sum of money in 1988. Her father's maisonette in South Kensington, which she sold for £210,000 and a small cottage in the Dordogne which she sold for a further £12,000. She also had a large sum of money she'd made from a music-publishing deal back in 1985. Around £80,000.'

Ana held her breath.

'However, Bee appears to have had an expensive lifestyle. Her monthly outgoings were substantial and seem to have eaten into a large chunk of her inheritance. And then' – he swivelled a large document towards her – 'she purchased this in, aaah, 1997.'

On top of the document was an estate agent's particulars – a chocolate-box cottage, painted fondant pink, covered in Albertine roses. £125,000.

'She paid cash for it. It was the only property she ever bought. She preferred to rent . . .'

Ana stared at the cottage in disbelief. The writing above the picture named the location as Broadstairs, Kent.

'. . . I think it may have been purchased on a whim, to be frank. As far as I'm aware she never visited it. Shame – it's awfully pretty, don't you think?' He turned it towards himself to appraise it, and Ana could almost see what was in his head: the image of him, his young wife and their two children enjoying lovely weekends away together at the seaside.

'Can I keep this?' she asked, staring in wonder at the particulars of the cottage.

'Well, I, aah, I don't see why not. I have no need of it.' He slid it across the desk towards her and she slipped it into her bag. 'So,' he said, 'all in all, including the cottage, your sister's estate has a net value of around £148,000. Plus, there are still some active royalty accounts which bring in another £1,000–2,000 per annum. Also, there was one other, slightly smaller matter. Your sister had a cat. He was called, aaah, John, I believe.'

Ana sat up straight.

'She was unable to keep him in her new flat, due to the tenancy agreement. In fact, that was the last time I spoke to her – her landlord was threatening to evict her if she didn't rehouse her cat, and she wanted my advice. And I'm afraid that the only advice I could reasonably give her was that the cat would have to go. So she took him to her friend. A Miss Tate. I have her address if you'd like to contact her. She acted as Bee's witness on a number of occasions, you see . . .' He flipped through a pile of papers and transcribed an address from the file on to a piece of paper and handed it to Ana. 'You may want to contact Miss Tate to find out how she'd like the matter to be dealt with. As far as she was aware it was only going to be a temporary measure – just until Bee found herself a new flat.' He wiped away some sweat from his brow. The small room was unairconditioned and disgustingly hot.

'So the flat in Bickenhall Street was just short term?'

Mr Arnott Brown nodded. 'Yes, very much so. I know she had been looking at alternative properties to rent in the weeks before the, aah, incident.'

'When was the last time you saw Bee, Mr Arnott Brown?'

He pulled off his glasses and absent-mindedly wiped the lenses with a soft cloth. 'Well, aaah, I saw her very rarely, very rarely. Let's see. Hmmm – the last time I saw her was . . .' he consulted his desk diary, leafing clumsily through the pages with sweaty fingers '. . . there. Yes. It was in January. Just after she moved into the new flat. She lodged some paperwork with me. Tenancy agreements and such.'

'And how did she seem?'

'Seem? Well, aaah, like she always seemed, I suppose. You know . . .'

'No. I don't know. I haven't seen her since I was thirteen.'

'Oh. Oh, I see. That's, aaah, that's, hmmmm. Well – Bee was always very exotically dressed. Very theatrical, you might say. And somewhat – mercurial.'

'What do you mean?'

'One could never quite predict what sort of mood she might be in. Some days she was exuberant and other days she would be rather withdrawn – easily distracted. And she would always insist on smoking in here, although it's absolutely forbidden, you know, and awfully dangerous. My wife always knew when I'd had a meeting with Bee because I'd return home reeking like an old ashtray.' He did a strange, snorty thing, into his fist. 'She was very open, which could prove somewhat disconcerting. She would think nothing, for example, of using very, aaah, strong language and asking somewhat – personal – questions.'

'But that day. In January. The last time you saw her. How was she then? How was her mood?'

'I'm afraid, Miss Wills, that I really do not recollect. But if you're asking me if she appeared to be on the brink of, aaah, taking her own life, then I would have to say, no. Most definitely not.'

A nasal voice on Mr Arnott Brown's intercom informed him that his next client had arrived. He smiled apologetically at Ana. 'I'm afraid we'll have to call it a day now, Miss Wills. I'll get all this paperwork to your mother's solicitor. If you could just sign these release papers, to authorize everything. Here. And – here. Super. Thank you.' He unfurled himself from his desk and saw Ana to the door. He grasped her hand in his and shook it warmly. 'And may I just take this opportunity to say, Miss Wills, how terribly, terribly sorry I was to learn of Bee's death. She was a very unusual character, but I have to confess to having been awfully fond of her. She had a way of making one feel very, aaah, special. Do you know what I mean?'

Ana nodded, shook his hand again and left his office, thinking sadly to herself that, no, actually, she had no idea what he meant as she'd barely known her and how much she was starting to wish that she had.

8

At the other end of a cobbled alleyway around the corner from Mr Arnott Brown's office was a pretty Georgian square. Ana took a right and found herself in a quiet residential street lined with diminutive Victorian council flats, with tiny balconies entwined with ivy and passion-flowers. Children played in a small playground fronted by a sign declaring 'Adults Permitted Only if Accompanied by a Child.' The sun had come out again, and Ana pulled off her cardigan.

As she walked a delicious smell suddenly wafted towards her: fresh bread. She hadn't eaten anything at all that day, and her hangover was giving her a most impress-ive appetite. She followed the smell into an art gallery housed in an old Methodist chapel and found herself in a peaceful, almost monastic courtyard, lined with wooden sculptures and large potted trees. There was a small kitchen at the back of the courtyard, serving a limited menu of healthy-sounding things, and there was hardly anybody here.

Ana ordered a pasta and wild-mushroom bake, and as she waited for her food to arrive, she looked around her and began to feel overcome by a sense of her surroundings. She was in London. She was in the city where Bee had gone when Ana was four years old. The city that had broken her mother's heart – twice. And Ana was on her own – and it wasn't that scary. Ana had always thought of London as this mysterious place that swallowed people up like a big, black hole, that took away their values and their emotional depth, dressed them up in stupid clothes, hooked them on alcohol and drugs, infected them with viruses that didn't even *exist* in Devon and then, when there was nothing left of the person they'd once been, spat them out the other end. That's what London had done to Gregor, according to Gay. And that's what London had now done to Bee, too. But try as she might, Ana couldn't hate the city for it, not like her mother did. In fact, there was something fascinating about this huge, unruly place of which she'd seen only a fraction.

A man wearing just a waistcoat and jeans sat above her on one of the fire escapes twanging on a guitar, and some windchimes tinkled from a fig tree: all very West Country, in fact – Ana felt almost at home. She settled herself at a wide wooden table in the shade and laid out Bee's things again. Her address book, notebook, camera, the *Rough Guide to Goa*. She thought of the anomalies, the inconsistencies, the cottage, the weekends away, the missing cat, and then she picked up the piece of paper Mr Arnott Brown had given her with the address of John the Cat's foster mother on it: Miss L. Tate.

She looked at her watch. 1.20 p.m. She had three hours before her train went, and it suddenly occurred to her that it wouldn't actually matter if she missed the four-thirty – she could get the five-thirty, the six-thirty, whatever. She should go and see this Miss L. Tate, this friend of Bee's. She'd like to meet a friend of Bee's. She might be able to shed some light on things. And she really wanted to see

Bee's cat, this creature who she'd apparently loved so much.

She pulled her *A-Z* out of her handbag and looked up Bevington Road, W10, the current residence of John the Cat. She found a payphone inside the chapel and dialled the number on the piece of paper. And then she remembered that it was the middle of the day, that Miss L. Tate was most probably at work, so she jumped a little when the phone was answered and a loud, raspy voice answered with an abrupt 'yup'.

'Um, hello. Is this Miss. L. Tate?'

'Who's this?' said a suspicious-sounding voice.

'My name's Ana. Ana Wills. I'm er, I'm Bee's sister.'

'Oh my God,' the voice screamed, 'Bee's sister! You really exist. I always thought Bee were making you up.' She had a very broad Leeds accent.

'Oh. Right. Yes. Well – I'm in London at the moment because I've been sorting out her stuff and I'm feeling a bit, er, confused . . . and I needed to talk to somebody – to somebody who knew her. And Bee's solicitor gave me your number because you're looking after her cat. And I wondered if I could meet up with you. Maybe. Or I could pop over? I won't stay long. Unless you're busy, of course . . .'

'No. No, I'm not busy. I'm bored off my tits, actually. Why don't you come round?'

Miss Tate lived just off Portobello Road. Ana didn't know much about London, but she knew that Portobello was cool, and this was confirmed resoundingly as she turned a corner and found herself slap-bang in the middle of some of the most frighteningly trendy-looking people she'd ever seen in her life. Ana tried to bolster herself up, but couldn't fight the ridiculous paranoid fear that one of these horribly self-assured people, one of these I-know-exactly-who-I-am-where-I-am-and-what-I'm-doing-here-type people was going to come up to her and take the piss. But nobody even glanced at her – which was a strange sensation for Ana, because everywhere she went in Devon, she was stared at remorselessly. There were three boys in particular, from the estate just outside Torrington, who tormented her every time she set foot out of the house. The ones with the ears and the red hair and the jewellery. Every time they saw her they would skid to a halt on their skateboards, scoop them up from under them and then just stop and stare at her as she walked past. And as she passed them, the tallest one, the one with the reddest hair, would hiss something, like 'Freak!' or 'Scarecrow!' or 'Skinny bitch!' Nothing very creative, but effective, none-theless. Ana decided she liked the anonymity of London's streets, where you could be tall or short, black or white, have pink hair or pierced cheeks and still nobody gave you so much as a second glance.

She followed Portobello to its northernmost point, past a few sad-looking stands selling what looked to her like stuff that even the least choosy of bag ladies would be embarrassed to possess, past a vegetarian restaurant with a queue outside, past record shops with Rasta colours in the windows, past a falafel restaurant, under a bridge and past a bustling market square filled with yet more painfully trendy people. The sky overhead was darkening, and it looked like rain, but it was still humid and sweaty. She zigzagged through a couple of scruffy streets until she found herself in Bevington Road, a dinky little curve of brightly coloured stucco houses facing a schoolyard.

Number fifteen was a lurid grass-green with mauve woodwork. She took the steps to the front door, rang on the bell and was buzzed in. The tiny stairwell took her to the top floor, where she was greeted by an open front door and the sound of stampeding wildebeest.

'Hello,' she ventured.

The herd of wildebeest stopped stampeding for a second and then began again.

Ana glanced around nervously. 'Hello.'

'Fuckcuntbollocks.'

Ana followed the rasping and stampeding through the tiniest, messiest living room in the world to an even smaller and messier bedroom, where objects were being thrown, seemingly at the hands of a poltergeist, here, there and everywhere.

'I've lost my cunting choker.' The rasping was definitely coming from somewhere in the room. 'It's not even mine. It's a Jade fucking Jagger. It's worth about two squillion fucking quid and I've got to give it back tomorrow. Fuck.'

A head suddenly appeared from underneath the bed, and a black hand was extended towards her across the top of the unmade bed. Its fingers were tipped with the longest, whitest nails Ana had ever seen, like five magic wands.

'Ana! Hi! Lol.'

'Lol?' repeated Ana, remembering the inscription in the Nigella Lawson cookbook.

'That's my name,' she croaked. She sounded like she

was losing her voice. 'Sorry about this. I've just done this live appearance on some kid's TV show and the stylist lent me this fucking stupid choker, and I forgot to give it back to her, and now I've fucking lost it. And I'm gonna be dead, soooo dead . . .' She grimaced.

Ana was too shell-shocked by the experience of meeting this dynamo of a woman and by the accompanying torrent of profanities to question what exactly it was she'd been doing on children's TV.

As Lol talked she got to her feet. She had waist-length platinum extensions tied high in a pony-tail, skin the colour of butterscotch, a sapphire in her nostril and matching bright-blue eyes, patently purchased from an optician and not formed in the womb. She was wearing a soft-leather bustier, exactly the same colour as her skin, and matching leather jeans covered in rhinestones. And, most impressively to Ana, she was about six-foot tall and thin as a stick of linguine.

'Oh. My. God!' Lol said, staring in amused shock at Ana. 'You look like my fucking negative!' And then she started laughing. Louder than Ana had ever heard anyone laugh before.

She strode around the clothes-strewn bed and grabbed Ana's hand, 'I have *got* to have a look at this,' she said, and pulled Ana towards a full-length mirror. They stood side by side, and there they were – perfect positive and negative versions of the same person – exactly the same height, exactly the same shape, black hair, white hair, white skin, black skin. For a second they both stared at the reflection with their mouths ajar – and then Lol started laughing again. She slapped her thighs. She wiped away tears with

97

the sides of her long-nailed fingers. She bent herself double. She grabbed on to Ana's arm and laughed a laugh so long and so silent and accompanied by so much painful arm-squeezing that Ana was beginning to worry that she was having some kind of a seizure.

Then she stood up straight again, pulled her face back into shape, shuffled around a bit, and eyed their reflections once more. Within two seconds she was bent double again, and this time Ana succumbed, too. It was one of the funniest things she'd ever seen, funny in the same way that seeing yourself distorted into a bulbous dwarf in a Hall of Mirrors was funny; funny in the way that wrapping elastic bands around your head was funny; funny in the way that blowing your cheeks up against a pane of glass was funny – just stupidly, childishly, unbelievably funny.

'Oh fuck – I'm going to wet meself,' wheezed Lol, now collapsed into a tangle of legs and arms on the floor. Ana was perched on the edge of the bed and had reached that convulsive, uncontrollable point when laughing stops being fun and starts to hurt. She looked down at Lol on the floor, at her abnormally long limbs and the bagginess about her tiny leather trousers, at the familiar impression made by her ribcage into her bustier and the lack of distinction between her calves and her thighs, and she suddenly thought, in the most overwhelming and entirely unexpected welling up of intense emotion that flickered around the sensitive lining of her belly like a feather duster, that she loved her, that she loved this girl who she'd known for less than five minutes, and with that shocking thought she felt the bruising in the back of her throat sort of catch and the tears in her eyes sort of tickle and suddenly she was crying. And the more she tried to stop crying the more she cried. She had no idea where the tears were coming from but they were thick and hard and they hurt.

Lol joined Ana on the edge of the bed and draped one extravagantly long arm around her shoulder. 'Oh pet,' she soothed, looking anxiously into her eyes, 'what's the matter, eh?'

Ana sniffed and wiped her nose against the sleeve of her cardigan. What *wasn't* the matter would have been a more useful question. She opened her mouth to speak but there was too much to say, so she closed it again. The reasons lined up in her mind, though, like a shopping list, to remind her.

I'm a gangling six-foot freak who gets stared at in the street and laughed at by little boys with piercing voices.

My father, whose height I inherited, whose legs I have, died ten months ago and I still miss him every day of my life.

The only boyfriend I've ever had dumped me just eight weeks after my father died.

My mother is an agoraphobic lunatic who walks in her sleep and thinks the world revolves around her.

I have no friends and no social life.

My sister, the only person who made it look as if being alive was any fun, killed herself.

I'm alone in a strange city and I know no one.

I'm scared, I'm confused, I'm dirty and I'm tired. And then you – you with the same arms and legs as me, the same bony torso and flat chest, you made me feel like a normal human being for a couple of minutes, like there wasn't just Ana, but that there was Ana and Lol, and for

99

the first time in ten months I laughed and for the first time in ten months I felt the same as somebody else. That's why I'm crying, that's what the matter is. And the saddest thing of all is that I already know that that was just a moment – it isn't the way things are going to be from hereonin, it's just the way things were for a brief moment, and it's those little tasters of normality that really, really kill me . . .

But she didn't vocalize her thoughts, and Lol was left to look for the most obvious reason for her tears.

'Oh pet,' she soothed, tears brimming in her own eyes now, 'I know. I know. She was my best friend, Ana. My best friend. I loved her more than anyone in the world. We were soulmates, the only people who really understood each other. Me and Bee – we were like sisters . . . we were . . . oh. I'm sorry. I didn't mean to say that. I mean, obviously, you were her sister. But . . .'

'It's OK,' said Ana, 'I know what you mean, it's fine.'

'She loved you, you know,' she said sniffing loudly into an old tissue. 'She really loved you. She kept this funny old rabbit thing, for years . . .'

'William.'

'Yeah. That's right. She took him everywhere. She had a party once and someone kidnapped him as a joke, and put him up for ransom, but she didn't think it was even slightly amusing. Oh no. She just lost it entirely. You should've seen her – screaming and crying. It was like that rabbit . . . I don't know, like he represented something to her that nobody else could ever have understood.'

It fell silent for a moment and Ana took in deep breaths, trying to control the overwhelming emotion charging through her system, trying to rein in the pain and force it back into the Pandora's box that Lol had inadvertently opened up. It was the first time she'd cried since her father's funeral.

She glanced around the flat, at the fuchsia walls and leopardskin curtains, the piles of clothes and shoes, perfume and jewellery. She looked at the photos pinned to the walls, smiling groups of people, small children, family. And then her eye was caught by a photo of Lol and Bee, arms round each other, champagne on a table in front of them, beaming at the camera, and Ana suddenly remembered why she was here.

'John?' she said, sitting up straight. 'Where's the cat?'

'Oh. Right. He's – out.'

'Out?'

'Yeah. You know. Out. Doing . . . cat stuff.' She shrugged and got to her feet. 'Listen – don't go anywhere, right? I'm just going to check the stairwell and the street for that fucking stupid choker. I don't really give a shit about it myself, but if someone found it and made off wi' it, I'd be fucked. What are you doing tonight, by the way?'

Ana shrugged and sniffed. 'Going home. I'm catching a train in an hour.'

Lol stopped still, her mouth opened wide and her eyes staring at her with exaggerated shock. She put her hands on her skinny hips and addressed Ana, sternly. 'No you are not, young lady.'

'I'm sorry?'

'I've been hearing about you for years. I've wanted to meet you for, like, *ever*. You can't go home yet. You're

Bee's fucking sister. D'you have any idea how exciting that is?'

'Yes, but . . .'

'Yes but nothing. You're staying here and I'm taking you out.'

'Yes, but – what about my mother?'

'What about your mother?'

'She's ill. She needs me. I can't just leave her.'

Lol smiled a warm smile and put her hand on Ana's shoulder. 'Look,' she said kindly, 'I know all about your mother. Bee told me everything. And I think your mother might benefit from a night alone. Oh – come on. Please stay. Ple-ease,' she wheedled. 'We'll go and check out old Lundarn Tan, togevver, like.' She smiled as she tried on a daft cockney accent.

Ana's thoughts veered dizzyingly between her sense of responsibility towards her mother and the realization that she wanted to stay. That she really wanted to stay. She wanted to be with Lol. She wanted to talk to Lol. All night. About Bee. About cottages and motorbikes and guitars. She wanted to go out with Lol. And get drunk. And not go home. Not tonight. She wasn't ready yet. A wall of resolve built in her chest. She was already nodding, without being aware of it, her mouth set hard, her hands wringing together. 'OK,' she said firmly, 'OK. I'll stay.'

'Good girl,' grinned Lol, squeezing her shoulders, 'top girl. I'll be back in a tick.'

'I need to phone my mum, though. Can I use your phone?'

''Course you can. It's over there.' Lol pointed at the window sill and smiled at Ana excitedly. 'I can't believe it,' she gushed, 'Bee's sister. In my flat. I'm so excited!' Lol squeezed her shoulder again and then went clattering down the stairs like a . . . like a skinny six-foot woman in wedge heels.

Ana walked to the window and found herself peering down through the sunroof and into the leather interior of a big black Lexus. She fiddled with her hair as she dialled her mother's number. The answerphone clicked on after two rings.

'Hi, Mum, it's me,' she began. 'I'm just phoning to say that I won't be home tonight. I'm staying another night. With a friend of Bee's. Everything's fine and I'll, er, see you tomorrow.' And then she hung up and felt her insides go all fizzy with the excitement of rebellion and change. Below her, the front door opened and then there was Lol, out in the street, peering at the pavement. The bright sunshine glittered off the rhinestones on her leather trousers and gleamed off her flawless skin. She was the most extraordinary-looking woman Ana had ever seen. And she wore her stature so differently to Ana – her shoulders back, her head erect, her heels high – almost like she was *proud* of her height.

She gripped the window frame and then noticed something nestled within the folds of curtain at her feet. An intricate band of turquoise feathers and translucent green beads threaded on to a delicate wire. A choker. She picked it up, feeling her spirits lift with the pleasure of being useful.

'Lol!' she called into the stiflingly hot street, 'your cunting choker!' Lol looked up at her and cackled. She cupped her hands together and Ana let the choker fall into them.

'Ana,' she grinned, 'I think I love you!' She kissed the choker and fastened it around her long, thin neck. A group of boys who'd been skateboarding all came to a grinding halt as they saw her walk elegantly back up the steps and into the house. They scooped up their skateboards and stared at her. Ana waited for one of them to say something. But they didn't. They just watched. And it wasn't until the door had closed behind her and she was half-way up the stairs that one of the boys spoke. He opened his mouth big and wide and emitted a single, breathless, overawed word:

'WO-OW!'

9

Lol, Ana soon realized, was a complete lunatic. She was thirty-three but looked about twenty-three and had more energy than a hyperactive, attention-deficit- disordered six-year-old on Red Bull. She was also disarmingly honest.

'You're not going out like that, are you?' she said, pointing at Ana's lank hair and grimy clothes in disbelief. 'Get in't shower, lass – I'll meck us some drinks.'

Lol's bathroom was a tiny damp tomb of a room with mildew on the ceiling and the widest array of beauty products Ana had ever seen. She encased herself in the shower cubicle and felt an overwhelming wave of relief as warm water ran from the crown of her head, down her face and over her tired body. She washed her hair with a coconutty Afro shampoo, scrubbed at her face with a grainy unguent that smelted of grapefruit and soaped her entire body with a translucent tablet of apple-scented soap.

Lol forced a drink into her hand as she emerged from the bathroom; a pale, lemon-coloured drink in a long-stemmed glass rimmed with glittering salt.

'Oh,' she said, staring at the drink, 'margarita. That's what Bee used to drink, isn't it?'

Lol nodded and took a slurp, her tongue snaking around the rim, collecting grains of salt. 'Sure was,' she said, 'and you're looking at the woman who taught her how to make them. Cheers,' she said, holding her glass aloft. 'To Bee. The greatest bloody girl in the world, the best friend I ever had. May her poor, beautiful soul rest in peace and may there be *rivers* of margarita flowing through the valleys of heaven . . .' They brushed their glasses against each other's and exchanged a fragile look. Lol was smiling, but Ana could see tears shimmering in her eyes.

'Right,' Lol exclaimed, putting down her drink and starting to unfurl Ana's towelling turban, 'what are we going to do with you then, eh?'

'What do you mean?'

'I wanna do you up,' said Lol, picking up strands of her wet hair and scrutinizing them. 'You're a pop star's sister – d'you know that? You should look like a pop star's sister. I've got two wardrobes full of beautiful clothes, and this is the first time I've ever met anyone I could lend 'em to. And besides – you look fucking awful, if you don't mind me saying. When was the last time you went to a hairdresser's?'

'Yes – but, I don't want to . . .'

'Don't worry,' Lol smiled, 'I'm not going to do anything over-dramatic. I'm not going to make you look like me or anything. Heaven forbid! I just wanna – polish you. D'you know what I mean. I wanna make you *shine* . . .'

She slathered a load of slimy stuff on to Ana's split ends and blow-dried her hair for about a quarter of an hour with a huge round brush until it lay gleaming on her shoulders like a black satin cape.

'Yasmin le Bon – eat your heart out.'

Then she applied some subtle make-up and forced Ana

into a brown, strappy chiffon top sprinkled with gold beads, which showed her midriff, a pair of very distressed vintage jeans with the waistband ripped off, and pointy-toed alligator-skin stilettos. 'Ooh, it's so nice not to feel like the only woman in the world with size eight feet, for a change,' she said, as she slipped Ana's long, thin feet easily into the shoes.

Ana watched her transformation in the mirror with wonder. It had never occurred to her that she could be scruffy and glamorous at the same time, that she could look so chic in a pair of jeans. Back home, girls either dressed down in student attire or dressed up in spangly New Look dresses and four-inch heels. You were either grungy or trendy. She liked this look, which was neither one nor the other. Her bony shoulders looked graceful under the barely-there chiffon, her pale stomach looked almost erogenous peeping between her top and trousers, and her legs looked shapely encased in pale denim on tiny, dainty heels. Lol had mascaraed her bottom lashes as well as her top lashes, making her eyes look enormous, and her hair looked shiny and wispy in a Patti Smith, Rock Goddess, kind of a way.

'And you cannot carry your stuff around in that.' Lol pointed disdainfully at her grubby tapestry rucksack. 'Here.' She chucked Ana a little gold clutch-bag. And then Lol stood and appraised her for a second or two, a smile spreading across her face. 'One last thing,' she said, walking towards Ana. She gripped Ana's shoulders and yanked them up, then she walked behind her and put a fist into the small of her back.

'What are you doing?' said Ana.

'I'm making you stand up straight. Your posture, Ana, is appalling. God has given you this fantastic, elegant, sophisticated body. Act like you're proud of it.' She backed away and appraised her again. 'That's better,' she said, 'now you like a propah Lundarn bird, like. Bee would be so proud of you.' Her eyes glazed over again and for a second she stared into space. 'Right.' She snapped out of her reverie and picked up her door keys. 'You and me, girl, we're gonna go out and be tall and skinny and black and white and scare the pants off all these poncey southern men. What d'you say?'

Lol took Ana to a members' club, a painfully, impossibly trendy series of distressed, shabby-chic rooms in an old factory in a decidedly insalubrious Ladbroke Grove back-street. Walking in with Lol, Ana noticed that for the first time since she'd arrived in London, she was being looked at – she was no longer invisible. And not just being glanced at but being stared at – with genuine interest – by men and women alike. And by some seriously stylish men and women, too.

'This,' said Lol, 'is about as London as London gets. Look at 'em – stylists, designers, retailers, restaurateurs, journalists, models, broadcasters. These are – I'm afraid to say – the people who make London what it is. Without these people, London would just be, you know . . . Leeds.'

Lol bought them a couple of margaritas, and they headed for a dark corner, spotlit through coloured gels and furnished with big brown leather sofas. Groovejet played quietly in the background, while opposite them two posh girls in Seventies throwback clothes made self-conscious roll-ups from mild shag and Rizlas.

'So – how did you and Bee meet?'

'Clubbing,' said Lol, simply, 'In the early Eighties. I can't remember a precise moment, though. We just sort of *merged*. She were wild back then, she really were. We were both part of the same scene for ages, all that New Romantic shite, Steve Strange, Philip Salon, Blitz and all that. But we became proper friends a few years later, after she asked me to work with her on "Groovin' for London".'

'So – what d'you do?'

'I am the world's least successful pop star.'

'What do you mean?'

'I mean – I left stage school fifteen years ago, I've worked non-stop since. I've been around the world about ten times, I've worked with some of the biggest names in the business, I've been credited on some of the most successful albums ever released. And I'm still £500 overdrawn and living in a grotty flat, just like I were the day I left college.'

'What've you been doing?'

'I'm a session singer, love. You know – the jobbing actors of the music industry. The faceless, anonymous providers of soulful harmonies, the unsung performers of those background noises that drown out the fact that the lead singer can't sing. Oh – and naff music for adverts, too, of course.'

'Adverts?'

'Oh aye. I've sung all sorts. Songs about deodorant. Songs about hair dye. Songs about tampons. You feel a right bloody fool singing those things, I can tell you, but it pays well.'

'God,' said Ana, dreamily, 'imagine getting paid to sing.'

'D'you like to sing then, Ana?'

'Uh-huh,' she nodded and took a sip of tangy margarita.

'Any good?'

She shrugged. 'Dunno. I think so. I've never sung in front of anyone.'

'Hmm. Now that's a situation we might have to rectify at some point. A good voice should never be wasted. It's like pouring Bolly down the sink.'

'What were you singing this morning, then?'

'Oh, my love – this morning were a real low point. Backing vocals for Billie Piper. It doesn't get much worse than that. She's a nice lass though, that Billie. Very mature. I told her about Bee. Didn't know who the fuck I was talking about, but did her best to sound sad, bless her heart. Ironic really, in't it? That could be *her* one day, it could be Billie Piper lying dead in her bed and nobody giving a shit and some little teenage superstar of the day saying, Billie Who? D'you know what I mean? That's the business. That's the life. That's just the way it goes. Chews you up, spits you out.'

Tears started plopping out of Lol's brown eyes, and Ana quickly handed her a tissue. The two posh girls opposite pretended not to notice but had stopped talking to each other and were sitting stock-still, like little rabbits.

'D'you think that's what happened to Bee, then? D'you think it was the music industry? I mean – do *you* think she killed herself?'

Lol shrugged and blew her nose noisily into the tissue.

'I don't know, Ana. I really don't know. It's all I've thought about for the last three weeks. I mean, it certainly looks that way. I can't see any other explanation. It's just really painful to admit though, in't it? It's like admitting that I wasn't a good pal. That I didn't really know her. That our friendship was a sham.' She sniffed and shot Ana a look. 'What do you think?'

'About what?'

'About Bee, of course. Do you think it was suicide?'

Ana shrugged. 'It's the only logical explanation.'

Lol nodded, sadly. 'It is, isn't it?'

'But why? Why would she have done something like that? I mean – did she *seem* unhappy?'

'The thing with Bee was that she was never really happy, was she? Not properly happy. Not after her dad died. And not really *before* for that matter. Except when she was young she used to drown it out by partying and drinking and sleeping around and being the original good-time girl. Then Gregor died and her career died and she never really recovered from it all.'

'But couldn't she have got help?'

'Oh – she did. Didn't she tell you?'

Ana shook her head.

'Yeah. She did three years of therapy – didn't get her anywhere. And she were on anti-depressants on and off for fifteen years.'

'Fifteen years?'

'Aye. Didn't she tell you that, either? Jesus. Yeah – Bee just sort of existed really. I don't mean to say that she went around being miserable all the time, or anything. She was still funny. She still enjoyed herself and was good company and all that. But she just sort of stopped . . . *developing*. She got set in her ways and didn't take risks. Didn't participate in life – just let herself get carried along by it.'

'So you're saying that Bee was depressed for half of her life?'

''Fraid so.'

'But that's shocking. Just shocking. Don't you think?'

Lol shrugged. 'This is London,' she said, 'depression's like the flu in a city like this. The norm. But actually, Bee did seem better for a while last year. Started talking about her career again, her future. And then she moved flat in January and seemed to go downhill again. Started obsessing about ageing, talking about plastic surgery. And she stopped going out. I used to try and get her to come out with me, but she said she was trying to save money. She'd invite me over there, but I . . . this'll make me sound bad, but I just *hated* that flat. I really did.'

'Why?'

Lol shrugged. 'I dunno, really,' she said, 'it were just a vibe. Something about the atmosphere. It were . . . *dead*.'

'Where had she been living before that?'

Lol shot her a strange look. 'What exactly did you two use to talk about? It's almost like you didn't know her.'

Ana shrugged. 'Well – I didn't really.'

'Well – she had this beautiful flat in Belsize Park. It was so gorgeous, all bright and posh and lovely.'

'Did she own it?'

'Nah – she never bought anywhere. She were too much of a free spirit to get lumbered with a mortgage. I never understood why she moved from there to Baker Street, though. And it were all so sudden. You know. One minute she was settled and sorted. She had her cat and all her lovely things. And then she just up and left, overnight. Left half her stuff behind, by all accounts. And moved into that pigging awful place. God – I hated that flat . . .'

'But did she seem unhappy enough to – you know?'

Lol shook her head and shrugged. 'As I say, she was never really a content soul. But I thought she'd learned to live with that. And she certainly didn't seem to be any *worse*, you know, like she was spiralling downwards or anything. But, you know, when something like this happens, you start thinking about every little thing, don't you?' She turned suddenly to Ana and looked at her desperately. 'Ana,' she said, 'there is one thing. Something I've not told anyone else. One little thing. I mean, I don't know if it was what caused it or anything like that, but . . .'

Ana nodded, encouragingly.

'. . . I think it might have been my fault.'

Ana frowned at her. 'Don't be silly,' she said, 'how could it be your fault?'

'Because . . . because, oh God. Listen. D'you promise you won't tell anyone else what I'm about to tell you? Not your mother, not anyone?'

Ana nodded forcefully.

Lol took a slurp of her margarita. 'Well,' she began, 'it were the Wednesday before she died. I'd not seen her for a few weeks because I'd been out of the country, on tour, and she turned up on my doorstep first thing and she were in a right state, crying and shaking and everything. And she had her cat with her. She said that her landlord had been tipped off that she were keeping a cat in that flat and had let himself in and threatened to kick her out if she didn't get rid of him. So she begged me to look after him, just for a couple of weeks, just until she found a new flat. And I said yes. And she looked so relieved and everything and I just felt, you know, really pleased to have been able to help her out.

'So, after she left I put all of John's things out – his bowl and his basket and all that. And he made himself at home. And then I went out that afternoon, to my voice coach and . . . and – oh God' – she sniffed again and rubbed her face into her crumpled tissues – 'I'd left the window in my hallway open a crack. Just a crack, because it gets so blinking hot in that place. And the hall window looks over the back of the house. And when I got back – and I don't know how he got through it 'cos he's a fucking big cat, I mean – *huge* – but he weren't in the flat and he weren't anywhere, so he must have. And I searched everywhere. I were out in the street until ten o'clock that night, until it got dark, and he was nowhere. And then all the next day. And Bee sent flowers. On the Thursday. While I were looking for her cat. Beautiful flowers with a note saying how grateful she was to me and how she knew that I wasn't that keen on cats and how much it meant to her that I'd taken him in and how she wouldn't have wanted to have left him with anyone else – and there was this, too.' She pulled open an embroidered silk purse and pulled out a piece of paper, torn from a magazine. She handed it to Ana. 'She said she'd torn it out ages ago, had been meaning to give it to me for months.'

The clipping was entitled 'True Friendship' and was

taken from a letter from Kingsley Amis to his friend, Philip Larkin:

I enjoy talking to you more than to anybody else because I never feel I am giving myself away and so can admit to shady, dishonest, crawling, cowardly, unjust, arrogant, snobbish, lecherous, perverted and generally shameful feelings that I don't want anybody else to know about; but most of all because I am always on the verge of violent laughter when talking to you.

If you were here, I keep thinking, we would spend the time in talk and drink and smoke, and I should be laughing A LOT OF THE TIME, and I should be enjoying myself A LOT OF THE TIME.

Lol pointed at it. 'Look,' she said, fresh tears springing to her eyes, 'look. If you were here,' it says. *If you were here.* God, that gets me. Because I wasn't there, I really wasn't. See, me and Bee, we'd always been the 'single girls', you know, the eternal bachelor-girls. We always made time for each other. And then, last year – I fell in love. For the first time. I mean, I'd had obsessions before, and passion and all that. But with Keith I just knew I'd found my soulmate. He's a Romany,' she grinned, through her tears, 'a real, proper Romany. And he's an astrologist. Really successful. He's got syndicated columns all over the world. And I'm out of the country a lot, on business. And before, I'd always make sure that when I was around I spent time with Bee. But since I met Keith – well, he's the one I want to make time for. I didn't have enough spare time to share it between both of them. And something had to give. And it was Bee. So what with her not wanting to come out, and me being with Keith and that fucking awful flat, well

– I'd hardly seen her at all. And that clipping' – she pointed at it again – 'it was a cry, don't you think? A cry for help? And there's me lying to her, telling her John's doing really well. When he's probably flat on his back in a gutter somewhere.' She sniffed and dragged a finger across her nostrils.

Ana handed the clipping back to Lol and she folded it sadly and put it back in her purse.

'So, the next day, I put up posters on trees and that. I started knocking on people's doors. I went to the local vet. To the RSPCA. The PDSA. I know I should have told Bee, but I just couldn't. She loved that cat like a kid, d'you know what I mean? But when he hadn't turned up by the Friday, I just thought . . . you know. So I told her, and she lost it, Ana – I mean, big-time lost it. It was terrible. She didn't get angry with me, though. She didn't blame me or anything. She kept blaming herself. It were almost like she was saying that she were a bad mother or summat. She came round that afternoon when I was out and she scoured the area, too. I didn't get back till late on the Friday night, and the next thing I heard was a phonecall from the fucking police on the Tuesday evening – saying she were dead. Saying she'd been dead since Friday. Saying she'd died all on her own.' Lol blew her nose again and rubbed her eyes. 'So even if she didn't kill herself, even if it *was* an accident, it was still my fault. Because I lost her cat, I lost John. And I made her miserable. And she died like that – miserable, and all alone, Ana. Isn't that the worst thing to imagine? Someone you love, dying all on their own?'

Ana nodded, tears catching in her throat as an image

of Bee's bed floated into her consciousness once again.

'I tried phoning her all weekend and there was no answer. I just presumed that she'd gone to see you, so it didn't worry me too much and . . .'

Ana turned to Lol. 'Sorry,' she said, 'can you say that last bit again?'

Lol looked at her. 'I said that it didn't worry me too much when she didn't answer the phone because I presumed she'd be in Devon. With you.'

Ana's jaw fell open. 'Oh, now – this is too weird, too, too weird.' She told Lol about what Mrs Tilly-Loubelle had said. And then she told her everything, about the cottage and the song about Zander and the trip to India. Lol knew nothing about any of it and was completely silenced by the information.

'I'm gobsmacked,' she said, her eyes wide with confusion, 'totally, completely and utterly *gobsmacked*. And I thought it were weird,' she continued, 'the way you've been asking me all these questions about Bee, as if you didn't know her. And you mean to say,' she squeaked incredulously, 'that Bee was disappearing off somewhere every weekend and lying to me about it? Me – her best friend? And that that mare had a lovely little cottage in the country and she never told anyone. God, you know, I always wondered what she'd done with all that money from her dad. I couldn't work out why she was always talking about being broke. And she was always, *always* going on about going to India. It was like her big dream. And she fucking went and didn't even tell us. I am outraged, Ana – outraged. You know what we've got to do, don't you?' she said.

Ana shook her head.

'We've got to go. We've got to go to this Broadstairs place and find this cottage. I'll bet you anything it's where she was going every weekend. She probably had a secret lover or something. This Zander bloke. I bet it was him. You said you found some keys in the flat?'

Ana nodded, numbly.

'So. We've got a photo. We've got keys. We have to go.' Lol was growing more and more animated as her tears dried up and her plan took shape.

'Yes,' said Ana, 'but when? I've got to go home tomorrow.'

'Oh, don't be daft. You can't go home now. Not now. We've got a mystery to solve.'

'Yes, but – what about Mum?'

Lol raised her eyebrows to the ceiling again. 'You sound like a scratched record, d'you know that? What about Mum, what about Mum?' she mimicked Ana's middle-class tones. 'What about your bloody mother? How old is she?'

'Sixty.'

'Can she walk?'

'Uh-huh.'

'Can she use a toilet?'

'Yes.'

'Can she cook for herself.'

'Mm.'

'Has she got friends? People to look out for her?'

'Yes – loads. Everyone in Torrington thinks she's wonderful.'

'So – she'll be all right for a few days then, won't she?'

'She'll give me hell, you know.'

'Oh, big-fucking-deal' – Lol drew a newspaper with her hands – 'I can see the headlines already – "Horror of Sixty-Year-Old Woman Shouting at Adult Daughter". How old are you, Ana? Twenty-four, twenty-five? And you're still scared of your mum. Honestly, girl – you should be ashamed of yourself. And, quite frankly, if you don't mind me being completely honest with you for a moment, your mother doesn't *deserve* your concern. Not after the way she treated Bee. Particularly after the funeral incident . . .'

'What funeral?'

'Gregor's funeral, of course.'

'Yes, but that was Bee's fault. She attacked my mother . . .'

'And can you blame her? It was the most shocking thing I have ever witnessed, and if I hadn't seen it with my own eyes . . .'

'What?' said Ana. 'What happened?'

'Well – what did your mother tell you happened?'

'That Bee threw her out of the chapel of rest, that she hurt her, that she screamed at her in front of everyone.'

'And why d'you think she might have done that?'

Ana shrugged. 'Because she didn't want her to be there? Because she was ashamed of her. Ashamed of *us*.'

'Is that what she told you?'

'Uh-huh.'

Lol raised her eyebrows. 'That woman,' she said, 'that woman should be . . . she should be – *God*. I dunno. She's a *disgrace*. Look. Your mother behaved appallingly at Gregor's funeral. She were sobbing and wailing and crying out "my husband, my husband", when everyone knew that he *weren't* her bloody husband *at all*. And she were making such a racket that one of Gregor's friends, this really lovely guy called Tiger, he went and sat next to her to try to calm her down. Apparently he just said, is there anything I can do for you, maybe you'd like some fresh air — that sort of thing. I mean, he wasn't being even slightly rude. And he put an arm around her shoulder, like this. And she *slaps* it away and turns round to him and starts really laying into him . . .'

Oh God. Ana already knew what was coming. Her mother's abundant charm was a barely existent membrane over her hateful innards. When she turned, she turned.

'She said, "Get your disgusting AIDS-ridden hand off me, you snivelling, malnourished, frankly rather unattractive *excuse* for a man." And then told him that he should hurry up and die and stop being a drain on the National Health. And then she stood up, in front of everyone, in front of all of Gregor's friends, and accused them all of turning him into a pervert against his will and of deliberately infecting Gregor with their 'rancid virus' so that they could get their hands on all his money.'

'No!' said Ana.

'Yes,' said Lol, 'she fucking well did. Oh Ana, I tell you, it were one of the most shocking things I have ever seen in my life. I wanted to hit 'er. I really did. And then I saw Bee getting up from her seat, and her face went all sort of twisted up, and she just grabbed your mother by her arms, like this, and frog-marched her out of the chapel. Told her she didn't ever want to see her again. Told her she was disowning her. I wanted to cheer, I really did. But it weren't exactly appropriate, you know . . .'

Ana's face felt slack with shock – not shock that her mother was capable of behaving so badly, but shock that she'd missed out on a relationship with Bee because of it, that the infamous and much-vaunted bruises on her mother's arms, far from being an acceptable reason to sever ties with Bee, were the exact opposite. And that she'd been stupid enough to believe her mother's version of events in the first place.

'So,' said Lol, 'that should give you a fresh perspective on things.' She picked up her bag. 'I'm going to get us some more drinks now, and by the time I get back I expect you to have made the right decision. All right?'

'All right.' Ana's hands shook as she picked up her margarita and drained it of the last few drops. The enormity of what Lol had just told her was hitting home. Everything could have been so different.

She watched Lol sashay across the room in her blue chiffon gypsy top and indigo jeans, her white pony tail and long diamanté earrings swinging from side to side, and the eyes of every person in the room on her. Lol knew no fear. She didn't see obstacles in life – only opportunities. She wasn't just Ana's physical negative, but her mental negative, too.

Ana looked around her at the other people in the bar. Strangers. Dozens of them. Strangers with strange lives who lived in flats she'd never visit and had jobs she'd never heard of. This was Bee's world, she realized, this city of transients and trendies, exclusivity and anonymity, this city where it could take two hours to visit a friend living three miles away but less than thirty minutes to get a fresh lobster delivered to your front door. And not only did she want to know what this city had done to her big sister, but she also wanted to know *it*. She wanted to feel at home here. Like Bee had. She wasn't ready to go home. She wasn't ready to face her mother. She wanted to stay.

'I'm staying,' she said firmly, when Lol returned with two more margaritas. 'I'm staying.'

Lol threw her arms around her, and the two women hugged. 'Nice one, girl, nice one. Now we've just got to sort out a plan. We'll go on Sunday, right? I've got to work tomorrow and I'm off on Monday.'

'Off?'

'Yeah. I'm going to St Tropez for a few days. To a recording studio.'

'*Really?*' Ana's mind was boggling with the glamour of it all.

'Uh-huh. I'm going to be staying in a *belle époque* mansion on a cliff overlooking the sea with a swimming pool and a maze and fountains and everything.'

'Wow,' said Ana.

'Yeah. Downside is I'm going to be there with a bunch of foul-mouthed, beer-swilling Scousers with too much money in their pockets and too much coke up their noses. But I'm not complaining. Not at all. And I'll find you a place to stay. I'd offer you my flat, but it's a shithole and, anyway, I don't want you living on your own. Not a country girl like you in a city like this. Have you got any money?'

Ana thought guiltily of the £7,350 sitting in her suitcase at Lol's flat, and nodded.

'Excellent. Leave it with me. And we'll get Flint to drive.'

'Flint? Who's Flint?'

Lol raised her finely plucked eyebrows. 'Don't ask. Just a guy. A guy with a really big car. So – a toast,' she grinned, raising her glass towards Ana's, 'a toast to us – the Cagney and Lacey of W10.' They laughed and clinked glasses, and then Lol turned to Ana and looked serious.

'Do you forgive me?' she said.

'What for?'

'For not being a good enough friend to Bee? For being selfish? For losing the cat? For breaking Bee's heart? For letting her down?'

'Oh Lol – don't be silly. It wasn't your fault. Look – Bee would have kept searching for that cat if it had taken her for ever. It wasn't the cat. It was something else. And that's what we're going to search for in Broadstairs. OK?'

'OK,' said Lol, 'OK.'

And then their conversation was interrupted, as a floppy-haired man in a T-shirt and Bermuda shorts approached them. 'Excuse me,' he said in a German accent, 'my friend and I' – he indicated another floppy-haired man standing at the bar – 'We were wondering. You two are very beautiful and also very tall. Are you by any chance – models?'

'No, love,' said Lol wearily, flipping her ponytail over her shoulder, 'we're not models. We're something much better than models. We're undercover detectives. But don't tell a soul. All right?'

Ana and Lol waited until the confused-looking man wandered back to his friend before looking at each other and dissolving into cackles.

10

Flint pulled his car up alongside the flower-seller and climbed out.

'Morning there,' said the bearded man who ran the stall. 'How are you today?'

Flint shrugged and slipped his hands into his pockets. 'Not bad,' he said, 'you know.'

'The usual?'

Flint scratched the back of his neck. 'Yeah,' he said, 'cheers.'

The man looked at Flint curiously, but said nothing. He pulled ten tall stems of candy-pink roses from a green bucket, selecting the fattest buds, and tied them loosely together with cream ribbon. Flint handed him a £20 note and took the flowers and his change.

'If you don't mind me asking,' said the man, after a long pause, 'the flowers. Nearly every day for the past three weeks. Who are they for? Wife? Mum? Girlfriend?'

'No,' said Flint, 'they're just for a friend.'

'A good friend, by the look of it.'

'Yeah,' said Flint, 'one of the best. Too good for me.'

'How's that?'

'Oh. You know. It's easy, isn't it? So easy just to be – you know – selfish . . .'

'Oh well. There aren't many of us around who aren't

selfish, mate. It's the human condition. Self-preservation. You gotta put yourself first – nobody else is going to.'

'Yes but – it's *wrong*. Just because it's the human condition, it doesn't make it right, you know. We should be able to rise above it. Look out for other people.'

'So,' said the florist, 'what happened then. What was it?'

'Overdose.'

'Suicide?'

Flint shrugged. 'We're not sure yet.'

The florist sucked in his breath. 'That's bad,' he said, 'that's very bad. But you can't tie yourself up in knots over it. For a person to do something like that – well, they've reached rock bottom, haven't they? There's nothing anyone can do when someone's reached the end of the line.'

'Yeah there is. There's always something someone can do. You never heard that story about the man on the bridge? And that other guy who talked him down?'

'Yes – but what happened after? That's the real question. He stopped him that time, but who the hell knows what happened next? Eh? Next time the guy was feeling down? And there was no one there to talk him out of it? You know – this friend of yours – how d'you know you hadn't already saved her a few times already? How d'you know you haven't said a kind word at the right time, taken her out for a drink on a bad night, given her something to look forward to when there was nothing? Eh?'

Flint shrugged. The man's words were of no comfort to him. 'I was supposed to be looking after her,' he said. 'It was my . . . *job*.'

'What – literally?'

'Yeah. At one time. I was her minder, you know. Not

for a while, not for years, but I never really lost that feeling that she was my responsibility. She didn't have anyone else, you see . . .'

'Listen, mate. You can't be everywhere at once. You can't protect people from everything. Believe me. I've got three kids. I know. And it doesn't matter how much you want to control things, people will make their own decisions, ultimately. It's all about choice. People make choices and other people *cannot* take responsibility for that.'

'Yeah,' said Flint, running out of steam now, patting the flowers up and down against his forearm, enjoying the feel of the silky petals and prickly leaves tickling his skin, 'yeah. Maybe you're right. But it doesn't make it any easier to sleep at night. You know . . .'

The florist nodded and smiled. 'Yeah,' he said, 'I know.'

'But – thanks. For the chat. Thanks.'

'No problem. See you tomorrow, then, mate?'

'Yeah,' he said, tapping the flowers harder and harder against his arm, 'yeah. See you tomorrow.'

He climbed back into his car and drove slowly to the car park, his tyres crunching against loose chippings on the road. He parked the car and began the walk across the cemetery to Bee's grave.

11

Lol was as good as her word about finding Ana somewhere to stay.

The room she found wasn't particularly nice, but it was (according to Lol) in a good part of town, near Ladbroke Grove. 'West is Best, that's what I always say,' she'd said.

Lol couldn't go to the house with her because she was working, but drew her a detailed map. It was in a small modern terrace just opposite Latimer Road Tube station. 'It's ex-Local Authority, but you'd never know it. And Gill keeps it spotless.'

Gill was an ex-flatmate of Lol's from 'fucking aeons ago'. She was small and skinny and pretty in a washed-out sort of a way. Her hair was fine and brown with bright ash highlights. She was wearing those neat little jeans that small, skinny, unglamorous women always wear, with blue flip-flops and an orange-jersey top with gold and black braiding around the neckline. She wore plain gold studs in her ears and a tricolour Russian wedding band on her little finger and had on no make-up. She looked about thirty.

'I didn't really want to have to let the room out at all, but I was made redundant a couple of months ago and now I've decided to go back to college to do a counselling course. So I need every penny I can get at the moment. D'you smoke?' She was Scottish with a sweet, childlike voice and walked around with her hands shoved into her pockets like a little schoolboy.

'No,' Ana said, and then corrected herself, 'well – only sometimes, and definitely not in the house if you don't want me to . . .'

'No – God, no. I want you to smoke. I've just given up and I need to at least be able to smell it. I miss the smell of it so much. This is the kitchen . . .'

Small, neat, modern, and with a large window over-looking a small, neat garden.

'I'm really, really sorry about your sister by the way. She was an amazing person. I can't believe it. I really can't. And this is the living room . . .'

Mint-green walls, pale-ash floors, lots of bookshelves, photographs of family, sporting trophies of some kind, small yellow futon.

'And not leaving a note, or anything. That must be terrible for you to deal with. This is the downstairs toilet . . .'

Pine seat, quilted toilet paper, chrome toilet-brush, pink festoon blind.

'And how's your poor mother taking it? Lol tells me they hadn't spoken for an age. She must be devastated. Here's my bedroom . . .'

Lavender walls, wrought-iron bed, broderie anglaise cushions, soft toys, exercise bike, rowing machine.

'It's always so much worse when someone goes when there are still unresolved issues. Bathroom . . .'

Victorian-style claw-footed bath, sponge-printed por-celain chamber-pot, stripped-pine dresser, pink bath towels, contact-lens containers.

'And this is yours . . .'

It was the smallest room Ana had ever seen, but it was neat and clean and prettily decorated with yellow walls, a single lime-green futon and a very narrow wardrobe.

'I know it's a bit small, but my sister lived here for a while a couple of years ago and she was very happy. And it's nice to have the futon, in case you have people round . . .'

An image of Gill's sister throwing a party in this cupboard of a room, inviting lots of people over to hang out and drink punch on her weeny futon flashed through Ana's mind and she had to stop herself laughing.

'It's really sweet,' she said. 'I like it.'

'Och – and it's ever so convenient for everything round here. There's a big Sainsbury's just around the corner, and the Tube just over the road. It only takes a few minutes to get into town. And there's a great wee gym a few roads up. And if you're still around next weekend it's the carnival, or "Carnival" as the trendy types around here like to call it. We're right in the thick of it here – the atmosphere is amazing. How long are you planning on being here?'

Ana shrugged. 'God. I don't know. At least a week, I suppose.'

'That's perfect for me. I've a long-term tenant moving in in September, so that couldn't be better. So . . . what do you think? Do you want it?'

'Well – do you want me to want it?'

'Oh aye. Definitely. Any friend of Lol's is a friend of mine. And I'd rather live with a friend than a stranger. How does a flat £100 for the week grab you . . . ?'

Ana thought that it grabbed her tightly round the throat

and made her want to shout '£100 – for a cupboard – are you fucking *joking*!' But instead she nodded and smiled and said, 'Fine. Fine. And I've got the cash.'

'Great,' replied Gill, 'we'll sort that out later, I'm off to the gym now. And then I'm meeting a girlfriend for lunch. I probably won't be back till early evening – so make yourself at home! Oh – and if you're gonna do any sunbathing in the garden, don't wear anything too skimpy. There's a guy across the way who likes to get his cock out and slap it about a bit at the merest glimpse of female flesh. You have been warned.' She beamed and giggled and scooped up her gym bag, leaving the house with a tinkly 'cheerio'.

Ana found herself alone in her temporary new home. She unpacked her few possessions in her tiny room and then wandered around a bit, looking at Gill's trophies and medals – it looked like she was an athlete of some kind. And then she picked up a magazine, the walkabout phone and a glass of tap water and ventured out into the garden.

The magazine was called ES. She flicked through it. 'Hoxton vs. Notting Hill' said a headline. Underneath were pictures of very thin girls with flicked hair and plucked eyebrows wearing very odd clothes and standing in very uncomfortable-looking poses. The text ran:

Ever since the global success of Richard Curtis's Notting Hill, the spotlight of cool has shone a little less brightly on the streets of W11 . . . pink stucco and scented candles, pashminas and Patty Shelabargers, the Cross and Kate Moss, have lost the style race to the mean streets of London EC1. The Hoxton girl has taken control of the Monopoly board of London fashion . . . think scuffed stilettos and ankle socks . . . think uncompromising wedged hair – think Tracie singing 'The House that Jack Built' in '83 . . .

Think 'What a pile of old bollocks,' thought Ana. And then she smiled as she mentally applied the same frothing-at-the-mouth-style commentary to her home county.

. . . the Barnstaple woman has taken control of the Monopoly board of North Devon fashion . . . think comfy shoes and support tights . . . think uncompromising shampoo and set . . . think Ethel off *EastEnders* doing karaoke at the Queen Vic in '83 . . .

She smiled to herself and put the magazine down on the grass. And then she felt her stomach clench with anxiety. She couldn't put it off for another second. She had to phone her mother. She took a deep breath, squared her shoulders and punched in her mother's phone number. 'Please,' she whispered to herself, 'don't pick up, *please, don't pick up . . .*'

'Mum,' she began, addressing the answerphone, breathing a sigh of relief, 'it's me. I'm sorry I didn't phone yesterday, it's just that I've been . . .'

'Anabella!'

Ana jumped as her mother's harsh voice came booming out of the receiver.

'What the *hell* do you think you're playing at?!'

'I . . .'

'You are the most useless, selfish girl I have ever known. I ask you to do one thing. ONE THING. And you make a mess of it. This really is quite unacceptable, Anabella, quite unacceptable. I've been worried SICK. I want you home today, Anabella. Do you hear me?'

'I . . .'

'Not another word. Not one more word. There's a train from Paddington in an hour and a half. I want you on it.'

'I . . .'

'Not one more word. You're coming home.'

'NO!'

'YES!'

'NO!'

'YES!'

'NO! I am not coming home, Mum. I'm staying here. For a few days at least. I am not coming home. So you're just going to have to look after yourself for a while. Do you understand?' A tiny, shell-shocked moment of silence indicated to Ana that her words had made an impression.

'What do you mean, you're staying?'

'I mean, I've rented a room in a flat and I'm staying.'

'What flat?'

'Gill's flat. She's a friend of Lol's. And Lol was Bee's best friend.'

'And where is this flat?'

'It's in Ladbroke Grove.'

'Never heard of it. What's this Gill like?'

'She's very nice. She's Scottish. She's an athlete.'

'Hmmmm. And this *Lol*?' – she expelled the word like phlegm – 'what about her?'

'Lol is . . . she's' – Ana found herself smiling – 'she's *amazing*. She's really funny and really beautiful and really confident and she can sing and . . .'

'Yes, yes, yes. I'm almost out of polenta, I've only a couple of brushes' worth of toothpaste left and if I don't get some seed down by tomorrow we can wave goodbye to our lawn next year. And as if I didn't have enough to worry about, I'm nearly out of toilet paper and couscous, too. I can last a few days, but after that, well . . . But I shouldn't imagine that any of that is of even the slightest interest to you. What the *hell* are you doing down there anyway?'

Ana bit her lip, unsure whether or not she should tell her mother what was going on. 'Look, Mum. There's all this weird stuff. About Bee. So we're going down to the coast to see if we can find out what's been happening . . .'

'We?'

'Yes. Me and Lol and Flint.'

'And *who* is Flint?'

'He's another friend of Lol's. I haven't met him yet . . .'

'Ridiculous name. He sounds like a caveman. Anyway – everything's arrived. All of Belinda's things. They got here yesterday afternoon. But I'm a bit concerned that some of it might have gone astray. All Gregor's furniture for example. And her memorabilia. There doesn't appear to be very much here.'

'No, Mum. That's all there was. She didn't have very much stuff.'

'I see. And the papers? What's happening about the papers? I still haven't seen anything, you know – not a thing.'

'Mum,' sighed Ana, 'I hate to break this to you, but I don't think anyone cares.'

'Of course they care. They're obsessed, these days, the papers, obsessed with celebrity – any celebrity.'

'Yes, but Mum – Bee wasn't a celebrity.'

'Of course she was.'

'No, Mum – she was an ex-celebrity. Nobody cares about ex-celebrities.'

'What – not even when they're dead?'

'Not even when they're dead.'

'Oh.'

'Look. Mum. This call's going to cost a fortune. I'm going to go now.'

'Oh. I see. Will you . . . will you call me again? Soon?'

Ana felt herself softening as her mother's pathetic, childlike side came out blinking into the open. 'Of course I will. I'll call you.'

'Good. Because I'm feeling rather low. About everything. I feel like I've lost everything. D'you understand? Everything. And now you've gone, too. And I'm all alone . . . all alone . . .'

'I'll be back in a few days, Mum, I'll . . .'

'. . . How you could do this to me, I just don't know. It's that city. That *evil* city. It sucks people in. It destroys people. It's the devil's own playground. It's . . . oh *God*! I'm so alone, Anabella. I'm so entirely *alone*. I don't know if I can cope. I don't know what's going to happen to me. I'm scared. I'm so, so scared. I can't sleep at night, I can't . . .'

'Take a pill, Mum. Just take a pill,' sighed Ana, as her mother began to lose her austere façade and go into emotional meltdown. She always did this. She would start off with her lips pursed together like a drawstring bag, spitting out her words like bitter little fruit pips and then, if that didn't work, she'd let her face collapse into a tragic sack of despair and start talking about 'how alone' she was. There was no middle ground. No point at which Ana could begin to communicate with her in a reasonable manner. She didn't want to listen to this. She didn't *have* to listen to this. She had more important things to worry about.

'Bye, Mum.'

'No. Anabella. Don't go.'

'I'll phone you in a couple of days.'

'No! *Don't.* Stay on the line – I insist . . . I . . .'

Ana pulled the phone away from her ear but she didn't put it down immediately. She listened first to the muted sounds of Gay softly sobbing as she replaced the receiver. And she knew what Gay was sobbing for. Not for Bee and not for Ana, but for herself. Because as long as Gay had had Ana upstairs in her bedroom being useless, then there was always going to be someone worse off than she was. And without Ana upstairs in her bedroom being useless, it was just Gay, a sad and lonely old woman, too chock-full of neuroses to go out of her front door, who'd failed at everything she'd ever attempted, whose daughters couldn't bear her and who was now, for the very first time in her life, all alone.

Ana imagined her mother there, alone, in her finely decorated home. She imagined the thud of the *Telegraph* landing on the doormat like it did every day, at nine on the dot. She imagined the smell of Gay's peppermint tea, and the lopped-off tops of people's heads passing by their front window on the way to the paper shop next door and the sound of church bells on Sundays being carried on the breeze from St Giles in the Wood.

It already felt alien, only two days into her absence. And then, as she lay there on Gill's cream deckchair, drinking up the sun, she thought of last night, of her shiny hair and her snakeskin stilettos, her chiffon top and her gold clutchbag. She thought of her strong feelings for Lol and the way everyone had stared at them and the guy who came up and asked them if they were both models. She thought of holding on to Lol's arm in the midnight breeze, of giggling together and singing Groovejet, 'If This Ain't Lo-ove', together at the tops of their voices, until a blonde woman in a satin camisole top opened a window and shouted at them to shut the fuck up. She thought of the minicab that picked them up at one in the morning, driven by a guy from Serbia with enormous brown eyes, who showed them pictures of his little daughters and his beautiful wife and explained how he was staying in a hostel with sixty other men, sharing a room with five, some of whom cried themselves to sleep every night, and how he was the lucky one because he could speak English and had a car. She thought of winding down the window and feeling the warm night air billowing through her smoky hair and watching young Londoners reeling around the streets in denim jackets and midriff tops and dyed hair. She thought of going back to Lol's little flat and watching her make a big fat spliff with oily pungent grass the likes of which she'd never seen in Devon and smoking it with her while they listened to Lol's demo tapes, the sash window in the living room heaved wide open, letting in drifts of warm city air, and the occasional sounds of partygoers on their way home. She thought of how she'd started getting the spins and had sat with her head over the toilet for a few minutes before feeling normal again, and how Lol had laughed and called her a lightweight, and told her how ashamed Bee would have been and how she was going to have to toughen her up.

And then she thought of *last* Friday night. She thought of her mother calling her down for dinner and the two of them eating together in silence. She thought of getting into bed at midnight, still wide awake and listening to the sounds of Torrington on a Friday night – silent but for the occasional passing car. And she thought of that hollow feeling, that sense of uselessness and emptiness, that sense that nothing good was ever going to happen to her again that kept her blankly sleepless until one o'clock, and never thinking for a second that just a week later she'd be here. In London. Sitting in a deckchair in a garden in Ladbroke Grove. Living with a woman from Perthshire and about to have an adventure with a six-foot black singer and a mysterious man called Flint.

And at this thought she felt her heart fill up with joy, and an incredible feeling of well-being suddenly overcame her. She closed her eyes and let the rays from the sun kiss her all over her face while the noises of urban life – the high-pitched squeal of black cabs, the rhythmic thud of distant bass, the sonorous rumble of double-decker buses and the shouts and hollers of a nearby game of basketball – seeped into her consciousness like the soundtrack to some classic film that people had been recommending to her for years but she'd only just got around to watching. And now she was wondering why she'd waited so long.

'Bee,' she whispered to herself, as she hugged all these feelings to her chest and realized that there was only one thing missing, 'I wish you were here.'

Lol took Ana out again that night. They went for cocktails at a snazzy bar by a smelly canal next to a noisy bus station, full of loads more trendy types. Why did trendy types insist on hanging out in such grotty areas? They talked about Bee and they talked about Keith – who was currently holed up in a cottage in Cornwall trying to make the deadline on an astrology book he was writing – and they talked about their plans for the following day. Then Lol called a cab at ten, insisting that she and Ana both go home, get some sleep. They had an early start the next day.

When Ana got back to Gill's that night, the little house in Ladbroke Grove was in darkness. She took off her snakeskin stilettos and tiptoed slowly up the stairs towards her tiny bedroom. As she neared the landing she saw that Gill's light was still on, and as she approached her door she could hear music. And squeaking. And groaning. And sucking. And slapping. And banging.

Ana felt slightly shocked. Obviously there was nothing that shocking about a thirty-year-old woman having sex on a Saturday night, but Gill just hadn't seemed the type, for some reason. There are some people in life who you can easily imagine having sex and some that you just can't, and Gill definitely fell into the second category. She seemed too clean, too fresh, too sporty, too neat, the sort of person you couldn't imagine pooing, or farting, or having smelly trainers, either.

When Gill came back from her lunch that afternoon, they'd chatted for a while, and Ana had discovered that Gill used to be a gymnast. She'd represented Great Britain at the Barcelona Olympics and had been working as a personal trainer at the local gym before the redundancy. The counselling course she was about to start was actually sports counselling (Ana had wondered what that was. 'My swimming coach never hugged me'?), and Gill spent 90 per cent of her free time at the gym and at the local swimming-pool. Her fridge was full of energy drinks and yoghurt and fresh fruit, and she had about ten pairs of dinky little size-three trainers lined up in her bedroom, none of which looked like they'd ever been worn. She was wholesome and fit and the sort of person who made you feel like a big, smelly, unhealthy monster.

Which was why it seemed weird that she'd be doing something as base, animal and generally messy as having sex.

Ana pushed down slowly on her door handle, trying desperately not to put Gill and her lover off their stroke. She eased open the door, gently hit the light switch and was about to close the door behind her when the sound of male laughter made her suddenly stop in her tracks. Because it wasn't just the sound of one man laughing. It was the sound of *men* laughing. Together.

As she stood in her doorway, statue still, not knowing where to look, not knowing what to do, Gill's bedroom door suddenly flew open, and there in the doorway, silhouetted from behind and absolutely stark-bollock naked, stood a man. A big black man. With huge muscles. And a shiny chest. And thighs so large that his legs didn't close properly. His head was shaved and he had a little strip of goatee on his chin.

'Hi,' he beamed at Ana, cupping his rude bits with his hands. His voice was mellifluous and his smile captivating.

'Hi,' said Ana.

'Sorry. I – er – didn't know there was anyone else in the house. I'm just – er –' He indicated the bathroom with embarrassed eyes and then skipped off down the hallway, the moonlight gleaming off his two perfect buttocks as he ran.

'Oh fuck. Ana. Sorry.' Gill appeared in the doorway, wrapped in a duvet, her hair all over the place, a fag in one hand and about as pissed as Ana had ever seen anyone in her life. 'God. Shit. Fuck. I forgot about you.' She giggled and shuffled towards the door. 'That was Tony,' she slurred, 'and this' – she stepped aside and gestured towards her rumpled bed and the second naked black man lying on it – 'is . . . is – wash your name again?'

'Marcus.'

'Marcus,' she said, smiling and swaying. 'Look. I hope we didn't dishturb you, Ana. I mean – things must be tough for you right now. Her sister died,' she said, turning towards her bed to address Marcus. 'She took an overdose and she died.'

'No shit,' said Marcus.

'Uh-huh.' Gill's duvet was beginning to slip a little and Ana didn't know where to look when a tiny little pink nipple suddenly popped out. 'Look,' she continued, taking a big drag on her cigarette, 'you should get ta bed. We're finished in here now. We willn't dishturb y'anymore. You sleep tight now, y'hear.' She gathered up her duvet and got on to her tiptoes and kissed Ana warmly but wetly on the cheek. 'Night night. Say night, Marcus,' she said, turning towards the bed again.

'Night, Marcus,' said Marcus.

At which Gill dissolved into hysterical laughter and closed the door behind her.

12

Ana's alarm woke her up at eight-thirty the following morning. She tried to turn over but her back screamed out in agony. She'd never slept on a futon before but had always been under the impression that they were supposed to be much more comfortable than normal beds. What a load of old bollocks *that* was.

She could hear some kind of activity downstairs, and then she suddenly remembered – last night – Tony – Marcus – Gill's nipple. Jesus. Had that really happened? Really and truly? She slipped out of her bed and padded softly to the bathroom, looking around her gingerly for any errant naked men, but everything seemed back to what she supposed was normal. Early morning August sunshine streamed through the spotless windows, the air smelled of Ambi-pur and Mr Sparkle, and Gill's bedroom door was wide open and displaying a gleaming white, freshly made bed.

After an invigorating shower she made her way warily downstairs, just in time to see Gill, her hair in a perky ponytail, her body encased in an immaculate little Ellesse gym ensemble, glugging down a glass of something golden in colour and glowing like the healthiest woman in the world.

'Morning!' she chimed, as she spied Ana coming towards her. 'Juice?' she said, proffering the jug.

'What's in it?'

'Mango, kiwi, papaya, egg yolks and honey.' Gill counted off the ingredients on her fingers, jauntily. 'The best hangover cure known to man. Have some – it's yummy.'

Ana nodded mutely and accepted a glass.

'There's bagels, too. Fresh. I picked them up earlier on.'

Earlier on? Earlier on? How much earlier could it be than it already was? Ana was feeling strangely out of kilter. It was nine o'clock in the morning. A mere ten hours ago this woman had been off her tits and having sex with two men. And now here she was, up and about, buying bagels, making juice and looking like the neatest, sweetest little PE teacher you could ever hope to meet.

Ana stood for a moment or two, feeling utterly shell-shocked. She hadn't, had she, imagined last night? There *had* been two men in Gill's bed? She *had* been smoking a cigarette? She *had* been pissed senseless? Ana *had* seen her nipple, hadn't she? Maybe Gill had no recollection of it, maybe she had memory loss? But no – surely not. It was one thing to forget how you got home, but to forget a *ménage à trois*? It simply wasn't possible.

'Anyway. I'm off to the gym. I'll see you later?'

Ana was about to nod, and then suddenly remembered that she wasn't going to see her later. She told her about Broadstairs.

'Oh – *Flint's* driving you, is he?' she said. 'You'd better keep an eye out for him.'

'What do you mean?'

'Flint's a very naughty boy. Don't let that gentle-hearted-giant act fool you. OK?'

144

Ana nodded, uncertainly.

'OK then. I'll see you tomorrow. Have fun!' she tinkled, before bounding out of the door with her gym bag.

Ana finished her juice and poured herself another glass. Gill was right. It was delicious. Then she helped herself to a gorgeous warm bagel. It was all gooey with cream cheese and salty with smoked salmon, the crust a perfect chewy shell, the inside soft and glutinous. She wolfed it down and then had another one. Ana could hardly remember the last time food had tasted so good. She pushed open the kitchen door and felt the early sunrays already burning her skin. It was going to be another scorcher.

She took her juice upstairs to her bedroom and started to pack for this peculiar daytrip, panicking as she suddenly realized that she'd run out of knickers and cursing herself as she pulled the little silver camera she'd found in Bee's suitcase from the bottom of her tartan suitcase.

'Fuck,' she muttered to herself. She'd forgotten all about it.

She went to the hallway and phoned Lol.

'Look,' said Lol, 'don't worry about it. There's one of those one-hour places at the bottom of your road. Bung it in there now and we can collect it later. There was something I wanted to do before we set off, anyway.'

'What's that then?'

'Never you mind,' said Lol, 'we'll be round in about twenty minutes. Flint's just got here.'

'So, what's this Flint like then?'

'He's very tall, he's very quiet and he's got a very big car. Let's leave it at that, shall we? See you soon.'

*

Ana found the photo shop and also, much to her joy, a pound shop, where she picked up ten pairs of cotton knickers for £5. She was half-way through a third bagel and another glass of Gill's juice when a horn sounded in the road outside. She grabbed her bag and rushed to the door, and stopped in her tracks when she clapped eyes on the most massive Mercedes she'd ever seen in her life. It was dark blue with tinted windows and a sort of stretched bit in the middle. It was very shiny and disgustingly ostentatious.

Lol unfurled herself from the back, lifting a huge pair of black sunglasses from her nose and grinning at Ana. She had a big sunflower in her hair. 'Darling,' she drawled in a mock-posh accent, 'how are you? You look simply divine. Mwah. Mwah. Do get in.'

Ana threw her bag in first and climbed in after Lol. 'Oh. Wow. Fuck,' she exclaimed, looking around her at the mahogany-trimmed interior, the discreet lighting, the buttons and the knobs. 'Are we really going there in this?'

'Uh-huh. Better get used to it.'

'Wow.' She ran a hand over the soft-leather upholstery. 'Wow.'

'That's three wows, Lennard. Did you get that?' Lol knocked on the glass partition with a chunky diamond ring. 'Three wows. *You* might be losing it, but your car can still do it for you.'

'Ha. Ha. Ha.'

Ana watched as a tinted glass partition slid down and the back of a man's head was revealed. It was a large square head set on a wide neck and supported by vast shoulders. It was covered in short, thick, dirty-blond hair peppered with a smattering of grey.

'Flint,' said Lol, moving closer to the partition, 'this here is the World Famous Ana. Ana – this here is the – er – well – this is Flint.'

'Nice to meet you at last,' said Flint, turning round stiffly to flash a quick smile at Ana. His voice was deep and coarse. And he was beautiful. Ana gulped.

'Nice to meet you, too.'

'I'm really, really sorry about Bee,' he said.

Ana shrugged and smiled tightly. 'Me, too.'

'Flint was Bee's driver back in the Eighties, when she was famous,' said Lol.

'Aaah,' said Ana. She stared at Flint's ears. They were surprisingly delicate for such a burly man.

'Anyway,' said Flint, leaning forward to find a button on his dashboard, 'it's too early for conversation for me, so I'll leave you two girls to it. Keep your heels off the upholstery. Keep your hands off the champagne. Ashtrays are in the armrests. And give us a shout if you need a pitstop.'

'Sure thing, Mister Flint,' said Lol, and then the partition slid back across the car and it was almost as if Flint had never existed.

Lol turned to Ana. 'Oh, bloody Nora,' she said, a smile creeping across her face, 'hark at the colour of you. You look like a fucking beetroot. But just forget about it, all right. That bloke might look like butter wouldn't melt, but he's a sly old bugger. Don't fall for the act. OK?'

'Jesus,' said Ana, 'that's exactly what Gill just said, too. What is he? A serial killer?'

'No,' said Lol, 'not a serial killer. He's a serial *shit*.'

'Well, anyway. He's not my type, I can assure you.'

'Good,' said Lol, as she folded her long legs up under her and started fiddling with a pop-out tray in the inside door, 'OK, then. What have we got here?' She ran a fingertip across the surface of the mahogany-topped table and held it towards Ana. 'A-ha! Colombia's finest.' A film of white powder clung to her skin. 'Without fail,' she said, wiping it off on her jeans, 'every time I get in this car. God, I *hate* this stuff, I really do. I mean – is there such a thing as a celebrity who doesn't do coke?'

'Celebrities?'

'Yup. That's what Mister Flint there does for a living. Drives celebrities around.'

'Really!'

'Don't sound so excited. He doesn't even get to see them half the time. Just has to clear up all their coke and spunk and puke after they've gone.'

'Ooh,' grimaced Ana.

'Exactly,' said Lol, turning to face the window. 'Oh. Look. We're here already.'

Ana looked out of her window. They'd pulled up on the side of a grimy main road lined with electrical repair shops, minicab offices and West Indian bakeries, and were parked next to a large flower-stand.

'Where are we?' asked Ana.

Lol indicated a sign just behind her with her eyes. It was painted with the words 'West London Crematorium'.

'Is this where . . . ?'

'Uh-huh,' said Lol, 'thought you might like to say hello. And goodbye.'

Ana nodded slowly. She was going to see Bee's grave. She hadn't even *thought* about seeing Bee's grave.

She bought a bunch of orange gladioli and then wondered if they were quite suitable. For a dead sister. Or for a dead popstar, for that matter. Did anyone leave gladioli for Diana? She'd never seen gladioli tied to railings or on the side of the road, either, come to think of it. Maybe they were all wrong. A floral faux pas. 'They're beautiful,' said Lol, 'orange was Bee's favourite colour.'

'Was it?' said Ana. 'Really?'

'Yeah,' Lol nodded. 'Well. One of them, any road.'

The two women began walking. 'Isn't Flint coming?' whispered Ana.

'No. Flint likes to do things like this alone. You know?'

Ana didn't really know but nodded anyway. They were heading down a meandering gravel driveway, flanked by plane trees and cypresses. The sunlight dappled on to lush green grass. A few other people were here, too, clutching flowers. The graveyard stretched out in front of them for miles.

A crunching on the gravel behind them warned of an approaching car. They moved on to the grass and looked behind them. A funeral cortège. A coffin piled high with red roses and a large floral structure that spelled out the word 'MUM' lay in the back of the leading hearse. Lol put her hand to her heart and cast her eyes downwards, standing still until the entire procession of cars had passed them by. When Ana looked at her again her eyes were damp with tears. 'Sorry,' she sniffed, wiping them away, 'I'm an emotional old bugger sometimes.'

Bee's grave was to the west, in the shade of a sycamore.

She lay between her father and a man called Maurice Gumm who'd been born in Tobago in 1931. Her grave was a flat marble plaque, flush to the grass, engraved with the wording that Ana's mother had chosen:

BELINDA OCTAVIA BEARHORN
1964–2000
BELOVED DAUGHTER & SISTER

SHE BROUGHT JOY TO MILLIONS WITH HER BEAUTY,
HER TALENT AND HER JOIE DE VIVRE

SHE WILL BE MISSED FOREVER MORE

'*Joie de vivre*'? thought Ana. Wasn't '*joie de vivre*' a rather odd thing to put on a headstone? A small bunch of loosely tied pink roses rested on her grave.

'Who d'you think left those?' said Ana.

Lol shrugged.

Ana placed her flowers next to the roses and dusted some dirt off the plaque. She felt strange. She knew she should be thinking about Bee right now, but she wasn't. She was thinking about her father. She was thinking about rushing to Bideford General from her flat in Exeter with Hugh when the phonecall came, and getting there just in time to say goodbye, just in time to tell him she loved him, to squeeze his liver-spotted hands while they were still warm. She was thinking about going to the Co-Op with her mother and picking out the oyster-coloured marble with the pink veins, the gold-leaf lettering, the wording. Identical to Bee's. Cut from the same stone, engraved with the same lettering. Her mother's choice.

Her mother's taste. Ana's mother had impeccable taste. She knew how she liked things.

Tears started tickling at the back of her throat. Lol squeezed her shoulder. 'D'you want me to leave you?'

'Uh-huh,' Ana gulped. 'Just for a minute.'

'I'll see you back at the car.'

Ana listened to Lol's footsteps receding across the crunchy gravel and bowed her head. And then her shoulders started trembling and shaking as tears erupted from the very pit of her stomach. The tears she hadn't cried at her father's funeral. The tears she hadn't been allowed to cry because her father's funeral had been all about her mother.

He'd keeled over in the garden while digging up hyacinth bulbs – it was ironic that he should have been preparing so vigilantly for the next season when he wasn't to last the day. He'd been taken by ambulance to Barnstaple General Hospital but had died two hours later while waiting for an emergency heart bypass. He had been eighty-two years old. It had been a quick and relatively painless death, exactly the death that Bill had always said he wanted. He'd never been a burden to anyone, never inadvertently hurt anyone, never forgotten himself, humiliated himself or soiled himself.

During the last few years of his life, Bill had started to stoop, and Ana had forgotten how tall her father actually was. As she watched his long coffin being slipped from the hearse on to the shoulders of six strong men, she'd felt strangely proud of his stature and, for the first time in her life, she'd felt proud of her own gangling body, long hands and large feet, which echoed those of her father.

Ana had always known that her father would die while she was relatively young, that he wouldn't be there to see weddings and grandchildren, but when it came it was still a massive shock which, combined with her already self-obsessed mother's rapid descent into an almost psychotic state of self-indulgence, had forced Ana rudely off the path to adulthood she been successfully following. Well – successful-*ish*. A going-nowhere job at Tony's Tin Pan Alley selling drum kits and synthesizers to spotty sixteen-year-olds, a damp flat with a shared bathroom and a six-year relationship with Hugh, the highly intelligent but occasionally overbearing guy she'd lost her virginity to. But since she'd lost her going-nowhere job, her damp flat, her overbearing boyfriend and her father, all within the space of three months, she'd done nothing to get her life back on track. Instead of finding someone to look after her mother, getting herself a new flat and looking for a new job, she'd spent all her time in her bedroom writing songs – trite, sentimental, self-indulgent songs. Terrible songs. She had boxes of them under her bed. Dozens and dozens. They were so bad that she couldn't even bear to look at them.

When she wasn't writing appalling songs, she was reading books – voraciously, two or three a week, from the local library. She could have fooled herself into believing that she was improving herself, expanding her mind, but the only books she ever read were crime novels. Patricia Cornwell. Ruth Rendell. P. D. James. Agatha Christie. And books about serial killers, too. Jeffrey Dahmer. Dennis Nielsen. Charles Manson. Ted Bundy. Ed Gein. Her mother called her a 'ghoul', but Ana was just compulsively fascinated by the workings of minds and souls darker than hers.

Ana had never been a particularly gregarious or fun-loving girl. Her school reports had told of a bright, sweet-natured girl with an amazing talent for music-writing, singing and playing – but suggested that her social skills could be improved upon. People had always described her as 'shy', 'quiet', 'studious', 'creative'. Since her father died, though, these adjectives had transmuted, subtly, to 'strange', 'odd', 'peculiar' and 'weird'.

Living alone with her mother had a lot to do with it. She and her mother were so diametrically opposed in every way – physically, socially, sartorially, intellectually – that they could find no common ground whatsoever. Bill had always acted as a kind of buffer between the two women – he'd understood so well what made each of them tick – but without him there, the house on Main Street was a cold and unhappy place.

'Oh God, Dad,' Ana whispered to herself, 'I miss you so much, Dad, I miss you *so much*.' Ana was convulsing now, her stomach feeling bruised by contractions as tears that she hadn't cried when she'd needed to came erupting to the surface. She choked and coughed on them and her whole body shook. For ten months she'd sat on these feelings, kept them to herself. She'd wanted to break down a long time ago, but Hugh had told her to be strong, told her that now was a perfect opportunity to grow, to become adult. When all she'd wanted to do was curl up in a ball in his arms and let him hold her like a baby, he'd forced her to restrain herself. And to prove to him that she could be strong, that she could be a woman, she'd done as he said.

And denied her own grief. And then Gay had started going downhill, and she'd moved home, and there was no room for anyone's emotions other than her mother's in that house. Ana wasn't allowed to *feel* – all she could do was keep her head down and try not to antagonize her mother. This was the first time, Ana realized, since her father had died, that she'd been in a position just to . . . just to . . . 'Oh God, Dad,' she sobbed, 'what am I supposed to do without you – I don't understand – how am I supposed to be able to live without you?'

Ana stayed like that, her shoulders heaving, her stomach aching, her head bowed and her knees bent, for another ten minutes, as she emptied her soul of all its pain, until she heard footsteps on the gravel behind her and pulled herself together. She took a deep breath and wiped the tears from her cheeks and pulled her hair away from her face.

And as her tears began to subside and her vision cleared, she glanced down once more at the slab at her feet and felt suddenly gripped by the greatest, most overwhelming sense of loss – not of someone she'd known and loved, but of someone she *should* have known and loved, and she found herself whispering to Bee, one single and entirely unexpected word: 'Sorry.'

13

Flint screwed the empty crisp-packet into a tiny ball and squeezed it into the ashtray next to a scrunched-up Twix wrapper and a few pellets of greying, hardened chewing-gum. He searched his pocket for a toothpick and found one, using it to investigate the crisp-retaining crevasses between his teeth. Lol was in the back of the car, and Ana was walking back towards them. Fuck, she was tall. Very tall. Taller than Lol, because she was wearing flat lace-ups and Lol always wore those bloody great skyscraper heels. And she was nothing like Bee. In fact, if someone had given you a picture of Bee and asked you to come up with a woman who was the complete opposite of Bee in every way, Ana would have been the result. Not his type. Not his type at all. But quite interesting. Interesting the way her nose protruded from her face almost like a spout, like a beautiful but functional spout. And her eyes were a fascinating shape – like soft little triangles, resting on their sides. And such an amazing shade of hazel. Almost yellow. Long thick eyelashes. And not a scrap of make-up. Flint admired that in a woman. She was quiet, too, had a sort of dignity about her. Not like Loud-Mouth Lol and Gibbering Gill. Flint liked quiet women – you never knew what was going on in their minds. That was the trouble with most women – they just wanted to tell you what they were thinking all the fucking time.

As Ana got nearer Flint noticed that her eyes were red and raw and felt a flash of empathy as tears started to stab at his own eyes. He cleared his throat abruptly. He'd cried more in the last three weeks than he'd ever cried in his life before. Enough crying. More than enough. He slid open the partition and glanced backwards. 'Are we ready?' They nodded and he put the car into gear and pulled away. He was feeling strangely intrigued by Ana, this awkward-looking sister who Bee claimed to have spent every weekend with for the last ten years but who hadn't actually seen Bee since she was thirteen, but he wasn't much of a one for making small talk, so he switched on the intercom, unwrapped himself a stick of Wrigley's, folded it into his mouth and listened, instead.

'You all right?'

Sniffing from Ana. 'Yeah. Sorry. I'm fine.'

Sound of nose being blown.

'What was it like, Lol? Bee's funeral?'

Short silence.

'The weather was nice.'

'How many people came?'

'Me. Flint. Gill.'

'Is that all?'

'Uh-huh. We were pretty shocked. We thought you and your mum were going to come. We thought there'd be more people from home. You know, from Devon. Relatives. Family friends. I'd have invited other people but I didn't know who else there was. I thought your mum was going to handle it all . . .'

'I wanted to come. Mum couldn't – but I wanted to . . .'

'So – why didn't you?'

Brief silence.

'Too scared, I guess.'

'Scared? Of *what*?'

'Scared of being alone, scared of London, scared of death, scared of Bee's friends, scared of the train journey. You know – just *scared*.'

'You silly arse.'

Wry laughter. 'I wish I'd come now. Now that I know it's not scary. I really, really wish I'd come. Only three people. That's so . . . *awful*.'

Another brief silence.

'And what about London? Bee's London friends? What about all those people in her address book?'

Sound of Lol sighing.

'Look. Ana. Your sister. She was my best friend, right. Truly, the best friend I had in the world. I'd have done anything for her and she'd have done anything for me. But – and please don't take this the wrong way – she could be a bit of a cow.'

Flint nodded and smiled to himself in the front seat.

'Particularly in the early days, when she was much younger. She'd walk over people, use people. She were so bloody ambitious. And she pissed a lot of people off. I didn't want to start going through her address book and hearing people telling me they didn't want to come to Bee's funeral because they didn't like her, because she'd hurt them. D'you understand?'

Flint nodded his agreement and swept the pavement with his eyes. Summer – he loved it. Girls. Flesh. Everywhere.

'So, how come she never fell out with you?'

'I knew how to handle her. That was the thing with Bee. She was this really special person and most people just handled her all wrong. Made excuses for her. Made a fuss. Treated her like a fucking princess. When all she wanted was an equal. A pal. Someone to have a laugh with. And, most importantly, someone she could trust. It was an education seeing what happened to Bee when her single came out and she was famous overnight, it really was. The way all these wasps came out of nowhere. Bzzbzzbzz. Bluebottles. Stinking great flies. It's fucking nauseating the way these people come climbing out of the woodwork when they get a sniff of money. They crawl out and they treat you like the centre of the fucking universe, like their life's purpose is your happiness, your comfort, your every whim and desire. And then when she stopped making money they wouldn't even give her 50p for her bus fare. D'you know what I mean?'

'But she can't have fallen out with everyone, surely?'

Lol sighed. 'I don't know, Ana, all right. All I know is that since her father died I only ever saw her on my own or with Flint. She never talked about anyone else. She didn't trust anyone else. And now – well – it looks like she didn't trust me, either.'

'So – are you telling me that the reason no one came to Bee's funeral was because no one liked her?'

'That's the long and short of it.'

Short pause.

Whisper from Ana. 'That's so terrible ... imagine being alive for thirty-six years and only having three friends ...'

A particularly ripe blonde caught Flint's eye, then. Tall,

athletic-looking, tanned, tight cotton sundress, tennis shoes – posh. Ponies. Public school. Lovely. Flint had a particular thing about posh girls. And they seemed to have a particular thing about him. She saw Flint staring at her and flushed slightly. Flint laughed under his breath as he pulled away from the traffic lights.

'Flint.' Lol opened the partition and leaned towards him with one of her 'how can you resist me I'm so adorable and I'm about to ask you a really annoying favour' faces on.

'Ye-es.'

'Can we have some music in the back?'

'Yes.' He sighed and switched on the radio. Groovejet. Had to be. Everywhere he bloody went this summer. *Big Brother* and Groovejet.

Ten minutes later, he pulled up outside the photoshop on Latimer Road and watched as Lol and Ana both unfurled themselves and scuttled into the shop together like a pair of exotic stick insects, music blaring from the back of the car and everyone stopping to stare at them as they passed, wondering who they were. Flint sighed and wiped a slick of sweat off his upper lip with the back of his hand. A minute later they emerged from the shop, flapping photographs around and acting in a generally overexcited manner.

Lol threw herself into the back of the car. 'We got pictures!' she squealed, so loudly that Flint had to put his hands over his ears.

'Jesus, Tate,' he said, 'calm down, will you?' He picked the photos out of Lol's hand and looked at them. Ana slid into the passenger seat and looked over his shoulder. She smelled of Gill's house – of fabric conditioner, of fresh bedclothes.

'God,' Ana said in a whisper as Flint flipped through the pictures, 'Bee looks so . . . so grown-up. Her hair's really different. I always thought she'd still have that black bob she used to have.'

'Nah,' said Lol, taking the pictures as they circulated her way, 'she got rid of that when she turned thirty.'

Flint swallowed and felt it catch at the back of his throat as he looked at Bee in the photos. She looked beautiful and was, of course, immaculately dressed in every picture. Her hair was decorated with fresh tropical flowers, fat white camellias and sprigs of mauve bougainvillea and, most surprisingly, she looked rapturously happy. He couldn't remember the last time he'd seen her looking that happy. He flicked faster and faster.

Bee on a beach.

Bee in a restaurant.

Bee haggling with a market trader.

Bee on a bridge.

Bee wearing a bindi.

Bee eating a coconut.

And then, finally, a couple of photos from the end of the pile, there was a picture of a man. They all stopped breathing. Lol shrieked, 'Ohmygod, it's a fella. It's a fucking fella!', and grabbed the picture from his hands.

He was in his early forties, his hair nearly completely white and shorn close to his head. He was wearing long shorts with trendy sandals and a brightly coloured Hawaiian shirt, with a pair of those cool, popstar type sunglasses on his head. He was sitting outside a restaurant, with one leg crossed high upon the other one, in a classic groin-display position, and he was looking slightly cross. He wasn't particularly good-looking and he wasn't ugly. He looked like a tosser.

'Who is he?' Ana asked, urgently.

Flint leaned in towards Lol and took another look at the picture, before Lol snatched it away, again. He rubbed his stubbled chin. 'I've got no fucking idea,' he sighed, 'I've never seen that man before in my life. Maybe it was just some bloke she met on holiday. Maybe she got chatting to him at that restaurant and she took his picture. He's not in any of the others.'

'Yes,' said Lol, impatiently, 'but who took the others? Bee must have been with someone . . .'

'Not necessarily. Bee wasn't shy of strangers. She might just have got other people to take those pictures for her.'

Ana shook her head. 'No,' she said, 'no. She looks too . . . relaxed, too aware of the person taking her picture. Look – you can see it in her eyes . . .'

'What?'

'Excitement. Or something. Understanding. *Love.*'

Flint grunted, cynically. 'That was just Bee,' he said, 'a born flirt. And boy did she love the camera.'

'Look!' said Ana suddenly, tapping at a photo of Bee patting a mangy old street dog.

'What?'

'The ring. *This* ring,' she pointed at the diamond band she was wearing on her own finger, 'she's wearing it in these pictures. On her engagement finger.'

'And where did you find it?'

161

'In her airing cupboard. In the inside pocket of an evening jacket. She's wearing an engagement ring.'

Flint shook his head, again. 'She was in India – on her own. She probably just put it on as a precaution, so people would think she was married.'

'Maybe it's Zander!' said Ana.

'Who the hell is Zander?' said Flint.

'We don't know,' said Lol, 'but she wrote a song for him, apparently. A love song. Ana found it in her flat.'

All three of them fell silent for a moment, until Lol spoke. 'Chop chop,' she said, slapping her thighs. 'Enough talking, let's get going. I can't stand this suspense for another fucking second.'

Ana climbed into the back of the car and they pulled away and started the drive out towards the coast.

14

October 1997

Bee pulled the helmet from her head and ran her fingers through her hair.

'Mrs Wills.' A small man who looked somewhat like an overgrown baby bounced out of his Ford Puma and headed towards her with his hand outstretched. 'Tony Pritchard. Did you find it all right?'

Bee rested the helmet on the seat of her bike and shook his hand. 'No problem at all. I've had a lovely ride down actually.'

'Good, good.' He began looking around him, over her shoulder. 'Are we expecting your husband, Mrs Wills?'

'No,' smiled Bee, unzipping the top portion of her leathers, 'no – he wasn't feeling too well. We decided it would be better if he stayed at home.'

'Of course, of course. I perfectly understand. Well, if you're ready?'

She followed him towards the house.

'Wheelchair ramp,' he said, pointing out the wheelchair ramp. 'Handrails, as you can see, from the gate all the way through the house. Does your husband have any, er, mobility, in his legs?'

Bee shook her head.

'I see. I see. Well – I think you'll find everything he needs has been installed. This cottage was adapted for the needs of a paraplegic lady.'

'Yes,' said Bee, 'I know.'

'But the particularly nice thing about this paraplegic lady is that she was also an interior designer.' He swung open the front door and for the first time since Bee had reached her decision, she felt completely convinced she was doing the right thing. It was even nicer inside than the photographs from the estate agent had suggested. Far from the institutional, linoleumed and stain-proofed atmosphere she'd half-expected, the cottage was stylish and snug, with higgledy-piggledy ceilings and cream carpets.

'No expense was spared in adapting this property, and everything has been thought of. Everything is low-level, every room has an emergency contact button, the security system is state of the art. Come and look at the kitchen. I think you'll find it very impressive.'

Bee followed him through.

'The previous owner was a very keen cook – but so was her husband – so they had this installed. Look.' He ran a Formica work-surface up and down on parallel tracks screwed into the wall. 'And look. Even the hob is adjustable. There are two sinks, at different levels – so there's no excuse for your husband not to do his share of the washing-up.' He laughed. 'Now do come and see the garden. I think you'll find it particularly delightful.'

Bee nodded and swallowed a smile. Estate agents. Honestly. What were they like? 'Particularly delightful.' Did he honestly expect Bee to believe that he used that sort of language in the normal course of things? That after his wife served him his dinner he said, 'Thank you darling – that was particularly delightful'? Or while he was watching football in the pub with his mates: 'Well – that header into goal really was particularly delightful.' Bee had seen enough estate agents over the last few weeks to know them quite well. The way they tidied up the loose ends of their accents, the not-quite-cool grammar-school air about them, the pastel-coloured shirts, discreet gold jewellery, unisex hairdresser hair, Lynx deodorant. Paul. Dave. Phil. Steve. Tony. Mark. Lots of Marks. Mainly Marks, in fact. This Tony – he wasn't as bad as some. He wasn't wide. He wasn't slick. He was wearing a wedding band and was probably a very good husband, probably had a couple of little ones and probably crawled to his mother-in-law, who even now, after all this time, still thought her daughter could have done much better than him.

'Do you have children, Mrs Wills?' he asked, leading her out to the garden.

Bee shook her head. 'We've got a cat, though.'

'Oh. Lovely. This is a cat's paradise out here.'

Bee looked round her and decided. Immediately. This was the house she wanted. A ramp extended from the back door out along a gravelled path that ran through a hilly green lawn. To the east was a small cluster of apple trees, a few swollen, stubborn fruit still clinging to their branches. Surrounding the lawn was a horseshoe of dahlias, geraniums, pansies and violets. Gaudy flowers. Her mother would have hated them. To the west was a billowing vista of patchwork fields and in the far, far distance, the bruised outline of the sea, frothy under a darkening sky.

She spun round to face the house again. Fondant pink and chunky, striped with white, like a gigantic French Fancy. And then she turned to face Tony. 'It's beautiful, isn't it?' she sighed, pulling a strand of hair off her face.

'Stunning,' he agreed. 'Possibly one of the nicest out-of-town properties of this age we've ever had on our books. And all the adjustments are so unobtrusive. And as for this view . . .'

They both turned to look at it again, casting their eyes upwards as a few fat droplets fell from the sky. 'Shall we go indoors?'

Tony took Bee upstairs, showed her the stair-lift, the easy-access bath, the special toilet and the spectacular view from the bedroom windows, now rain-splattered and obscured. It was almost dark outside now as the cloud thickened overhead, and Tony switched on a few lights. Bee paced around on her own for a while, letting the cosiness overwhelm her. He'd love it here. This was no compromise. This was no sad, secret, sordid place. They wouldn't have to pretend here, pretend to be happy. They actually *could* be happy. Imagine Christmas Day in front of that wonderful open fireplace with fairy-lights draped all over the place and Bing Crosby on the CD. Imagine summer afternoons in that garden, pottering around, sunbathing, playing Frisbee. Well – maybe not playing Frisbee. But just imagine, thought Bee, imagine the times they were going to have here. Together. Just the two of them.

'I want it,' she said to Tony as she descended the stairs. 'I want to buy it. I want to offer the full asking price. And I want to pay cash.'

Tony did his best not to look overexcited and got to his

feet. 'Fine,' he said, 'fine. That's great. And I've got to say – an excellent decision. Absolutely excellent. Well – we'd better get back to the office then. Get things going.'

He wandered around, switching off lights, and saw Bee to her bike under his umbrella. As she straddled it and perched her helmet on her head he looked at her, and a small smile began to play on his plump lips. 'Has anybody ever told you that you look like Bee Bearhorn?' he said.

Bee smiled. 'Bee who?' she said.

'You know – Bee Bearhorn. That singer from the Eighties. With the bob and the red lipstick. "I'm groooooving, for Lon-don, for Lon-don, all night."' He smirked as he finished his painful rendition of her one and only hit.

Bee grimaced and laughed. 'Never heard of her,' she said. 'She sounds awful, though.'

'Yeah,' laughed Tony, heading back towards his car in the rain, 'yeah. She was.'

15

It only took about half an hour to find Bee's cottage once they got to Broadstairs. The estate agent's particulars described it as being 'in a secluded location about half a mile from the charming, Dickensian seafront.' They stopped a few times and shoved the particulars under people's noses until finally someone said, 'Oh yes, I recognize the place,' and pointed them in the right direction. And they knew for sure they'd found the right place when they pulled up outside the cottage and saw Bee's huge Honda sitting in the driveway, wearing its canvas overcoat.

'What the fuck is that doing here?' said Flint, climbing from the driver's seat and walking towards the bike.

The canvas was covered in grime and dead insects. Flint brushed them off and started pulling the cover away from the bike. Ana watched him with interest. It was the first time she'd seen him standing up, and Lol hadn't been exaggerating. He was absolutely enormous. He was wearing knee-length khaki combat shorts, a grey V-neck T-shirt and a pair of Velcro sandals. His calves were the size of cantaloupes and his shoulders reminded Ana of those old Kenny Everett sketches with the US military man in the tank. She felt a sudden overwhelming urge to go and stand next to him, so she could feel for the first time what it might be like to be petite. His face was handsome but craggy, the face of a fine-featured young man who'd lived a little too much. His eyes were the murky blue of a newborn baby's and he had a small scar near the corner of his mouth which pulled his cheek into an unintentional puckered dimple.

He was incredibly good-looking.

If you liked that sort of thing.

'Have you got the keys, Ana?' he said, turning to her and making her blush. Again. Damn. She dipped her head quickly into her rucksack to conceal her embarrassment and rifled around clumsily for the clink of keys. 'Here.' She waved them at him and started grinning inanely. This man really was obscenely sexual. He oozed it. He stank of it. He may as well have been walking around with a twenty-inch erection growing out of his forehead.

'OK, let's go.'

'Look,' Lol was saying from where she stood near the front door, 'what the bloody hell's this – isn't it a wheel-chair ramp?'

They all looked down at it. 'Hmm. Dunno.'

'Looks like one.'

'Could be.'

Ana slid the Yale into the lock and they all breathed a sigh of relief when the door slipped open without an alarm going off.

The three of them started wandering around the cottage. 'Wow,' said Lol, 'this is so lovely.' And it was. About a million times nicer than the grim old flat in Baker Street. The walls were painted in warm shades of cranberry and plum, the floors were cream-carpeted, the furniture was cartoonish – fat lipstick-pink sofas and a distressed mahogany dining-table laden with three-foot gothic candlesticks. The ceiling had been painted with a *trompe l'œil* sky and clouds, and a Tuscan sunset glimpsed through straggling vines was painted on to a rough-hewn wall on the far side, decorated with bunches of bloomy plastic grapes. Enormous paintings depicting just a single, lushly painted piece of fruit hung from the walls – a three-foot pomegranate, a huge misshapen apple with mottled red and green skin, the lime-green, pip-speckled insides of a hairy kiwi. One wall was draped with a real tiger skin, decapitated and spreadeagled across the wall. Candelabras sprouted from plaster. Junk-shop chandeliers hung from the ceiling.

'This is Gregor's furniture,' muttered Flint.

'What?'

'All this stuff – these sofas, the paintings, chandeliers – all Gregor's old stuff, from his place in Kensington. Old stage props and bits of scenery, most of it – look' – he picked up an enormous gothic candlestick and waved it around airily – 'tin.'

'Shit. You're right,' said Lol, glancing around, 'I thought she'd left all this behind on her travels or put it in storage or something. Good grief,' she said, pointing at a metal contraption by the stairs, 'will you look at this – a bloody lift. Bee had a bloody lift in her house. What d'you reckon she used that for, then? When she'd had a few too many? God – that's so Bee to have a lift. I can just imagine her, looking at the stairs and thinking, "I don't wish to walk, I shall *glide* . . ."'

Ana was in the kitchen now, looking at all the strange fixtures, the adjustable work surfaces and the two sinks at differing levels. A pile of glossy cookbooks sat on a big wooden table. The cupboards were full of condiments. Soy. Pepper. Olive oil. Lime juice. Pine nuts. Ground cumin. Sundried tomatoes. And breakfast cereals – tons of it. Variety packs and Frosties and Golden Nuggets. The fridge was empty save for a packet of eggs and a squeezed tube of tomato puree. And there wasn't a cocktail shaker or a bottle of tequila anywhere in sight. Everything about this house was diametrically different in every possible way to the flat in Baker Street.

She tried another one of the keys on her bunch in the back door and pushed her way out into the garden. It was beautiful. Very compact and mature and well-tended. In a shed at the farthest end Ana found a lawnmower and rows of tiny pots and trowels and quilty gardening gloves, secateurs, twine and compost. The garden shed of an active and enthusiastic gardener – it looked just like Gay's garden shed at home.

'Jesus Christ!' Ana heard Lol's ear-shattering tones behind her. 'Could this girl be any more fucking mysterious. I mean – *what* is this?' She held aloft a pair of boxer shorts, greying, flimsy and somewhat small. 'There's a whole fucking drawer of these upstairs. And you should see the bathroom.'

'What?'

'Just come and have a look, will you?' Lol grabbed Ana's hand and dragged her up the stairs. 'Look. There's a fucking door in the bath, Ana. What's that all about then? A door. In the bath. And look at the size of the flush on that toilet. And these railings, look. Here. And here. And all these fucking buttons everywhere. And have a look at this.' Lol pulled Ana into a small bedroom at the other end of the corridor. 'Look!' The room was painted bright blue. Posters of Radiohead and Teenage Fanclub, Buffy the Vampire-Slayer and the *X-Files* decorated the walls. There was a TV and a sound system and an enormous chest of pine drawers with fat handles. And a large, white and distinctly surgical-looking bed tucked into a bay window.

'I mean – what the fuck is this, Ana? Was Bee shacked up with Christopher Reeves or summat?'

Flint walked in, looking more animated than Ana had seen him looking all day. 'This is totally fucking weird. Look what I just found in Bee's wardrobe.'

'No way,' gasped Lol.

Flint was holding aloft a pair of trainers. Trainers. 'Uh-huh,' he said, 'and look at this.' With his other hand he held out a sweatshirt. A grubby sweatshirt with mud on the front.

'OK,' said Lol, collapsing on to an armchair, 'now I'm seriously spooked. We've entered the Twilight Zone, d'you realize that? We're in *Tales of the* fucking *Unexpected*. My head hurts.'

The three of them fell silent.

'This *is* Bee's house, in't it?' said Lol.

Flint and Ana nodded.

'Right,' said Flint eventually, slapping his large-hock-of-Norfolk-ham thighs with his five-Cumberland-sausages-on-a-dinner-plate hands, 'I think we should take a couple of rooms each and search them for anything out of the ordinary. Then in an hour or so we'll meet downstairs and take a look at what we've found. OK?'

'OK?'

*

Ana took the bedrooms, Flint took the living room and the garage and Lol took the bathroom, kitchen and garden shed. For an hour no one spoke. Instead the cottage was filled with the sounds of floorboards creaking, the toilet being flushed every now and then and general industriousness. It was a strange hour or so as Ana once again found herself sifting through Bee's underwear, picking through her books and CDs, feeling her clothes and examining her toiletries. But this was so different to clearing out the flat in Baker Street. On Thursday her sister had been a stranger. Apart from the moment when she'd stood and stared at Bee's pubes in the bath, there'd been an unsettling numbness to her activities. But things had changed, already, just three days later. Ana herself felt unburdened, particularly after her tears at Bee's grave, and now every object, every item felt imbued with some kind of magical, desperate poignancy. And Bee was growing in her head moment by moment, turning from a two-dimensional cartoon character into a real human being. She opened a bedside drawer and passed her hand over the contents. Hairgrips, one with a black hair still attached, elastic hair-bands, sleeping pills, crumpled-up tissues, toenail clippers, a photo of Gregor. In Bee's wardrobe were more clothes, but simple clothes here – jeans, sweaters, a long denim skirt, walking boots, even some thermal underwear.

A thorough search of Bee's bedroom revealed nothing, so Ana moved along the corridor towards the blue bedroom. There was a smell in here – a sort of stale smell. Nothing gut-churning, just the whiff of bedclothes a couple of weeks past their wash-by date. It smelled like

173

the bedroom of a teenage boy. It *was* the bedroom of a teenage boy. There were socks on the floor, trainers under the bed, CDs out of their cases, dirty mugs on the TV. Ana pulled open drawers and found several more pairs of unsophisticated underpants plus various items of male clothing of the casual and unfashionable variety – old T-shirts, unbranded jeans, shapeless jumpers.

She fiddled with the bed a bit, pressing levers, until it suddenly boinged upright and scared her half to death. 'Jesus,' she muttered, clutching her heart. The evidence was mounting up very rapidly. The wheelchair ramp, the weird bath, the lift and the hydraulic bed – who lives in a house like this, indeed?

She sat down on the bed and went through the bedside drawer. An empty spectacle case. A dead fly. A calculator. A CD-Rom. There were books piled on top of the unit, books like *Conspiracy Theories – Secrecy and Power in America*, *The Case for Mars: The Plan to Settle the Red Planet and Why We Must* and *Apollo 12: The NASA Mission Reports*.

In the cabinet underneath were textbooks with titles like *Elementary Linear Algebra with Applications*, *Schaum's Mathematical Handbook of Formulas and Tables*, and *Applied Linear Statistical Models*. A few notebooks underneath were full of scribbled algebra, that looked too technical and complicated even to bother flicking through. And there at the bottom sat a school exercise book with a typed label attached that nearly made Ana gasp out loud. 'Zander Roper, Form 5L.'

Zander.

The same Zander Bee had written a song for.

He wasn't a man at all. He was a child. She grasped the exercise book to her chest and ran downstairs.

All three of them sat blankly in the living room, surrounded by an assortment of disparate and eclectic objects. It felt like they were playing some very surreal, very sombre parlour game. Even Lol was quiet for once.

Lol had found some bird-spotting handbooks that had been well-thumbed, a pair of binoculars, a whole heap of prescription drugs, a pile of plastic sheets and another set of notebooks covered in algebra. And Flint had collected some watercolours, painted directly into a pad of cartridge paper, watercolours of the garden, the view, the cottage and Bee. Bee sunbathing on a deckchair, Bee at the kitchen table, Bee asleep in front of the fire.

'Jesus,' said Lol, picking one up, 'these are just beautiful. Just absolutely beautiful.'

She let it drop to the floor and held her head in her hands, sighing loudly. 'Well,' she said, 'it's all crystal-fucking-clear now, in't it? Bee spent every weekend for the last three years with an incontinent, bird-watching mathematician called Zander who had a crush on Gillian Anderson and could paint like Michelangelo. Oh – and she wrote a love song for him, too. Of course. It all makes perfect fucking sense. It's as clear as the fucking North Circular in the rush hour . . . Jesus . . .'

'D'you think . . . ?' began Ana, about to form the most obvious of all possible questions.

'Don't even go there, Ana,' said Lol, using her hands to demonstrate her confusion. 'I don't even want to think about it. If this Zander kid was her son then it throws the last fifteen years of my life into complete mayhem. If she had a kid and didn't tell me, then nothing in the world makes sense any more . . .'

Flint got to his feet and stretched. Bits of his huge body audibly cracked and Lol winced. 'And where are you off to?' Flint was reaching for his car keys.

'The pub.'

Lol rolled her eyes. 'Oh – that's typical, that is. We've come all the way down to Broadstairs, we've found out that our best friend was living a secret bloody life, we've got all this stuff to do and you're going to the fucking pub!'

Flint rolled his eyes back at Lol. 'How about you just stop talking, just for a second and think. Just for once, Tate.'

'All right, Lennard. I've stopped. I'm thinking. And er – sorry, but nowt's come to me. Just the fact that you're like a fucking dehydrated homing pigeon when it comes to the boozer.'

Flint sighed. 'It's a Sunday lunchtime. This is a small village. And what do people who live in small villages do on Sunday lunchtimes?'

Ana nodded and smiled. 'They go to the pub.'

'Exactly, Ana – they go to the pub. And what else do people who live in small villages do?'

'Have sex with their sisters,' sneered Lol.

'Apart from that.'

'Their dogs?'

'They gossip, Tate. They gossip. Someone's bound to have seen something, to know something. So – are you coming?'

Lol sighed and got to her feet. 'Yeah yeah. All right. Let's do it. But remember – we are going to get seriously stared at. The whole pub *will* fall silent the minute we walk in, every person *will* turn around and fix us with an impassive gaze designed to scare us out of town, and the only sound we hear *will* be the ticking of the clock over the bar. We are not only strangers, but we are three very, very tall strangers who are going to turn up in a stretch limo with tinted windows. And one of us is black. They're going to assume we're gangsters and call out the sheriff. OK?'

Flint and Ana nodded.

'OK, then. Let's go.'

There were three pubs in the village, which threw them a bit. Two of them were restaurant pubs, with full car parks and children running around in beer gardens, so they headed for the Bleak House, a small cream pub with curtained windows. Flint pulled the Mercedes up on the pavement and a few passing villagers stopped and watched with interest. 'See,' hissed Lol, 'and we haven't even got out the pigging car yet. Oh bugger, I wish I was wearing something else.' She fiddled with her thin cotton top, pulling it down over her midriff, and slid her sunglasses from her head to her nose. Ana looked at her with surprise. She was nervous. Fearless, loud-mouthed, extrovert Lol, was nervous.

She caught Ana looking at her. 'What?'

'Nothing,' said Ana, 'nothing. It's just that I've never seen you look so – uncomfortable before. I didn't think you were bothered what people thought of you.'

'Yeah, well. I'm not. Not in London, anyhow. It's small towns. I hate 'em.'

'Why?'

She shrugged. 'I dunno. I suppose it's because I come from a small town.'

'But I thought you were from Leeds?'

'Yeah – from a small town just outside Leeds. It were bad enough being black there. But being black and skinny and nearly six-foot tall. It were hell.'

'Really?' asked Ana in wonder. She found it hard to imagine that Lol could ever have felt anything but confident and beautiful.

'Oh aye. I got loads of shit.'

'What sort of shit?'

'Oh, you know. Kids. Comments. Being shouted at on the street. That sort of thing.'

Ana nodded. 'I get it, too,' she whispered. 'Comments. Stares.'

'Yeah,' said Lol, 'I could see that in you when I first met you. I could see *me* in you when I first met you.'

'What d'you mean?'

'Well – I wasn't always so blinkin' gorgeous, you know. I mean – those contact lenses aren't just for show – I'm half-blind wi'out them and when I first left home I used to wear these glasses like paperweights, and I had this flippin' great Afro that I used to scrape back in a ponytail. And make-up! You should have seen the state of me. I used to go to Woollies and buy all that white-girl make-up, all blue eyeliner and that, trying to make myself look like Lady Di – and pink blusher! Bright fucking pink, it was. I didn't really know who the hell I was then. And then I came down to London and I fitted in. I could be whatever and whoever the hell I wanted to be. That's why I love London so much. In London I can *be*. D'you see what I mean? I can look as freaky as I like and there's always going to be someone looking freakier. I can be as loud as I like and there'll always be someone louder. I can be tall as I like and there'll always be someone taller. On the other hand, there'll always be someone richer, prettier, happier and nicer, too. But nobody gives a shit anyway. The only true currency in London, Ana, is celebrity. The only thing that makes one Londoner look at another Londoner with any interest, is celebrity. And even then they try to pretend to be unimpressed. Try to pretend they haven't noticed them. But out here' – she turned and looked through the window – 'anyone who's different in any way is a sort of celebrity. Gets talked about, stared at, bothered. And I hate it. I really hate it.'

'Any chance of you two getting out of this car any time today?' said Flint, his enormous head appearing at the window.

Lol took a deep breath and turned to Ana and smiled. 'Pretend you're Madonna – that's what I always try to do – pretend to be Madonna, then it dun't matter about the staring.'

Sure enough, everyone in the pub did stop talking when they walked in. But then, there were only four people in there and it didn't look like they'd been talking to each other anyway. The barmaid, a young girl of about eighteen, looked up at them with interest as they approached. Her expression told them that she didn't see the three 'strangers' as a threat but as an opportunity for something unusual to happen. And her face perked up even more when Flint opened up his mouth and flashed her one of his electric smiles.

'Hiya!' she beamed, her steamed-pudding breasts swelling visibly under a tight Lycra vest inscribed with the golden word 'Angel', 'what can I get you?'

'Watch this,' whispered Lol, nudging Ana in the ribs, 'Flint's about to switch it on. Pass me a bucket . . .'

'I'll have a pint of Export please and my two friends here will have . . .' He turned to Lol and Ana and raised his eyebrows at them, Roger Moore-style.

'Same please,' said Ana.

'Vodka and cranberry, please,' said Lol, adopting a strange, Joanna Lumleyesque accent.

'Oh. Sorry. We haven't got cranberry' – the girl's face blanched with the disappointment of not having cranberry and then brightened slightly – 'we've got blackcurrant, though.'

'What – blackcurrant *juice*?'

'Yes. No. I'm not sure. I'll just ask.'

She scuttled away then and Flint gave Lol a stern glance. 'Oi – Scary Spice – leave the poor girl alone.'

'Sorry Mister Flint sir,' said Lol, stifling a giggle and nudging Ana in the ribs again.

'Angel – is that your name?' Flint pointed at her vest-top.

Lol raised her eyebrows at Ana.

The barmaid giggled and started pouring a pint. 'Nah,' she beamed, 'my name's Louise. But my friends call me Lou.'

'So – Lou – are you a local?'

''Fraid so,' she sighed, 'I've lived here all my life.'

'Bit dull is it?'

'You could say that, yeah.' She placed a full pint on the bar and started pouring another one. 'It's like *Night of the Living Dead* round here sometimes.'

'And what do you do? Around here? Anything going on?'

'Nah. Nothing. The only action is up on the seafront, but even that's pretty non-existent.'

'So if anything unusual was to happen in the area, you'd notice?'

'Oh yeah. Definitely.'

Flint beamed at the barmaid again and Ana saw her cheeks flame scarlet.

'You could be just the girl I'm looking for then.'

'Oh yeah?' She laughed and her blush increased.

'Yeah. We're looking for some information. About the cottage down on Broad Lane.'

'Hark at Inspector Morse,' whispered Lol into Ana's ear, stifling another giggle.

'Which cottage is that, then?'

'The pink one. The pink one with the motorbike outside.'

'Oh yeah. Yeah – I know the one. That's £5.85 for the drinks, please.'

Flint passed her a tenner. Ana noticed that he deliberately brushed the side of her hand with his fingertips as he handed it over and she noticed that Lou almost visibly jumped, like she'd just had an electric shock.

'D'you know anything about it? The cottage.'

She shrugged and slammed the cash register shut. 'Like what?'

'Like who lived there?'

Lou rested her elbows on the top of the bar and put her face in her hands, looking up at Flint with wide eyes, her sun-burned breasts quivering urgently. She grinned up at him. 'Are you coppers?' she asked.

'Nah,' grinned Flint, taking a big macho slurp of his lager and wiping his mouth with the back of his hand, his eyes glued to Louise the whole time. 'Look. Lou.' He leaned down towards her so that their noses were almost touching. Ana noticed that Louise stopped breathing. 'Are you any good at keeping secrets?'

She nodded, her eyes widening by the second.

'Look. Our friend. Well – she died last month.'

'Oh God – I'm really sorry.' Lou clutched her heart with her hand.

'Yeah. Thanks. And the thing is that since she died, we found out some really weird things about her.'

'Oh yeah?' If Lou's eyes had opened any wider, her eyelids would have slipped irretrievably behind her eyeballs.

'And one of them was that she owned that cottage. The pink one.'

'Oh right. You mean the woman with the black hair and the motorbike?'

'Yeah. That's the one. Did you know her?'

'No. She wasn't around all that often. Only at the weekends, I think. Mrs Wills – that was her name.'

'That's my mum's name,' Ana whispered in Lol's ear.

'And who did she used to stay with?'

'What d'you mean?'

'I mean – when she was there, in the cottage. Do you know who stayed with her?'

Lou shrugged. 'I never saw anyone. There was an ambulance there sometimes, though.'

'An ambulance?'

'Yeah. You know. One of those like they take old people about in. Not like an emergency ambulance or anything.'

'Like they might take disabled people about in, you mean?'

'Yeah. That's right.'

'But you never saw anyone getting in or out of it?'

'No – I mean, I saw it arriving and that, and the ambulance people helping someone out, but it was all on the wrong side, facing away from me, so I never saw anyone getting in or out. I just kind of thought it was an elderly relative or something.'

Flint nodded and looked very serious. 'And did you ever speak to Mrs Wills? Did she ever come in here?'

'Nah. Not in here. But I used to see her sometimes, on her motorbike – just passing through. Or at the Spar, a couple of times. Not to talk to or anything, though. She was very pretty. How did she – if you don't mind me asking – how did she die, exactly?'

'Well – we don't know – exactly. That's what we're trying to find out.'

'She didn't – well, she didn't die in the cottage, did she?'

'No – she died in London. In her flat.'

'God. I'm really sorry. She was so young and so pretty and everything. You must be gutted.'

'Yeah. We are.' Flint turned to look at Ana and Lol, and Louise looked at all three sadly.

'Look,' she began, 'I get off in half an hour. If you want I can take you round to see some people. People who might know more than me. You know – busybodies and that.' She giggled and Flint smiled, and she giggled even more.

'Really?' he gushed. 'Would you? That would be fantastic, wouldn't it, girls?' He spun round and they nodded eagerly. 'OK. Great. We'll be here, in the corner, when you're ready.'

'OK,' she beamed, 'brilliant.'

He was about to turn away and then he stopped, turned back, looked straight at Louise's tits and grinned. 'Have you ever thought about changing your name?'

Louise flushed and giggled and hid her face, and Lol stuck her fingers down her throat and gagged and headed towards the back of the bar. 'Christ, Lennard, you really are vile, d'you know that?' she said, as they sat down.

'Just doing what was necessary. That's all.'

'Oh. Bollocks. Couldn't you have just said, "Hi – d'you know anything about the woman who used to live in the pink cottage on Broad Lane?" Did you have to get yer knob out and start waving it around in front of the poor girl. And you're thirty-six years old in case you'd forgotten. You could have fathered her and another half a dozen like her by now, you sick fuck.'

Ana looked at them both in amazement. 'Don't you two ever stop arguing?' she asked.

Flint and Lol looked at each other and laughed. 'No,' they both said in unison. 'Not while we still get this much pleasure out of it, at any rate,' said Lol, and they both laughed again.

And then Ana looked at them, at big, flash Flint with his scarred cheek and mad Lol with her platinum glued-in hair and her big raspy laugh and she thought, these are Bee's people – I'm sitting here in a pub in Kent with Bee's people. And Bee's dead. How weird is that? And just think, she thought, if I'd stayed in touch with Bee, if I hadn't let my mother's neuroses influence me, if I hadn't believed her lies, if I hadn't been so lazy, if I'd had more strength of character, maybe I could have been sitting in a pub with Bee's people and *Bee*. I could have known Flint since I was a teenager. I could have known Lol when she was my age. I could have been someone for Bee to talk to, someone for her to tell her secrets to. I could have ridden pillion on her bike down to Kent and we could have done whatever it was she was doing here together. I could have been at her flat in Baker Street on that night, on 28 July, and I could have saved her. I could have saved her . . .

16

January 1998

Bee ran round the cottage one last time, making some final adjustments. Puffing up cushions, straightening curtains, switching on a table-lamp, switching off a table-lamp. It was a glistening winter's morning, and a fine layer of snow lay all over everything. It was 8 January but Bee had bought a Christmas tree anyway, just a small one, and put it in the corner decorated with gold sequinned stars, tiny white fairy-lights and these really cute little fluffy baubles she'd found in Paperchase. A huge fire was crackling away in the fireplace and there was a chicken roasting in the oven.

My God, thought Bee, it's finally happened – I've turned into my mother. She shuddered at the thought and pulled the curtain back again to peer out into the road. She looked at her watch. 11.15 a.m. Where the hell were they? They'd been due at eleven. And then she heard a crunching, of tyres on grit. A small white ambulance, emblazoned with the legend 'High Cedars' pulled into her driveway. They were here. Oh God. They were here. She let the curtain fall and smoothed down her hair, her neat blouse, her smart tailored trousers. She looked down at her feet – pumps – flat navy pumps. Weird. And then she caught sight of herself in the mirror. At the pale, unlipsticked mouth, the softly mascaraed eyes, the discreet gold earrings. She did. She looked just like her mother. Oh Jesus. She pulled on a coat, took an enormously deep breath and strode out into the driveway.

'Hi,' she said, putting out a hand to the care assistant who was unlocking the back of the ambulance. 'Belinda Wills. Nice to meet you. Did you have a good journey down?' I wish it was you, she thought, looking at the pimple-faced boy, I wish it was you. I wish that all I had to do was shake *your* hand and welcome *you* into my home and make *you* chicken. That would be so easy. So easy compared to what I have to do now.

She peered into the ambulance over the care assistant's shoulder, and there he was. He caught her eye and looked away again.

'Zander!' she said, trying to inject her nerve-wracked voice with enthusiasm and lightness. 'At long last. Welcome.'

17

Carol in the Spar knows everything. Absolutely everything. She knows that Mrs Wills – Belinda – bought the cottage in October 1997; that Tony Pritchard from the estate agent up on the seafront sold it to her. She knows that she bought her curtains from the posh interiors shop on the High Street and she had a mural done – Carol saw the van – 'Specialist Paint Effects', it said. She knows that Mrs Wills had originally been due to move in with her husband – but he'd never been seen, maybe they split up or something, she didn't like to ask. And then in January 1998, this boy had started visiting. Yes – that's right. A disabled boy. That's £1.20, love, thanks. About twelve years old. Although it was hard to tell, with him being in a wheelchair and everything. No – she never met the boy, never even saw him really, except from a distance. He turned up on Saturday mornings and left on Sunday nights, and then Mrs Wills went home on her motorbike, with her cat strapped on the back in a box. She'd been into the Spar a few times, not regular or anything, for tea and sugar and basics like that. Not with the boy, though, and she was always in a hurry to get back. Carol asked after the boy sometimes – she'd say, 'How's your boy?', and Mrs Wills would always smile, that beautiful smile of hers, and say, 'He's fine, thank you for asking.' She didn't chat but then Londoners don't, do they? And as for who the boy was –

well – she presumed it must be her son but no, she didn't know that for sure. That's £3.74 please, love. Thanks, love – say hello to your mum. And did you know, says Carol, did you know that apparently Mrs Wills – Belinda – used to be a popstar? Yes. She was a popstar in the Eighties. She had a hit with that song, you know, 'Groovin' for London', or something, wasn't it? Carol wiggles her hips and giggles. You could tell it about her, when you thought about it, she says. She had that quality, you know – star quality. Even in her old Barbour and wellies – she was definitely a star. Oh yes. Definitely . . .

Lol, Ana and Flint all flopped on to the lipstick-pink sofas and sighed in unison.

'Barbours. Wellies. Weekend trysts with Tiny bloody Tim.' Lol kicked off her stilettos and massaged the soles of her feet. 'Fuckin' hell, Bee. What the fuck were you playing at?'

'So. What d'you think? Was he her son?'

Both Flint and Lol shook their heads vehemently.

'Why not?'

'Because Bee was never pregnant, that's why. A small matter of biology.'

'So why the hell was she spending weekends with this boy? I mean – why?'

Flint rubbed his face into his hands. 'I can't get my brain round any of this stuff right now. There's nothing we can do today to answer any of these questions. I think we should just chill out, get something to eat, watch a bit of telly. And then tomorrow, we can phone around some children's homes, hospitals. That sort of thing.'

'That's the first sensible thing you've said all day, Lennard,' said Lol. 'I'm going to have forty winks in the garden.' She pulled herself to her feet and put her hands on her hips. 'What are you two going to do?'

Ana and Flint looked at each other and shrugged. 'Fancy a ride?' said Flint.

'I beg your pardon?' said Ana.

'On the bike. D'you fancy a ride on the bike? I've got keys. Bee gave me a spare set. We could go down to the seafront, get some chips or something. Go for a paddle?'

'Oh,' said Ana, flushing slightly, 'yeah. Why not?'

'OK, then. I'll just go and get the bike ready. I'll be a couple of minutes.'

'Yeah,' said Lol, addressing Flint's back, 'and you make sure you look after her all right. No showing off. All right? And none of your macho bullshit. Stick to the speed limit. No wheelies and no monkey business. And get us some dinner, will you? Get some pizza or summat. I'm fucking starving.'

A couple of minutes later, Ana opened the door to find Flint outside, sitting astride the enormous red and yellow Honda, revving it urgently and proffering a crash helmet.

She walked towards the huge machine in wonder. She'd always had a bit of a thing about motorbikes and this really was a fine specimen. 'Wow,' she said, running her hands over the brightly coloured paintwork, 'this is incredible.'

'It is, isn't it?' he said, 'And you know the funny thing that just occurred to me. This monster probably belongs to your fucking mother now. Do you think she'll like it?' He grinned his grin and Ana laughed, the image of her mother mounted on this huge beast of a machine running through her mind. 'I can't imagine Bee on this, either,' she said. 'She was so tiny.'

'Yeah. She did look a bit out of her league on it. But she loved it. It was the first thing she bought after her dad died, after she inherited all his money. She really hated cars, you see.' He stroked the bike, tenderly. 'Hop on.'

Ana didn't need asking twice. She threw one long, spindly leg across the bike. 'Ooh,' she said, settling herself into the pillion seat and pulling on the helmet, 'it's ever so comfy.'

'Blimey,' said Flint, staring at Ana's knee, which was jutting out at a 90° angle and resting very nearly in the crook of his knee, 'Bee's leg only used to come up to there.' He indicated his hip. 'You ready?'

Ana jiggled around a bit and nodded.

'Arms.'

'What?'

'Put your arms around me.'

'Oh. Yes. Right.' She gently brought them round and strapped them round Flint's substantial torso. He was wearing just a T-shirt and she could feel everything: every last rib, every muscle, the beating of his heart, the warmth of his blood, the dampness of his sweat.

'Tighter.'

She fastened them tighter, and now she was close enough to be able to smell him, her nose only a centimetre or two from his T-shirt. She breathed in deeply and held his smell in the back of her throat, like cigar smoke. He smelled of unponced-about man. A bit musty, a bit sweaty and run all the way through with a seam of the indescribably delicious smell of sun-warmed flesh.

The sun was starting to get low in the sky and it cast long shadows on the country lanes. As they neared Broadstairs it hung over the sea and threw a Lucozade glow over the bustling seaside resort. Ana's heart filled with joy as she saw the sea, as the smell of brine hit her nostrils and the agitated squawk of seagulls assaulted her ears. She missed the sea.

They parked the bike by the seafront. Flint ran his fingers through his tufty hair and laughed. 'I must look a right state.'

'I've got a comb, if you like.'

'Cheers.' He took it from her and combed his hair. Ana watched him. It was a vain thing to do, she thought, but he made it look unconsidered and masculine. 'Thanks.' He passed it back to her and they stood and surveyed the view for a while. The sea breeze was taking the edge off the late August heat and Ana felt herself shivering a little. 'What sort of things do you like doing at the seaside then, Ana?'

She shrugged, felt her head tie itself up in a knot as she tried to find an answer to Flint's simple question. What do I like doing at the seaside? She thought desperately, what the hell do I like doing at the seaside? And why the hell is this man making me so nervous? She glanced at him. He was squinting into the distance. Not many men fell into the category of 'handsome'. It was easy for a woman to be thought of as 'beautiful'. Just by not being 'ugly' and making an effort and being young-looking and having nice hair and a good figure, a woman could be described as beautiful. But it was different for men. Men could be cute, or good-looking or sexy, but rarely handsome. And Flint was handsome.

Ana didn't really like handsome men. Or even good-looking men, come to that. She found something offensively ostentatious about an overtly attractive man. She liked nice but strangely unattractive men who had 'something about them'. The sort of unattractive men who had that verging-on-arrogant air of confidence instilled by late-in-life mothers. Interesting men. Men with opinions and ideas. Men who liked to talk. Intense men. Educated men. Intelligent men. The sort of men who didn't have a problem going out with women taller than them. The sort of men that other women didn't fancy. Usually of quite an undernourished appearance, with the type of skin that tended away from tanning. Often with thin wrists and oddly fleshy mouths. Men who didn't gossip, who didn't bitch.

Men like Hugh.

There'd been good-looking blokes at college, guys that all the girls had fancied, but she'd never looked at them in that way. Attractive men came from a different planet in Ana's opinion and she was as likely to be attracted to one as to a Tibetan goat herd.

But Flint was – Flint was – good God, she had no idea what Flint was. He was interesting, she supposed. There was something going on there, something underneath the bulk and the scars and the 'cheers, mate' persona. Something that unnerved Ana. Messed with her cognitive functions. Her ability to form reasonable responses to ordinary questions. Like the one he was still waiting for her to answer right now. What sort of things did she like doing at the seaside? She shrugged. She gave up.

'Whatever,' she said, finally, her voice emerging as a gruff whisper that sounded like a Jack Russell coughing.

'Well,' he said, 'I'll tell you what I like doing at the seaside. I like going to arcades.'

That figures, thought Ana, picturing him wearing out his thumb-pads on a space-invader machine or kicking the shit out of a virtual Ninja. Or something.

'Have you got any moral objections to gambling? As a concept?'

She shook her head.

'Got money on you?'

She patted her tapestry rucksack and nodded.

'Cool,' he said, 'let's go.'

Broadstairs was prettier than your average seaside town, prettier than Bideford, thought Ana, where she'd walked on the beach with Tommy and her father in the winter, throwing sticks for the dog, bashing the sand out of their shoes before they got into the car and getting a pie on the way home. Steep cobbled streets ran away from the seafront, where bow-windowed, knock-kneed cottages lined the lanes.

'Did you know,' said Flint, 'that Dickens wrote *The Olde Curiosity Shoppe* here? In Broadstairs?'

'Did he?' said Ana, 'really?'

'Uh-huh.'

'How did you know that?'

Flint grinned. 'I dunno,' he said, 'I thought everyone knew that.'

'Oh,' said Ana, 'right.'

She glanced at people as they walked and wondered what they were thinking, wondered what sort of a couple she and Flint made. Pretty eye-catching, she imagined, her being so tall and him being so huge, clutching their crash helmets. Nobody would guess, she was sure, that she was just waste-of-space old Ana Wills, unattractive and disappointing second daughter of Gay Wills, naïve country bumpkin and pretty much born-again virgin. She probably looked like she lived in some funky, stripped-floorboarded flat, like she had loads of cool friends who all got stoned and went to parties together and like she had sex with Flint about twenty times a day while drinking tequila from the bottle and listening to really loud music.

Ana suddenly felt like a character in a film. A little fizz went down her spine.

The feeling soon evaporated as they entered the arcade. That smell. That smell of teenagers' trainers, cold metal and dirty money. And the noise – not just the rings and clunks and clinks of the old days, but the new sounds too; booming American voices, rapid gunfire, explosions, thwacks, grunts and groans of Japanese warriors. This was home. This was Devon. This was Bideford and everything she hated about it. Bored teenagers and displaced aggression.

She posted a £5 note into a change-making machine and listened to the jackpot noise of coins being returned to her. And then she looked around for Flint but couldn't see him anywhere. She looked at the Tekkan machines, the Sega Rally cars, lined up together at the far end. She looked at the pinball machines, Time Crisis, some big thing that looked like an army tank, but he was nowhere to be seen. Growing a little concerned now, her hands full of sweaty ten-pence pieces, she walked around the circumference of the arcade, and then she stopped in her tracks and just stared for a while at what suddenly struck her as one of the most endearing images she'd ever seen in her life. It was Flint. He was sideways on to her, wearing a very earnest expression and patiently depositing two-pence pieces into a penny cascade machine. As she approached, a precariously quavering lip of coins crashed noisily into the metal spout in front of Flint. She saw him bunch up his fists triumphantly before scooping up the money and counting it.

'24 pee,' he grinned at her, '24 pee! I'm 10 pee up!'

He looked like a little boy in his Gap Kids-style outfit. He was so excited. Ana wanted to hug him, wrap her arms around him and tuck her head into the crook of his enormous shoulders. He grinned at her again before turning back to the slot with a fistful of two-pence pieces. Bless him to death.

She tore her eyes from him and headed towards a one-armed bandit in the corner where the shadows concealed her scarlet blush and the metal stick in her hand cooled her sweaty palms.

18

They found a pizzeria but it wasn't due to open for another half an hour.

'Fancy getting a drink somewhere?' asked Flint.

They found a big noisy boozer a couple of streets away, and Ana offered to get the drinks in. It was the least she could do, she said, after all the petrol Flint must have used getting here. He watched her at the bar from a small table in a corner, watched her fiddling inside her old tapestry rucksack for a purse, rubbing self-consciously at her elbows as she waited to be served, smiling tightly at the barman and then walking back towards him ever so carefully, a pint in each hand, careful not to spill a drop, careful not look at Flint.

'I got us some crisps, too,' she said, dropping a packet of salt and vinegar on to the table from underneath her arm.

'Ah,' smiled Flint, 'a girl after my own heart – a pint of lager and a packet of crisps. Lovely.'

She picked up her pint and tipped at least a quarter of it down her throat. 'Argh,' she exclaimed, 'I needed that.'

'Yeah,' laughed Flint, 'I can see that. You're not really like your sister, are you?'

Ana laughed, too. 'Aren't I?'

'No. Your sister was more of a cocktail girl. A high-maintenance woman, really.'

'Yeah,' said Ana, 'I can imagine.'

'And your sister was a real loudmouth, too. Like Lol. Can you imagine it? When the two of them got together?' He winced and they both laughed. And then they both stopped laughing and fell into a sad silence. Flint cleared his throat. 'So,' he said. 'What sort of things have you been up to with Lol? In London?'

'Oh. We've been to a couple of bars. In Ladbroke Grove.'

'What – like, poncey places you mean?'

'Well – not really. Just sort of – fashionable places, I guess.'

'Yeah. I know the sorts of places you mean. All scabby second-hand furniture and rank canals.'

'Yeah,' smiled Ana, 'something like that.'

'If you don't mind me saying, Ana – those sorts of places don't seem very – you. I mean, from the look of you – you're more of a pub girl, aren't you?'

Ana smiled. 'I'll try to take that as a compliment,' she said.

'You want to come out with me one night, when we're back in London. I'll take you to some proper London places. There are some amazing pubs in London. And some of the best beer. You've seen a bit of Lol's London – I want to show you a bit of mine.'

'Yes,' Ana said, shyly, 'that would be nice. Thank you.'

Flint eyed her as she picked up her pint and took another sip. He'd enjoyed this little sojourn at the seaside with Ana. It was nice to get away from the indefatigable Lol for a while. Lol was great but she was also one of those people who didn't leave any room in a situation for your own interpretation of things. You always got Lol's version whether you wanted it or not. But with Ana, he'd been able to absorb the odd English seaside atmosphere, the sunset, the smells and sounds. Like being on his own, but with someone.

And there was something about her, he thought, but he found it impossible to put his finger on it. She was quite posh. But not *posh* posh, not public school and fine blonde hair and skiing-tan posh. Not the sort of posh that he usually liked. Just a sort of low-key, middle-class, slightly hippified posh. And it wasn't really about her looks. It wasn't about what she had, as such, but about what she *didn't* have. Like experience. Like sophistication. Like a sense of herself. Like the way she'd blushed just now when he'd suggested this drink. He'd almost been able to see her thoughts through her eyes – 'If I walk into a pub with you, we'll have to have a conversation, and that means I'll have to reveal myself to you, and that makes me very nervous.' She didn't give anything away and, in a world full of people prepared to bare their souls at the drop of a hat, she was coolly refreshing.

Flint had lived in London for most his life. Born and bred in Enfield, he now lived in Turnpike Lane. All his life he'd only known London girls or girls who'd chosen London for what it could offer them. But Ana hadn't chosen London. She was here because of circumstance, not because of ambition or greed or thrill-seeking.

'Have you ever thought about living in London, Ana? Leaving Devon?'

She shook her head. 'No. Never.'

'God, you know – call me small-minded, but I really can't understand that.'

'What?'

'Living in a small town and not being fucking desperate to get away. I mean – what exactly is the attraction?'

Ana shrugged. 'I've never really thought about it.'

'What do you do?'

'What d'you mean?'

'In Devon? Who do you live with? What do you do for a living? Who are your friends? Boyfriend? You know – tell me about your life.'

Ana smiled wryly and took another slurp of beer. 'You don't want to know,' she said.

'Yeah,' he said, 'I do.'

'Well,' she began, smiling with embarrassment, 'I used to have a life. Quite a nice life, actually.'

'Oh yeah?'

'Uh-huh. I had this really nice flat in Exeter. And a job.'

'Doing what?'

'I worked in a music shop. I was the assistant manager.'

'What sort of music shop?'

'You know – guitars, organs, drum-kits. That kind of thing. It wasn't exactly a *career* or anything, but I liked it. I had a little car. I had friends. I had a boyfriend.'

'Called?'

'Called Hugh.'

'And what was he like?'

'Hugh? Well – he was – *is* – great. He's a research scientist. Unbelievably intelligent. And funny. And a good cook. Yeah – Hugh was great.'

Flint watched her as she talked about Hugh, watched the way her cheeks flushed crimson and she suddenly found a dozen things to do with her hands.

'So what happened?'

'Oh. You know. We grew apart.'

'How come?'

'Well – everything sort of changed, after my dad died.'

'Shit yeah – I forgot that your dad died, too.'

'Uh-huh.'

'Sheesh. How?'

'Heart attack. Nothing very exciting. Not like Gregor. But he was eighty-two years old, so it was – you know?'

'Still though – what a shame.'

'It was,' she said, 'it is. He was the nicest man in the world. The nicest man ever. He was like my best friend. I know that sounds weird. But he wasn't like other men of his generation, you know, the war generation. He was different. He even used to come out to the pub with me and my friends sometimes and they all loved him. He was one of those old men who wasn't scared of the new world – he was excited by new technology and new music and new ways of doing things and looking at things. It was like he found the patterns of change exhilarating and life-affirming rather than threatening. I think I did that for him, I think having a child so late in life did that for him. And even though I'd always known he'd go soon, while I was still quite young, it still came as a shock. So, after he went, everything kind of fell apart a bit.' She blushed and cleared her throat and took another large slurp of her lager.

'So?' said Flint.

'So what?'

'So what happened with Hugh?'

'Oh, well, you know – I got compassionate leave from work and it just sort of went on and on and on, and the longer it went on the less I could cope with the idea of going back to work, dealing with the public. So I resigned. And then my mother developed agoraphobia and I had to go home. To look after her. So I went home ten months ago. And me and Hugh tried to make it work for a while. But I think he got fed up in the end.'

'Fed up with what?'

'Well – with me being such a misery-guts, I suppose. With me not being fun any more and not making any effort. He just gave up, and I haven't spoken to him for weeks now.'

'That's a bit rough, isn't it?'

'What?'

'Hugh. Giving up on you when you really needed him?'

Ana shrugged and rubbed her elbows again. 'I've never really thought about it like that. I was always a bit of a burden on him, really and I suppose it was just . . .'

'What do you mean – a burden?'

'I mean – he's really, really intelligent and all his friends were really intelligent, too – they were all scientists and engineers and that sort of thing – all a few years older than me, and I was always a bit – out of my depth, I guess. I wasn't much good. I couldn't cook and I didn't know anything about politics or world affairs or wine or . . . or . . . *conspiracy theories* and all that stuff they liked talking about. I always thought he deserved someone a bit more sophisticated than me, a bit more mature. I think I dragged him down a bit . . .'

Flint exhaled through puffed-out cheeks. 'Well, well, well – poor old Hugh, eh?' he said, having already decided that the bloke was obviously a complete cunt.

'Yeah. I guess so. Poor old Hugh.'

'But what do you *do*, Ana?' Flint asked. 'I mean – what do you actually do all day?'

Ana shrugged and looked embarrassed. 'Look after my mum. Go shopping for her.'

'Yes – but the rest of the time – what do you do? Have you got a job?'

She shook her head. 'I've been meaning to start sending out applications. But I haven't got round to it.'

'And what about your old friends, in Exeter – do you still see them?'

'No,' she said in a very small voice, 'not really. They tried. But I think they kind of gave up on me too, eventually. I haven't really been very good company, since my dad died. You know? But anyway,' she said forcefully, 'enough about me. More than enough about me. What about you?' She looked directly at Flint. 'What about your life?'

Interesting, Flint thought, the way she'd opened up like that, just for a moment and then snapped shut again, like a fly-trap. She was quite obviously depressed, although she hadn't admitted it to herself yet. That's even if she knew it. He ignored her last question.

'So. Let me get this straight. You haven't worked for nearly a year. You live at home with your mum. You've got no friends and you never go out.'

'Yup.'

'Christ. That's tragic. That's one of the most tragic things I've ever heard. How old are you?'

'Twenty-five.'

'Twenty-five. Jesus – what would I give to be twenty-five again. You wait – one day you'll be my age – thirty-six – and you'll be wondering what the fuck happened to your youth, where'd it go. Can I tell you the worst thing about getting old, Ana? They try and make out that ageing is all about gain – gaining experience, wisdom, happiness, all that. They're lying. All getting older is about is loss. Losing things. Losing your hair, your figure, your looks. Losing your sight. Losing your hearing. Losing your mother, losing your father. Losing time to experience things. Losing touch with people, losing your mind. And the worst thing of all – losing memories. The more time you've got to look back on, the less you remember. Whole days, weeks, months that you have no recollection of. People you've spent entire days with, worked with for months, slept with, partied with . . . Fuck, Ana. You should be living life. Not wasting your youth. You'll regret it one day, you really will . . .'

Ana smiled tightly and to Flint's horror her eyes suddenly filled up with tears. She cleared her throat and looked away abruptly.

'Sorry,' he said, 'I'm sorry. I didn't mean to give you a hard time, really I didn't. It's just – people not making the most of what they've got – it annoys me. It winds me up. I don't believe in God, Ana, in the bible, but if there was to be one commandment from on high, it should be that – Thou Shalt Make the Most of What Thou Hast.'

'Oh yeah. And what exactly have I got to make the most of?'

'Do you want me to make you a list?'

'Yes.'

'OK, then. OK. Youth.'

'Not all it's cracked up to be.'

'Beauty.'

'Yeah. Right.'

'What – you don't think you're beautiful?'

'Er, no? Not even slightly.'

'Why not?'

'It's my nose . . .'

'You don't like your nose?'

'No – I hate it. Look.' She turned round sideways to show Flint her profile. 'I look like a . . . a buzzard or something. It's like a beak. It's disgusting.'

Flint shook his head and laughed. 'Women! Jesus. What are you like? Well – for what it's worth, I think it's a very beautiful nose. It's elegant. Regal. Dignified. It's like you.'

She blushed. Vividly. 'And, of course there's the fact that I look like a giant coat-stand.'

'You mean you don't like being tall?'

'Well, it's not so much the tallness as the tallness combined with the thinness.'

'Jesus,' said Flint, 'did you know that London is literally bursting at the seams with women who would sell their *lungs* to have your figure?'

'Yeah. Sure.'

'No. Really. For a hell of a lot of women, your shape is an absolute ideal.'

'But that's ridiculous. Why?'

Flint shrugged. 'Because that's what models look like, I suppose, and some actresses.'

Ana looked unconvinced. 'So. Carry on. Other things to make the most of . . .'

'Your freedom.'

'I haven't got freedom.'

'Of course you have.'

'I haven't. My mother has my freedom.'

'Oh yeah. And what does she do with it?'

'She keeps it in a little box under the stairs.' She smiled wryly.

'Your mother sounds like a bit of a nightmare, if you don't mind me saying.'

'She is.'

'So why d'you stay?'

She shrugged. 'Because she needs me.'

Flint took a deep breath. 'Are you sure it's not because you need her?'

'I'm sorry?' Ana's eyes boggled.

'To hide behind.'

'I don't get your point.'

'I mean — are you sure that you don't just use your mother's agoraphobia as an excuse to keep away from the real world? Because you can't deal with it?'

'Jesus,' said Ana, 'what is this? The Anthony Clare Show?'

'No. It's what your sister used to say about you, actually.'

'What — Bee?'

'Uh-huh. She was very concerned about you.'

'You are joking, right?'

Flint shook his head.

'Jesus,' said Ana, 'ever since I got here, all I've heard is how great Bee thought I was.'

'Well – she did.'

'But she didn't even know me.'

'She knew enough. And she lived with your mother, too, remember.'

'Yeah, but – she had no idea about anything else – she didn't know about Hugh and my job and my life.'

'No,' said Flint, plainly, 'she didn't. But she knew what it was like to lose a father and she knew what it was like to live with your mother and she knew what *you* were like. You know those meetings you all used to have, in Bristol and places like that?'

'Yeah?'

'She used to come back in tears sometimes. Usually because of your mother. But other times because she was sad about you. She said you were like this pale, beautiful little ghost, that she just wanted to pick you up and stick you under her arm and take you back to London with her. And she said she felt really bad because she never knew what to say to you, how to talk to you. She wasn't the most maternal of people, but she always had this huge soft spot for you.'

'Huh – well – you could have fooled me. She didn't even use to *look* at me unless it was to take the piss.' She was looking at her watch again. 'Oh look,' she said, 'it's seven o'clock. That pizza place will be open now. We should get back. Lol'll be starving.' She already had her rucksack on her lap, the conversation was over. For now.

They finished their drinks, picked up their crash helmets and headed for the pizzeria.

19

Bee descended the stairs of her Belsize Park flat in her satin dressing-gown, a mug of Earl Grey in one hand, John in the other. Summer should have been over by now, but it wasn't. After a dismal August, the sun was out every morning, the temperature not dropping below 73°C. It was like a little freebie from the weather gods and London was fully appreciating it. The sun was glowing through the stained-glass panel above the front door, casting pools of coloured light all over the pale wooden floor of the spacious hallway. Wendy the Reflexologist, who lived in the ground-floor flat, was listening to some kind of bongo-y 'world' music – very loudly. Bee was sure that Wendy the Reflexologist didn't actually like world music but had obviously decided that it fitted her image.

A pool of letters lay on the doormat. Bee leaned down to gather them up and quickly let John drop to the floor when she saw an envelope addressed to her – in her mother's handwriting. Bee hadn't heard from her mother since Gay had written to tell her that she was contesting Gregor's will. That was nearly ten years ago now. This had to be something pretty serious. She ripped at the Basildon Bond tissue-lined envelope and pulled out the neatly folded little letter, handwritten on heavy blue paper.

'Dear Belinda,' it began,

I shouldn't suppose that the following news is of very much interest to you but I thought it only polite to inform you that my beloved Bill passed away on Sunday. It was fast and relatively painless and he had a good, healthy, long and happy life. I should count my blessings, but can't help feeling robbed and very, very bitter. First Gregor, then you (you may as well be dead) and now my wonderful, wonderful Bill. My life really is one long tragedy . . . The funeral is to be held on Thursday at St Giles (Bill always loved that church and he got on so well with Father Boniface) but I don't suppose you'll have any interest in attending. Still — I thought you should know.

Your mother,

Gay

Bee collapsed on to the bottom stair and clutched the two sides of her dressing-gown together over her chest. *Ana*, she thought immediately. Poor Ana. Her mind filled with images of pale little Ana, with her knobbly knees and gawky features, sitting there during those dreadful family meetings in the Eighties, so quiet and perfectly behaved. And so much like her father.

She stared into the distance for a while, stroking John, absent-mindedly, trying to decide what to do. It was Wednesday. The funeral was tomorrow. She had nothing planned for tomorrow. She could go. She could get on her bike and go. To Devon. She could. She squeezed her eyes closed and tried to imagine the scenario. Tried to imagine standing there in the graveyard at St Giles, her mother dressed in head-to-toe Escada sobbing dramatically at her side, sad, lanky Ana on the other. She imagined going back to Gay's perfect townhouse on Main Street afterwards, the big, squishy sofas covered in huge jacquard cushions with glossy tassels that Bee happened to know had cost £85 each. Wandering around disconsolately on expensive cream Wilton in the glow of fat-bottomed table-lamps. Making polite, muted conversation around a coffee table covered in expensive little objects, tiny lumps of carved marble and beautiful engraved silver boxes that seemed to perform no function whatsoever other than to give her mother something extra to dust and polish and arrange. Standing drinking sherry beside the huge open fire carved out of the wall, flanked by big baskets full of dried roses and shiny brass things for stoking the fire. And remembering all the time her mother's *rage* if any one of these pointless, spotless objects were moved by so much as a millimetre.

She tried to imagine her mother, moving from person to person, around her lovely home, dabbing daintily at her nose and soaking up the sympathy and the attention like a delicate sponge. Gay had her own personal fan-club in Torrington, people who could see no bad in her. People who thought she was an angel. People who truly believed her claim that her charmed life had been 'one long tragedy'.

And then she tried to imagine what it would be like after all the villagers had left, when the canapés had been cleared away and the caterers had packed their van up and it was just her and her mother and Ana. And she would have to speak her mind. She knew it. 'You didn't deserve that man,' is what she'd have to say, 'he was too good for you and you treated him like shit, like you were ashamed of him. You never appreciated him while he was alive and now he's dead all you're interested in is milking the situation for your own benefit, for the attention. Exactly like you did with Gregor. You fucked me up and now you're fucking up poor Ana. You make me sick.' That's what she'd say. And every word would be true. Which was why she couldn't go. She couldn't do that to her mother. Not at her husband's funeral. It wasn't the right time.

Bee picked up John and went back up to her flat. Ed was just emerging from the bedroom, scratching at his cropped, silver hair and yawning.

'Thought you'd been abducted by aliens,' he said, heading towards the kitchen.

'No,' she said, 'no. I got some bad news. In the post.'

'What sort of bad news?' Ed's disembodied voice came from the kitchen, where Bee could hear the click of the fridge door being opened.

'It's my stepfather. He died.'

'I didn't know you had a stepfather.' Ed emerged clutching a carton of orange juice and a cold sausage.

'Uh-huh. My mother's second husband. Ana's dad. He was very old.'

'So – are you going to the funeral?'

She shrugged. 'I should,' she began, 'for Ana's sake. But I really, really don't think I can face it.'

'What. Your mother?' He put the sausage in his mouth and left it there.

'Yeah. My Mother. But Ana, too. I feel so bad about Ana. *For* Ana. She's going to be so alone and I really want to see her, so badly. But I'm scared, because I've got no idea what to say to her. I mean – where do you start, after ten years?'

'Why don't you just write her a letter or something?' He scratched his arse with his spare hand and wandered back into the bedroom, leaving an aroma of bedsheeted-man in his wake.

A letter, thought Bee. That wasn't a bad idea. She showered and breakfasted and saw Ed off at the door at eight o'clock.

'You off to Broadstairs this weekend?' he asked, while he adjusted his tie and switched on his mobile phone.

'Uh-huh. I'll be back early Sunday, though. D'you fancy coming over? We can get a late dinner.'

'Er – I'm not sure. I'll have to check.'

'With who? Tina's not around.'

'Well – she might be. Her flight's due in on Monday morning, but you know what she's like. If she can get an earlier flight, she will. I'll check. OK?'

'OK,' said Bee, a pout forming on her plump lips. 'But try, won't you? Please.'

He kissed her forcefully on the lips and smiled at her. 'I always try, Bee. You know that. Have a good weekend, OK, and send my love to Zander.'

Bee sighed as the door closed behind him and she heard his footsteps taking the stairs, two at a time, running away from her and towards his other life – his real life.

And then she made herself another mug of Earl Grey and walked to the desk in the window. She lit a cigarette and searched around in the drawers and filing trays. Paper. Writing paper. She must have some writing paper some-where. She finally found some old bits of loose A4. She placed one in front of her and picked up a blue rollerball. The sun shone through the window and across the paper, making it look very white and very empty. She hadn't written a letter for ages. How the hell did you write a letter anyway? Jesus. She went to the kitchen and made herself some toast.

Then she fed the cat.

Then she filed her nails.

Then she opened the rest of her mail and made a couple of phonecalls. Then she took the rubbish out and had a little chat by the trees in the sunshine, with Wendy the Reflexologist.

And then it was nearly lunchtime. So she made herself some more toast.

And then she went back to the desk, where the sheet of paper stared blankly at her. She sat down and eyed the paper up. She didn't like this paper. She wanted to use nice paper. She pulled on some sandals and a pair of sunglasses, slicked some deodorant under her arms and headed for the stationer on Haverstock Hill – where she spent nearly half an hour looking at their small selection of writing paper. She finally settled on a pad of silky mauve paper with contrasting burnt orange envelopes. And she bought a 'With Sympathy' card, with a picture of a single white lily on the front.

By the time she'd done a bit of shopping, bought herself some flowers and picked up her dry-cleaning it was nearly three in the afternoon. She made herself another mug of Earl Grey, lit another fag, spread out her mauve paper and stared at the blank sheet in front of her. And she stared at it and she stared at it and she stared at it.

'Jesus,' she exclaimed jumping to her feet in frustration. 'Why is this so fucking difficult?' But she knew exactly why it was so difficult. This was Ana she was writing to, little Ana. Little Ana who was now big Ana, big Ana who had a life and a job that she knew nothing about. Little Ana who she'd effectively abandoned twelve years ago when she'd fallen out with her mother. Little Ana who she'd never bonded with. Little Ana who was her sister, for God's sake. Her only sister. It wouldn't be enough just to write a line of condolence. Ana deserved more. An explanation. A background. Some history. She picked up her pen and finally started writing.

After she'd finished, she read it through about thirteen times before finally folding it into a square and slipping it inside the 'With Sympathy' card.

It was heavy, she knew that. But it needed to be. There was no point being half-hearted about it. Anything else would have sounded trite, would have sounded like the Bee that Ana probably remembered from those awful meetings, the preening, shallow, ambitious Bee. The Bee who thought she didn't need anyone who couldn't further her career. The Bee who was more concerned with impressing the trendy people she used to surround herself with than the feelings of her gangling, awkward adolescent sister. The Towering Twiglet. That's what she used to call her. And laugh. Out loud. Bee blushed at the mere thought. Poor Ana. And she was probably stunning now, she thought. Twenty-five years old and with legs up to here and those amazing yellowy-hazel eyes. She addressed the envelope and licked a stamp and took the letter down to the box on the corner. Post it now. Before she had a chance to change her mind.

And then she went back to her flat and made herself a margarita and waited for the evening to wear itself out so that it would be tomorrow. The day that Ana got the letter. The day that something might change and something good might happen. Maybe. For the first time in years she had something to look forward to. Maybe. A letter from Ana. Maybe. Or a phonecall. A chance to put something right. She'd done it with Zander. Made things right with Zander. Maybe she could make things right with Ana, too.

Maybe.

20

'Look what I found.' Flint was standing in the living room of Bee's cottage, triumphantly holding aloft a small mobile phone.

Lol threw down her slice of pizza and grabbed it from his hands. 'That's Bee's phone,' she cried, 'where did you find it?'

'In the storage compartment under the seat of her bike.'

'God – I can't believe she'd just have left it there – she was addicted to this sodding thing.' She started tapping numbers into the phone until it beeped and lit up. 'It's still got some juice,' she said, 'let's have a little look, shall we?' She sat back down and Ana slid across the sofa to peer over her shoulder.

'What are you doing?'

'I'm just checking through her directory, to see if there are any names I don't recognize . . . Aha!' she exclaimed. 'Who's ET? ET home? 0208 341 6565 – isn't that Highgate? It is, isn't it? Did Bee know anyone in Highgate, Flint?'

Flint shrugged. 'Not that I'm aware of.'

'OK, what about ET work? 0207 786 2218 – that's the West End, in't it? Soho? Well – there's only one way to find out who they belong to.' She started tapping in some more numbers and then straightened her back and cleared her throat.

'What are you doing?'

'I'm phoning it, doofus-features, what' you think I'm doing?'

'Yeah – but what are you going to say, exactly?'

'I dunno,' she said, 'I'll wing it, I guess.'

'OK,' said Ana, wedging herself between the two of them before they started bickering again, 'we should really decide which number to dial first and what we're going to say.'

'Right,' agreed Lol, switching off the phone. 'It's a Sunday and the Soho number's probably an office number, so let's call the Highgate number. OK?'

Flint and Ana nodded.

'And what are you going to say?'

Lol shrugged. 'I dunno. What d'you think I should say, Ana?'

'How about just being plain, you know? Just saying who you are and how you found the number and why you're calling.'

'Brilliant!' she beamed, before handing it over to Ana. 'You do it,' she said, 'people respond better to a posh accent.'

'I'm not posh,' exclaimed Ana.

'No – but you know what I mean.'

Ana shrugged and took the phone. 'OK,' she said, before dialling the number. 'It's ringing.'

She took a deep breath while she waited for the phone to be picked up. This could be it, she thought. Finally. After all this wild-goose chasing and all these dead-ends, at last they were going to talk to someone who might have some idea what exactly Bee had been up to for the last three years of her life.

A man picked up. 'Hello.'

Ana widened her eyes at Flint and Lol to indicate that she'd got through.

'Oh. Er. Hi,' she began.

'Hello.'

'Hi. Erm. My name's Ana Wills. I don't know if you've heard of me.'

'No,' he said, bluntly.

'Well, I'm the sister of – well, half-sister, to be accurate – of Bee? Bee Bearhorn?'

'Oh.'

'And, well, this is her mobile phone I'm calling from.'

'Right. Good.'

There was something very disconcerting about this man's manner. 'Yes – and your number comes up as the last number to phone her on this, er, number.' Ana took another deep breath before she ended up saying 'number' again.

'OK.'

Jesus – this was possibly the most monosyllabic person Ana had ever encountered. 'And that's why we're calling you. Just to . . . er . . . we wanted to . . . er . . . I mean, we wanted – who *are* you?'

'I'm sorry?'

'No. Sorry. I didn't mean to be so blunt. I just meant, well – who are you in relation to Bee? Exactly?'

'Well. Yes. I see. I could probably make it, yes.'

Ana scrunched up her face in confusion. What on earth was he talking about? 'I know it sounds weird, but we really need to know who you are. I mean – obviously you might just be her plumber, or something. Are you?'

'What?'

'Nothing. Sorry. I just need to . . . who *are* you?' she asked again in desperation, thinking what an awkward tool of communication the phone could be sometimes.

'Yes,' said the deadpan man, 'tomorrow would be fine. How about midday?'

'What?'

'At my office. Yes. Do you have my office address?'

'Er – no.'

'52 Poland Street. Uh-huh. The bell says Tewkesbury. Ed Tewkesbury Productions.'

'PEN!' Ana mouthed urgently at Lol, who threw her one. '52 Poland Street?' she repeated back to him.

'That's right.'

'Ed Tewkesbury Productions?'

'Uh-huh.'

'Midday tomorrow?'

'Yup.'

'So you want to meet me, tomorrow, at midday, at your office?'

'Yes, please. That would be great.'

'And your name is?'

'Ed Tewkesbury Productions. Yes. That's right.'

'So you're Ed?'

'That's correct, yes.'

'And how exactly did you know my sister?'

'Great. That's great, then. I'll see you tomorrow. Bye.'

'No – hold on – wait a minute!' But he'd gone. Hung up.

'Jesus,' said Ana, switching off the phone and flopping backwards into the sofa. 'That was officially the weirdest person I've ever had a conversation with.'

'What' he say? What' he say?' squealed Lol.

Ana shrugged. 'Absolutely nothing. Just to meet him at his office tomorrow. At midday.'

'And he didn't say who he was?'

'Ed Tewkesbury?'

Flint and Lol both looked at each other and then turned back to Ana and shook their heads. 'Never heard of him,' said Lol.

'Me neither,' said Flint.

'Well,' sighed Ana, 'we will have by this time tomorrow.'

21

At eleven o'clock the following morning, Flint and Ana dropped Lol off at her flat. Her flight to Nice was at three that afternoon and she wanted to shower and pack. They pulled up outside her house on Bevington Road.

'Now,' she said to Ana, 'I'll have my mobile with me so just phone me, right. I want all the developments. I want to know what's going on. I cannot believe that I have to go away. Now. Just when you're about to find out what's happening. And you – Lennard' – she leaned in towards the partition – 'you look after this girl, OK? Don't let anything bad happen to her and *behave yourself.*' She gave him a big smacker on the cheek and then smiled at Ana. 'I'll be back on Thursday, right, and I'll phone you the minute I get in. And promise me, Ana, *promise me,* that whatever you do, you *don't go home.* OK?' She gripped her hands and stared deep in her eyes.

'Promise,' Ana said.

'Good,' said Lol, grabbing Ana's shoulders and giving her a huge bear-hug. And then she picked up her handbag and got out of the car. Ana felt her gut suddenly clench up with anxiety. Lol was going. Lol who'd looked after her and taken her out and made sure that she didn't feel scared and alone in a big strange city – her new friend, Lol.

Ana sat in the back of Flint's car sadly watching her new friend climbing the steps up to her bright-green house. She stuck her head through the window as Lol put her key in the door. 'Have a good time,' she said sadly, 'I'll phone you.'

Lol pushed the front door open and blew her a kiss. And then she disappeared. And Ana was all alone in the world again. She suddenly felt like crying.

She breathed in when she saw Flint turning around in the front. 'Can I interest you in a seat up front?' he said, eyeing up the passenger seat and smiling kindly.

Ana nodded. 'Thanks,' she said. She picked up her rucksack and slid into the front seat. Flint looked at her with concern. 'You all right?' he said.

'Yeah,' she said, 'I'm fine. I'm just – I think I might miss Lol.'

'Don't you worry about a thing, Ana,' he said, grinning at her, 'I'll look after you, I promise.'

Ed Tewkesbury's office was housed in a wide, five-storey Deco office block squeezed, like *War and Peace* between two novellas, between a sandwich bar and an Italian restaurant. Flint held the door open for Ana as the Intercom buzzed to let them in. A uniformed security guard on the front desk directed them to the fifth floor, which they reached by a tiny mirror-lined lift.

'He might not know that Bee's dead, you know?' Flint said. 'We might be the bearers of bad news.'

The lift pinged and slid open and they stepped out into a plush reception area. A girl with platinum-white hair with black streaks in it looked up at them brightly from behind a glass-brick desk. She was wearing one of those headsets like Steps wear in their videos.

'Hi!' she beamed, 'can I help you?' As they approached Flint noticed that she smelled overpoweringly of strawberries.

'Yes,' said Ana, 'we're here to see Ed Tewkesbury.'

'And do you have an appointment?'

'Uh-huh. He said to meet him here at twelve. At noon. Midday.'

All three of them turned their eyes towards a large chrome clock on the wall to the left. It was dead on twelve. And noon. And midday.

'I'll just try him for you. Who shall I say is here?'

'Ana Wills and Flint Lennard. Thank you.'

Flint and Ana both stood smiling at her as she tapped numbers into her switchboard. 'Hi, Shona, it's Amber here, I've got an Ana Flint and a Leonard Wills here to see Ed. Cool. Cool. Cool. Uh-huh. Cool. OK.'

'Hi,' she beamed again, 'Ed's just finishing off in a meeting. He'll only be five minutes. Would you like to take a seat?' She pointed behind them at a denim-covered sofa with contrast stitching and rivets and huge pockets on the arms. Trade magazines were spread in a fan on a glass-brick table. Flint picked up a copy of *Broadcast* and started flicking briskly through it. He didn't like offices. They made him feel uncomfortable. He'd never had to work in an office in his life, apart from one week – well, three and a half days actually – on a YOP scheme when he was sixteen, working at a firm of accountants in Palmers Green. He'd had to wear a suit that belonged to his cousin Paul. Paul was a slight boy at least four inches shorter than Flint and with a habit of letting his cuffs trail in his food judging by the encrustations that Flint had had to scrape off with a knife before he could even contemplate putting on the jacket. Unable to stomach the prospect of wearing Paul's stinky nylon shirt, too, Flint had worn one of his own frayed-cuff school shirts, and his mother had tried to tame his tufty, Glen Hoddle-esque coif with some of his dad's old Brylcreem from a tin that had been rusting in the bathroom for ten years. He'd looked a complete clown and had been treated accordingly, particularly by the snobbish secretaries with the frilly-collared blouses and stiff hair. They'd made him stick stamps on envelopes and clean the fridge and take things to the post office every five minutes and make them tea in their prissy little cups and saucers, and he'd hated every second of it. He'd thrown a box of PG Tips – leaf, not bags – all over the desk of one of the secretaries, called her a 'fucking balloon-faced old trout' and stormed out when she'd chastised him for taking a personal phonecall and as he'd walked out of the musty-smelling building and into the fresh crisp air of a January afternoon, he'd felt like the guy in *Midnight Express*. He'd joined the army the same day.

'Hi.' An anorexic-looking woman in turquoise pedal-pushers and a black knitted halter-top was standing in front of them, with one skeletal little bird-hand clutching a folder and a big coldsore on her lip. 'I'm Shona, Ed's PA. He's ready to see you now – would you like to follow me?'

Flint and Ana both stood up and smiled at Shona and then at one another. This was it. They didn't talk as they made their way behind the upsettingly thin figure of Shona, down a muted corridor. She knocked on a pair of double doors at the furthest end and a brusque male voice said 'Come.'

It was a huge office with windows on both sides, one set overlooking the street below and the other a fire-escaped courtyard. They looked around them, absorbing the heavy limestone linen curtains, the biscuity calfskin sofas, the custom-made galvanized steel chandelier, the five-foot pewter candlesticks and the screen-printed canvases. It looked more like the bachelor penthouse of an over-bonused city boy than an office.

'Hi, Ana, nice to meet you.' A small man emerged from a booth in the corner of the office, smiling minimally. He was slim and well-dressed, with cropped white hair and wire-framed glasses.

He was the man in Bee's India photographs.

'Ed Tewkesbury.'

'Hi,' said Ana, turning to catch Flint's eye, 'this is Flint Lennard – he was a very good friend of Bee's.'

'Hi,' he said grimly, slipping an insubstantial little hand inside Flint's large paw. 'Nice to meet you, Flint.' Flint looked down at him. He didn't like him. He let his hand drop and put it in his pocket.

'So,' said Ed, clasping his hands together and trying to look relaxed, 'a drink? Tea? Coffee?'

They both shook their heads. 'Are you sure? No? OK. I'll have a tea please, Shona – jasmine. Thanks.' Shona left the room and Ed turned and smiled his painful smile at Flint and Ana.

'So,' he began, 'you're Bee's sister are you?'

Ana nodded and perched herself uncertainly on the edge of the calfskin sofa.

'I'm really, really sorry about what happened.'

'So you heard then?'

'Yup. There was a bit in the Times. I was shocked. Absolutely shocked. When you meet someone as alive as Bee, you just can't even contemplate something like that happening. It's tragic.'

Ana nodded again. There was a short silence. Ed sat down in his chair, ostentatiously. 'So. I have to admit to being rather curious about your phonecall. It was all very mysterious. What can I do for you exactly?' He was still smiling that awful fake smile, and it was blatantly obvious that underneath the smooth exterior, he was absolutely shitting himself.

Flint opened his mouth to say something but Ana had already started talking. He turned to watch her. Her ears were protruding from her straight black hair like little white handles. They were slightly sticky-outy. They were unbelievably cute.

'Well,' she began, 'the thing is, we found Bee's mobile phone at her cottage in Broadstairs . . .'

'I see.'

'Did you know,' asked Ana in surprise, 'that she had a cottage in Broadstairs?'

He puffed and smiled again, 'Well, yes, she did mention it. I think . . .'

'And we went through her directory – and yours were the only two numbers we didn't recognize.'

He suddenly stiffened. 'How did you know that it was my number in Highgate?'

Ana shrugged and looked at Flint.

'We recognized the area code,' he said.

'Ah. I see. OK.'

'So what was your connection? With Bee?'

'Well,' said Ed, stretching out on his leather chair, 'my connection with Bee was rather – er – tenuous you might say. I don't think I'm going to be of much assistance.'

'So,' said Flint, losing his patience now, 'how did you know her?'

'On a purely professional basis. We were working on a series of nostalgia shows for Channel 4 – you know – the hits and TV shows and adverts from a certain year. We approached Bee to appear in the 1985 programme. She declined. I took her out for lunch, to try to persuade her. And well – if I'm to be entirely honest, because I really wanted to meet her. I'd had an almighty crush on her when I was younger, you see. So I took her out for lunch and she said, Absolutely no way. The past was the past, she said, and that's where she wanted to leave it. I got the impression she wasn't particularly proud of her pop heritage. She struck me as someone who liked to look forward rather than back. So we parted company there and off she went. We made our nostalgia series without her.

'But then in January we were approached by Sky to produce a similar series – but less documentary-style, this time, and more MTV-video-jock style, and it occurred to me that Bee would make a fantastic presenter. She was a beautiful woman and so charismatic. It surprised me that someone hadn't already asked her. So I phoned her and couldn't get through on her mobile. I phoned a number of times during those few days. Really frustrating. You know – we had a deadline, we had to get the project off the ground, and I needed confirmation from Bee that she was interested. But I never managed to get in touch. And, you know, she didn't have an agent or anything. So I had to leave it. Go with someone else. And the next thing I heard of Bee was that she'd . . . died.' He held out his hands, helplessly.

Flint looked at him, his eyes slanted with anger. He'd known it. With every fibre of his body. From the first moment he'd set eyes on that photograph of him, yesterday morning, he'd known he was a slimy bastard. And now he'd proved it. Lying. He was lying. Flint's hand went to the buckle of Ana's rucksack, where the packet of photos was currently residing. Ana's eyes darted to his hand and then to his eyes. She nodded imperceptibly.

'So,' began Ana, looking Ed squarely in the eye, 'you've only actually met Bee once?'

'Unfortunately for me – yes.' His eyes darted away from hers, and he focused on Shona, who'd just walked back in with a big yellow mug full of steaming jasmine tea. 'Aah, Shona, wonderful. Thank you. Yes – just the once, though as I say, I'd rather I'd known her better.'

'Are you sure there wasn't more to your relationship?' asked Ana, watching Flint slip the photos from her bag.

'Absolutely,' he grimaced, taking a big slurp of tea, far too quickly, and burning his mouth in the process. 'Ow, shit,' he hissed, letting the mug clank heavily on to his desk and covering his lips with a hand.

'So, it's quite strange then, wouldn't you say, that you appear to have been on holiday with her? To India?' Flint got to his feet and let the photos fall on the desk in front of Ed. Flint watched Ed closely, could almost see the various options running through his mind until, eventually, his face slumped with the realization that there was nothing he could say to negate the fact that he'd been lying.

'Aaah,' he said finally, picking up the picture of himself and looking at it. 'I see.'

'OK,' said Flint going back to the sofa, 'can we start this conversation again, please?'

Ed sighed and let his face fall on to his fist. 'It was her idea,' he began. 'She insisted on keeping the whole thing secret. I wanted to go public months earlier, but she wouldn't let me. If there was one thing you could say about Bee, it was that she liked to keep her life compartmentalized.'

'So,' said Ana impatiently, 'what was going on?'

'Well – *we* were. *We* were going on. But I was – am – married. That's why I was so cagey when I spoke to you yesterday. My wife was standing right next to me. And I would have left her – Tina – I was prepared to leave her from the minute I met Bee, but she kept putting me off, she wouldn't let me.'

'How long?' said Ana. 'How long did you two . . . ?'

Ed sighed, opened a drawer, pulled out a packet of cigarettes, offered them around, lit one, exhaled. 'Three years.'

'*Three years?*' said Flint, incredulously.

'Uh-huh.'

'So you were together? When she lived in Belsize Park?'

'Yup. I paid the rent on that place, in fact.'

'Really?'

'Yes – well, I spent a lot of time there and she was always short of cash so . . . you know, it wasn't like I was paying her or anything. It was just a practical arrangement.'

'Is that why she moved out?'

229

Ed shrugged. 'I don't know. The money probably. And maybe she was looking for some kind of fresh start. Or something . . .'

'And how did you meet?'

'Well, that's the thing, you see. That's the thing . . .'

'What thing?' asked Ana, impatiently.

'The way we met – it's got everything to do with why she wouldn't let me into her life, why she wouldn't let me leave my wife.'

'What was it?'

Ed shook his head. 'I can't,' he said, 'I can't tell you. I always swore to Bee, swore I'd never tell anyone. I can't . . .'

Flint felt himself running out of patience – and he was a very patient man. He got to his feet again. 'Listen,' he said, using his bulk rather than raising his voice to intimidate Ed, 'Bee's dead. And we've got no idea why. And you seem to know a whole load of shit about her life that even her closest friends and family' – he nodded towards Ana – 'didn't know about. If you've got any respect for us and for Bee you'll tell us what you know.'

Ed shook his head and stubbed out his half-smoked cigarette 'No,' he said, simply, 'I can't. I made her a promise.'

'Did it have something to do with you? Bee's death? Huh?' Flint could feel a rage building and tried to swallow it. He felt a hand on his bare arm. It was Ana.

'Look,' she began soothingly, addressing Ed, 'has this got anything to do with Zander?'

Ed started. 'What?' he said. 'You know? You know about Zander?'

Flint heard Ana breathe in. 'Uh-huh, yeah – we know about Zander.'

Flint had stopped breathing. Brilliant, he thought to himself admiringly, what a brilliant manoeuvre.

'Well, then, you don't need me to tell you anything else, do you?' There was sweat rolling down Ed's temples and along his jawline. He was finding this whole experience deeply stressful.

Flint looked at Ana. 'Well, yes – we do actually. Like how can we find him? How can we get to talk to him?'

'No,' said Ed, bluntly, 'no way. I only ever met him once. Her son was her own affair, and she hated the idea of anyone else having anything to do with him. So, no – leave well alone. Trust me. Zander's a difficult boy – very angry, very . . . cruel. He wouldn't take kindly to being unearthed. And he's fine where he is. Leave him alone. Really. Trust me . . .'

Flint sat down. Ana looked at him and then back at Ed. 'Bee didn't have a son,' she said.

'Try telling that to Zander,' sighed Ed.

'No – but really – she didn't.'

'Look – you've just told me that you knew next to nothing about your sister. So take it from me. She had a son. His name is Zander. He's fourteen.'

'No no no,' said Flint, getting to his feet, 'that's bollocks. That is such bollocks. I've known Bee for more than fifteen years. I've known her, see, and she was never pregnant. Ever.' Flint was starting to sweat now, as he began to doubt his own recollection of the major life events of his closest friends.

Ed shrugged. 'What can I say? She had a son. I met him

once. He existed. Sometimes it's impossible to know everything about your friends.'

'Yes, but – there's secrets and then there's going around with a fucking great lump in your frock for nine months. I mean – Bee was only tiny – I'd have noticed.'

'Maybe she went away? Maybe she had her baby some-where else?'

'No,' said Flint, 'no, because she never went anywhere. Never went anywhere for longer than a couple of weeks and no – because that was 1986, see, and 1986 was the year that . . . well . . . No way – there's no way . . .'

Ed shrugged again and sighed, and Flint wanted to hit him. How could this small, smug man, sitting here in his poncey *handbag* of an office, this little weasel who'd known Bee for, like, two seconds, possibly think he had anything to say on the subject of Bee Bearhorn? And particularly on the subject of Bee Bearhorn *circa* 1986, which Flint happened to know had been the worst year of Bee's life and a year in which they had been almost inseparable.

Ana put her hand on his arm again. Soft, fluttery hands. 'What happened to him – to Zander?' she asked Ed. 'Why was he disabled?'

Ed shrugged. 'Just came out that way, I suppose. He was in a home from birth, as far as I know. Bee only regained contact three years ago. Around the time that I met her.'

'And where did you meet her, exactly?'

'At the children's home. Where Zander was living. I was there making a documentary, and she was visiting Zander. That was when I met him – the only time I met him. Look,' he said, 'I'm not going to tell you where to

232

find him, but I'll tell you everything else. About Bee. And Zander. Everything I know. OK?'

Ana glanced at Flint and then nodded. 'Sure,' she said, 'OK.'

Ed sat up and stubbed out his cigarette. 'Let's get some lunch. Japanese all right?'

22

June 1997

Bee parked her bike and dismounted. She pulled a bag from the pannier on the back and walked towards the house. It was beautiful place, turreted and gargoyled and slightly enchanted-looking. She crunched uncertainly across the gravel driveway to the front entrance.

'Good morning,' she said to the blue-uniformed nurse on reception, 'my name's Belinda Wills. I have an appointment with Dr Chan. About Alexander Roper.'

The nurse smiled. 'Yes, certainly. Do take a seat.' She indicated a row of plastic chairs behind her.

'Actually,' said Bee, 'I was hoping I could get changed first. You know. Get out of these leathers. I don't want to frighten him, or anything.' She laughed nervously and the nurse smiled and pointed her towards the ladies.

Once in there, Bee started feeling sick with nerves. What was she doing? What in the name of God was she actually doing? This was a ridiculous idea. Bee had had some ridiculous ideas in her time, done some foolish and ill-advised things, but this really took the double-chunky-chocolate-chip *stupid* biscuit. Her heart raced and her hands shook as she tried to unzip her leathers.

'Fuck,' she muttered under her breath, 'fuck.'

She finally managed to slip out of them and then fiddled

around in the bag she'd brought with her for her 'Belinda Wills' outfit. Tailored black trousers, grey polo-neck jumper, flat lace-up shoes. She grimaced at them. Flat shoes – she hated flat shoes. They made her look like a pygmy. And polo-necks – yuck. She looked mono-bosomed in a polo-neck, like a little boy with a giant Swiss Roll stuck up his jumper. She put on the hateful clothes and then tried to do something with her hair, something to make her look less like a coke-sniffing advertising executive and more like the schoolteacher she was claiming to be. She combed it till it went limp and then slicked on a bit of pearly lipstick. Her eyes, without the thick black eyeliner she normally wore, looked like two currants pushed into the white dough of her unfoundationed, unblushered face. Yuck yuck yuck. Still – she wasn't here to be admired, she was here to be accepted and this was the only way. The only way.

Bee took a very deep breath and looked in the mirror at Belinda Wills one more time before tucking her hair behind her ears and going back to reception.

Dr Chan was a tiny woman, smaller even than Bee. She had short black hair and was wearing glasses. She also had a large mole on her cheek with one wiry hair growing out of it.

'Good morning, Mrs Wills.'

'Dr Chan. Thank you for seeing me. And do call me Belinda.' She oozed a smile and squeezed the doctor's hand.

Dr Chan's office looked out over a gorgeous, rolling, landscaped garden, dotted with nurses and children playing, some in wheelchairs, some with sticks and some running around freely.

'This is a lovely place,' said Bee.

Dr Chan looked behind her and nodded. 'It's certainly the nicest place I've ever worked. So. How are you feeling?'

'Nervous,' admitted Bee with a grimace.

'I'm sure you are. Now – I know you've already spoken at great length about Zander's problems to Dr Whitaker.'

'Zander?'

'Yes. That's what he likes to be known as.'

'Oh,' said Bee, 'right.'

'He's a very depressed, very angry child. He has his reasons, obviously, but don't let his woe-is-me victim persona make you think that he hasn't had his fair share of attention. He's a nice-looking boy and he's highly intelligent. Many, many couples have expressed an interest in adopting him since his grandmother passed away but he's refused every opportunity to make a life for himself outside of this hospital. Potential adopters have either, according to Zander, been too fat, too stupid, too ugly, too quiet, too old, too young. He doesn't want to live in Oxfordshire, in Cheshire, in London, in York. He doesn't like their other children, he doesn't like their furniture, he doesn't like their dog. Any excuse, any reason. So don't feel too sorry for him. There are an awful lot of people in this hospital and outside this hospital who've done more for Zander over the years than could ever be reasonably expected.

'And you mustn't think for a minute that he sees your visit as exciting or even vaguely interesting, come to that.

So don't expect an emotional meeting. He'll probably do his best to ignore you. He'll attempt to undermine you, intellectually. He'll want to test you, to see how far he can push you, possibly even humiliate you, OK?'

Bee nodded.

'Are you sure, Belinda? Are you sure you want to do this?'

Bee nodded again. And then shook her head. And then laughed. 'Sorry,' she puffed, 'it's just very frightening.'

'Yes,' said Dr Chan, 'it is. But if I didn't truly believe that there was some potential for a positive outcome, I would never have allowed this to happen. You're going to have to persevere. If you're going to do this, you need to be committed to going all the way. Yes?'

'Yes.' Bee nodded more forcefully. 'Yes. All the way. That's what I want. Definitely.'

Dr Chan smiled. 'Good. That's good. So' – she started getting to her feet – 'shall we go?'

'Yes,' Bee grabbed her bag and crash helmet. 'Can I leave these here?'

'Sure.'

They walked down a long, wood-panelled corridor. Bee tried not to catch the eye of any of the children they passed. Bee found disability absolutely terrifying. And then, as they turned a corner, she saw something even more worrying to her. A pile of aluminium boxes. Some cables. A stand-mounted light. A young girl wearing headphones and carrying a clipboard. A camera.

She stopped in her tracks. 'Er – Dr Chan. What exactly is going on here?'

'Oh,' smiled the doctor, 'nothing to be alarmed about. Just a TV crew. They're making a documentary.'

'A documentary? About what?'

'About High Cedars. About us. It's for daytime TV – heartwarming stories and such. It's not something I would have wanted, but it's great publicity. The directors insisted. Shareholders and all that.'

'Yes, but, I don't want to be filmed. I mean, I really, really don't want to be filmed.'

'Don't worry,' Dr Chan smiled warmly. 'Everything's already been approved in advance. They can't film anyone who hasn't given their written permission. And Zander has his own room – you'll be perfectly private – I promise you.'

'Are you sure?'

'Absolutely.' She smiled again and continued. Bee followed her down the corridor towards a lift. The second floor was more modernized than the ground floor, looked more like a hospital and less like a boarding school.

'OK. This is it.' They stopped outside a door. 'This is Zander's room. Ready?'

Bee tugged at her polo neck and smoothed her hair and wiped her sweaty palms against her gabardine trousers. Her heart was racing so fast she thought she might be having one of her panic attacks.

After twelve years of guilt and thinking and imagining and planning and hoping, this was it. Finally. She was going to meet Zander. Jesus. She was *going to meet Zander*. In a few seconds she'd be in a room with Zander, looking into his eyes.

What was she going to see in them?

She was terrified.
She took a deep breath.
'Yes,' she said, 'yes. I'm ready.'

23

The room was small and sunny and modern. There was a TV in one corner, a Playstation and a computer, and posters on the wall. It was the bedroom of a normal young boy. Except for the hydraulic bed and the smell of disinfectant in the air.

'Zander. Good morning,' Dr Chan said, breezily.

A very small boy turned to face them from the computer he'd been working at. He had dead-straight brown hair cut in an unflattering style that covered half of his face. He was wearing glasses and a too-large checked shirt. But he had a delicate face, a finely sculpted nose sprinkled with freckles and wide-set, piercing blue eyes.

'Good morning, Dr Chan,' he said, glancing at Bee momentarily before turning back to his computer.

'You've got a visitor, Zander.'

Bee arranged her face into what she hoped might look like a non-threatening expression, but all her facial muscles felt tight and unyielding.

'This is Belinda, your auntie,' continued Dr Chan, 'remember? We've talked about Belinda?'

'Yes, Dr Chan. I remember talking about Belinda.'

'Belinda's come all the way from London, just to see you. Don't you think it would be polite to at least say hello?'

He turned slowly in his chair and eyed Bee up.

Bee's heart missed a beat and then started racing again. She'd been expecting him to be fragile, vulnerable, sad. But this boy looked so . . . strong. So assured. So cold. He didn't look like a child. He looked like an adult.

'Hello, Belinda,' he said sarcastically, and then turned away again.

'Zander . . .' Dr Chan began.

Bee put her hand out and touched her arm. 'Don't worry,' she mouthed. And then she walked towards Zander and sat on the edge of his bed, within his range of vision. There was a slick of sweat on her upper lip and she could feel a dampness under her arms. 'Hi, Zander,' she began, 'what are you doing?' She indicated the screen with her eyes.

'I'm researching Robert K. Meyer's inconsistent arithmetical theory.'

'Aaah,' said Bee, 'right.'

'Yes, you see, Meyer was more interested in the fate of a consistent theory, but there proved to be a whole class of inconsistent arithmetical theories; Meyer and Mortensen in 1984, for example. Meyer argued that these theories provide the basis for a revived Hilbert Program.'

'Aah.'

'Yes. Hilbert's program was widely held to have been seriously damaged by Gödel's Second Incompleteness Theorem, according to which the consistency of arithmetic was unprovable within arithmetic itself. But a consequence of Meyer's construction was that within his arithmetic . . .'

'That's enough, Zander. You're just showing off. And

turn that computer off.' Dr Chan strode towards him and put a finger out towards the power switch.

'No!' he exclaimed. 'Don't. I haven't backed up my spreadsheets. I'll do it.' He hit a few buttons, sulkily. 'There. It's off. Are you happy now?'

'Yes, thank you, Zander. Now, I'm going to leave you and your aunt alone together, to chat. OK? I'll be back in an hour or so and we can all go and get some lunch. All right?'

'Do I have a choice?'

'No. You don't have a choice.'

'Well, then, why bother asking me?'

'Fine,' said Dr Chan tersely, throwing Bee a look, 'I'll see you in an hour, then. And if you need anything, just hit that bell.' She pointed at a buzzer on the wall.

'Who are you talking to – her or me?'

Dr Chan raised her eyebrows and left the room.

Bee wanted the earth to open up and swallow her. Dr Chan's presence had given the situation a layer of insulation. Now it was raw and unprotected.

Zander wheeled towards her and then came to an abrupt halt a few inches from her feet. The room was entirely silent. He stared at her, his head on one side, rubbing the top of one of his ears between his fingertips.

'So,' said Bee, in an attempt to soften the malevolent atmosphere, 'this is a nice room you've got here.'

'I don't believe you're my aunt,' he said.

Bee blanched and gulped. He knows, she thought, *he knows*. 'I'm sorry?'

'It's bullshit that you're my aunt.'

'And what exactly makes you say that?'

'Well – everyone in my family was pig-ugly. You're far too good-looking to be related to me.'

Bee tried to control her facial muscles, to look unfazed. Stick to the story, Bee, she told herself, just *stick to the fucking story*. 'Yes. Well. We had different mothers your mother and me. I never even met your mother.'

'Bullshit.'

'I didn't. I mean, I only just found out that she existed and . . .'

'Bull. Shit. Big steaming pile of it.' He wiggled his fingers to demonstrate the steam coming off the shit.

Bee forced her fingers into the collar of her polo neck, trying to relieve her claustrophobia. 'Look. I don't know what else to say. I mean . . .'

'Huge, vast mountains of hot steaming rancid fly-infested bullshit . . . Tons of it. Piles as big as the Himalayas. Everywhere. Urgh . . . urgh . . . urgh' – he put his hand to his throat and pretended to choke – 'the ammonia, the poisonous, noxious, choking gases coming off those piles of shit . . . Help me, I'm choking, choking to death on it . . . urgh . . .'

And as Bee looked at this puny, disabled little boy, with his withered legs and his too-big shirt and his stupid glasses, this little boy who she owed so much to, who she'd taken so much from and who she'd spent the past twelve years fantasizing about, she stopped feeling nervous and started feeling irritated, and suddenly and overpoweringly wanted to punch him in the face. Really hard.

'OK, then, Mr Know-All,' she snapped, getting to her feet, 'if I'm not your aunt, then who the fuck am I?'

'Well, that's a very good question. An excellent question.

Maybe you could answer it? My guess though is that you're either a) an undercover reporter – something to do with all those TV airheads hanging around the place – but I have to concede that it's unlikely you'd have undertaken such a sophisticated ruse just to talk to little old me. Or b) that you're a sick sexual pervert who wants to put her hand in my knickers and feel my impotent little willy.'

'Jesus Christ!' said Bee, 'that's disgusting! How old are you?'

'I'm twelve years old, thirteen in July. But I have the intellect and vocabulary of a thirty-year-old. If that's what you were asking . . . So? Was I right? Are you a sick pervert?' He threw her a lascivious look. 'Because I really don't have a problem with it if you are – sexy-legs . . .'

'Oh. Jesus. You are disgusting.' Bee folded her arms and eyed him with contempt. 'Do you talk to the doctors and nurses like this?'

'No. I'm just rude to them. But then, they're not as good-looking as you – and they don't lie to me.'

'I am not lying to you, how can I prove it to you? I mean, how . . .' She broke off half-way through a sentence when she heard a knocking at the door.

'Enter,' said Zander, wheeling himself towards the door.

'Oh. Hi. Sorry,' said a smallish man with close-cropped grey hair, 'I'm looking for Tiffany Rabbett's room.'

'Two doors down. You can't miss it. It's very *pink*. It's Tiffany's life ambition to one day be a Barbie doll. Not to actually *walk* or live a long and healthy life or anything. Just to be a doll.'

The man looked at Zander in amazement. 'Er, right. Yup. OK. Thanks.' He started to back out of the room.

'Hey, hey, hold on. Wait a minute,' Zander called after the man's receding back.

'Yes.'

'Are you with the TV crew?'

'Uh-huh. I'm the producer.'

'D'you want a really good story for your show?'

He smiled and edged into the room. 'I'm always interested in hearing a good story.'

'Well then. Get this. This woman,' he pointed at Bee, 'she's my mother.'

'You what!' cried Bee, jumping to her feet.

'Yes,' said Zander, 'but she's too ashamed to admit it, because she hasn't been a very good mother.'

'He's lying,' said Bee, turning to face the producer, 'I'm his aunt, actually.'

Zander tutted extravagantly. 'Yes, well, that's the story she's concocted. Because it's a hard thing to admit, isn't it? That you gave your baby away because he wasn't perfect, because his little legs didn't work properly.'

'He's lying. He is. Honestly. Lying. You can ask the doctors. They'll tell you. He was paralysed in an accident . . .'

'And so this woman gives away her imperfect little baby boy and he goes into a home and nobody wants him. Nobody wants a baby that can't walk, that can't be potty-trained, do they? And then one day, say, oooh, twelve years later, that woman finds herself all alone and getting old and decides to find her baby. And here we are. Our first meeting. Our first reunion. Isn't it joyful to behold? Aren't you moved? Don't you think your viewers would just love this little scene?'

'I am not his mother. I'm his aunt. Why are you lying like this, you little shit?' Bee hissed.

'Aw,' said Zander. 'See? Isn't this sweet?'

'Look. I'm sorry,' muttered the producer. 'I've obviously interrupted something. I'll just go to Tiffany's room now.'

'No. Don't go,' said Zander, 'I want to be on TV. Can't I? Please? Please Mr Hot-Shot TV Producer – I want you to make me a star.' He crossed his arms across his chest and fluttered his eyelashes at the man.

'Sorry, son. No can do. We're doing Tiffany and that's that. Besides, I think you and your mother have got some talking to do, haven't you?'

'I am not his mother,' shouted Bee, 'I am *not* his fucking mother.'

'Hey,' said the man, suddenly stopping in his tracks and giving Bee a strange look. 'Aren't you Bee Bearhorn?'

'Who's Bee Bearhorn?' said Zander.

Bee's jaw dropped. This was getting worse and worse. Worse than she could ever possibly have imagined. She stared at the man in horror. 'No,' snapped Bee, 'I am not Bee Bearhorn. And I am not this little monster's mother either. Now, if you'll excuse me, I'm going to get some fresh air.'

'Who's Bee Bearhorn?' said Zander again.

Bee stormed past Zander and the man and stomped out into the corridor.

'I said, "Who's Bee Bearhorn?"' Zander's voice followed her down the corridor.

'You are, aren't you?' said the man, hot-footing it after her, 'you *are* Bee Bearhorn?'

'Please – leave me alone.'

'I was a fan. Please – stop . . .'

Bee ignored him and kept on striding.

She needed a fag. Now.

Her fags were in her bag. In Dr Chan's office.

Fuck.

'D'you smoke?' she said, spinning round on her heel to face to him.

'Er – yeah.'

'Can I have one?'

'Yeah,' he said, 'sure.' He began feeling his shirt pockets. 'You can't smoke in here though. You'll have to go outside. There's a balcony just through here.' He steered her down another corridor.

On the balcony he passed her a cigarette and watched her closely while he lit it for her. Her hands were shaking as she took the cigarette from her lips to exhale.

'Fuck,' she exclaimed, leaning against the railings of the balcony and staring out into the distance. 'Fuck. That was a nightmare. What a cunt that kid is.'

'That's a bit harsh, isn't it? He's only a child.'

'No he's not. He's a demon. He's Rosemary's fucking Baby.'

'And who are you then – Rosemary?'

'No I am not. I am not that little fucker's mother, all right.'

The man put his hands up in surrender. 'Sorry. Right.

Not another word. But you are Bee Bearhorn, right? I'd recognize you anywhere. I was a great fan, really. I even bought your third single.'

Bee exhaled and turned to smile at him. 'Ah,' she said, 'so it was *you*, was it?'

He grinned and shrugged. 'What can I say? I was a huge fan. I wanted to single-handedly revive your career.'

'What a mug,' she said, grinning at him.

'Yeah,' he said, 'I guess. I'm Ed by the way. Ed Tewkesbury.'

'Hi, Ed.' She turned and shook his hand. He had small, cool hands.

'Hi, Bee. Wow,' he grinned, 'I'm a bit starstruck. This is amazing, I mean . . .'

'Look. Ed. All that stuff in there just now' – she indicated the general direction of Zander's room – 'you won't, you know? . . . I mean, that was all really personal stuff and I don't want . . .'

Ed put a finger to his lips. 'It will go no farther than this balcony. I swear.'

'Really?'

'Uh-huh. Do you honestly think that I would dob Bee Bearhorn in it? No way. Nuh-huh. My lips are superglued.' He sealed them with his fingers. 'And just to prove it,' he said, reaching into his pockets and fishing out a small card which he passed to her, 'here's my number. And my address. And if you ever see any evidence anywhere that I've spilled a word of this to anyone, you have my express permission to come round and chop out some of my vital organs. OK?'

She took it from him and smiled again. 'OK. And I would, you know? I'd enjoy it, too.'

'Oh, no doubt . . . no doubt. Look. I'd better get back in there. I'm only here for a day and my team's waiting for me. Good luck, Bee Bearhorn. With everything. It's been an absolute honour meeting you.'

'Likewise. And thank you, for, you know . . .' She sealed her lips with her fingers.

'And look – if you're ever in London and want to be taken out for a really good meal, you know, no strings, just grub – you've got my number. Yeah?'

'Yeah,' she said as he turned to leave, and she listened to his squeaky footsteps on the vinyl-floored corridor, until the sound disappeared.

She turned back to the railings and stared across the landscaped grounds and out towards the countryside for a while. Ashford town centre was a small clump of grey and brown buildings in the farthest distance. She watched a Eurostar train speeding towards the station while she smoked her cigarette deeply and slowly, savouring every moment of not having to go back to Zander's room. Yes, she'd been warned in advance. Yes, she'd been told he was difficult, precocious and angry. But still she hadn't been prepared for that. She'd fantasized about this moment for so long that it had become almost romantic. She'd been expecting to get inside his angry shell, to break down his defences. She'd been expecting tenderness, deep emotion, tears maybe. She'd been expecting one of the most moving, monumental days of her life. She most certainly had not been expecting to feel this – this annoyance and plain old-fashioned *dislike*.

She wasn't going to give up, though – no way. She was going to see this through to its conclusion – whatever that might be. She stubbed out her cigarette on the metal railings and straightened herself up. She was going to deal with this little boy. She wasn't going to let him – excuse the expression – walk all over her. Although it often didn't feel like it, she was an adult. And Zander was a child. She could do this.

She walked back to his room, took a deep, deep breath and opened the door.

24

Zander was sitting at his computer, and spun around in his chair when he heard the door go. He grinned at her. He looked quite sweet when he smiled.

'This is getting better and better,' he said, happily.

'What on earth was all that about?' she asked, angrily. 'How dare you go around telling people I'm your mother?'

'Well,' said Zander, 'how dare you go around telling people you're my aunt?'

'I am . . .'

'No you're not. And I've got the evidence to back it up now, thanks to our smarmy TV producer friend.'

'What do you mean?' Bee perched on the arm of a chair.

'Recognize this?' he turned back to his computer and hit a button.

Nothing happened for a while, and then some music started playing. Zander shut his eyes and swayed his head as the intro began. Bee recognized it immediately. Of course. It was her song. It was 'Groovin' for London.' It was Groovin' for fucking London.

'Where the fuck . . . ?'

'Aah,' said Zander, 'the wonders of modern technology.' He turned and fiddled with his mouse for a while. 'Recognize this, too?'

It was 'Space Girl', her shockingly bad second single.

'But where . . . ?'

'WAV files. I just downloaded them from the net.'

Bee looked at him blankly. She knew absolutely nothing about computers.

'Techno-bimbo?'

'I beg your pardon?'

'You? Are you a techno-bimbo? I.e., is your experience of digital communication limited to thumbing through the *Yellow Pages* for dress shops?'

She looked at him blankly again.

'Look,' he said, moving slightly so that she could share his view of the monitor. 'I ran a search for Bee Bearhorn and it brought up all these results.'

'And what are all these?'

'They're websites.' Zander clicked on his mouse twice, and the screen changed. Slowly, line by line, a picture emerged. It was Bee. A publicity picture taken at the height of the campaign for 'Groovin'.' Some graphics popped up underneath, THE UNOFFICIAL BEE BEARHORN SITE in huge sparkly disco letters.

'Hmmm,' said Zander, rubbing at his chin and turning from the screen to Bee and back again. 'Looks a lot like you, wouldn't you say? Except obviously, you look a lot *older* than her.'

Bee slanted her eyes at him – he really did know exactly how to get to her.

'Yes, in the time it took you to smoke a fag . . .'

'How . . . ?'

'I can smell it on your breath – you stink, d'you know that? Like a dirty old ashtray. Anyway – in the time it took you to smoke a fag and take another minute off your already curtailed life expectancy, I have managed to dis-

cover everything there is to know about Bee Bearhorn.'
He started scrolling down the screen. 'Yes – let me see.
Born in 1964, in Devon. Only daughter of Gay and Gregor
Bearhorn. You moved to London in 1979 when you were
fifteen years old and soon found yourself absorbed into
London's burgeoning club scene. I believe you were some-
thing of a 'wild child'. You founded a few bands from the
years 1979 to 1984, mainly New Wave, New Romantic
and punk bands, all of which disappeared without trace.
But you were disgustingly ambitious and never gave up.
In 1985 you sent a demo tape of one of these bands, The
Clocks – g-reat name by the way – love it' – he winked at
her and she gave him the finger – 'to Dave Donkin at
Electrogram Records. He liked you but not the other
greebos in the band, so you abandoned them and were
signed up as a solo artist. What a sweetheart you are. This
was about the time that you adopted your trademark black
bob.' He threw her a disparaging look. 'What happened
to that then?' he asked, pointing at her hair.

'It looked fucking stupid so I got rid of it.'

'Hmmm. So. Your first single "Groovin' for London"
was released in October 1985 and spent five weeks at
number one, before being toppled by "The Power of
Love" by Jennifer Rush. The single sold in excess of
750,000 copies. Realizing that there was more money
to be made in the songwriting side of things than the
poncing-about-wearing-stupid-clothes-and-miming-on-
Top-of-the-Pops side of things, you rejected your label's
suggested song for your second single and insisted on
using one you'd written yourself. It was called "Space
Girl". It made number thirteen in the charts in March

1986 and sold around 150,000 copies. Your third, also self-penned single, "Honey Bee" was released in July 1986, got to number 48 and sold 24,000. Electrogram Records promptly dropped you, and your pop career came to a grinding halt.

'Still. It wasn't all dull, dull, dull after that, was it? Your father, the revered theatre director Gregor Bearhorn, developed full-blown AIDS shortly after the disastrous flop that was "Honey Bee" and you devoted yourself full-time to caring for him in his dying days. Gregor finally passed away in late 1988 and you inherited shedloads of money. You eschewed all the traditional routes that ex-popstars take – no pantomime for you, no marrying a rich record producer or presenting on VH1. You just . . . disappeared. Completely disappeared. Probably to spend all your dad's money. On cocaine or something, probably. Or – if I'm to believe the ridiculous story you told the staff here to get a crack at me, to become a schoolteacher and decide that you were related to my dead mother.'

Bee sighed. OK. Plan A had gone distinctly pear-shaped. And she didn't have a Plan B. 'Who writes this shit anyway?' she said, gesturing dismissively at the screen.

'This particular piece of shit was written by . . .' – he scrolled down to the very bottom of the screen – 'some sad loser called Stuart Crosby. He's a "big fan" – he made the quotes with his fingers – 'of yours, apparently. How sad is that? To be a 'big fan' of some has-been, one-hit-wonder old tart who no one's heard of for more than a decade. Huh . . . People . . .'

Bee thought about slapping him. Round the face. *Really* hard. So that it left a big handprint. So that he'd start crying. Just like a big baby. God, she'd love to.

'Anyway. I have a new theory about you now. You're not my aunt. And you're not my mother. And, to be quite frank, I really don't give a toss who you are. My theory is that you're just rich and lonely and feeling guilty about contributing nothing to this life, except a couple of mediocre – and I'm being kind when I say that – mediocre songs. You're just a shallow London ex-celebrity with a big gaping hole in your life. And you want to do good. I also believe that it's you who's been sending me those big, anonymous postal orders every Christmas. Ta for those by the way – they've been very useful.' He gestured at his PC and his TV and his Playstation. 'Those are my theories, Miss Bee Bearhorn, and I don't care whether I'm right or wrong, they're the ones I'm working with.'

Bee opened her mouth to argue with him but then shut it again when she realized that his theory was perfect. Just perfect. She let her shoulders slump forward in a gesture of acquiescence. She shrugged, sniffed. 'Well,' she said, 'I haven't really done much in my life to be proud of.'

He smiled at her triumphantly. 'You know,' he said, 'I think this might work. I *like* the idea of being your little project. I like that you used to be famous. I like that you haven't got any kids of your own. I like that you're stinking rich. I like the fact that you're guilty about your pointless existence and that you want to use me to assuage that guilt. It's all great stuff. It all puts me in a very comfortable and fortunate position. And I actually quite like you . . .'

Bee was gratified to note that the cocky little shit had the decency to blush. She was also surprised to feel a flush of pleasure in her own stomach.

'So,' he continued, 'I'll play along with this "aunt" thing. And you'll play along with me. OK?'

Bee's eyes turned to slits as she looked at him. 'What?' she said suspiciously, 'what do you want from me?'

'I want you to take me away from here.'

'What!'

'I'm serious. I want you to take me away from here. Not permanently or anything. Just now and then. You know.'

'Where?'

Zander looked into Bee's eyes for a moment, before turning around and wheeling himself towards the window. 'To a house,' he began, 'somewhere small, cosy. Warm. Somewhere quiet. Near the sea. Somewhere with a garden. And a bird-table. Somewhere private. Somewhere where everybody doesn't know my business. I've been here for ten years,' he said, turning to face her again, 'do you realize that? Pretty much all my life. And the only place I've ever been is to hospital or on stupid daytrips with all the other cretins in this place. And everyone stares at you when you're out with that lot. They think you're just a stupid spastic, just a brain-dead vegetable. And this place is very pleasant, I can see that. My grandma chose this herself just before she died, and she went to see *loads* of places. And this was definitely the best. It's a nice building and they try to make things as nice as possible. But it's not a proper home, is it? I mean – is it? I don't want to sound like I feel sorry for myself, or anything, but I haven't anyone. No family at all. No one to take me out of here occasionally and make me feel . . . special. I want my own life. A special little private life. Away from here. D'you see? Do you?'

256

They stared at each other for a while. There was a vein throbbing on Zander's temple, and his hands were clenched into fists. He'd dropped the façade, and for the first time since Bee had walked into his room, she felt that the real Zander was talking to her.

A smile played at the corners of her mouth.

'What?'

'Oh, nothing.'

'It's not funny. What are you smiling at?'

She opened her lips and beamed at him. 'Has anyone ever told you that you look really cute when you're begging?' she said.

'Oh, piss off, you old Pop Tart,' he said, but he was smiling as he said it.

Ed took Flint and Ana to a shockingly expensive Japanese restaurant just around the corner from his office. It was packed full of businessmen and they were served by a tiny woman in a blue kimono. Ed ordered the most expensive sushi sets for the three of them and insisted that Ana eat even the pieces that scared the living daylights out of her – pieces filled with huge, violently orange fish-eggs; or draped with skinny, naked pairs of prawns with the heads still attached, two sets of beady eyes gazing at her in confusion; things wrapped in glossy emerald seaweed and things swathed in rubbery slices of suckery octopus. Ana had only ever had sushi once before but that had been from Sainsbury's and she'd been less than impressed. Now she finally understood what all the fuss was about.

'Enjoying it, Ana?' said Ed, waving his chopsticks at her beautifully presented plate.

'Yeah,' she said, 'it's incredible. Much better than the supermarket stuff.'

'Oh God,' he said dismissively. 'Supermarket sushi is an *aberration*. Sushi should *never* be put in a fridge. The key to sushi, the magic of sushi, is in the warmth of the hands of the sushi chef. The fish is important, the rice is paramount, but put even the finest sushi in a fridge and it dies, Ana. It just dies.'

Ana glanced at Flint. He was making disparaging, sneering faces at an oblivious Ed. He hated him. Really hated him. She stifled a smile under her hand. 'Enjoying your sushi, Flint?' she said, clearing her throat and covering her mouth with her hand again.

Flint grunted and nodded.

Ana smiled again and then put something into her mouth that looked like a damp puppy's tongue sitting on an oblong of rice. 'Ouurghhh . . .' she suddenly murmured through her mouthful, 'thish ish fuffing gorshuss, wharrishitt?'

'Er . . .' Ed picked up the photo-illustrated sushi menu and started looking at it, 'it's er. . . .'

'It's toro,' said Flint, quietly.

Ana looked at him quizzically.

'Toro is the meat from the tuna's belly. There's not much of it, so it's a real delicacy. It should taste . . . buttery?'

'Ouurghhh,' said Ana, nodding and swallowing and taking a slurp of Kirin. 'That's exactly what it tastes like – freshly churned butter.'

Ed looked at Flint in surprise. 'Know a bit about Japanese food then, Flint?' he asked.

'Yeah. Well' – Flint slipped a pearly-pink piece of pickled ginger into his mouth – 'I was out there for a while, you know. You pick things up.'

'You went to Japan?' asked Ana, unable to mask the surprise in her voice.

'Yeah. I was there in 1984. For a year.'

'Really?'

'Uh-huh. In Tokyo.'

'Doing what?'

'Teaching, mainly.'

'Teaching what?'

'English.'

'Wow.'

'Yeah.' He shrugged and dunked a salmon roll in his soy. 'Long time ago, though, that.'

Ana looked at him in wonder. Flint had lived in Japan. For a year. He'd been a teacher. She wondered what else he'd done. She'd just assumed, rather narrow-mindedly, that he'd sort of been *born* behind the wheel of his limo, that he hadn't existed before he met Bee. She tried to imagine Flint as a fresh-faced twenty-one-year-old, teaching English to a rapt group of wide-eyed Japanese children, walking the streets of Tokyo, towering over everybody else. She really didn't know a thing about him. Or his relationship with her sister, come to that. She was about to ask him another question about Japan but he forestalled her by addressing a question towards Ed.

'So – you never actually heard Bee admit that Zander was her son?'

'Well – no, not in so many words. But I always referred to him as her son and she certainly never corrected me.'

'And what about the father? Did she ever say anything about Zander's father?'

'No. I asked. But she refused to tell me anything about Zander. Refused to talk about him, full-stop.'

'Isn't that a bit weird? If you were the only person in her life who was aware of Zander's existence, what would she have had to lose by telling you about him? I don't understand.'

'Look,' he said firmly, 'I'm as confused as you are. I

never understood why she refused to talk about him. But in the end I respected her need for privacy, for *secrecy*, whatever her reasons. And why would the boy have lied, anyway? Why would Bee have spent all that time with him, bought a house for him? He was a horrible little bastard, so it can't have been because she liked him – there's no other explanation.'

Flint and Ana exchanged a look. He had a point.

'So, what happened to you and Bee?' asked Ana, 'Why did you split up?'

Ed grimaced momentarily and he dabbed at his mouth with his napkin. 'Ah,' he said, 'now there's a story. Another beer, anyone?'

26

January 2000

Bee let the ring on her wedding finger glint and glitter in the muted light. She smiled. It was very traditional, classic, not what she'd have chosen, but still stunningly beautiful. And at least it was platinum, not gold. She hated gold.

'Hi.' Ed came back from the toilet and slid into his seat. Bee smiled at him. It was incredible, she thought to herself, how when she'd first gone out with Ed – to this exact same restaurant, actually – she'd thought he was vile, a puny little coke-sniffing media-weasel. The idea of having sex with him had made her feel quite queasy, in fact. Having dinner with him was just something that had to be done to ensure that he never spilled the beans to anyone about Zander. But he'd grown on her imperceptibly during the course of that first evening. She'd gone from finding him smug, arrogant and bland to seeing him as a sweet, confused, kind-hearted man who wasn't really very happy. Someone who just wanted to be loved. Unconditionally. Someone who didn't know how to show his vulnerability. Someone just like her, in fact.

By the time they'd checked into a hotel, drunk another bottle of champagne and fallen noisily and clumsily into bed with each other, she'd been more than happy with the situation. And when, after their next meeting, he'd told her he loved her and wanted to leave his wife for her, rather than running a mile in the other direction like she usually did when men told her they loved her, she'd actually found it quite sweet.

As the months went by she'd found herself anticipating his phonecalls and his visits with more and more enthusiasm. And then, at some vague point, she'd fallen in love with him. She'd fallen in love with a short, bald, married man. Funny old world.

And now, here they were, nearly three years later, engaged and about to go public. They'd just had their first proper holiday together. To Goa. It had been the most amazing two weeks of her life, two weeks of normality, of feeling like a real person, and two weeks in which it became obvious to Bee that she needed this man in her life. Properly. Not part-time.

So when Ed handed her the ring, nervously and uncertainly, at the airport on their way out, she'd grabbed it with both hands and grinned from ear to ear. Marrying Ed had suddenly gone from being an utterly ludicrous concept to seeming like the best idea in the world. He was going to leave his wife, the moment they got home, leave her. He'd had enough. Tina was a wonderful person, as he kept telling Bee, but her desire for a baby had destroyed their relationship. She'd had three courses of fertility treatment in the last year, despite the fact that the gynaecologist had told her she only had a one-in-a-thousand chance of ever conceiving and carrying a child. Now she was talking about finding a surrogate mother.

Ed couldn't stomach the thought – his baby, in another woman's womb. Not to mention all the potential emotional anguish and pain. And what if the mother changed her mind, kept the baby – it would destroy Tina completely. And without the incessant obsession with reproduction, the doctor's appointments, the thermometers, the test-tubes, the tears and the never-ending waiting as Tina's periods became the focus of their lives, there was nothing left . . . absolutely nothing.

Ed had convinced himself – and Bee, who'd never been happy with the idea of Ed leaving Tina – that it was in Tina's best interests for him to leave. She'd be happier without him. She was only thirty, she had plenty of time to meet someone who might be prepared to do the surrogate thing or go through the treatments all over again. So he was going to leave her. The minute he got back from Goa. And tonight was going to be their first meeting as legitimate lovers, a celebration of their freedom.

The champagne that Bee had ordered while Ed was in the toilet arrived. He looked at it strangely. 'Did you order that?' he said.

Bee beamed at him and nodded.

He sighed and rubbed his face into his hands. 'I wish you hadn't, Bee,' he said.

Bee felt her stomach clench itself up into a knot.

'There's something I need to tell you.' Ed crossed his arms in front of him and stared at Bee. 'Everything's changed,' he said, simply.

Bee stopped breathing momentarily, felt herself begin to panic. She forced a tight smile. 'And what exactly does that mean, Mr Tewkesbury?'

'Tina's pregnant.'

Bee smirked. 'Oh,' she said, 'don't be daft.'

'I'm not being daft, Bee. It's true. She's pregnant.'

'But – how? It's been months since your last treatment.'

'I know.'

'So – how?'

Ed dropped his eyes to the tablecloth.

Bee raised hers to the ceiling.

Stupid question.

'She's having triplets.'

'But, that's the silliest thing I've ever heard.'

'Yes. It is, isn't it? It's mad. But it's true. It's . . . it's a miracle, Bee. That's what the doctor said. Somehow all the treatment she'd been having – well, she got sort of super-fertile, I suppose. And now she's pregnant. And we're having triplets.' His voice was going up an octave with every sentence. His hands were flittering around. His face was animated. He was excited. He was trying his hardest to hide it, but he was absolutely overjoyed.

'But I thought, you know, you and Tina . . . ?' She was about to say, But I thought you and Tina didn't have spontaneous sex any more, I thought you only had sex with test-tubes and speculums, but she knew the moment she opened her mouth how that would make her sound. Stupid. Stupid with a big fat capital S. Stupid like all of those thousands of other stupid, stupid women who believed their married lovers when they said they didn't have sex with their wives.

She felt sick. Violently sick. She could feel the tomato

and basil soup she'd had for lunch lurching around in her stomach, creeping bile-like up the back of her throat. She took a large sip of champagne.

'So – what . . . what are you going to do? I mean – are you going to stay?'

'With Tina?'

'Yes, with Tina,' she snapped.

Ed sighed and slid his hands across the tablecloth towards hers. She snatched hers back into her lap.

'Well?'

'Shit, Bee, I don't know. I mean – I've wanted to be with you from the first moment I saw you. I've been ready to walk away from Tina and be with you and you've kept me at arm's length. And now – it's like – I mean – *three babies*, Bee – three babies. I made three babies. *We* made three babies. Me and Tina. I can't . . . it's . . . it's just so incredible. It's a miracle.'

'But you don't love Tina.'

'I don't. No. Well, I didn't. I didn't love the Tina who put her desire to have a baby ahead of everything. The Tina who only remembered I existed when it was time for me to wank into a jar. But this Tina – this Tina with three babies inside of her. You should see her, Bee – she's happy – she's glowing – it's like she's been reborn and . . .'

'Oh God, stop it, Ed – please, just stop . . .' Bee put her head into her hands.

They were both silent. A waiter poured some more champagne into their glasses. 'Are you ready to . . . ?' he began.

'No,' snapped Ed, 'no. Sorry. Not just yet. Thanks.'

'Certainly, sir.'

Ed sighed and held Bee's gaze for a while. He was quite obviously about to say something horrible.

'I want a clean break, Bee.' Yup, thought Bee, there it is. 'I want to start again, with Tina. And that means . . . you know?'

'Yes, Ed. I know what that means.'

'And the flat. I don't want to pay for the flat any more. It's not that I resent paying for it. It's just that I don't want to have to hide anything any more. D'you see? From Tina? I want . . .'

'You want to erase me from your life entirely.'

Ed stopped for a second and stared at Bee. 'Yup,' he said eventually, letting his head fall on to his chest.

These moments, thought Bee, these moments in life, soap-opera moments – they look so exciting when you see them on the television, at the cinema. But when you're actually living them, they're just so horribly hollow and bleak. And kind of, well . . . bland.

'I never wanted this to happen, Bee. I never wanted to abandon you. I wanted to look after you for ever. I wanted to be with you for ever. I love you so much, Bee . . .'

Bee looked up into Ed's eyes, his funny little mouse-eyes. And he did. He did love her. He was telling the truth. And she wanted to be angry with him, for loving her but still leaving her, but she couldn't. Because, she suddenly realized, like she was awaking from a dream, that this was never going to have worked out. Of course it wasn't. She'd been fooling herself. And in a way, the only reason she'd allowed herself to fall in love with Ed in the first place was precisely because he *was* married, precisely because she'd never be able to have him, properly. If only they'd met under different circumstances, if only what happened in 1986 hadn't happened, and Zander hadn't existed, and her whole life hadn't turned into one great conglomeration of lies and deceit, one dizzying maze of separate compartments, she could have married Ed. She could have had a normal life where she spent weekends at home with her friends, a life where she knew her family, a life where everyone she knew knew everyone else. But 1986 had happened and Zander did exist and she was never going to have a normal life. And she had no one to blame but herself.

Tears started plopping down her cheeks and she tried desperately to stop them. She hated people to see her cry. And she'd never cried in front of Ed before.

He looked at her with alarm. 'Shit, Bee, I'm sorry. I'm so, so sorry.'

'Don't be, please,' she sniffed, dabbing at her eyes with her napkin. 'It's not your fault. It's my fault. And I understand. I wouldn't want you to leave Tina now, abandon your chances of having a family and a life. Really. I would hate that.'

'Oh, Bee.' He stretched out a hand again and this time Bee let him hold hers.

'I've made such a mess of everything, Ed. I had it all. And I've messed everything up. In the space of thirty seconds I messed up my entire life . . .'

'What do you mean, in the space of thirty seconds?'

'Oh nothing. Nothing. Just. God. Shit. This is horrible, isn't it? I mean isn't this – just horrible?' She sniffed again and laughed, and Ed gave her hand a squeeze. 'Look,' she said, regaining her composure, 'it's better this way, you know. I think I'd fooled myself into believing that things would work out for you and I, but they wouldn't have. Not really. It would never have been right. It would always have been a bit of a . . . you know, a mess. It's better this way. It's better.'

'I'm going to miss you so much, Bee Bearhorn. So much you wouldn't believe it.'

'Yeah right,' she said, picking up her champagne glass, 'you wait till you've got three little buggers running around the place morning, noon and night – you won't have a chance to miss me.'

'Bee,' he said, squeezing her hand even harder, 'I am going to miss you until the day I die. You're the most amazing person I've ever known.'

Bee shook her head and smiled. 'No,' she said, 'I'm not. And if you really knew me, if you really knew what sort of person I've been, you'd walk out of here now and breathe a great big sigh of relief. Because I'm bad, Ed. I'm B.A.D.'

'No you're not,' he said, 'you're more than the sum of your life history, Bee. Somewhere underneath all that armour, you're still the same person you were when you were a child, before you'd had a chance to make any mistakes. And you should remember that. Stop letting yourself be weighed down by the things you think you did wrong. Stop being a victim of your own fallibilities. You should. Your whole life will just . . . just . . . you know – *stagnate* if you don't move on. If you don't start again. Bee. Please. Please try to make yourself happy. For me.'

Bee looked at Ed and forced a smile. 'Don't you worry

about me, my lovely Teddy Tewkesbury. I'm going to be just fine. Honestly. Just fine.'

They squeezed each other's hands and smiled grimly, each one of them wholly aware that she was lying through her teeth.

27

'Jesus,' said Flint, pulling on a pair of sunglasses as they walked away from the Japanese restaurant and towards his car, which he'd parked in the NCP in Brewer Street.

'I mean,' began Ana, her mind boggling so hard it hurt, 'what . . . ? It's all so . . . it's just so . . . Jesus.' She did a double-take as her eye was caught by a window display of chrome and leather bondage gear and pictures of half-naked men with shiny chests and body piercings. Good grief.

'Christ, that bloke's a tosser.'

'What,' said Ana, teasingly, 'didn't you like him?'

'Him? God. No. I. . . . Oh, very funny,' he said, when he noticed Ana smiling at him. 'Was it that obvious?'

'Uh-huh. It was this obvious.' She extended her arms.

'I don't trust him, not even a tiny bit. And did you notice how close together his eyes were? And how he was all sort of . . . clammy?'

Ana smiled again. 'I thought he was all right,' she said.

'What. Really?'

'Yeah. I just think he was unbelievably nervous. I think Bee gave him a huge secret to look after and he was scared he was going to blow it. I think he really loved Bee – he was just protecting her.'

'Hmm,' said Flint, unconvinced. 'And did you believe what he said – about the boy?'

'What d'you mean?'

'I mean – why would she say that he was her son, when I know for a fact that he couldn't possibly have been?'

Ana shrugged. 'Maybe it was easier to lie than to admit the real truth? And are you sure she couldn't have . . . you know?'

'Absolutely. Totally. A lot of shit happened to Bee in 1986. Big shit. And having a baby was not part of that shit, I can assure you.'

'What sort of big shit?'

'Oh, you know. Having two flop singles. Being dropped by Electrogram. Being slagged off by the national press. Public humiliation. Her father being diagnosed with HIV. The usual sort of shit.'

They'd reached the car park and were heading up a urine-soaked stairwell.

'Fancy a drink?'

Ana stopped in her tracks. 'What?'

'A drink. D'you fancy one?'

'Oh. Right. Yes. But – what about your car? I mean, you've already had a couple of beers and . . .'

'No – not here. In Turnpike Lane.'

'What Lane?'

'Turnpike Lane. It's where I live. We can drop the car off and I'll take you to my local. What d'you think?'

'Oh,' said Ana, 'right.'

'So? Yes or no?'

'Er,' Ana looked at her watch for some inexplicable reason, 'er . . .'

Flint stopped and turned towards Ana. 'Look. It's not a big deal. I'm going home anyway, and I just thought it'd be nice to have a drink, that's all. No pressure . . . no big deal . . .'

Ana chewed her lip. She'd just assumed that after this meeting with Ed, Flint would be desperate to offload her, to drop her back at Gill's and get on with his life. His invitation had thrown her entirely. But then, she thought, what else was she going to do this evening? Stay in on her own? Sit on her futon all night staring at the walls?

'No – no. I mean. Yeah. Sure. Why not? Where is this Turnpike Lane place, anyway?'

'Oh,' said Flint, turning away and smiling slightly, 'it's a shimmering oasis in the enchanted woods of north London. A verdant, romantic corner of the city peopled by poets and artists and intellectuals . . .'

'Really?' said Ana, her eyes widening at the prospect.

'Nah,' said Flint, 'it's a total khasi. But it's my khasi and I love it.'

Ana was amazed by how long the journey to Turnpike Lane took. They'd been driving for ever – how could they possibly still be in London? The scenery changed as they drove and became incrementally and undeniably uglier and uglier the further they drove. Turnpike Lane itself neither turned nor piked and was the complete opposite of any lane that Ana had ever seen, a wide and unattractive road lined with kebab shops, Turkish supermarkets, burger bars and launderettes.

The heatwave was showing no signs of abating. Buffed black girls in silver trainers shouted into mobile phones, smoky-windowed cars drove past full of music, olive-skinned men in thin shirts stood on pavements outside cab offices, smoking and watching the world pass them by. They parked Flint's limo in a lock-up garage behind a petrol station and walked towards his road. Flint lived in a small flat in a small house in a small, one-way, dead-end road. There was something very strange, very intimate about going to someone's home when you'd only known them in one particular context, and particularly when that person had been expecting to come home alone. Flint unlocked the door and ushered Ana inside.

'Fancy a quick beer before we go out?' he said, leading her towards his kitchen and stripping off his T-shirt as he talked.

Ana nodded and looked away, feeling suddenly hot and flustered with embarrassment. Flint's bare chest was tanned to the colour of strong tea, and he was wearing silver dog-tags around his wide neck. He was in extraordinarily good shape for a man of thirty-six. He turned to lead her through the house towards the garden and presented her with a smooth, muscled back. A few stray hairs grew from his shoulder blades and another scar, long, thin and trimmed with pinprick suture marks, ran from his spine to his side. They squeezed through a hallway packed with large objects – a bicycle, a car-jack, a few large cardboard boxes, a hoover and a set of golf-clubs.

'Do you play *golf*, Flint?' Ana asked in surprise.

'Uh-huh. One of the many advantages of not having a day-job. Civilized mid-week tee-times. Piss-weak lager all right?' he said, crouching down to pull a can of Heineken Cold Filter from the fridge in his small, basic kitchen and offering it to her. She nodded, taking it from him, enjoying the icy cold of the metal in her hot hands. She glanced around her as Flint pulled some more lager from an Unwin's carrier bag on the floor and popped them into the fridge, can by can.

The kitchen was unfitted and cheap. A large water-heater took up the only wall space in the room, leaving Flint's groceries displayed endearingly in piles along the work surfaces: chopped tomatoes with herbs, chopped tomatoes with garlic, chopped tomatoes with basil, whole plum tomatoes, fusilli, penne, Spanish onions, tinfoil, Desiree potatoes, carrots, garlic bulbs in a net bag, a dead basil plant on the windowsill. And then she noticed a little pile of teas next to Flint's kettle – peppermint, rosehip, camomile, mango and apple – and for some reason they made her feel the same way she'd felt when she'd seen him in the arcade in Broadstairs pushing two-pee pieces into the penny cascade. Like she just wanted to hug him to death. Ana had always found something stupidly, wonderfully vulnerable about men's groceries. She'd been the same about Hugh's things – she'd go to his flat and go all gooey over his choice of butter, his little cans of spaghetti rings, the shaving foam and soap he chose.

She followed Flint through the flat towards a door at the back. She glanced quickly at a cluttered bookshelf in the hallway as she passed and just had time to spy *Midnight in the Garden of Good and Evil*, a biography of Hugh Hefner, the screenplay of *Pulp Fiction*, *The Prime of Miss Jean Brodie* and the *Oxford Dictionary of Quotations*. Wrong again, thought Ana – she'd have put money on two Andy McNabs, a John Grisham and the Guinness Book of Records *circa* 1989. She really must stop jumping to conclusions about him.

On a table by the back door was an ancient PC, a pile of reference books and a shelf loaded with files.

'Are you studying something?' said Ana, pointing at the desk.

Flint scratched his head. 'Yeah. I'm . . . er . . . I'm taking a degree course, actually.' He looked slightly embarrassed.

'Oh,' said Ana, trying not to let her surprise show too blatantly in her voice. 'In what?'

'Psychology. It's, er, just a correspondence course, but it fits in with my lifestyle, you know – working nights, free days . . .'

'Which year?'

'Just starting my third year. Yeah . . .' He picked up a reference book absent-mindedly and then put it down again. And then he turned away and walked towards the back door.

Outside was a tiny, overgrown garden. A railway track ran behind the fence at the bottom, and the sound of children playing in an abandoned carriage echoed around the whole area. In the garden next door, two smaller children screamed as they climbed up and slid down the same plastic slide over and over again.

'Fucking school holidays,' muttered Flint, stretching backwards into a threadbare brown upholstered armchair, kicking off his shoes, and cracking open the lager.

His feet, Ana couldn't help but notice, were two of the most beautiful things she'd ever seen in her life: brown, smooth, hairless, like they'd never sweated in a pair of ill-fitting shoes, like they'd spent their entire lives walking unshod through soft talcum sands. And his skin had the most beautiful satiny sheen. And his thighs were. . . .

Enough! Ana tore her eyes away from his groin and focused on a particularly perfect pink rosebud on the bush behind him instead. Is this what it was like for men, she wondered, constantly assailed by the sight of bare flesh? The embarrassment, the desire, all those thoughts in your head that had no place being there. It was impossible to ignore, the satin silkiness of his tanned flesh. So hard to take your eyes off it and, like those men who big-busted women complain about for talking directly to their breasts, Ana now found herself talking to Flint's skin and muscle tone and bigness.

'So,' he said, twanging the ringpull on his lager with his thumb, 'what now?'

'Sorry?'

'In the Great Unsolvable Mystery of Bee Bearhorn? What do we do now?'

'Find Zander?'

'Find Zander. Right. OK. How?'

Ana shrugged. 'No idea. All we know is his age and his name. And that maybe he lives in a home in Kent and . . .'

'No!' said Flint, clicking his fingers and suddenly looking uncharacteristically animated. 'No! I've got it! That documentary. The one that Ed was there to film.'

'Of course! We can find out from that.'

'Yeah – there must be some kind of archive or information service about old TV programmes.'

'Yes. Definitely. There's bound to be. I can look into it tomorrow.'

'D'you know,' said Flint, 'it's got to the stage when I almost can't imagine ever finding out what happened to

Bee. D'you know what I mean? Like it's going to be a mystery for ever.'

Ana nodded. 'Flint?' she said after a short pause, bringing her face closer to his. 'Can I ask you something?'

'Sure.'

'Do you – do you think she killed herself?'

'Nah,' he replied instantaneously, and much to Ana's surprise. 'No way.'

'Why are you so sure?'

'Why the hell would someone like Bee kill themselves?'

'And why the hell would someone like Bee drink so much tequila and take so many prescription drugs that she'd end up dead? And why did it take so long for anyone to find her? And why has she got so few possessions? I mean – I spent a whole day in Bee's flat and from what I saw she didn't have much of a life. I've spent the last ten years imagining Bee's life. I imagined someone who'd put down roots, who had a relationship and a beautiful home, hundreds of friends. I imagined her going to parties and clubs and being . . . someone. And – well – what was it actually like, her life? What little you knew of it, anyway. Who were her friends? Where was everyone when she died? I mean – where were they?' Ana stopped suddenly when she realized that she'd started shouting and was actually half-way off her stool. Where the hell had that come from? She sat back down and smiled apologetically at Flint. 'Sorry about that,' she said, 'I didn't mean to shout. I just – I need someone to explain how this could have happened. Explain her to me.'

Flint rubbed his hand across his stubble and regarded

Ana with steely eyes. 'OK,' he said. 'Where d'you want me to start.'

'Well – what sort of a friend was she? To you?'

Flint sighed, sat back. 'Bee was – Bee was a good friend. The sort of friend I like. Self-sufficient. She was the most independent person I've ever known. And she took people as she found them. No unrealistic expectations. She used to say that that was the key to happiness – not having expectations of people – that way you could never be disappointed. She didn't seem to need anyone. She didn't cry. She didn't talk about herself. You might not speak to Bee for weeks but then you'd phone her and she'd just be happy to hear from you. No recriminations. She never put people on guilt trips. But on the other hand – she'd forget your birthday, forget stuff you'd told her last time you saw each other. But that never bothered me because I'm just as bad.'

'And what exactly did she do for the last few years, after Gregor died?'

He shrugged. 'Not much. She did quite a lot of fund-raising stuff for AIDS research for a while, organized balls and charity events, that sort of thing. And then she took guitar lessons for a while, was going to try to get back into the music industry. She had a few collaborations with producers and musicians, it almost looked like something was going to get off the ground, but nothing ever did. I think she just used to read a lot, watch videos, write songs. And obviously for the last three years she was maintaining two totally secret relationships.' He shook his head slightly in disbelief. 'She basically went from being a complete wild child to being a recluse.'

'But didn't you worry about her?'

He shook his head. 'No,' he said, 'that was the thing about Bee. She went out of her way to make sure that nobody ever worried about her. She hated the idea of being a worry, being a burden. She was one of those people who just sort of floated along the top of life, who never really touched the ground – do you know what I mean? She just always gave off this aura of – all-is-wellness, I guess. Bee was always OK. Bee was always cool. Things didn't get to her. She was *unemotional*.'

'And what about men? What about her love life? Was there anyone apart from Ed?'

Flint exhaled and rearranged himself on his armchair. 'Bee was what you might call asexual, I suppose. She didn't have sex. She didn't have relationships.'

'What. Never?'

'Not after her father died, no. She just lost all interest in men. She used to say to me that she didn't care if she never had sex again as long as she lived.'

'What about before that? Before her father died?'

'Flings. Here and there. Nothing important. I don't think Bee ever had a proper, grown-up, full-on relationship in her life.'

They sat together in silence for a while, absorbing this sad little fact. A thin cat tiptoed swiftly across the back fence, silhouetted by the sinking sun. A light was switched on in an upstairs flat, flooding the garden with a sudden, unkind light. The temperature had started to drop and Ana shivered in her sleeveless cotton top.

'Shall we get out of here?' said Flint, 'I could do with a change of scenery.'

Ana nodded.

'D'you want me to lend you a jacket? – you're going to freeze in that top.'

Flint threw her a blue fleece as they passed his bedroom and she wrapped it around herself. It was huge and very soft. When he turned away she lifted the sleeve to her nose and sniffed it. It smelled of him, exactly how he'd smelled on Bee's bike yesterday. She put a hand into a pocket and pulled out an old bus ticket and a purple disposable lighter.

Flint sighed and picked it off Ana's palm. 'Ha,' he began, 'you know, I've never smoked a fag in my life, but I always kept a light on me – for Lady Bee. She always used matches, but sometimes, towards the end of the evening, when she was a bit – you know – the worse for wear, you wouldn't want her going anywhere near fire, if you know what I mean. She nearly set her fringe alight once. So I used to carry these around – for her.' He bounced the lighter up and down in his hands for a few seconds, staring at it intently and then he pulled her hand towards him, peeled apart her fingers, dropped the lighter on to her palm and closed her fist back up again, like he was rewrapping a present.

'Don't you want it?'

'Nah,' said Flint, 'nah. I'll be finding them all over the place, those fucking lighters, you wait and see . . .'

Ana brushed his bare arm with her hand and Flint gave her a tight, brave-little-soldier smile and then they left and headed for the main road.

28

'So,' said Flint, as they strode briskly up the road, 'how tall are you, exactly?'

'Five foot eleven and a half.'

'Blimey.'

Flint's local was an ugly old Victorian boozer called the Freemasons Arms. It was the sort of pub that Ana would usually avoid, with curtained windows and a bar lined with silent, red-faced men in threadbare sweaters and old shoes. Flint bought them a pair of pints and whisky chasers and led them through the quiet bar to a room at the back, where a few younger men played pool and talked to each other instead of staring into space. And Ana wondered at which point a man went from drinking at the pub *with* his mates, to just drinking in the same pub as his mates.

A solitary woman sat alone in the corner filing very long fingernails and drinking Smirnoff Ice from the bottle. She gave Ana an exaggerated double-take as she walked in and then eyed her slowly up and down.

Flint became surrounded, momentarily, by men who patted him on the back and shook him by the hand and asked him where the fuck he'd been. 'Just keeping my head down, mate, you know . . .' he said, smiling at each of them. He introduced Ana to everyone and they all nodded and said 'All right?' and Ana felt flattered that Flint hadn't felt the need to justify her presence by introducing her as Bee's sister, that he was obviously happy to let his mates think that he was 'with' her.

He ushered her to the table furthest from the pool table with his hand on her elbow, reminding Ana of those tabloid pictures of Madonna's boyfriend steering her about the place as if she was a slightly doddery old woman who might just go walking into a wall without him there to guide her, instead of the feistiest woman in the world. But every time Flint touched her, Ana found a small loop of film replaying in her head – an image of her, unpopping the buttons on Flint's fly, one by one, and sliding her long fingers inside and . . .

'I've got a suggestion,' he said, letting his emptied shot glass bang heavily on to the table.

Ana jumped. 'Oh yes.'

'It's quite radical.'

'Right.'

'How's about – and just tell me if you think this is ridiculous – but how's about, you and I, tonight, getting very, very, very drunk, and how's about you and I, tonight, not talking about Bee? You know. Just having normal conversations. About normal things.'

'Like what?'

'God. I dunno. Like the telly. The news. Celebrities. D'you like talking about celebrities?'

Ana shook her head.

'Shame – I'm very up on celebrity gossip. Women tell me that my encyclopaedic knowledge of celebrity trivia is one of the most attractive things about me. I was hoping you might want to test me.'

'Sorry,' shrugged Ana, apologetically. She could feel

herself reddening and thrust her face into her pint glass. Was that flirting just then? Was he flirting with her? Why else would he say that he wanted her to test his trivia knowledge, having already informed her that his trivia knowledge was something that women found attractive about him? It was almost equivalent to him saying, Women find my enormous dick very attractive – would you like me to slip it in? Almost.

But no. No way. There was no way that a man like Flint would be flirting with her. Of course he wouldn't. Flint was a man. A real man. A man with needs and desires that someone like Ana would never be able to satisfy. Ana tried for a moment to imagine the type of woman that might be able to satisfy Flint and came up with a picture of someone so entirely different to her that it made her feel like crying.

'So,' said Flint, looking at her with a disconcertingly wicked glint in his eye, 'what shall we talk about?'

'You,' said Ana, more loudly and vehemently than she'd meant to. She lowered her voice. 'Let's talk about you.'

'Ooh' – Flint sucked in his breath and smiled at her – 'that's not exactly my favourite subject.'

'Why not?'

'Oh, you know. Skeletons. Closets. That sort of thing.'

Ana thought back to the warnings that both Lol and Gill had given her about Flint and felt her curiosity intensely stimulated.

'I told you all about me yesterday,' she said, 'it's only fair you tell me a bit about you.'

He smiled. 'You know what?'

'What?'

'Bee always had this theory, right. About people – she always compared them to clothes. Some clothes, she said, you'd try on, and you'd know within a few seconds whether or not they suited you. Other clothes you'd think suited you but then you'd take them home and realize that they didn't go with any of your other clothes. But the best clothes were the ones that always suited you, that never went out of fashion and that made you feel good every time you put them on even when they shrunk in the wash. She said me and Lol were her favourite old clothes. But that she still loved trying on new clothes. Making impulse purchases. Do you see what I mean?'

'No,' said Ana.

'Well, basically, she reckoned that pretty much everyone could be interesting for half an hour. What you did with them after that was irrelevant. But she was always willing to talk to new people. It was her speciality. She used to say it was all in the questions – you had to ask the right questions. If you asked people boring questions, then you'd get boring answers. So – it's' – he craned his neck around the corner to view the clock above the bar – 'five to eight. From now until twenty-five past, you're allowed to ask me anything you like.'

Ana looked at him.

'Go on, then,' he teased.

'OK,' she said, 'OK. Tell me about . . . Japan.'

'What d'you want to know?'

'How come you went? Why did you come back?'

'Shit,' said Flint, sucking in his breath, 'that's a good question – that opens up a whole can of worms. Right. Well. I'd been in the army . . .'

'Really?'

'Uh-huh. For three years. Hated it. So I left. When I was twenty. And things went . . . well, it was tough coming out, you know. I had no useful skills and no work experience that was of any interest to anyone. So I went on the dole and then I got in with the wrong people, as they say.'

'What sort of people?'

'Oh. You know. Bad people.'

'What sort of bad people?'

Flint smirked and took a sip of lager. 'It's funny,' he said, 'but for some reason I feel really embarrassed talking to you about all this.'

'Why?'

'I dunno. It's just – you're so . . . kind of *untainted*. I guess it's because you're a country girl. You've never lived in a city . . .'

'Exeter was a city.'

'Yes, but you know what I mean – you're just not urban. You make me think of cornfields and village fêtes and macramé pot-holders . . .'

'Oh – thanks!'

'No – but you know. You're clean. And the way my life was then – it was dirty. And I'm so used to it and everyone I know is so used to it and it just really brings it home to me, just exactly how rank it all was, when I'm sitting here talking with someone like you. Yeah. Drugs,' he said suddenly, as if he was trying to get it over with, 'I was into drugs.'

'What sort of drugs?'

He shrugged. 'Heroin. Pills. And drink. And a bit of

petty crime. Everything, basically. And in quite a big way. I was a mess, really. It was all a mess. People dying and that. And then, you know that scene in *Trainspotting*, when his mum and dad lock him up in his room. Well, my mum did that to me. And while I was locked up, going through hell, I got this idea in my head. It was after watching something on the news about Tokyo, I can't remember what it was about. But I just remember thinking how clean it looked. How clean all the people looked. It looked so hygienic, like a huge hospital or something. And that became my obsession. I started reading up all about the culture and history and everything. Spent every day at the library. Everything about the place struck me as being the complete opposite of my life in London. And then my mum – God bless her soul – she was my saviour. She was doing all this overtime, telling me it was for a holiday for herself, and then one day she came home with a present for me – a one-way ticket to Tokyo. So I went.'

'Really. And what was it like?'

'Fucking nightmare.'

'You're joking.'

'Yeah. At first. The one thing I hadn't found out about the place before I went was how *expensive* it is. A flat like mine, you know, piddling little shoebox, ten miles from the centre, was like about £250 a week. So I had to get a job, pretty sharpish, and the only thing I could find was door-work. You know, working as a bouncer, which wasn't exactly what I'd had in mind. Those Japanese businessmen – Jesus, can they drink. And they got so drunk. Made us lot look like teetotallers. Picking fights. Puking up. Falling over. But still – it was clean – and there were no drugs to speak of. And the women were – God, you know, just beautiful . . .'

'Oh,' said Ana, immediately putting Flint into the same category of old and ugly men who went out to Thailand and the Philippines to buy young, beautiful wives, and feeling vaguely and inexplicably disappointed in him.

'To look at, obviously. I didn't touch. Not at all. They're so vulnerable, those women. And so small. You felt like you'd break them. And anyway – I like a woman with a bit more – oomph.'

Ana smiled.

'So I took a course and started teaching English during the day and doing the door-work in the evenings.'

'What else did you do?'

'Ate sushi. Drank green tea. Went to the gym. Learned Kendo.'

'Oh yes? How far did you get?'

'Black belt.'

'No!'

'Uh-huh. It's the fittest I've ever been. I was in amazing shape, and it was like the smack and the booze had been washed out of my system months before, in my bedroom in London, but being in Tokyo cleansed my soul. Shit – that sounds really wanky, doesn't it?'

Ana shook her head. 'No it doesn't. Not at all.'

He looked pleased that he hadn't sounded wanky. 'So – after ten months I decided to leave. It was such a weird place, Tokyo – they're all bloody mad over there. I knew I was better when I could see how fucked up their society was, when I could see it objectively. And I was missing home, missing my mum, missing London. Missing the dirt, actually. Ironically. But I've found that when you're clean inside, the dirt outside is just sort of . . . comforting. Do you know what I mean?'

'I'm not sure that I do, actually.'

'No. I don't suppose you would.'

'So what did you do when you got home?'

'Well, I'd really enjoyed the teaching and I thought about doing that again, English, to foreign students. But I didn't have the right qualifications over here. So I got a job with this limousine company. As a driver.'

'Why that job?'

'I dunno, really. I've never thought about it, particularly. It just seemed like a nice job. You know – the isolation, the nice motor, the smart uniform. I felt like I was damaged goods, and it just seemed to fit me, as a job. It seemed to be the right sort of job for a reformed character. It made me feel like Robert de Niro actually,' he grinned, 'especially when I was driving around at night, through the city. It can be a very romantic job sometimes, you know.

'Bee used to say it was the best feeling in the whole world, being driven around the streets of London in the back of my car, music playing, not having to speak, not having to do anything. Just sitting there watching the world go by, thinking her own thoughts. She used to say that London always seemed like a film when she was in my car, like a beautiful dream, and all the people on the streets looked like actors – it was like having a layer of insulation between her idea of what life *should* feel like and what it actually felt like. There were never any disappointments in the back of my car, that's what she always used to say . . .'

He fell silent for a moment and fiddled with a beer mat. 'D'you miss her?'

'Every second of every day.' His voice stayed steady but Ana noticed a film of tears spring to his eyes. He cleared his throat and took an abrupt sip of his lager.

'Tell me about when you first met her. Tell me what she was like.'

Flint craned his neck again to view the clock in the bar. 'How are we doing on that half-hour?' he said jokingly.

'Plenty of time,' said Ana. 'We've only done half of it.'

'Well – according to Bee, the first time we met was when I collected her from the airport after she'd been in Germany. But I think that was another driver. She had a terrible memory, that woman. The first real memory I've got of Bee, though, was this day when I had to take her to the dentist. That woman, I tell you, that woman was just obsessed with her fucking teeth. It was unreal. I swear to God half her fortune ended up in the pockets of nice Jewish men in Harley Street. She said she had toothache, so I drove her over there and two hours later she comes out and she's all wobbly and all over the place. The dentist had only taken her fucking wisdom teeth out while she was sitting in the chair.' He winced. 'Her face was all puffed up down this side and she could hardly talk and there was all this drool' – he demonstrated it with fingers on his chin – 'pouring down her chin. So there's this tiny little woman wearing a black leather trenchcoat and black shiny boots, with her boobs hanging out of this tight corset thing, with her face all fat and swollen with drool all over her chin. And then she started crying, too, so there was mascara running all down her face, and she's going,' he adopted a mincey accent, '"Oh Flint, I hurt, Flint, I hurt so much I want to die," just on and on and on and on, like a scratched record. So eventually I stopped the car and I turned around and I said, What the bloody hell do you want me to do about it? And she sits there looking all shocked like I've just slapped her, or something – all hurt and injured. And then she pulls herself up, like this, trying to make herself look tall, and she says, I'll tell you what you can do about it, *Flint*. You can take me into that bar over there and buy me 8,000 fucking margaritas and stay with me until I've drunk them all. OK?

'And we both just stopped, then, and she stared at me until I couldn't stand it for another second. And I said, Can I laugh at you now? And she just looked at me all sniffy and serious and said, Yes, you may laugh at me now. And I tell you what – I just lost the plot – totally. I don't think I've laughed so hard before or since.

'So anyway, we walked into this bar, and I knew what we must have looked like to other people – this big bloke with a scar on his cheek holding up this tiny beat-up little woman in head-to-toe leather who's so woozy she can't walk in a straight line. So, of course, everyone just stared at us, and I tell you what – that was the moment when I knew that Bee was special, that I wanted to get to know her. She was this famous popstar and she honestly didn't give a fuck about people seeing her looking like a crack-head whore. All the money that her label invested into creating and maintaining her image and she didn't give a flying fuck. I loved that . . .

'So. We stayed in that bar all afternoon, and she wanted to know all about me – my family, my childhood, my girlfriend, my hopes and dreams. She was so easy to talk to, that woman, so excited by people and life and all the . . . I don't know – all the little stuff. She liked detail. Not that she'd ever remember any of it afterwards.' He smiled. 'You could never just tell her that you'd met a girl in a bar and gone to bed with her. It would be, What bar? Who spoke first? What were you drinking? Whose place? What colour sheets? What fucking colour was her fucking bush? She honestly asked me that once . . .' He laughed and then fell silent, staring at the grubby pattern on the carpet. 'Fuck. I'm going to miss her. I'm going to miss her so much. Still,' he said, snapping out of his reverie, 'we're breaking the rules here, aren't we? We weren't supposed to be talking about Bee. And – oh look – my half-hour's up. Time to get another round in. Same again?'

At eleven o'clock, Ana and Flint spilled from the pub and into the slightly chilly outside air. Flint had offered Ana his sofa for the night, but she'd declined, and they were now waiting for a cab to take her back to Ladbroke Grove.

'So,' said Flint, 'tomorrow. Daytime. We'll do some research, yeah? Maybe I'll come over to Gill's – she's got the Internet, hasn't she?'

'Uh-huh.'

'I've got a job tomorrow night, but you could always come out with me, if you fancied it?'

'What d'you mean?'

'I mean sit up front with me, in the passenger seat.'

'But – won't your client mind?'

'Nah. They won't even know you're there. And besides

– it's my car. I can have whoever the fuck I want in it.'

'OK. Maybe.' Ana didn't want Flint to think she was leeching on to him. 'But definitely, tomorrow, research.'

'OK. I'll phone you. Tomorrow. Yeah?'

'Yeah. Tomorrow.'

'Good. Well – it's been an experience, hasn't it?'

'God – that's an understatement. Sunday morning feels like years ago now, doesn't it?'

'Uh-huh. Oh look – cab.' Flint strode out into the road with one large arm held aloft. It pulled up beside him and he gave the address.

'So,' he said, letting Ana into the cab, 'see you tomorrow. And sleep tight.' He closed the door on her and leaned into the open window. 'And thank you.'

'What for?' laughed Ana.

'For being such great company. I've had a really good night.'

'Really?'

'Yeah. Really.' He stepped on to the pavement and started to walk away, but Ana felt suddenly compelled to ask him something. 'Flint?' she called out, gripping the edge of the open window.

'Yes, sweetheart,' he said, turning back to her.

'Were you . . . were you ever in love with Bee?'

He laughed. 'No,' he said, 'no. I've never been in love with anybody.'

And then, before Ana had a chance to check the expression on Flint's face as he said it, the cab pulled away and bore her homewards. And as the cab drove on, Ana wondered to herself how anyone who was friends with a man like Flint could ever possibly want to kill themselves when all they'd have to do, she was sure, was phone him up and talk to him and everything in the world would be just fine . . .

29

'That'll be £18.60, please, love.'

Ana's eyes boggled slightly, but she pulled out her purse anyway and took out a £20 note. 'Bloody hell,' she said under her breath as she got out and walked towards the house. Twenty quid! For a cab ride. This city really was taking the piss.

As Ana regarded the little house on Latimer Road, she suddenly felt like she'd been gone for ever. And in a strange, heartwarming way, it almost felt like home. She picked up her rucksack and made her way inside. Once again, all was in darkness. She went to the kitchen and poured herself a couple of big glasses of water to thin out all the whisky she'd drunk and then found, much to her delight, a couple of plates of yummy things in the fridge – M&S party food, little sausages, terriney-salmony things, bits of battered fish. In the dishwasher were a few used champagne glasses and in the bin lots of empty crisp wrappers and houmous pots. Gill must have had some people round. And, in true Gill style, had cleared away every last crumb and wrapping. She grabbed a couple of nibbly things and took them upstairs. And, almost like a *déjà vu*, as she grabbed the handle of her bedroom door, she could hear groaning. And grunting. And slapping. And moaning. And giggling. Lots of giggling. No, thought

Ana, no way. She couldn't be. Not again. And surely not on a *Monday night*.

She let herself silently into her bedroom and breathed a huge sigh of relief as she let her rucksack fall to the floor and flopped on to her futon. She felt utterly exhausted, mentally and physically. She felt like every last drop of energy she'd ever possessed had been wrung out of her, like she'd never be able to stand up again. And she really wanted a bath – she hadn't had a bath since last week, since Torrington. She wanted to run herself a huge, steaming, foamy bath and lock the door and read her serial-killers book and not get out until she'd turned into a prune. But she couldn't. Because she was living in a house with a nympho, and she was too scared to open her bedroom door for fear of who she might find herself bumping into.

Slowly and painfully she started to peel off the clothes she felt like she'd been wearing for about three years, and she had her top half-way over her head when she heard a gentle knock at her door. Her heart stopped beating for a millisecond.

'Yes,' she said cautiously.

'Ana – it's Gill, can I come in?'

Oh God, thought Ana, oh no. What does she want?

'Yeah,' she said, slipping her top back on, 'sure.'

The door creaked open slowly and Gill crept in.

'Oh,' said Ana, jumping slightly and clutching her chest. Gill was wearing nothing but a pair of purple satin knickers and a matching bra, with one strap hanging off her shoulder and the majority of her breast on display. There was gingery lipstick streaked all over her face and bits of paper streamer in her hair. And she hadn't, Ana couldn't help but notice, done her bikini line.

'Hi,' she smiled crookedly, lurching a bit from side to side, 'I heard you coming in and I just thought I'd see how you were.'

'Oh,' said Ana, covering half her face with a hand and feeling unbelievably claustrophobic, 'oh, I'm fine. Really – fine.'

'Good. I've been a wee bit worried about you.'

'Oh. You didn't need to worry. I've been . . .'

'You shoulda been here earlier on, Ana – you missed a *hoot*.'

'Oh?'

'Yeah – I had a hen night here, for my friend Cathy. It was *hilarious*. We had a stripper and everything. You'd have loved it.'

'Oh. Yes. That is a shame . . .'

'And how wuz Broadstairs? Did you find anything interesting?'

'Yeah,' began Ana, realizing immediately that this response would only lead to a full-length conversation, the prospect of which, in the current circumstances, she couldn't quite stomach. 'Well – sort of. Not really. No . . .' She shook her head dismissively. 'You know . . .' she petered out.

'Oh well,' slurred Gill, 'it was worth trying, I guess. And how was the delicious Flint?' she asked in an innuendo-laden voice, accompanied by a grotesque Carry-On wink.

'What do you mean?'

'Feisty Flint?' she giggled. 'Did he behave himself?'

'I don't know what you're talking about.'

'Oh come on – you know what I mean. Did he try to – you know?'

'What?'

'To get into your knickers, of course.'

'No!' snapped Ana. 'Of course he didn't. Look,' she said, 'what exactly is it with Flint? I mean, why are you and Lol so mean about him?'

'Och – we're no mean about him. We just like taking the piss, that's all.'

'Yeah – but why? He seems perfectly all right to me.'

'Yes. But that's exactly it. He seems ever so nice. But he's not. He's a complete tart.'

'A tart?'

'Och. A right old slapper. He'll shag anything that moves.'

'Flint?'

''Course Flint. If it's got a pulse and a hole – he's in there. And actually, it doesn't even need to have a pulse. Just the hole will do.'

Ana face crumpled with confusion.

'We've all had him, you know.'

'Sorry?'

'Flint. All of us. Me. Cathy. Lol.'

'Lol?'

'Uh-huh – and Bee.'

Ana suddenly felt like she'd been kicked in the chest by a shire horse. She gulped as an image of a tiny Bee writhing around under a huge naked Flint flashed through her mind. 'No . . .' she managed to croak.

'Aye.'

'But – I mean – how do you know?'

'Cuz she told me, silly. That's what girls do, isn't it? Talk about stuff. Yeah. Bee and Flint had their moments. D'you see what I mean now? Keep away from Flint. You're a nice girl and he'll take advantage of you if you let him . . .'

'Well,' said Ana sniffily, regaining her composure, 'I've got no intention of letting him do anything. I'm really not interested in him in that way.'

'Good,' said Gill, finally realizing her bra strap was hanging down and snapping it back on to her shoulder, 'that's good. But I tell you what – if you want a nice, no-strings shag, you could do a lot worse than Flintypoos. He's fucking great in the sack. And his bits are all in proportion, if you get my drift.'

A click from across the hallway drew their attention away from Flint's proportions and towards Gill's bedroom.

'Oh, Lloyd, sorry. I was just talking to my lodger.' In the doorway stood a black guy. He had small dreadlocks, a long face and quite thin legs. 'Lloyd – this is Ana – Ana – this is Lloyd.' They both smiled politely at each other and said 'Hi.'

'Lloyd was our stripper tonight.' She turned and grinned at him saucily. 'But I've kidnapped him, see. Kept him all for myself. Anyway – I'll let you get to bed now. You must be knackered.' She got on to her tiptoes and left another big wet kiss on Ana's cheek. 'You sleep tight now.'

'Yeah,' said Ana, trying to wipe the wet kiss away surreptitiously, 'yeah. You too.' She was just about to close the door when Gill suddenly turned round again.

'Ooh,' she said, 'I nearly forget to tell you. Your mother called.'

'Oh God – when? What did she want?'

'Oh, she just wanted your address. She said she had some mail to forward on to you. She's ever so nice, your mother, isn't she? Really friendly. Anyway. I've got sex on a stick waiting for me next door. N'night.'

She waved at Ana and closed the door behind her, and Ana collapsed on to her bed in a state of total and utter shock. What was her mother up to? This 'having some mail to forward' thing sounded highly suspicious – Ana didn't get any mail. And Flint. Jesus. Horrible. He just didn't feel like . . . Flint any more. He didn't feel like a protector, he felt like a predator. He'd had sex with pretty much everyone Ana had met since she'd arrived in London. He'd had sex with Bee. And he'd lied to her. Told her that Bee was asexual. What else had he lied about or omitted to tell her?

She pulled off her clothes, pulled back her duvet and fell into a deep and instantaneous sleep.

30

Flint awoke at nine the next morning feeling strangely energized. Which was weird, because he usually woke up feeling like a ninety-year-old man with emphysema.

He made himself a cup of mint tea and a bowl of Alpen, picked up the *Independent* from his doormat and made his way out to the garden, where he sat on his armchair in his boxer shorts and soaked up a few early morning rays. He looked ahead of him at the stool he'd brought out for Ana to sit on last night. It was still where she'd left it, directly opposite him, her empty lager can on the ground next to it, and he could almost see her sitting on it – all hunched and awkward, her legs all twisted around themselves, picking at her fingernails, covering her face with her hands every few seconds, blushing constantly. He smiled to himself at the image.

He was just about to bring a spoonful of cereal to his lips when something hit him on the back of his neck. Something wet and cold and heavy. He looked up for a large bird but couldn't see anything. He put his bowl down on the grass and gingerly put a hand out to his neck. He prodded a bit and cringed. There was something there. Something squidgy and wet and disgusting. He grimaced and very, very gently picked the thing up between two fingernails. It was a large lump of wet pink toilet paper. And at the same moment that he worked out what it was, another large lump landed on the grass at his feet and he heard the snorty sounds of stifled laughter. He looked up again. Two small faces in the top-floor flat disappeared.

'I saw you, you little fuckers,' he yelled.

More snorty laughing noises.

Flint decided to play along with them. He pretended to go back to reading his paper and eating his cereal. And sure enough, within a few seconds two little heads had appeared at the top window, one little hand clutching another blob of wet paper. Flint immediately leaped from his seat, took two giant strides backwards and lobbed his missile at them. It hit the smallest boy square in the face, before dropping off and on to the windowsill below.

The two boys stopped smirking and started grimacing.

'You're messing with the wrong man – I'm a trained marksman.'

'Ya mother,' said one.

'I beg your pardon,' said Flint.

'Ya mother.'

'What?'

'Ya mother ya mother ya mother.'

'What *about* my mother?'

The two boys fell silent for a moment and exchanged a confused glance.

'Ya mother is a *fanny rash*,' said the small one, eventually, before both of them dissolved into hysterical stifled laughter and closed the window behind them.

'Jesus,' he muttered under his breath, 'Jesus Christ.' He took his cereal and his paper into the kitchen and finished his breakfast in there.

Later on, he phoned his mother to tell her that she was

a fanny rash, and she laughed so hard she nearly wet herself.

'*Where are you?*' Ana shouted into the phone.

'Drinking espresso in the sunshine, with only a scabby old Scouser to spoil the view.' Lol's voice was a tinny echo on the other end of the line.

Ana could hear a man swearing in the background, and Lol started cackling. 'Fuck off, soft lad. Go and find a car to nick or summat,' she cackled again. 'So – talk to me Ana. Tell me what's happening. What've I missed?'

Ana filled her in on all the events of the previous day.

'Jesus,' breathed Lol, 'that's unbelievable. You mean she'd been seeing that bloke for *three years*? But – when? How? I don't understand.'

They chatted for a while about Zander and the children's home, too. And the obvious question soon arose. 'Flint won't accept the possibility that Zander might be Bee's kid,' said Ana.

'Well – I have to say that for once I agree with him. I mean – I know I spend a lot of time out of the country and everything, but even someone as dense as me would've noticed something like a pregnancy. So what are you going to do? What's next?'

'Well,' Ana began, 'Flint's coming over in an hour and we're going to do some research on the Internet – see if we can find out what children's home Zander lives in.'

'Top idea,' said Lol, 'good work. And how is Flint? Is he looking after you properly?'

'Oh yes. Totally. He took me out last night . . .'

'Oh – he took you out, did he? And I sincerely hope he behaved himself . . .'

Ana blushed, in spite of the 500 miles and body of water that separated her from Lol. 'Of course he behaved himself,' she murmured, 'I really don't think he sees me like that, you know. I don't really think I'm his type, you know . . .'

Lol made a strange Marge Simpson-esque noise down the phone, and Ana could hear that she had her lips tightly pursed. 'Just be careful, that's all. You've got enough on your plate right now without having to worry about old slinky-knickers Flint trying to schmooze you into bed.'

Ana grunted and blushed even more.

A voice called out something in the background. 'Hmm,' said Lol, noisily slurping down her espresso, 'I've gotta go. My golden tonsils are required in the studio. Phone me again tomorrow, won't you? And look after yourself. Mwah.' She blew a kiss down the line, and then she was gone, leaving Ana standing there wondering, with a strange sense of shame mixed with excitement, why exactly old slinky-knickers Flint *hadn't* tried to schmooze her into bed and what exactly was wrong with her.

Flint got to Gill's at twelve. On the way there he bought a box of little Portuguese cakes from the place by the bridge up on Golborne Road. As he handed the white card box to Ana at the door of the house, he felt like Tony Soprano.

'Hi,' she said. She was wearing the same jeans and top she'd been wearing last night, and all weekend, come to that. Flint had never before met a woman who appeared to have so little interest in clothes. Her feet were bare and her hair was tied back in a ponytail. It looked nice. Off her face. Gave her a sort of ballerina look.

'Your hair looks nice,' he said, dropping his car keys into his pocket and following her into the living room. 'It suits you – up like that.'

She didn't say anything.

'Gill not here?' he said, looking around the empty room.

'No,' she said, 'she's at the gym.'

'Yup,' he said, 'that sounds like our Gill.'

'Do you . . . do you want a cup of tea or something?' Ana said, fiddling with her earlobe.

'Yeah. Great. We can have the little cake things, too.'

She nodded distractedly and padded into the kitchen, clutching the box tentatively like it was a dirty nappy.

Flint sat down. Something wasn't right. With Ana. She seemed awkward. Well, she always seemed awkward, actually, that was nothing new. But she seemed extra-awkward.

She came out with a tray with a couple of mugs on it and the cakes arranged on a plate.

'So – how are you getting on here with Gill. You happy?'

She shrugged. 'Haven't really been here enough to form an opinion. But it seems all right. Gill's . . . nice.'

'Yeah.' Flint leaned forward and helped himself to a cake. 'I like Gill, too. She's as mad as a hatter, but I like her.'

He bit into his cake and the room fell silent. He couldn't think of a thing to say to her. 'Are you all right?' he managed, eventually.

'Yeah,' she said, 'I'm good. I'm great.'

He looked across at her and felt a sudden wave of

warmth and compassion for her. Poor girl. One minute she'd been living her funny little half-life in Devon, thinking her sister hated her, and the next she'd been uprooted and transplanted to one of the biggest, noisiest cities in the world, was living with strangers and discovering that her sister's entire life was a lie.

He put down his cake and walked over to where she was sitting on a low cushion thing. He crouched down and put an arm around her shoulder. She flinched. He put another hand on her knee and squeezed it. She stiffened.

'Are you missing home?' he asked.

She jumped slightly and looked him straight in the eye. 'God. No,' she said, 'not even a tiny bit. I'm just tired, that's all.'

He removed his hand from her knee and looked her in the eye. 'Look,' he said, 'I know this must all have been quite hard going for you. And I just want you to know that I'm here. If you need me. If you want to talk. Or cry. Or anything. OK?'

She didn't look him in the eye this time, just sort of shrugged and nodded. And then, before he had a chance to push it any further, the doorbell rang. Ana looked at him and then at the door.

'Expecting anyone?' said Flint, getting to his feet and going to peer through the window.

She shook her head. 'Who is it?' she said.

'I dunno,' said Flint, 'some weird-looking bloke.'

'What does he look like?'

'Kind of geeky. Skinny. And he's wearing really weird clothes.'

Ana got to her feet and walked towards the window.

She peeled back the curtain and looked through the glass and suddenly jumped and flattened herself against the wall. 'Oh my God,' she whispered, 'it's Hugh!'

'Hugh who?' said Flint, peering out again.

'You know – Hugh Hugh.'

'Ah. Right. That Hugh. *Your* Hugh. Yoo-hoo, Hugh,' he tinkled camply, pretending to wave at him.

'Don't!' said Ana, slapping his hand away from the window. 'And don't answer the door,' she said. 'Please. I don't want to see him.'

'I think it's a bit late for that,' he said, grinning and waving at the man who was now staring at them through the window. He was short. That was the first thing that Flint noticed. Not just shorter than Ana, but properly short. And his head was a strange shape – kind of like someone had tied a belt around the middle of it, really tightly, when he was a baby. And it was just a little too large for his tiny sloping shoulders. His hair had a strange sort of kink to it, which he'd tried to tame by combing it down flat to within an inch of its life. And he had a very high domed forehead with freckles all over it.

Also, as if God hadn't given him enough to deal with on the physical front, he was horribly dressed. He was wearing a sort of cagoule thing. In this weather. It was red and white. And tight black jeans. And chunky-looking lace-up shoes constructed from a kind of porous brown leathery stuff. He had a small rucksack on his back and, oddly enough, he was wearing an earring in his left lobe that didn't go with the rest of him. Almost as if he was saying 'Hey. I'm a cool dude – I just can't be bothered to look like one, OK?'

He was staring straight past Flint, and at Ana.

'Oh God,' she muttered, crossing her arms and going to the front door. Flint sat himself back down on the sofa and waited.

'Hugh,' he heard Ana saying, breathlessly, 'what on earth are you doing here?' And then Flint heard something that sounded like one of those pantomime dames talking – like a *Monty Python* woman. Flint put his hand over his mouth to stop himself laughing out loud.

'Flint,' said Ana, walking back into the room, crimson-faced, 'this is Hugh. Hugh. This is Flint. Flint was Bee's best friend.'

'Nice to meet you.' Hugh grinned at him with crooked, grey-coloured teeth. Was he putting that voice on? Was it a joke? Flint didn't know whether or not he was supposed to be laughing. He decided not to.

'Flint, did you say your name was?' Hugh furrowed up his big, freckled brow and put a hand out towards him. He had peculiarly hairy hands and a very strong handshake and didn't seem at all phased by the fact that Flint was nearly a foot taller than him. There were two types of unattractive men in this world, Flint had noticed: those who were painfully aware of the fact and tried their hardest not to draw attention to it and those who walked around like George Clooney was their ugly younger brother or something. And this guy – well – he definitely fell into the second category. He had no idea he was ugly. He had all the confidence and swagger of a handsome Italian playboy. He thought he was fantastic. And good on him, thought Flint, smiling and giving his hand a good hard shake, good on him.

'What are you doing here, Hugh?' said Ana, flopping on to the sofa.

'Well, your mother asked me to come, actually.'

Ana raised her eyebrows and tutted. 'I should have guessed. Jesus.'

'She's worried about you, Ana. That's all. She just asked me to pop in on you, see where you're living. Find out what you're doing. She's just lost a daughter. I don't think she particularly wants to lose another one just yet.'

'She's not losing me, for God's sake. I'm trying to find out what happened to Bee.'

'What do you mean? Bee's dead. Isn't that the end of the story?'

'No,' she snapped, 'no – that's far from the end of the story. Look,' she said, sighing, 'you must be knackered – d'you fancy a cup of tea or something?'

He threw her an incongruously flirty, fluttery smile. 'I'd love one, Bellsie. Thank you.'

Ana shot Flint a look. He raised a quizzical eyebrow at her. Bellsie? She got to her feet. 'Flint will fill you in on everything that's been happening, won't you, Flint?'

'Yeah. Sure.' Ana left the room and Flint ran through the bare bones of the story – the cottage, Zander, Ed – and Hugh maintained a high level of very intense eye contact with him throughout, rubbing his chin occasionally and saying 'hmmmm', as if he was Hercule bloody Poirot. He seemed to think that Flint and Ana had just been sitting around waiting for him to turn up and sort everything out.

'Well,' he said, 'the first thing you should do is find

out about the documentary this Ed chap said he was producing.'

'Yup,' said Flint, patiently, 'we were working on that one.'

'You could probably find everything you need on the Net.'

'Uh-huh, yeah. That's why I'm here today.' He gestured towards Gill's PC sitting in the corner.

'Woah,' said Hugh, getting to his feet, 'look at that old dinosaur. Fantastic.'

'Yeah,' continued Flint, suddenly and inexplicably feeling the need to impress this self-assured and very young man. 'We were going to look up TV-scheduling sites, you know, see if there was some kind of archive service or . . .'

Hugh was already shaking his head and taking a seat at the desk. 'No no no,' he said dismissively, hitting buttons in an infuriatingly confident manner, 'waste of time. Even if there were such a thing, you'd never be able to find it. You're much better off running a search for this Ed chap's company. Oh God,' he muttered, 'she hasn't got her modem switched on. Any idea where it is, Flint?' he said, wheeling his chair backwards and looking under the desk.

Flint didn't even know what a modem was. 'Er, no,' he said, 'no idea. Ana!' he called.

'What?' Ana emerged from the kitchen with a mug of tea.

'Any idea where Gill keeps her modem?'

'Her what?' she said, looking at Flint.

He shrugged, behind Hugh's back.

'A modem,' said Hugh in a pompously patient tone of voice, 'it's the hardware that connects your PC to the Internet. It's like a box. It's . . . aaaah . . .' He found something under the desk and reached underneath to fiddle with it, 'excellent. OK. We're all ready to go.'

Flint and Ana stood hovering above him clutching their mugs of tea as Hugh bashed away at the keyboard. Flint stared at the top of Hugh's huge head and tried to imagine Ana and Hugh writhing around in bed together, Ana's beautiful tendrilly fingers running through the thatch of brittle brown straw that passed for Hugh's hair. He imagined Hugh's little falsetto voice cooing 'Bellsie, Bellsie' as he exploded inside of her and he suddenly and violently wanted to be sick. Jesus, he thought, surely Ana could do better than this.

'Okie dokie,' said Hugh, 'Ed Tewkesbury Productions – here we are.' Hugh hit a button on a side panel and a list of productions came up. 'Hmm,' sneered Hugh, 'classy.'

Ed's company, it seemed, made a speciality of producing programmes about drunken English people embarrassing the nation in various corners of the globe, and programmes about people with really boring jobs being followed around all day by cameras, and programmes about stag nights and hen nights and people with bizarre sexual preferences living in Berkhamsted.

'That must be it,' said Ana, pointing excitedly at a section entitled '*High Cedars*'. '*High Cedars*,' it went on to say, 'was first broadcast on BBC1 in the summer of 1997. This seminal documentary, filmed over twelve weeks at High Cedars Residential Home for Children in Ashford,

Kent, kept the nation emotionally gripped for the entire season with daily viewing figures averaging 3.3 million and set the standard for every human-interest docusoap to follow.'

'Well,' said Hugh, with a ring of self-satisfaction in his voice, 'that's that then. You've got your children's home. Let's run a search for it, shall we?'

He tapped the name of the home into a box and then clicked on a site on a list. A crested logo came up and a heading saying 'High Cedars'.

'There it is,' he said smugly, 'it's all yours.'

The site gave a phone number.

'So,' said Ana, turning to look at Flint.

He shrugged and looked over at the phone.

'What am I going to say?'

Flint puffed. 'Ask to speak to Zander, I guess.'

Ana made a cute little face at him, turning her mouth downwards and widening her eyes nervously.

'I don't mind doing it,' he said.

'No,' she said, and he saw her take a deep breath, 'no. I'll do it. OK. And what if he's not there? I mean, what if I can't talk to him? What shall I say?'

Flint saw Hugh open his mouth to say something and quickly cut in. 'Make an appointment,' he said, 'or something.' He set his jaw defiantly and out of the corner of his eye, saw Hugh raising an eyebrow.

'OK,' said Ana, 'OK.' She walked over to the phone, and the room became completely silent as the two men watched her dialling the number. Flint held his breath. This could be it. Ana might be about to talk to Zander.

'Oh,' she began, 'hi. I wondered if I could talk to Zander

Roper. Please.' She turned and hit Flint with a big grin that instantly warmed his heart.

'Erm – yes, that's the one. Yes. Who's calling?' She turned and made a panicked face at Flint. 'Oh it's er' – she gestured madly at Flint for him to come up with an identity for her – 'it's er . . .'

'Aunt,' he mouthed at her.

'Aunt,' she said, 'I'm Zander's aunt. Yes. Mrs Wills. That's right. I'm Mrs Wills.' She threw an oh-my-God-I'm-free-wheeling-like-a-motherfucker-somebody-please-help-me face at Flint and he smiled at her and gave her the thumbs-up. 'Oh,' he heard her say, 'right. I see. OK. And why is that, exactly? I see. I understand. No. No. That's fine. OK. And thank you so much for your help. Yeah. Bye.'

'What?' said Flint, unable to control his curiosity, 'what did she say?'

Ana flopped down on the sofa and fanned her blazing cheeks. 'He's not taking phonecalls from Mrs Wills.'

'What?'

Ana shrugged. 'I dunno. That's all she said. Zander has requested that phone calls from Mrs Wills not be put through to him.'

'So he doesn't know that she's . . . dead. Jeez.' Flint ran his fingers through his hair and exhaled heavily.

'D'you think I should have told the receptionist? About Bee?'

'No,' Flint shook his head, 'no. If we're going to talk to Zander we need to take him as we find him. You know. And I think news like that would be best coming from you, rather than a nurse.'

'So? Now what?' said Ana.

'Well,' began Hugh, 'we should probably –'

Flint cut in. 'Did she say anything about visitors?'

Ana shook her head.

'I think we should pay a little visit. What d'you think?'

'When?'

'Tomorrow – I'm not working during the day. Is that OK with you?'

Ana nodded. Hugh cleared his throat. 'I have to leave tonight, unfortunately. Early meeting tomorrow morning. So I'm afraid that . . .'

'Do you think they'll let us talk to him? Without an appointment?' said Ana.

'Let's talk about it tonight, eh? In the car?'

Hugh, now unhappily picking up the complicity between Ana and Flint and the fact that he was somewhat excess to requirements, took his mug of tea and sauntered over to the sofa, where he started fiddling around in the voluminous pockets of his cagoule. He eventually pulled out a small packet of Rizlas and a pouch of tobacco and proceeded to make a neat and very professional little roll-up.

'So,' he said, lighting it, inhaling and then picking a piece of tobacco off the tip of his tongue, 'Bellsie. Are you going to phone your mother?'

Ana tore her eyes away from the screen and looked at Hugh pointedly. She tutted. 'Yeah,' she said, 'I suppose so.'

'She really is very worried about you, you know.'

'Yeah. Sure she is. She's not worried about me. She's just worried about herself. About her shopping . . .'

'Well – don't you think that's fair enough? I mean to say, she *is* all alone.'

'And whose fault is that?'

'Ooh,' said Hugh, inhaling and scowling, 'that's a little harsh, wouldn't you say? The poor woman's lost a husband and a daughter within a year. That's tough for anyone.'

'Well – she should have been a bit nicer to both of them while they were still alive, shouldn't she? I really think that if you haven't appreciated people while they're living, you've got no right to mourn them when they're dead.'

'She loves you, you know.'

'She does not. She doesn't love anyone.'

'She does. She cried, Bellsie. She did. Cried.' He ran his fingertips down his cheeks to demonstrate the tears.

'Jesus – what is this? Bee ignores me for ten years, cuts me out of her life and all of a sudden the world and his wife is telling me how much she loved me. Now my evil witch of a mother, who won't even let me touch her, is bursting into tears and claiming undying love for me. I should have come to London a long time ago . . .'

Hugh rested his roll-up in an ashtray and walked towards Ana. 'Bellsie,' he said, massaging her bare shoulders with his funny, muscular little hands and making Flint's flesh crawl, 'come home. Eh? Come home with me now?'

'No,' said Ana, more firmly than Flint had heard her say anything up to that point, 'I'm staying. And I'm not coming home until I find out why Bee died.'

'Aah,' said Hugh, reaching back into his cagoule pockets, 'that's another reason why your mother sent me.' He pulled out a sheaf of paper and handed it to Ana. 'It's the coroner's report. On Bee,' he added, unnecessarily.

Flint jumped from his chair and stood next to Ana while she opened the letter with slightly trembling hands. 'Oh God,' she said, and Flint found himself, before he'd even had a chance to think about it, putting an arm around her shoulders and giving them a reassuring squeeze. It was the first time he'd touched her bare flesh, and it was nice. She didn't seem to notice. She unfolded the letter and held it up for both of them to read. Flint's eyes scanned the typewritten report, looking for the bottom line, looking for the verdict.

'Suicide,' said Ana, suddenly, the tip of one finger hitting a spot further down the sheet. 'Well – there it is. . . .' She sat down heavily on the sofa, and her lanky body collapsed in on itself. Hugh plonked himself down next to her and started stroking her hair.

Flint felt himself go numb. Bee had killed herself. But – she couldn't have. Of course she hadn't. I mean. Just. She couldn't have. He took the page from Ana's limp hand and surveyed it again, searching for something he might have missed, something that would tell him that she hadn't really killed herself, that it was an accident, that there was nothing Flint could possibly have done to have stopped it. Because as long as he'd been able to think of it as a tragic accident, then he hadn't had to accept any responsibility. As long as he'd thought that Bee hadn't meant to die, then the pain he'd felt had been the pain of futility instead of the pain of guilt and the pain of knowing that he hadn't been a good enough friend, that he hadn't phoned her for more than a fortnight before she died, that he hadn't been to her flat for weeks, that he'd just made assumptions that she was fine, that she was coping, that she was Bee and that Bee was always all right. Even when she left her beloved Belsize Park flat and moved into a desperately miserable flat that didn't suit her at all. Even though she hadn't had a boyfriend in years. Even though she had no job, no function, no purpose in life. Even though she'd been on anti-depressants half her life. Even though he couldn't remember the last time he'd seen her do that Bee thing of tossing back her head and opening up her mouth and laughing a laugh so loud that it scared the birds from the trees. That despite every warning sign that his so-called best friend was unhappy and spiralling downwards to somewhere dark and lonely, he'd just left her to it.

He held up the report and looked at it again. 'Diazepam 150 mg, Temazepam 300 mg, Paracetamol 310 mg, alcohol 25 units.' Jesus, he thought, that was certainly no accident. She'd taken at least eighty pills and the best part of a whole bottle of tequila.

He read on: 'Food contents largest amount first: uncooked fish, rice, wheat cereal, bread, cooked fish, seaweed, milk, tea, chocolate.' Oh God, thought Flint, these are the contents of Bee's stomach. This is what Bee put into her body on the day that she died, on the day she decided that she didn't want there to be a tomorrow. Flint could feel tears bruising the back of his throat. Wheat cereal. She'd eaten cereal. And chocolate. And seaweed. And uncooked fish. Sushi. She'd eaten sushi. He gulped. It was a shared passion. He'd introduced her to sushi way back in the Eighties when there were only about five Japanese restaurants in London. He'd taught her how to pick up the sushi and dunk it so that the soy didn't touch

317

the rice. He remembered her picking up a large glob of acid-green wasabi with her chopsticks, murmuring, 'What's this green stuff?', before popping it in her mouth too fast for Flint to tell her not to. She'd turned purple when the horseradish heat had permeated her nostrils, puffing and panting like a sweaty horse, her eyes bulging and watering, swearing and not caring that everyone in the restaurant was looking at her. He remembered her hitting him with her little handbag and blaming him for not telling her, and he smiled to himself.

How could he have let her do this? They'd been so close, particularly after the events of 1986. How could he have let their bond whittle itself down to such a spindly little thing? Because he was selfish, that's why. Selfish selfish selfish. All he cared about was his car and his kendo and his degree course and keeping his life all neat and well-ordered. That was why he was friends with Bee in the first place – because she was low-maintenance. And that was why he didn't have many other real friends. Because they were all too much like hard work. They made demands, and, Flint suddenly realized, he'd cut himself off from any sort of relationship that would call on him emotionally in any way. But that wasn't an excuse. It just wasn't. He was a bad person. As simple as that.

'Are you OK?' Ana and Hugh were both looking at him with concern. Flint looked down and realized that the coroner's report was screwed up in his fist. And then he realized that he was crying. He loosened his grip on the paper and wiped away the tears with the back of a fist. 'Shit,' he said, 'sorry. It's just . . . it's – poor Bee,' he said, looking Ana desperately in the eye, 'd'you know what I mean? Poor poor Bee.'

Ana nodded and picked up his big hand in her thin hand and rubbed it and squeezed it, and Flint looked at her and decided that the new Flint started here. He was going to be a good person, from this point on.

'Funny old world, isn't it?' said Hugh, pulling the report gently from Flint's open hand as if it was a surrendered gun.

Flint looked at Old Domehead and nodded.

Hugh stayed all afternoon. Flint wanted to like Hugh, would have been happy to have let Hugh grow on him, but it didn't happen. Instead, every moment spent in his company increased his dislike of him by leaps and bounds. He didn't dislike him the same way he'd disliked Ed – that had been to do with Ed's creepiness and the general lack of trust he felt towards him. The dislike he had for Hugh was based purely on the fact that he wasn't good enough for Ana, but that he obviously thought he was much better than her. He patronized her. He acted like Ana was just the luckiest gal in the world to know him, should be so grateful that he'd packed his horrible little rucksack and come all the way down here to check up on her. And in fact, seeing Ana with Hugh just served to crystallize the feelings he'd been having ever since he'd first set eyes on her. Seeing her with someone so wrong gave her a context, made him see clearly what was right for her. And suddenly Flint knew – *he* was right for her. And how weird was that? Bee's sister. A girl who didn't wear make-up. A girl with half a centimetre's stubble growing under her arms. A girl who wore the same clothes three days on the trot. A very tall girl. A very shy girl. A girl who was so different to his usual type in every way it was almost comical.

Flint had a mate called Terry who always went against the grain, girl-wise. He fancied Phoebe in *Friends* instead of Rachel. He fancied Willow in *Buffy the Vampire-Slayer* instead of Buffy. He fancied Carmella in *The Sopranos* instead of Dr Melfi. And now, with Ana, he could almost understand where Terry was coming from. There was something fascinating about the 'other girl', the supporting actress, the less obvious choice. For years Flint's mates had given him a hard time about Bee, couldn't understand how he could just be 'friends' with such a 100-per-cent babe. And he hadn't even bothered trying to explain, because he didn't really know himself. And if he'd told the same friends that he was now fantasizing about Bee's odd younger sister, they'd have had him sectioned.

He asked himself if these feelings were related in any way to Bee's death – some kind of strange knee-jerk reaction to loss and grief. But the answer was no. He just liked her. A lot. On many levels. Plain and simple. Full stop.

At about four o'clock Gill had come back from the gym with her friend Di, and Hugh had suddenly and repellently turned his attention away from an oblivious Ana and towards the two women. Neither Gill nor Di were exactly oil-paintings, but he was still way out of his depth. But Hugh wasn't even vaguely aware of his limitations, or the fact that Di and Gill both made gagging gestures at each other the moment he walked out the door to use the toilet.

Hugh finally left at 5.30 p.m. In a sudden and entirely unaltruistic moment, Flint offered him a lift to Paddington. And he deliberately didn't invite Ana, sensing that she wouldn't appreciate it, but also because he was hoping to get a bit of insight into her from Hugh while they drove the three-quarters of a mile to the station.

Hugh liked his car. Even Mr Cool personified wasn't able to feign indifference to a stretch Mercedes with tinted windows.

'This must lap up the old juice,' he said, touching it gently with one hand.

'About ten miles to the gallon – in town.'

Hugh sucked in his breath. 'Still,' he said, 'I guess the punters in the back pay for that?'

'And the rest,' said Flint, laughing and holding the passenger door open for Hugh.

'So,' said Hugh, in a pitiful attempt at blokey bonding, 'have you ever had a female passenger who didn't have enough cash on her?' He winked obscenely.

Flint knew exactly what he was getting at but refused to humour him. 'No,' he stated simply, 'everything's paid on account, through management companies and record companies. I don't deal in cash.'

'Oh,' said Hugh, rubbing his hands over his jeans, 'right.' He turned to look out of the window.

'So,' said Flint after a couple of moments' silence, 'how long have you known Ana?'

Hugh shrugged, still smarting from Flint's rejection of his all-blokes-together comment. 'Seven years,' he said, 'eight. Something like that.'

'Really?' said Flint, in surprise. 'So – since she was eighteen? Or younger?'

'Yeah. First loves,' he smiled.

'You mean – you were Ana's first boyfriend?'

'Yup. I taught her everything she knows.'

Oh grim, thought Flint. And if that's really true then get the girl to therapy – now. She must be traumatized.

'She tells me she used to live in Exeter?'

'That's right. Just up the road from me. She left Exeter when her father died.'

'Yes. She said. It sounds like she had a pretty tough time.'

Hugh shrugged. 'I dunno,' he said, 'Bill was very old. Eighty-four or something. It's not as if Ana wasn't expecting it.' He sighed and craned his neck to view two skinny girls in pedal-pushers and cropped tops tottering down Clarendon Road with a Rottweiler puppy.

'Yes, but – everyone's going to die at some point. Knowing it doesn't make it any easier when they do. And it sounds like she was particularly close to her father.'

'Yeah – she was. Unhealthily close, I often used to think.'

'Why d'you say that?'

'I don't know. It just didn't seem right somehow, a young girl spending so much time with such an old man. Although Bill was a very charming, very er . . . switched-on old man. But I think she depended on him too much.'

'And you?'

'What about me?'

'Did she depend on you? I mean – eight years – that's a long time to be with someone.'

322

Hugh puffed and scratched the back of his neck. 'Yes,' he said, 'yes, she did. Unfortunately. I always tried to encourage Ana to be independent. To stand on her own two feet. I think she expected rather a lot of me in the weeks after her father passed away. Expected me to hold her up, somehow.'

'Well,' said Flint, 'isn't that normal? To be expected? You were her boyfriend, after all?'

Hugh shrugged dismissively. 'I don't like to be used,' he said, and Flint wanted to punch him. 'And I have no respect for people who can't look after themselves, emotionally. If you don't do it for yourself then you never grow as a person. You never develop. And Ana was in dire need of development.'

'What do you mean?'

'Well – she's rather immature. For her age.'

'No she's not.'

'She is. And excuse me if I sound rude, but you don't really know Ana, do you? The only reason why Ana ever managed to make a life for herself away from home was because she had me. She'd never have done it on her own. *I* got her job for her, *I* helped her find a flat. All our friends were *my* friends. I thought her father dying, having to deal with his death, would be the making of her. But it wasn't, I'm sad to say. The minute I wasn't there to support her any more she let it all fall away. Reverted to teenagedom and moved back home.'

Flint opened his mouth to say something, then snapped it shut again. He wanted to say – is it any wonder that Ana didn't develop when she had a boyfriend like you? Is it any wonder she gave up on everything after her father died, when the one person in the world who claimed to be on her side abandoned her? And cut all this 'independence' bullshit, he wanted to shout, the reason why you let Ana throw her life away was because you wanted to shag around. You wanted to shag around and you didn't have the guts to dump her so you waited until she was at her most vulnerable and let her do it for you. You snivelling little shit . . .

All of a sudden Ana's life story opened up like a book in front of Flint. Put down by a vain, preening, neurotic mother. Abandoned by a glamorous, unattainable elder sister. Her personality swamped by an overbearing, self-styled Svengali of a first boyfriend. The only person who truly loved her was sixty years older than her, and he died. Having made her completely dependent on him, her boyfriend then cuts her loose just when she needs him most and, instead of being able to work through her own grief, she is summonsed to her childhood home to attend to the demands of her mentally unstable mother. A mother who has no interest in the emotional development or fulfilment of her daughter.

Jesus.

Paddington station loomed up on their left and Flint pulled up.

'Well,' said Hugh, extending a hand, 'Flint. It was nice to meet you.'

Flint hesitated and then gave Hugh his hand to shake.

'And thanks for the lift. Much appreciated.' He put his hand to his forehead and performed a daft little salute.

'No problem.'

Hugh lifted his rucksack from under his feet and let

himself out of the passenger door. 'And good luck,' he said, before closing the door, 'with tomorrow. Just call me if you need any help. You know?' And then he sauntered off with his rucksack slung nonchalantly over his shoulder, swaggering towards the concourse like Clint-fucking-Eastwood.

Flint shook his head, put the car into gear and headed back towards Latimer Road.

31

'You used to go out with *him*?' said Gill, looking at Ana in wonderment.

'Yes,' said Ana, a bit sniffily. 'We went out for about eight years.'

'Really?'

'What?' demanded Ana, knowing that Gill was getting at something.

'Well – he's a bit, you know . . . he's not . . .'

'He's vile, Ana,' said Di, tipping a can of Diet Coke to her mouth and emptying it of its last drops.

'Well,' said Ana, defensively, 'looks aren't everything, are they?'

'I'm not talking about his looks, sweetheart. I'm talking about him.'

'What about him?'

'He loves himself. And don't get me wrong. I'm usually quite partial to a man who loves himself. But only when they've got good reason. And that man has absolutely no reason, dammit.'

Gill dissolved into giggles and dropped half a vol au vent on the floor.

'Where on earth did you find him?' continued Di, obviously using the fact that she'd only just met Ana as ample excuse to be as rude as she liked. Ana felt her hackles rising.

'I met him at college,' she said, 'he's highly intelligent.'

'Yeah,' said Di, 'and so's Mr Spock. But that doesn't necessarily make him good boyfriend material.'

'Hugh's a good person,' said Ana, lamely, 'he's done a lot for me. He's a good friend and . . .'

'Sorry,' said Gill, wiping vol-au-vent crumbs from her fingertips into a piece of kitchen roll, 'we're no meaning to be mean, you know. But it's just that you're such a beautiful girl, you know, and you're so sweet and everything. I just kind of expected anyone you've been out with to be a – I don't know. A nice guy, I guess. A cute guy. Someone kind and gentle. Like you . . .'

Ana's tummy fizzed pleasurably. Kind and gentle? Beautiful? 'But I'm not . . .'

'Yes ye' are. You're gorgeous. Isn't she gorgeous, Di?'

Di nodded enthusiastically. 'You could be a model,' she gushed.

Ana looked at them suspiciously. 'You're both taking the piss, aren't you? You're winding me up.'

'No way,' said Di. 'I mean – you are 100 per cent gorgeous. Really. And I bet with a bit of make-up and some funky clothes . . .'

'Done that already. Lol got me all tarted up last week when I first arrived.'

'And?'

Ana shrugged.

'I bet you looked stunning, didn't you?' said Di, excitedly. 'Didn't you?'

Ana let a smile seep slowly across her face. 'Well,' she said, 'I wouldn't say gorgeous exactly. But I looked, you know – all right.'

'Ooh,' said Di, peering through the window, 'talking of gorgeous. The beautiful Flint returns.' She stood on her tiptoes to view the return of Flint, who was parking his car across the street.

'Sit down, you old slapper,' said Gill, dragging her down by the hem of her sweatshirt. 'He's too good for the likes of you.'

Ana stiffened as she heard Flint's footsteps heading up the garden path. She was still reeling from Gill's drunken revelations about him and his sexual behaviour last night, about his failure to mention at any point during all the incessant talking about her past the fact that he and Bee had had a sexual relationship. And she was also reeling from the faint stirrings of jealousy churning around inside her stomach. What was all that about? What exactly was this nagging, insistent little voice inside her saying, 'Why Gill? Why Lol? Why Bee? Why every woman in south-east England and not me?' When she'd first met Flint he'd given off 'unattainable' vibes, the kind of man who would only look at a woman if she was actually Christy Turlington's identical twin sister. Discovering that he'd sleep with a warthog if he could get it to stand still for long enough was really very disappointing.

But then he'd walked into the house this afternoon clutching a little box of cakes, with his big shorts on and his tufty hair, and those negative thoughts had melted away immediately. And then when he'd touched her – physically and emotionally – she'd had to resist the temptation to bury her head into his enormous chest and squeeze him half to death. And then Hugh had turned up, and at one point she'd walked into the living room and looked at the two of them side by side and, oh God – Hugh had looked so little and inconsequential and kind of . . . sad. She'd almost burst into tears seeing a man she'd loved unquestioningly and depended on so completely for so many years shrunken to such inadequate proportions in front of her very eyes. And not just shrunken but somehow tainted – almost, she imagined, like it might be to meet an idol in the flesh who you've only ever seen in airbrushed photographs before.

But Hugh's presence had done something else – formed a bond of complicity between her and Flint. For the first time, she felt like she and Flint were equals. Up until Hugh's arrival she hadn't been able to shake this feeling that Flint was just humouring her – that she was cramping his style in some way. Even after he invited her back to Turnpike Lane to go drinking, even after he introduced her to all his mates in the pub, even after he phoned her this morning, even after he asked her to go out with him tonight in his car, she still thought he was just being nice. Today she had suddenly realized that he wasn't just being nice, that he actually *wanted* it to be her and him, together.

Flint walked in and his eyes went immediately to Ana's. He looked at his watch. 'Ten minutes,' he said, grinning.

'Ten minutes for what?'

'To get your glad rags on and get going. Come on. I've got to be in Chepstow Road in half an hour.'

'What for?'

'A job. Now get going.'

'But why do I have to get changed?'

'No reason,' he said, unzipping a suit carrier and heading

towards the downstairs toilet, 'you'll just have more fun if you're glammed up. Trust me.'

'OK,' said Ana, blushing at Gill and Di's winks and heading up the stairs.

She unzipped her tartan suitcase and tipped the contents all over her bed. What kind of choice was this, she thought, picking up ludicrously, almost comically ill-matched garments and discarding them? She had two pairs of Bee's Indian harem trousers, a spare T-shirt, her khaki Lycra top, which she threw to the floor when she realized that it actually *smelled*, a load of diamond jewellery, the black sequinned jacket, three brightly coloured cotton Indian tops and her pyjamas. Bollocks, she thought, thinking of all those beautiful dresses and gowns she'd packed away at Bee's and sent back to Devon. But then she looked down at her legs and realized she couldn't have worn a frock anyway – nearly a week's worth of stubble – not just a hint of mousy growth but proper lesbian-rambler, boots-and-shorts stubble. So. Trousers. It had to be. She pulled off her cotton vest and slipped on an Indian top. Pretty, she thought, eyeing up her reflection, but not glam. She took it off. Then she took off her jeans and pulled on the harem trousers. As she looked at her reflection she suddenly remembered that harem trousers were just *stupid*. The sort of thing that probably seemed like a good idea when you were wandering around India with a bindi on your forehead eating lentils with your fingers, but get them home and you soon realize that they're an incredibly unflattering garment that makes you look like you've done a huge poo in your crotch.

And then she remembered Lol. Lol wore jeans all the

time but she always looked glamorous. She pulled her jeans back on. And then she spied the black sequinned jacket. She pulled it on over her bare chest and buttoned it up. She arranged herself into all sorts of unlikely positions in the mirror, checking that her boobs didn't fall out, and then she put on Bee's diamond necklace and Lol's snakeskin stilettos. Jesus, she thought, checking herself again, this either looks great or I look a complete tit. How were you supposed to know the difference, she wondered? Could she, she wondered? Could she really go out like this? With no bra on? No top? Well – she'd have to – she didn't have any choice.

She was about to let down her hair and comb it out when she suddenly remembered what Flint had said earlier on about it suiting her up, so she smoothed it down with her fingertips, put on a pair of diamond drop earrings, got halfway through her door, remembered she'd forgotten deodorant, slicked some on, put some spit on her eyelashes and then went clattering down the stairs.

'Ready,' she cried, grabbing her rucksack from the coat stand and piling into the living room.

'Oh. My. God,' said Gill, getting slowly to her feet, a copy of *Now!* magazine falling to the floor. 'You look amazing.'

Di's jaw was on the floor. 'I told you. Didn't I tell you? Fantastic, absolutely incredible.'

And then Flint emerged from the kitchen, gulping down a glass of water, and Ana nearly fainted. He was wearing a black suit, a white shirt and a thin black tie. He looked like Michael Madsen in *Reservoir Dogs*. He looked like the handsomest thing she'd ever seen in her life.

'Wow,' he said, looking genuinely taken aback, 'Ana – you look – wow.'

The two of them stood and stared at each other in wonder for a while, like a paused video, before someone hit Play and Flint looked at his watch and Ana said, 'Come on, we're going to be late,' and in a big fug of embarrassment and wolf whistles and silly comments from Gill and Di, they both bundled themselves out of the door and towards his car, desperately trying not to look at each other as much as they both desperately wanted to.

32

Flint's client was a model called Liberty Taylor. With her was her boyfriend, a weasely, pasty-faced boy with strange, combed-forward hair who was 'no one', according to Flint. How weird, thought Ana, to be 'no one' just because your girlfriend was skinny and pretty and got paid to have her photograph taken. Ana watched in wonder as the two of them emerged from a large white house with wrought-iron balconies, all unsmiling cool and tatty vintage clothes. She had it, she thought, peering curiously at Liberty, whatever it was that it took to be famous, she had it. Her hair was jet black and gelled into Marcel waves across her forehead, and she was wearing a flimsy, chiffony dress and shoes so strappy that they barely existed. She was unbelievably pale and had a pink blob in the middle of each cheek. Her boyfriend looked like a recalcitrant teenage brother who'd been made to dress up for the night. They didn't talk to each other as they left the house, just sort of wafted silently out and lowered themselves professionally into the back of the car as Flint held the door open for them. She heard the 'no one' boyfriend muttering 'Cheers, mate,' as the door was closed behind him.

'Where are we taking them?' Ana whispered to Flint as they pulled away.

'You don't need to whisper,' whispered Flint, turning towards her and smiling. 'They can't hear us.'

'Oh. Right.' She grinned at him, thinking, 'You are a juicy-rare-burger-and-thick-cut-chips of a man and I want to *eat* you.'

'We're going to a film premiere,' he said, 'some cockney-caper thing. Sunny Moore's in it.'

'Who's Sunny Moore?'

'Another model – I think they used to be flatmates, or something.'

'How do you know that?'

'I told you,' he smirked, 'I know absolutely everything about celebrities.'

'What – even stuff like flatmates?'

'Yup. Even stuff like flatmates. It scares me sometimes how much room in my tiny little brain is taken up by things like the name of Liz Hurley's new boyfriend.'

'Oh,' said Ana smugly, 'even I know that one – it's Hugh Grant, isn't it?'

Flint threw her a pitying look. 'You poor, poor little thing,' he said, 'you really don't know a thing, do you?'

'What,' Ana objected. 'But it is, isn't it? Liz Hurley does go out with Hugh Grant, doesn't she?'

'No, my child. Liz and High split up a few months ago and Liz is now going out with a guy called Steve Bing who is some hotshot Hollywood film producer. A big fella, a bit like me. He's also in line for about 14 billion or something when his dad pops off. They were first photo-graphed together, in much the same way as Jennifer Aniston and Brad Pitt, on a balcony at a charity rock concert.'

'Oh my God, Flint – that's sick – knowing that much about a pair of strangers is sick.'

'I know,' he said, 'I agree. But what's frightening is how

easy my brain finds it to absorb that sort of information and how hard it finds it to absorb important stuff.'

'You mean your studying?'

'Uh-huh. They say that your powers of memory are at their peak when you're twenty-six, and it's all downhill after that. Which in many respects is true. But if that really is the case, how come I remember so much trivia? It's all information, isn't it? It uses the same part of the brain. And I retain it perfectly. Yet give me an important fact and it's gone in seconds.' He clicked his fingers. 'It's a mystery to me, it really is. Oh. Hold on. Her ladyship is calling.' He looked down at the dashboard, where a little light was flashing.

'Yes,' he said solemnly into a tiny microphone.

'Oh,' said a breathy, Sloaney voice, 'yeah. Hi. Driver. Could we, like, er stop, please. At a chemist. I just have to . . . yeah . . .'

'No problem, Miss Taylor,' said Flint before pulling over at a big glitzy-looking place called Bliss that looked more like a nightclub than a chemist.

Liberty emerged from the back of the car like a frightened little bird. Rush-hour traffic whizzed by noisily and homeward-bound commuters surged past her. She looked frail and lost, like the Little Match Girl in a posh frock, and Ana suddenly felt inexplicably sorry for her. Before she'd even thought about it, she'd opened her door and was standing next to Liberty. 'Hi,' she said, 'I'm a friend of the driver's. Would you like me to go in there for you? I'm probably a little more suitably dressed for a chemist run.'

She grinned and the waif-like Liberty smiled wanly

at her. 'Would you?' she said, 'really?' Except she said 'Rarly?'

'Yeah,' said Ana, 'sure. Tell me what you want and I'll get it for you.'

'God – that's rarly sweet of you,' said Liberty, ferreting around in a tiny satin pouch for an even tinier satin purse with a minute zip that she could barely get a grip on. She opened it and pulled out a tiny crumpled £5 note and passed it to Ana. 'My fucking period's just started and I didn't bring any tampons. It's just sooooo fucking annoying. And Mr "I'm, like, a guy I can't buy things like tampons" in there' – she indicated the back of the car – 'refused to go in for me. Would you mind? SuperPlus? Non-applicator? Thank you. You're a complete star.' And then she stalked back into the car and pulled the door closed behind her.

Ana bought the tampons, thinking what a funny old world it was – one minute you're buying organic barley for your agoraphobic mother in Devon, the next you're buying jumbo-tampons for a supermodel in Marble Arch.

Liberty opened the car door as Ana knocked on it. 'Oh, you star,' she said again, grabbing the plastic bag and the change from Ana's hand. 'God, I just can't thank you enough.' Her boyfriend was sitting at the other side of the car, staring into the middle distance, sniffing loudly and sucking his teeth, his legs apart, one leg bouncing up and down to the music playing in the back. 'That's a fantastic jacket, by the way – where's it from?'

'Vivienne Westwood,' said Ana, feeling happy to be wearing a famous designer label and then feeling really annoyed with herself for being so shallow. 'It's my sister's. Was. My sister's.'

'Well – you should keep it – it rarly suits you. You look fabulous.'

For a second, the two girls stared at each other. Ana looked into Liberty's eyes and wondered what it would be like to be her, to be Liberty Taylor. And as she looked, she noticed with shock that Liberty was staring at her, doing exactly the same thing. Ana pinkened and smiled and closed the door gently behind her before climbing back into the passenger seat, feeling strangely substantial.

'Do you know,' said Flint, turning to smile at her, 'that a supermodel, a girl who has been on the cover of *Elle* and *Vogue*, a girl who is widely held to be one of the most beautiful girls on the planet, has just told you that you look fabulous?'

'Yeah,' she replied.

'Do you believe it now?' he said.

'Believe what?'

'That you're beautiful?'

'Oh,' she scoffed, 'fabulous is one thing. Beautiful is another. And anyway – she was talking about the jacket. Not me.' But even as she said it she knew it wasn't strictly true. Because suddenly, and for the very first time in her life, she actually felt like she might be beautiful. She really might be. Well, maybe not beautiful exactly, but, you know – not bad-looking. She smiled and turned her head to the window, watching the hordes of early evening office-bods scuttling around greyly, and felt positively serene.

*

They parked in a sidestreet around the back of Leicester Square, picked up a KFC and scoffed it in the front seat of the car, watching the world go by. After the premiere they drove Liberty, her 'no one' and a few other beautiful, sad-looking people to a club in Soho for the post-premiere party. As Liberty emerged from the back of the car she knocked on Ana's window.

'Hi,' she beamed, 'take this.' She handed Ana a sliver of white card. 'My friend Rosa's a scout for Models One. Give her a ring. I think she'd really like to see you. Yah?'

'Me?' said Ana, touching her chest with her palm, 'but I'm not . . . I mean . . . I'm . . . *my nose*,' she blustered.

'Yah. That's cool. They're looking for you know, what's the word, er . . . *edgy* – that's it – edgy girls. You know. Unusual. You've got a great look. She'll love you. Phone her. Yah?'

'Oh. God. Yeah. Well. Yeah. Thank you.' She took the card and stared at it for a while. When she looked up again, Liberty and her friends were all half-way up the steps to the club where a red-velvet rope was instantly unclipped for them to pass through.

'Yeah,' said Flint, one elbow resting against the window ledge, eyeing Ana sceptically, 'it wasn't you. It was the jacket. Right.' He rubbed the top of Ana's head with the palm of his hand. 'Well, well, well,' he laughed hoarsely, before steering the car deftly away from the front of the club and pulling out towards Piccadilly. 'Well, well, well.'

'So,' said Ana, feeling suffused with some ridiculous feeling of complete and perfect joy, 'where are we going now?'

It was eleven-thirty.

'D'you fancy getting in the back?'

'I beg your pardon?' teased Ana.

'Get in the back,' said Flint, 'I'll drive you around for a while. It's the best way to see London.'

'OK,' Ana grinned.

She sat smack in the middle of the black-leather seat and spread herself out a bit, running her hands over the leather pleasurably.

'Sit back, have a glass of champagne, listen to the music and just watch the world,' said Flint, 'just watch and feel . . .'

She opened the side cabinet and pulled out a half-drunk bottle of champagne. She poured herself a glass and then rubbed her fingertip across the mahogany tabletop. There it was, she thought, examining the white film: the ultimate urban experience. She put her fingertip to her lips and tasted it with her tongue, like she'd seen them do in films about a million times. It tasted bitter, salty. The end of her tongue went numb. She took a sip of half-flat champagne and turned her attention to the world outside. It really was very insulating in here, she thought, with these muted little lights and black upholstery and tinted windows.

They drove along a wide dual carriageway lined with imposing office blocks, past a big gothic church with a modern extension attached, past Woolworths' head office, Madame Tussaud's, the Planetarium. And then they turned right past rows of immaculately tended white houses. Lights twinkled in huge, uncurtained windows. Ana saw a cocktail party, a woman in a white dress tipping back her head and laughing uproariously at something an old man wearing a monocle had just said, and then circling her finger around the rim of a wine glass.

They passed the BBC building – she recognized it from pictures – and then turned into a sideroad and zigzagged around for a while. They passed fashion shops and fabric suppliers and canopied restaurants where people sat at pavement tables. She saw a man with black hair kiss the back of the hand of a girl wearing a blue and white dress. She smiled and put a chip in his mouth. He chewed it up and showed it to her on his tongue. She laughed.

A group of girls with highlighted hair strolled down the road, arms linked together, singing 'Tragedy' at the tops of their voices and then doubling over with laughter. One of them was wearing a diamond chain around her bare midriff, which sparkled in the orange streetlights. An African man wearing a jellabah and an embroidered cap hailed a cab and climbed in after his purdahed wife. Ahead of her, Ana could see the Post Office Tower.

She looked up, above the shopfronts and the restaurants, at the ornate floors above, the occasional stained-glass window or gothic turret, chipped gargoyle or leaded bow-window. She saw someone moving around in a high-ceilinged flat, talking to someone on the phone, smoking a cigarette. Living their life in the middle of a film set.

A mixed group of drunken youth tripped across Tottenham Court Road, still wearing their office clothes, their cheeks flushed with excitement and cheap All Bar One wine. A girl in a sleeping bag sat in the entrance of Heals, staring vacantly at the passers-by, whose pace picked up as they passed her. Inside a Seventies-style Italian restaurant a group of friends all looked smilingly at their plump, aproned waiter as he illustrated a story with his arms and his eyebrows.

A doorman outside a hotel hailed a cab for a couple dressed in fluorescent cagoules. She saw them mouthing 'Thank you very much' as he held the door open for them. And then she saw the doorman's face fall as he examined the tip they'd left in the palm of his hand.

The car headed back towards Soho, through deserted squares framed by enormous Georgian mansions. In a railinged square, lit by a single streetlight, a man and a woman argued. Flint took them through the red-light district. The car slowed down to a near-halt as pedestrians swarmed across the narrow roads and cars double-parked outside clubs and taxi offices. It was almost midnight on a Tuesday night, but it looked like every resident of London was out on the streets of Soho. A bulbous-eyed man with tattoos peered into the tinted windows of the car and waggled a large grey tongue at her, like a Maori. Ana flinched before remembering that he couldn't see her.

She stared into the empty eyes of a dark girl perched cross-legged on a high stool in the entrance of a strip club and wondered how she'd ended up there, and then lost herself briefly in thoughts of destiny and cause and effect and how maybe if that girl wasn't working in that bar, sitting on that stool at this very moment, maybe someone else on the other side of the planet would be unable to come up with a cure for cancer. Or something . . .

They flew back down Piccadilly and across Hyde Park, Knightsbridge and Sloane Street. Chanel. Ralph Lauren. Christian Dior. Versace. Names that were just the adverts in between the articles in *Marie-Claire* to Ana. And there they were, in the flesh – shining, bright, untouchable, like film stars.

As they sailed down towards Sloane Street and down the King's Road, Ana felt herself being lifted out of herself again, like that night in Bee's flat when she'd dressed up and drunk champagne and listened to Blondie. Nothing else existed – just her thoughts, the music and the moving scenery. But it wasn't just scenery. It wasn't just a mishmash of separate, unconnected activities and individuals. It was cohesive. It was life. All those buildings and cars and strangers. They were life. And they were magical.

They turned off the King's Road and headed for the river. The music changed again. 'Perfect' by the Lightning Seeds. And as the river came into view, as she set eyes on Albert Bridge and gasped at its almost saccharine prettiness, at the ruffled reflections of fairy-lights in the treacle-black water of the Thames, she sat back in the soft leather and let a smile play on her lips while the lyrics drifted into her consciousness and seemed suddenly to make sense of absolutely everything.

Ana gulped as the song came to a close. There was a happiness welling up in her chest that brought tears to her eyes. She felt overcome by intense emotion. By intense love. By an intense desire to feel that song, to live that song. Music had always conjured up a sense of another life for Ana, of other, *better* ways of feeling and existing and being. And now, for the first time in her life, she felt like she could take one of those songs and make it real.

'Flint,' she breathed into the Intercom.

'Your ladyship?'

'Let's go,' she heard herself saying, in a stranger's voice.
'Where?'
'Yours,' she said, 'let's go back to yours.'

33

He smelled her hair first. It was spread all over his pillow. Black and long and in need of a shampoo. He picked up a strand between his finger and rubbed it under his nose. It felt like satin knickers.

He manoeuvred his body slowly on to its side and looked at her. She was fast asleep, her long lashes resting against her cheekbones, her lips slightly parted. He looked down at her bare breast. It was tiny. But it did everything that a breast was supposed to do. It had a neat nipple that was in proportion to the size of the breast and was a nice caramelly colour. The breast itself was round and firm and the nipple tipped ever so slightly upwards, giving it just the right amount of perkiness. He cupped it with his hand and felt her heart beating underneath, a slow, resting beat in rhythm with the little puffs of breath that slipped between her lips.

Well, well, well, he thought to himself, smiling, I'm in bed with Bee's sister. As Old Domehead had put it so eloquently yesterday – it's a funny old world.

He took his hand from her breast and very quietly got out of the bed and headed towards the kitchen. It was eight-thirty. The kids next door were already screaming and shouting. A paddling pool had now been added to their artillery of annoying, noise-producing garden con-traptions. He made two mugs of tea and padded back to the bedroom, where Ana was just stirring. He grinned at her while she rubbed her eyes.

'Hi,' he said, handing her her tea.

'Hi,' she said, taking it from him and pulling the duvet up around her armpits.

'Well,' he said, 'this is a turn-up for the books, isn't it?'

'Mmm,' murmured Ana, taking a slurp of tea.

'How you doing?'

'Er . . .' – she grinned and put her tea on the bedside table – 'good. I'm good.' And then she beamed at him – a huge toothy, tonsilly grin, and for the first time ever Flint could see something of Bee in her.

'That's what I like to hear.'

'You know, Gill told me specifically not to do that.'

'What?'

'Have sex with you.'

Flint liked the fact that she said 'have sex' and not 'make love', surely one of the vilest expressions known to man. 'And why's that, exactly?'

'She told me you were an old tart. That you'd sleep with anything with a hole in it.'

'She said what?'

'She said that you weren't as nice as you seemed. That you weren't to be trusted.'

'And what exactly did she base that judgement on?'

'On the fact that you've slept with her. And Lol. And Cathy – whoever the hell Cathy is.'

Flint raised his eyebrows and groaned. 'Oh,' he said, 'for God's sake. I can't believe she told you that. That's so unfair.'

'But true?'

'Yeah it's true. But that was fucking aeons ago. We were all young. All in our twenties. Thought that sex was just a big game. And for a while, after I got back from Japan and I wasn't even drinking any more, it was the only vice I had. I slept around a lot when I was younger – a hell of a lot – it wasn't like I made a point of only sleeping with people I knew.'

'And Bee?'

'What about Bee?'

'You slept with Bee, too . . .'

'Oh. God.' He let his head drop on to his fist. 'Yes,' he sighed. 'I slept with Bee. Once. About a week after we met. And that was it.'

'Why?'

'Why what?'

'Why did you only sleep with her once?'

Flint thought about it for a moment. 'Because it seemed wrong.'

'Wrong?'

'Yeah. Not right. It was embarrassing. Awkward. A mistake.'

'And these days?'

'What?'

'Do you still – sleep around?'

He shrugged. 'Nah,' he smiled, 'not like I used to. I mean I still have my moments, you know. But I'm an old man now – it's not my *raison d'être* any more.'

'And when was the last . . . ?'

'About a month ago.'

'And she was . . . ?'

'She was Angela. She was twenty-nine. She'd hired the car for her hen night.'

'You know on Monday night, when I asked you about Bee? About whether you'd ever been in love with her? And you said you'd never been in love with anyone? Did you really mean that?'

'Uh-huh.'

'But – I don't really understand. I mean – you're thirty-six years old. How did you get to be so old without falling in love with anyone?'

'Ah, now. I said I'd never *been* in love. Not that I'd never *fallen* in love. I've fallen in love a few times.'

'What's the difference?'

'Well, one is a process. The other is a state. I've been through the process but never found the state. At one stage in my life I persuaded myself that maybe the process was the state and I married her.'

'What!'

'Yup – it lasted fourteen months.'

'Who was she?'

'A client. Girl called Ciara. She was a dancer. Irish girl.'

'So what went wrong?'

'We didn't like each other.'

Ana laughed. 'That simple?'

'Yup. That simple. We just woke up one morning and both decided that we really couldn't stand each other.'

'So – how do you differentiate between the process and the state?'

'You need to be able to differentiate between insanity and sanity. Because that's the difference between falling in love and being in love. One is a state of total and utter madness, the other a state of pure clarity and peace. Or so I've been told.' He smirked.

Ana smiled and rested her chin on her knees. 'Sorry,' she said.

'What for?'

'For giving you the third degree. It's just that Gill made you sound so awful . . .'

'Yeah, well – Gill's not . . .' He paused. '. . . Nothing.'

'Gill's not what?'

'Nothing,' said Flint. 'Forget I said anything.'

'No way! Gill's not what?'

He sighed. 'Gill's not . . . the type to take rejection very well.'

'What – you mean, she's tried and you said no?'

'Uh-huh.'

'When?'

'Oh. On a pretty regular basis. When she's pissed usually. When Gill's pissed she turns into a complete raving nympho.'

'Yeah,' smiled Ana, 'I've noticed. But from what I've seen, you're not exactly her usual type, are you?'

'You mean the black guys?'

'Uh-huh.'

'Yeah. Gill loves her black guys. And they seem to love her, too, actually. I mean – don't get me wrong – I do like Gill. You know, I've known her half my life. But when it comes to sex, she's a bit fucked up. I wouldn't pay too much attention to anything she says – she's got a skewed vision of sex. She seems to think it's an Olympic event.'

Flint took a sip of tea and looked at Ana. 'Here's a question for you,' he said, 'how come you're only asking me about all this right now – why didn't you ask me last night – before . . . you know?'

Ana grinned at him. 'Because,' she said, 'last night I wasn't really in the mood for talking.'

Flint smiled and took another sip of tea.

'You must think I'm dreadful,' said Ana.

'What?' laughed Flint.

'Last night. I don't really know what happened. I was just . . . overcome. Not that I didn't want to, before, or anything. I've been wanting to since I first saw you . . . oh.' She put her hand over her mouth and looked embarrassed.

Flint laughed. 'You dirty old mare,' he grinned. 'And I thought you were such a nice girl.'

'I am,' she insisted, 'I'm a very nice girl. In fact you're only the second man I've slept with.'

'I know.'

'What! How?'

'The delightful Hugh told me. He told me that he taught you everything you know. And I have to say that as much as it makes me want to hurl to admit it, or even to think about it, for that matter – he did a fine, fine job.'

'Last night,' said Ana, 'was nothing to do with Hugh, I can assure you.'

'Oh no?' said Flint, putting his tea down and grabbing Ana by the waist.

'No,' said Ana, passing her hands over his buttocks, 'what happened last night was the inevitable result of being driven around London in a stretch limo at midnight by a large handsome man in a suit, while drinking champagne and listening to good music. You've got no one to blame but yourself.'

'Is that what I've got to do every time I want to do this with you then? Take you for a drive?'

'No,' she said, looking confidently and directly into his eyes, 'only the first time. After that all you have to do is ask.'

Flint stared into her eyes. Who was this person? This person with sparkling eyes and ready lips? This person whose body he could feel underneath his, long and taut and accommodating? This person who was like Ana only different? Whoever she was, he liked her, liked her even more than the other Ana.

'Please may I have sex with you, Ana?' he said.

'You most certainly may,' she said, guiding him on top of her and, as she pulled his face towards hers and put her lips against his, Flint just wanted to punch the air and shout, 'You've come a long way, baby . . .'

34

They set off for Ashford at about eleven o'clock. As they headed across the M25, the sun blazing through the windscreen and turning the leather seats to the consistency of warm flesh, Flint kept his hand on Ana's knee and thanked God for automatic gears. He glanced at her briefly. The air-conditioning was ruffling the fine fringe of baby hair that grew from her hairline and she was smiling serenely. She looked across at him and squeezed his thigh and grinned, pulling a strand of hair off her cheek.

Now, thought Flint, this feels right. This feels really, really right.

Usually when he woke up in a bed with a girl, a little something inside him sort of died. Almost like that feeling you get when you go back to your car and see a ticket on the windscreen. You knew you were parking illegally, you knew there was a good chance this was going to happen, but that space – well – it was just there and you wanted it and you took it anyway. Waking up with Ana had been more akin to leaving his car on a red route and coming back to find someone giving it a full valet and Turtlewax – for free.

Ashford was about twenty miles from the M25. High Cedars was just outside Ashford, on the outskirts of a smart commuter village.

'Wow,' said Ana, as they approached a Jacobean

mansion up a gravel driveway. They drove through ornate stonework gates and grounds planted with cedars and fir trees. 'This looks more like a five-star country-house hotel than a children's home.'

A shiny-faced receptionist wearing a cardigan smiled welcomingly at them as they entered. 'Good afternoon.'

Flint looked at Ana, who looked nervous for a moment, before stepping forward confidently to the desk. 'Good morning,' she said, 'my name is Ana Wills. My sister – well, my half-sister actually – she was related to one of your . . . er, children. To Zander Roper.'

'Oh yes,' she said, 'Mrs Wills – she phoned yesterday, actually.'

'Well, actually, that was me. The thing is you see – Mrs Wills died.'

The receptionist threw her hand over her mouth. 'Oh no,' she said. Her eyes were open in horror and she looked genuinely shocked. 'How?'

'I'm afraid it was suicide.'

'Oh no. But that's terrible. She was such a beautiful woman – such a caring aunt. I can't believe it. Does Zander know?'

Ana shook her head. 'That's why we're here. We thought it would be best for him to hear it from someone who was close to Bee.'

The receptionist asked them to wait while she called a doctor, and then a few minutes later led them through to a large office on the ground floor, where a small Chinese woman with a hairy mole on her cheek greeted them warmly. She was called Dr Chan and she knew all about Belinda Wills, had first met her back in 1997 when she'd come to High Cedars to visit Zander. She was deeply, deeply upset to hear about Bee and even more shocked to hear that it was suicide. 'But – why?' she asked plaintively. Zander and Belinda had, apparently, had some kind of argument about a month ago and he'd refused to see her and speak to her since. They'd tried to get Zander to talk about it in his therapy sessions but he refused to say a word. Which was, according to Dr Chan, entirely in keeping with his personality. He was a 'very difficult child'.

'So – you're Belinda's sister, you say?'

'Half-sister, actually.'

'And Belinda was a half-sister to Jo Roper – Zander's mother. Families really are very complicated these days, aren't they?' Dr Chan smiled and picked up a phone. 'Zander needs to know about this as soon as possible. I'll just find out what he's up to this morning.'

She put down the phone and smiled. 'You're in luck,' she said, 'Zander's in the grounds right now – painting. I'll take you to him.'

They followed Dr Chan through sunlit, wood-panelled corridors, past a gravy-scented dining room where lunch was being prepared and out across landscaped gardens.

'He's down by the pond,' she said, leading them down a concrete pathway into the shade of a small clump of trees. 'I'll leave you to tell Zander the news, but if the situation feels like it's getting in any way out of control, just call out "Nurse" and someone will assist you.'

'What exactly do you mean by "out of control"?' said Ana.

Dr Chan stopped and turned towards them. 'Zander is an orphan. Not just an orphan, but the only member of his

353

family still alive. No brothers, sisters, grandparents. Just Zander. He had a terrible, terrible start to his life, and until Belinda tracked him down, he was truly alone. He was very resistant to Belinda at first, to the idea of having family. But, in his own, unconventional way, he grew very fond of her. She bought a house for him? Did you know that?'

They nodded.

'Yes, they spent most weekends together. And he seemed to be improving month by month. I have no idea what they argued about last month, but I'm sure that Zander imagined it was a temporary situation. He occasionally likes to punish those who try to help him. Keep people on their toes – that's the way he tends to work. But when he learns that she's dead, I really don't think anyone can predict how he'll react. He may take it in his stride. He may be very angry. Just be prepared for anything – OK?'

'OK.' Flint and Ana both nodded.

At the bottom of the path was a lichen-covered pond dotted with lilypads and punctured by weeping-willow tendrils. It was cool and shady. A young man in a wheel-chair sat facing away from them, stirring a paintbrush into a glass jar of minty-green water.

'Zander,' called Dr Chan.

The boy didn't turn round, just carried on stirring his brush in the water and contemplating the view.

'Zander.'

'Yup,' he said wearily, still without turning around.

'Zander – you've got some visitors.'

'Yippee.' He applied his brush to a watercolour tin on his lap.

354

'Sorry about this,' Dr Chan said under her breath, 'it's nothing personal, I can assure you.'

They followed her towards Zander and then stood in front of him. He was a nice-looking boy, maybe a bit small for his age, but with precise features and thick brown hair worn long around his ears and neck and tucked behind his ears. He was wearing a Teenage Fanclub T-shirt, jeans and Reeboks. His eyes, when he looked up at them, were a very pale blue. He fixed them both with the most intense gaze Flint had ever seen.

'What is this?' said Zander, outlining a lilypad on his cartridge paper with a stroke of green paint, 'a giant's convention?'

Ana suddenly snorted. Flint looked at her. She was laughing.

'Sorry,' she said. 'Sorry.'

'Ah,' said Zander, suddenly looking up and straight at Ana, 'at last – a woman who appreciates my puerile sense of humour. Maybe we should get married?'

Ana smiled and blushed.

'Ana,' said Dr Chan, 'is Belinda's half-sister. And Flint here is Ana's friend. He was, is, also a very good friend of Belinda's. There's something they'd like to talk to you about. Would you like to talk to them here or back in your room?'

'I have no interest in talking with anyone, anywhere, about my former "aunt". Thank you very much.'

'Zander,' said Dr Chan, 'I think you'll want to hear what Ana and Flint have to say.'

'Oh, will I? Really. OK, then. Since you seem to know exactly what I want to hear and what I don't want to hear, I presume there's no point in arguing.'

He began wheeling himself towards a bench. 'Sit down,' he said to Flint and Ana, with all the authority of a middle-aged bank manager. He looked at Dr Chan. 'You can leave us now,' he said. Dr Chan tutted and raised her eyebrows. 'Don't forget,' she said, tapping her watch, 'lunch in forty-five minutes,' before putting her hands in the pockets of her white coat, turning on her heel and heading back to the house.

Zander waited until she was out of sight before turning to regard Flint and Ana. 'Right,' he began, 'three things. First of all – who the hell are you two? And don't give me that half-sister bollocks. I've had it up to here with half-baked sisters and half-arsed aunts and second-hand uncles, OK? I know that Bee wasn't my aunt, so you can cut that crap, right now. Secondly – before you say anything about Bee, you should know that there is nothing she could say or that you could say on her behalf that I would want to hear – now, or ever. And thirdly – have either of you two got a fag on you?'

They shrugged and shook their heads.

'Oh well. It was worth asking. So,' he continued, 'is there anything you'd like to say, given what I've just said?' He looked at them glibly.

'Yeah,' said Flint, unable to contain his annoyance with this smug, arrogant young man, wheelchair or no wheelchair. 'Yeah, there is, actually. She's dead.' Ana threw him a look. He hardened his jaw.

Zander smiled momentarily, and Flint wanted to hit him. 'Sorry?' he said, still with that infuriating smirk on his face.

'Bee,' said Flint, 'she's dead.'

The smirk started to fade a bit, and Zander's face contorted itself into a look of disbelief. 'You're kidding, right?'

Flint shook his head.

'But – when? How?' Cracks were appearing in his supercilious demeanour.

'A month ago. 28 July. To be precise.'

'My birthday . . .' He trailed off momentarily, rubbing his chin absent-mindedly with the palm of his hand. He looked up at Flint with those ice-blue eyes. 'What happened?'

'She killed herself.'

Zander flinched and his eyes dropped to the floor. 'How?'

'Pills and alcohol.'

'Shit.'

Silence fell. A cricket chirruped in the background and a breeze ruffled through the weeping-willow fronds.

'Did she leave a note?'

'Nope.'

'So do you – do you know why?' said Zander, eventually.

'No,' said Ana. 'No – it doesn't really make any sense.'

'I do,' he said, his head dropping slightly into his chest.

Flint and Ana glanced at each other.

'What?'

'I know.'

'You know?' said Ana.

'Uh-huh.' He nodded his head, heavily. 'I know exactly why she did it.'

'Why?' demanded Flint.

'Why what? Why do I know or why did she do it?'

'Both, for God's sake,' hissed Flint. 'Both.'

Zander sighed and let his head fall on to his fist. 'Come

upstairs with me,' he said, 'come up to my room. I'll explain everything up there.'

'Here,' said Zander, wheeling himself away from his desk and clutching a thick wodge of purple paper, 'this was from Bee. She posted it to me with my birthday gift. Quite inappropriate I think you'll agree after you've read it.' He passed the purple paper to Ana. 'She sent me this, too.' He handed a sheet of white paper to Flint. It was a will, signed by Bee and witnessed by a Miss Taka Yukomo.

'Who the hell is Taka Yukomo?' said Flint.

Ana shrugged. 'I have no idea.'

'Sushi,' said Flint, clicking his fingers, 'the coroner's report said she ate sushi during her last hours. She must have taken the will down to the restaurant with her that night. Got a waitress to witness it for her. Posted it that night.'

'Yes,' said Ana, 'and Amy said she went out that night, at about nine o'clock. She must have decided to go out for one last meal. On her own . . .' She petered off as she felt tears threatening. What an absolutely tragic thought.

'Your mother's not going to like this, Ana.'

'What?' Ana looked over Flint's shoulder.

According to Bee's will, everything was going to Zander. The cottage. The money in her bank accounts. Her royalty payments. Her books and CDs. The £7,000 hidden under her bed in a cigar box.

'But I visited her solicitor,' said Ana, scanning the page, 'he said she hadn't made a will. That he'd advised her to and she refused. I mean – does this actually have any legal standing without a copy being lodged with her solicitor?'

Flint and Zander shrugged. 'I wouldn't worry about that right now, anyway,' said Zander. 'Read that letter first. Read that letter and then try making sense of things. It's quite rambling – incoherent. A bit of a stream of consciousness, you might say . . .'

Ana perched herself on the edge of Zander's bed and began reading.

28 July 2000

My dearest Zander,

I went to the shops on Tuesday, looking for a birthday present for you. I went into Hampstead. It was a beautiful day. I had lunch at a French café and sat outside on the pavement. I had a bowl of Vichyssoise. It was freshly made. It was delicious. With it I had an iced coffee, served in a glass mug with whipped cream on top. After lunch I went to Gap and bought you the enclosed clothes. I hope you like them. And then I just wandered around for a while, soaking up the sun, people-watching, window-shopping. I bought myself a pair of shoes from Pied à Terre and a dress from Ronit Zilkha.

You're probably wondering why I'm telling you this. Well – there is a reason. It's because now, from the perspective of today, I can see that Tuesday was a turning point in my life. And that wandering around Hampstead High Street that afternoon was the end of an era for me. And if I'd known it at the time, maybe I'd have appreciated it more.

Because – and I don't really expect you to understand this – you may have the intellect and bearing of a man of thirty but you still have the emotional capacity of any sixteen-year-old boy – because about ten minutes after I bought my shoes, I saw Ed. I saw Ed and Tina, and they had their three babies with them. Three tiny new babies in a huge buggy. Tina was adjusting the parasol on their pram and Ed was holding all the baby stuff. And then Ed

359

leaned down into the pram and I saw him smile, a smile of complete and utter adoration. And then they carried on walking and everywhere they went, people smiled at them, complete strangers smiled at them, because they had three perfect, identical babies and the two of them looked so proud and complete.

I was wearing pink-silk capri pants that cost me £140 and a black mesh vest that was £85. My shoes were pink stilettos from LK Bennet. £115. I spent half an hour doing my make-up that morning – the usual slap, you know – black liner, red lips, an inch of foundation. I'd just had my hair done at John Frieda, the day before. That cost me £90. It was pinned up with a big silk rose from Rosie Loves Johnny. £18.

Tina was wearing a pair of baggy leggings and a big vest with a pair of old sandals. Her hair was tied back in a ponytail and she was wearing no make-up. She looked knackered and her gut was enormous.

You can guess who looked the most beautiful.

Something inside me died then, Zander. Not because I felt like it should have been me or because I wanted three babies or anything. I got over Ed a long time ago, as you know, and I'm not the world's most maternal person. But my desire to keep taking the path I've been on for the last fifteen years just evaporated at that moment. The past fifteen years have been all about covering my tracks, patching things up, telling one lie to cover another to cover another to cover another . . . the past fifteen years should have been about building a life, growing, developing, taking whatever fate threw at me. But I haven't been able to do that because every move I've made, every decision I've taken has been about one moment in my life that can never be erased and can, I now realize, never be put right.

I got home that afternoon, and all I wanted to do was curl up into a ball and cry. But Mr Arif was here. In my flat. Just sitting there on my sofa. John got out last week. The porter found him wandering around on the third floor. I went looking for him and I found him at the porter's desk being hand-fed tuna chunks from a can. The porter must have told Mr Arif about him.

Mr Arif went mad. His face went all purple and his eyes were bulging and he was shouting, calling me a cheat and a liar, telling me he should kick me out. He scared me, and I'm a hard person to scare. He made me take John, there and then, in his box, and get rid of him. I took him to the cottage, that afternoon. I spent the night there with him, but at about six in the morning I woke up having a panic attack. For the first time in years. My heart was racing, I was sweating and I thought I was having a heart attack. I could hear noises out in the garden. I was paranoid. I thought I was dying, Zander. I was terrified. So I just threw on some clothes, put John in his box and left. I took the train, left my bike – I was in too much of a state even to get the key in the ignition – and went straight to Lol's. Asked her to have John for a while – which wasn't ideal – she hates cats, but what choice did I have?

I've just spoken to Lol on the phone. John's gone. She left a window open in her flat and he's gone. I'm devastated. It just feels like the end of everything. I know what you'll say – he's just a cat. Just a big old silly old cat. But he was more than that. Much more. I mean – what responsibilities do I actually have, Zander? None – that's right. No children, no mortgage, no job, no family. I'm not even really responsible for you. High Cedars is responsible for you. And come September, you won't need me at all. The only creature on this earth who I had any responsibility for, who needed me, and he's gone. Probably squashed flat somewhere in some dark lonely road. Or stolen. Stolen and sold to some fat woman who'll feed him cream buns and give him a heart attack.

I'm feeling heartbroken, Zander and so, so guilty.

Now that you're moving on with your life, now that you don't need me any more and now that I don't even have John to concern myself with, I can't see the point of lying any more. I've realized something this week – I've had enough. I've had enough of patching over things, of compromising, of living half a life. And in order to stop feeling like this I'm going to have to do something I never ever thought I'd do. Something that will mean the end of you and I. For ever. I'm going to have to tell you about 1986 . . .

35

December 1986

Bee hated this driving-on-the-wrong-side-of-the-road business. Especially in the dark. Especially when she was tired. Especially in a hire car that she'd only been driving for an hour. And especially when there were tears blurring her vision.

She'd landed at Bordeaux airport at nine o'clock and was now heading up eerily quiet Friday-night roads towards her father's house near Angoulême. The small granite towns that stood flush to the road were all deserted, even the occasional strip-lit café or bar was empty.

Gregor had bought his old townhouse about four years ago, had it renovated at great expense and now spent most of his time here. Bee couldn't see the attraction herself. She really wasn't that keen on France: French food, French architecture, the French countryside, French music – or the French themselves, come to that. She preferred Italy. Or Spain. Or Holland. Or anywhere, really, on the European mainland apart from France. Her father had, on the other hand, become a complete Francophile. He could speak fluent French and was a popular figure in his adopted second-home town, where he went everywhere on his pushbike in a beret and neckerchief, stopping just short of the stripy Breton top and the string of garlic around his neck. But there you go – each to their own.

She steered the Panda left into the dirt track that ran down the side of Gregor's house and pulled up behind his 1961 Alvis. All the lights were on in the cottage, and it looked warm and inviting on this cold, black night.

'Hi-ee,' she called, pulling her weekend case from the back seat and heading for the back door. Her father was standing in the kitchen, wearing a striped butcher's apron and stirring something in a huge blue le Creuset casserole pot. He looked at her through the steamed-up windows and his face split open into an enormous grin. He put down his wooden spoon, wiped his hands on his apron and came to the door.

'Hello, darling,' he said, smothering her in a big, fragrant bear-hug. He smelled of cologne and garlic. Bee squeezed him back, her arms barely meeting around his 50-inch chest.

'Hello, Dad.'

'You smell like a cigarette,' he said, grabbing her head and sniffing her crown, 'like a little red Marlboro. When are you going to quit?'

Bee ignored him and dropped her bag and her coat on a red chaise longue. He passed her a huge glass of red wine. 'What's cooking?' she said, kicking off her high heels and padding across terracotta tiles towards the stove.

'Oh,' said Gregor, smiling at her over his wine glass, 'just a little something I've been slaving over for an entire day, that's involved driving to three separate markets and bribing the farmer down the road with a litre of red.'

'There aren't any pig parts in it, are there?' she said, peering over the edge of the pot.

'What?'

'You know – trotters, ears, snouts?'

He laughed his laugh and Bee smiled at him. He was so much more mellow since he'd retired last year and since this place had finally been completed. He'd adored directing but had hated the financial responsibilities involved in his profession, had always borne the pressure to direct a profitable production very heavily. He used to have this air about him of someone who was trying too hard to look relaxed. His smiles had always looked a little glued-on, and his back had given him constant pain. Now he really was relaxed and it was a joy for Bee to behold. He and Joe spent most of their time here in the Dordogne, just shopping, cooking, reading and drinking. At home he went out to eat, saw friends, was on the board of a couple of AIDS charities and another charity for impoverished actors. He was finally, at the age of sixty-one, a truly, serenely happy man.

She looked up at her big bear of a father, at his cheeks all pink with kitchen steam and red wine, his thick salt-and-pepper hair, his wiry beard and his trendy Lacoste sweat-shirt tucked unfashionably into enormous corduroy trousers. He was wearing soft, pastel Burlington-checked socks on his size-eleven feet and his trademark neckerchief around his now-jowly neck. He looked a mess. A big, happy, lovely mess. She felt overcome by a wave of love and affection and planted a kiss on his hot cheek.

'Where's Joe?' She peered around the corner towards the living room. Joe was Gregor's partner of ten years' standing. He was a set designer, fifteen years Gregor's junior. Gregor could have had his pick of ambitious, beautiful, six-packed young actors, but he'd fallen for the slightly geeky-looking set designer, Joe, with his goatee and his little pigeon chest and his sensible lace-up shoes. When Joe and Gregor walked around together they looked like father and ever-so-slightly backward son. But Joe was actually highly intelligent, and he loved all the things that Gregor loved – France, food, people – Bee. He adored Bee, almost worshipped her, in fact. When her first single had come out, he'd spent the entire weekend in the HMV in Kensington High Street forcing complete strangers to buy it. He kept a beautiful scrapbook of every last piece of press and publicity she got, writing to magazines for back issues sometimes if he missed something. Joe was her greatest fan, greater even than Gregor. Bee thought of him as a slightly nerdy but lovely big brother.

'Oh. Joe's not here.'

'Where is he?'

'He's in Angoulême.'

Bee waited for Gregor to elaborate. He and Joe were usually completely inseparable. Bee couldn't actually remember the last time she'd seen one without the other. But Gregor didn't say anything, just started chopping a bunch of something green and leafy.

'Is it me?' she said, jokingly.

'Oh. Nooo. Don't be silly, Bee. No – he, er – he had some unexpected business to attend to.'

'Oh,' said Bee. 'Right.' She resisted the urge to pry any further. There was something untoward going on here. But she'd leave it for now. They could talk about it over dinner.

'So,' he said, going back to his pot, 'what has my little pop star been up to, eh? Fill me in, fill me in . . .'

Bee raised her eyebrows and flopped on to the chaise longue. 'You don't want to know,' she said.

'I most certainly do. I have no life of my own now I'm retired. I have to live vicariously through my daughter. Tell me all your adventures.'

Bee felt her bottom lip start to quiver. Her father was the only person in the world she could do lip-quivering stuff with, the only person she could be herself with. The meeting with Dave Donkin had been on Tuesday and so far she hadn't told anyone. Not Flint, not Lol, nobody, because she'd wanted to wait and tell her father first.

'They're dropping me, Dad,' she sobbed. 'The bastards are dropping me.'

'What?' He spun round.

'Electrogram. They're pulling the plug on the album. They're not renewing my contract. They're dropping me.'

'But . . . but what about your contract, darling? You signed a contract. They can't . . .'

'They can.'

'But surely they're obliged to record and release your album – at the very least.'

'No.' Bee shook her head and blew her nose snottily into the piece of kitchen towel her father had just handed her. 'No. I've been through all this with my solicitor, their solicitor, everyone. They don't have to do anything. It's all legitimate.'

Gregor perched himself gently on the edge of the chaise longue and put his arm around Bee. 'But . . . why?'

'Creative differences.'

'And what the hell does that mean?'

'It means that I want to be a song-writer but my songs aren't "commercial" enough for them, apparently, and as long as I refuse to be a little dolly-bird all dressed up by them and made up by them and singing some rubbish songs by them, they don't want to know . . .'

'Cunts,' said Gregor, squeezing her shoulder and running his hand over her hair. 'What utter cunts . . .'

Bee sniffed and snivelled and sapped up her father's sympathy like blotting paper. She knew that it wasn't all down to Electrogram, and she knew that her father knew it wasn't all down to Electrogram. She knew that both of them knew that she'd been a manipulative, short-sighted control freak and that she'd pushed Electrogram to the very limits of their patience. But they both also knew that now was not the moment for recriminations, that now was the moment for a father to hold his daughter and agree with her that the whole world was a big, fat bastard.

Bee let her head fall into her father's soft, warm shoulder and felt herself relax as his mouth connected with the top of her head in a big plunger-like kiss, almost as if he was trying to suck the hurt out of her and swallow it. She snuggled deeper into his big, comforting frame and felt at least some of the disappointment and deep, burning humiliation of the last few days start to melt away. Life was simple here, under her father's heavy arm, life was bearable, life was sweet.

'You'll get another deal in seconds' – her father clicked his fingers – 'you know that, don't you?'

She sniffed and murmured.

'Once word gets out about this, you'll have every record label in London, in the country queuing round the block to sign you up. You know everything's going to be OK, don't you? You know that you're a star, don't you?'

She sniffed again and murmured again. She didn't want to talk, she just wanted to sit here and listen to her father telling her that everything was going to be OK and that she was a star. He unpeeled himself from her slowly and got to his feet creakily. 'My cassoulet is calling,' he said, padding towards the stove and sprinkling something green on top of the stew before giving it a good stir. 'Hmmmm,' he said, tasting it from the lip of a large wooden spoon. He picked up a bottle of local Bordeaux and splashed it generously into the pot.

Bee held her crumpled tissue between her hands, which hung pathetically between her knees. 'I love you, Dad,' she sniffed.

'I should think so, too.' He winked at her and dropped another handful of green stuff into his stew.

They ate in the kitchen, by candlelight, listening to Ennio Morricone. It had started to rain outside, and heavy bullets of rain battered against the windows. A fire lit in a huge brickwork fireplace spluttered and hissed as raindrops fell down the chimneystack and the flames were ruffled by ghostly gusts of wind.

'So,' said Bee, now that the subject of herself had been fully covered and she felt she'd had enough paternal attention, 'what's the story with Joe?'

Her father got to his feet and collected their empty bowls, brushing breadcrumbs from the vinyl tablecloth with the side of his hand. 'I told you, darling. Something came up.'

'What is this, Dad? A soap opera? You can't get away with saying things like "Something came up" in real life, you know.'

He scraped chicken bones into the bin and sighed.

'What, Dad? What is it?'

He dropped the empty bowls into the sink and turned to look at Bee. He tried to smile but the result was so unconvincing that it made Bee want to cry.

'Oh God. Dad. What is it?' She got to her feet and put her hand on his arm.

He smiled at her again, a strained, apologetic smile. 'He's gone,' he said, patting her hand comfortingly. 'Joe's gone.'

'What do you mean, Joe's gone?'

'I mean – we're finished. It's over.'

Bee almost smiled. The idea of Joe leaving her father was so unlikely it was almost funny. Joe didn't exist without her father. 'But that's the silliest thing I've ever heard.'

Gregor sighed and picked up his wine glass. 'Isn't it just?'

'So, what exactly is going on? I mean – how could this have happened?'

'Oh, darling,' he said, his eyes falling to the floor.

'What! Will you please just tell me what's been going on?'

'I think you should sit down.'

Bee let her hand drop from his arm and lowered herself numbly into a chair. 'So?'

'So – he's been – er – Joe's been having, um, affairs, I suppose you'd call them.'

'Affairs?'

'Yes. Sleeping with other people. Behind my back.'

'But. That's not possible.' Bee found it hard enough to imagine Joe having sex, let alone having sex with nameless strangers behind her father's back. He just wasn't a sex kind of person.

Gregor smiled wryly. 'Oh, darling, I'm afraid it's more than possible.'

'But, who with?' Bee realized she was asking stupid questions, but she was just responding to what seemed to her to be stupid statements.

'Men, darling. He's been sleeping with men.'

'But – men that you know? Or strange men?'

'Strange men.'

'What kind of strange men?'

Gregor sighed and cast his eyes downwards into his wine glass. 'Strange men he meets in public toilets.'

'You mean – he's been *cottaging*?'

Her father nodded.

Bee shuddered. 'That's disgusting,' she said. 'That is *so* disgusting. How long has he been at it?'

'Years, apparently. Years. It's not entirely his fault though, darling. The sex side of things faded out quite a long time ago between Joe and I, particularly with my back troubles and . . .'

'That's not the point, Dad. That is *not* the point. If he was feeling unhappy about things he should have said something, talked to you . . .'

'But that's the thing. He *was* happy. As far as he was concerned it was a perfect compromise. He loves me. He's always loved me. He would never have done anything to hurt me. Which is why he chose to sate his, er, appetite in such an anonymous fashion. He never, ever thought it would impinge on our relationship . . .'

'But you found out. How? How did you find out?'

'Well, that's the thing, darling. That's the very, er, difficult thing.'

'Difficult?'

'Yes. You see, despite taking every precaution, despite being one of the most intelligent, most aware people I know, Joe somehow managed to become – infected.'

Bee's vision clouded for a second and she covered her eyes with her fingers.

'Yes – he got the test results last week. He's HIV positive, darling.'

Bee gulped, painfully, and dragged her fingers from her eyes to her lips.

'And you see, even though we haven't been all that sexually active as a couple over the years, that doesn't mean to say that we haven't had our moments, our occasional moments. And . . .'

'No,' said Bee, through her fingers, 'no . . .'

'Well, yes, darling. It does seem that way. And . . .'

'No . . . no.'

'Yes. But darling, you know as well as I do, they're already making huge advances in medicine and . . .'

'Palliative medicine, Dad. Drugs that make it easier for you to die, not drugs to help you live.'

'No. That's not true. There are developments every day. And I'm in the very earliest stages. I've only been infected for a short while. By the time the virus starts to develop . . .'

'Stop it! Stop it now. I can't listen to this.' She put her hands over her ears.

Gregor pulled them away. 'Everything's going to be all right, my sweet. I promise you. Everything is going to be just dandy.'

'No. It's not. It's not going to be all right. One minute you're a healthy middle-aged man enjoying his retirement and the next you've got AIDS and it's all that bastard's fault. That dirty bastard. He's disgusting. I mean – *cottaging*. In stinky, pissy, shitty toilets. After everything you've done for him. Fed him, clothed him, let him into a world he'd never have been welcome in if it wasn't for you. Given him a life – you gave him life, Dad. I hate him. I hate him.' Bee's face was scarlet and her face was wet with tears. 'I've never, ever hated anyone so much in my life.' Her fists were tight and hard.

'Please. Bee. Don't take this out on Joe. Don't be angry with him. It's not his fault. Blame God. Blame bad luck. Blame poorly constructed condoms. But please don't blame Joe.'

'Oh, but I do. I really, really do. Where is he?'

'Joe?'

'Yes, Joe. Where is he?'

'He's, er . . . he's at the hospital. In Angoulême.'

'What for?'

'You see, he's very, very ill. That's why he had the test. He's not been well for a while. He's had pneumonia.'

'How long has he been there?'

'A couple of weeks. I haven't been able to bring myself to see him yet.'

'But why didn't you tell me before?'

'You didn't ask, did you, my little popstar?' He smiled and rubbed the top of her head.

'But – I thought you said that it was in the early stages?'

'I said I was in the early stages. Not Joe. He's been infected for a couple of years, apparently.'

'Is he going to die?'

Gregor shrugged.

'I hope he does. I hope he dies.'

'Please, darling. Please don't say things like that. Please.'

'I couldn't bear it. If anything happened to you, Dad, I think I'd die. I really, really do.'

Her father reached into his enormous fridge and brought out a large ceramic dish. In it was a creamy-looking confection covered in curly chocolate shavings. He held it towards Bee and smiled.

'Cheesecake, darling?'

Bee woke up at four in the morning, sweating and barely able to breathe. She'd been having a nightmare. Dave Donkin had been straddling her father with a huge syringe in his hand. His face was painted red and he was wearing leather knickers. Her father had been crying and Bee herself had been trapped somehow and unable to do anything to help.

She looked around her as she awoke and couldn't remember where she was for a second. Then she remembered. Her heart started racing. Her neck was damp. She tried to swallow but there was no spit in her mouth. She grabbed a glass. Her hands were shaking. She spilt water all over the top of her duvet. Her heart started beating faster. An image of her father, jaundiced and emaciated, stretched out and wired up across a hospital bed, flashed through her mind. Her heart raced again. She clutched her chest. Another image flashed through her mind, of midnight toilets. She could smell the urine, hear the *drip drip drip* of a leaking pipe, and she could see Joe, skulking around. Squeaky clean Joe. Quiet-life Joe. Joe who she'd known since she was twelve years old. He'd infected the man who'd given him everything. Her father. The kindest, most generous, big-hearted and gentle man that Bee had ever known.

She clutched her chest again as her heart started beating so hard that she could feel it banging against her ribcage. She was going to be all alone. Her father was going to die. A long, painful, protracted death, and then she was going to be all alone. And her career – her career was over. She'd have nothing and nobody. She was going to end up all alone, all alone in a horrible flat somewhere. She'd probably die, too. Die young. And nobody would care. And why should they, she thought, pulling the duvet tightly around her with shaking hands, why should anyone care about her?

Her head filled more and more quickly with thoughts and images. All negative. All black. All telling her that the good times were over. For ever. Life now was going to be about illness and death and failure and poverty. She leapt from her bed and began to pace around the room. She paced and she paced, her head thick with panic. She put her hand over her chest and felt the insistent pounding. She was dying. She knew it. She could barely breathe. She was having a heart attack. Should she wake her father? Wake him? Tell him she was dying? No, she thought, no,

don't disturb Dad, just take deep breaths. Deep . . . deep
. . . breaths. In – and out. In – and out. Her vision started
to blur. Her breath was short and tight. She had no lung
capacity whatsoever. She sat on the edge of her bed. Her
heart was beating so fast now that she couldn't distinguish
individual pulses. Her chest felt like it was going to burst.
The sides of the room turned into a blue-black fuzz, her
body began fizzing like electricity was running through it.
Everything was closing in, everything was just. . . .

'Morning, darling.' Gregor strode into the room, holding
a tray. On it was an individual cafetière, a large blue mug,
three slices of thick-cut toast, a pot of quince jam and a
single fat white rose with pink-marbled petals.

He put it on the table by her bed and then pushed open
the oatmeal curtains.

'Urgh. God. Dad. Do you have to?' Bee opened her
eyes and then immediately forced a pillow over her face.
'What time is it?'

'It's half-past ten.'

Bee sat bolt upright. 'Really?' she said.

'Yes. And it's really a rather beautiful day. Not much
cloud around . . .' He peered upwards through the
window.

Bee felt like she'd been hit over the head with a mallet.

'How are you feeling?'

'Shit. I hardly slept. And I think I' – her thoughts fugged
over as she tried to remember exactly what had happened
last night – 'I think I fainted.'

Her father turned around in alarm. 'Fainted?'

'Yes,' she plunged her cafetière, 'in the middle of the

night. I was . . . worrying about things and then I think I sort of blacked out. I feel terrible.'

'What were you worrying about?'

Bee raised her eyebrows. Typical Dad. Mustn't make a fuss. Let's pretend everything's all right. 'You, you dick-head,' she teased. 'I was worrying about you.' She stirred milk into her coffee and took a sip. She paused before making her next comment. 'I wish I didn't know so much, Dad.'

'What do you mean?'

'About AIDS. I wish I didn't know so much. It makes it worse. All those times you took me to see Geoffrey and Bobby at Westminster. All those guys. Those guys who'd been spinning around to Donna Summer a year before in their satin shirts, without a care in the world. Lying there looking thirty years older than they were, like they were already dead. I wish I hadn't seen them. Maybe it wouldn't seem so real, otherwise . . .'

'Oh, darling. It's not really real, you know. Not yet. Not now.'

Bee clanked her cup down heavily on the bedside table. 'But it *is* real, Dad. It is so unbelievably real. It doesn't get much more real than this.'

Gregor shrugged and picked the rose off the tray. He put it to his nose and sniffed it. His eyes closed and his face lit up with pleasure. 'You know what, though, my sweet. It doesn't feel real. It really doesn't. And I much prefer it that way.'

He put the rose on her lap, smiled at her and quietly left the room.

36

Bee drove to the shops for her father that morning. He'd tried to dissuade her, especially after the fainting incident, but she wanted to get away. Sit somewhere and have a coffee on her own. She had so much to think about.

She eschewed the exotic and enticing *boulangerie, boucherie* and *patisserie* for the *supermarché*, where she wouldn't be required to use her excruciating, schoolgirl French. She picked up a mould-covered cured sausage in a strangulating net and a great hunk of stinky cheese, a jar of murky fish-stock and floury loaves of criss-crossed bread. At the till she pointed at a carton of Marlboros and bought a copy of the English *Times*. She loaded her groceries into the back of her car, took the papers and the cigarettes and found herself a seat in the front window of a small café.

'Un café . . .' she said, her face wrinkling when she realized she couldn't even remember the word for please – *por favor*? *Pourquoi*? She smiled extra politely at the waiter, hoping that this would make up for not saying please and pulled the soft top from her cigarettes. She lit one up and stared through the window for a while. The town was bleakly pretty in the clear December sun. Street lamps were festooned with white Christmas lights, and a layer of glittery encrusted frost lay over everything. A week before

Christmas. Her favourite time of year. Usually. She sighed and pulled the supplement from inside her newspaper. She flipped through it absent-mindedly, half-heartedly. The usual end-of-year line-up. Pages of moody black-and-white photojournalism. A picture of Challenger disintegrating over Cape Canaveral, heartbreaking portraits of Chernobyl victims, a joyful one of a jubilant Desmond Tutu. And then lists.

Who died.

What was hot.

What was not.

Trends. Stars. Films.

Music. The Hits. Aha. Madonna. The Communards. The Housemartens. The Misses. Starship. Nick Berry. The Worst of the Worst. The hits that made us scared to switch on the radio.

She smiled with a satisfying *schadenfreude* at pictures of Dr & the Medics and Nu Shooz and various other one-hit wonders, before turning the page.

And there she was. Oh God. She felt colour flood her face. A huge quarter-page picture of her, looking sulky in a black-satin puff-sleeved jacket with backcombed hair and a red pussybow tied around her neck. It was one of her most hated publicity pictures. The make-up artist had given her all this Siouxsie-Sioux eyeliner and cupid-bow lips, and she just looked . . . she looked like a complete cow, a horrible, hard-nosed bitch-cow. They'd obviously selected it on purpose.

What a difference a year makes [ran the text]. This time

last year Bee Bearhorn was being hailed as the face of new pop, Britain's answer to Madonna, a star in the ascendant. 'Groovin' for London' was a classic pop hit and Bee herself made a more than acceptable popstar. With her striking image and bolshie interview persona she was a pin-up for the boys and a heroine for the girls. And then came 'Space Girl'. It was bad. It was very bad. And just when you thought it couldn't get any worse, along came 'Honey Bee'. A lesson for upstart popstars everywhere. Just because you're pretty and look good in black PVC, doesn't mean you can write songs. Leave it to the professionals, eh? As for Bee – well, since she's just been dropped by her label like the proverbial warm tuber, we can confidently look forward to seeing her in the 'Whatever Happened To's' by the decade's end.

Bee dropped the magazine on the tabletop and felt her eyes fill up with tears. This was too much. This was much, much too much. Her waiter returned with her coffee. She pulled out her purse and grabbed a handful of random coins, letting them drop noisily on to the saucer. *The Times*, she thought in horror. The most popular broadsheet in the country. Her friends read the *Times*. Her fans read the *Times*. Her *mother* read the *Times*. Everybody read the fucking *Times* and now everybody would know. As if it hadn't been humiliating enough having two flop singles in the space of six months, being slagged off in the music press, Woolworths and Our Price sending back crates of 7-inches to Electrogram's distribution centre, being the butt of company jokes. As if just failing in the first place hadn't been bad enough, now this. In a national newspaper.

She stumbled from the café and back to her car. She wanted to go back to her dad's now. She wanted him to tell her that everything was all right. She didn't want to be on her own. She reversed out of her chevron parking-space and started the drive homewards. Tears kept spilling down her cheeks as she drove, and her heart began to race again. She kept thinking of everyone at home, all those people who'd been taking her so seriously a year ago, laughing at her now. Laughing behind her back. Laughing at her spectacular lack of talent. And then she thought of Dave Donkin's face. The way he tried to look like he cared. Like it broke his heart to let her go. Like if it had been down to him . . .

'Bollocks,' she shouted out loud to herself, wiping away tears with the back of her hand, 'big hairy bollocks.'

Mucus trickled from her nostrils and over her lips. She wiped it away. She took deep breaths. Her heart raced and raced and raced. Everything was falling apart. It really was. Falling apart at the seams. And her heart, she thought. There was definitely something wrong with her heart. She put her hand on her chest. It was beating hard, irregularly. She couldn't breathe. She was having a heart attack. She was. She knew it. A heart attack at the age of twenty-two. She was dying. She was going to die. Here. In France. In a Fiat Panda. Jesus. Jesus Christ. She had to get back. She had to get home. To her father. She put her foot on the accelerator and wound down her window. Fresh air. The road started to twist and turn as she drove through wood-land. She heard her tyres squeaking against the tarmac.

She had to get home. She couldn't die here. Not here. Not in a car. All on her own.

She turned a corner, her wheels just gripping the slushy road. She turned another. And then – Jesus – Christ. What . . . a white van was hurtling towards her. A big white van. On the wrong side of the road. It was on the *wrong side of the road*. She hit her horn with the heel of her hand and turned the steering-wheel, violently, 90 degrees. The white van turned, too, and as it veered off the road she came to an abrupt stop about two inches from the trunk of a huge oak-tree. Her head bounced off the windscreen and her breath left her with a jolt as her breasts hit the steering wheel.

For a moment everything was eerily silent. She rubbed at her forehead and then at her ribs. But she was fine. And then, just as she was about to put the car back into gear and carry on, she heard a strange muted thud. And then another one. She twisted her head to look behind her. Clouds of dirt hung in the air. The white van was nowhere to be seen. The sides of the road fell away in a steep incline. No, she thought. No – it couldn't have. She was sure. There would have been more noise. No, she decided, the van was fine, on its way into town. The van was fine.

She put the car into first, took a deep breath and began the journey back to her father's. And it was only as she pulled back into the road and found herself automatically taking the left-hand lane that she realized that the van *hadn't* been driving on the wrong side of the road.

She had.

381

BABY'S MIRACLE ESCAPE AS FAMILY PERISH

A six-month-old child was the only survivor of a tragic road accident which killed four other members of his family yesterday. Two members of the Roper family from Tenterden in Kent and two members of the Wright family from Tunbridge Wells were on their way to a rented farmhouse in the Dordogne region of France, where they were planning to spend the Christmas and New Year holiday together. Their rented minibus came off the road at a sharp turn on a road just outside the town of Ruffec and tumbled more than eighty metres down a rock-and-dirt-covered ravine. Baby Alexander Roper was thrown free of the bus in a child's car seat. His condition today was described as critical.

His parents, Joanne and Rupert Roper, and aunt and uncle Beverly and Tim Wright, were all killed immediately by the explosion, which destroyed the minibus.

French authorities will be launching an inquiry into the accident. No one else is being sought in connection with the incident.

37

A chill ran down Ana's spine and she let the newspaper cutting fall on to the bed.

'Oh my God,' she murmured.

'Fuck,' said Flint, sitting heavily on Zander's bed. He ran his finger through his hair and exhaled loudly. Outside a child screamed with laughter.

Zander looked from Ana to Flint and to Ana again, his face alert with anticipation. But they remained silent, absorbing the full horror of what they'd just read.

'I kept expecting her to call,' said Zander, 'I had it all planned, what I was going to say to her. How I was going to make her feel. I was going to destroy her. Because I knew exactly how to get to her, you know? We had this . . . *connection* – and I knew just how to hurt her. I was going to take what little hope she had left and annihilate it. I was going to tell her I hated her. That she was ugly. And old. That I wanted her to be dead . . .' He petered out pensively. 'But she didn't phone. And after a while I just . . . It doesn't read like a suicide note, does it?' he said urgently. 'I mean – there was no way of knowing from that that she was about to do something so terrible? And even if it had been more explicit, it would have been too late because it didn't get here until the following Monday, so she must have posted it *that day*, you know, that exact day, so . . .'

It fell silent again and Zander looked desperately from one to the other, waiting for some kind of response. But Flint and Ana were still too shocked to speak.

'I was going to forgive her, you know?' Zander said, quietly.

'Really?' said Ana, finally lifting her gaze from the floor.

'Yes.'

'But how? I don't understand how anyone could . . .' She indicated his wheelchair with her eyes.

He sighed and looked up at the ceiling. 'Obviously I've given this one hell of a lot of thought and as time's gone by my view of the situation has become – characteristically, I suppose – rational.'

'But how can you rationalize something so appalling?'

'Look at it like this, Ana. Supposing what happened on that road in France hadn't happened, supposing I'd been able-bodied and brought up amongst a loving family, who's to say that it wouldn't have been me driving a car recklessly somewhere? Who's to say that *I* wouldn't have turned out to be some wild child rebel, stealing cars, speeding around, killing people? There's no way of knowing, and that's what makes it impossible for me to judge Bee. And, to use a cliché, you don't miss what you haven't had. Ironically enough, Bee gave me the only experiences of my life to date that I will ever miss. I had nothing to feel nostalgic about before I met Bee, nothing to look back on, no real history. D'you see? Bee took everything away from me, but because I had no experience of the things that she took, I can only judge her on what she *gave*. And she gave me a lot.'

'Like what?'

'Well – she inspired me, I suppose. She challenged me. And she brought out the *best* in me. I don't generally make it my business to make people happy, but there was something about Bee that just made me want to please her. I liked to see her smile. I liked to see her relax. I liked to make her laugh. I loved being with her. I loved *her* . . .' He cleared his throat and Ana watched a blush spread over his face. 'If it wasn't for Bee – well . . . I'm leaving here in a couple of weeks, did you know?'

'What do you mean, leaving here?'

'I've got a place at St Andrews. To study mathematical science. She insisted that I go.'

'Congratulations!'

He blushed again. 'Yes. Thanks. I just got my A-level results – I got four 'A's, top of my school.' He beamed at them proudly. 'I'll be the youngest student there, which is something of an achievement.'

'Who's going to, you know, look after you?'

'Well – there are three other disabled students at St Andrew's – we'll all be sharing a specially adapted house. There'll be a live-in nurse, but generally I'll be very independent. Oh – and I've got a new wheelchair on order. Seven grands' worth. It should be here next week. It's going to be *wicked*!' He grinned at them and suddenly looked like a sixteen-year-old kid instead of an old man. And then his face fell. He paused and fiddled with the hem of his T-shirt. A tear slipped down the side of his nose. He sniffed and used the bottom of his T-shirt to wipe his cheeks. 'Sorry,' he said, 'I'm sorry. God – how embarrassing.' Ana put a hand on his pale forearm. 'I can't believe she doesn't exist any more. How can Bee not exist?

It doesn't seem possible. Do you believe in heaven, Ana?'

Ana shrugged. 'I'm not sure about heaven as such, but I do sometimes get this strange feeling that people are watching me. You know. Dead people. Not in a spooky, ghostly sort of way, just in a sort of calm way, like I'm in a play and they're in the audience. It's a feeling of not being alone, rather than a belief that we'll all meet up again, one day. If that makes any sense?'

Zander nodded.

'What about you – do you believe in heaven?'

Zander laughed. ''Course not,' he said, 'I'm a scientist. How can I believe in heaven? But I like your "play" analogy. I feel like, if I allow myself to believe that Bee *is* watching me, then she'll continue to exert her positive influence on me. And my family. I can make them proud of me, make something of myself – for them. Yes,' he said, his face brightening slightly, 'Bee could be my "guardian angel" if you like. I like that idea. Thank you, Ana.'

She squeezed his arm again and then slipped her hand into her jeans pocket.

Flint looked at his watch. 'Sorry, mate,' he said, 'we're going to have to push off now – I've got a job at seven.'

'Sure, sure. Of course. I'll come with you to your car, if that's all right?'

As they said their goodbyes in the car park, Zander looked at both of them, warmly and with a hint of embarrassment. 'Could I – could I ask you a favour?'

They nodded.

'Well – if it's agreeable with you, I'd really like to keep in touch with you both. I don't mean like I want to be a big part of your lives, or anything,' he gulped, 'just, you know, the odd phonecall, or, maybe, if you're ever in Scotland . . . do you play golf, Flint?' He addressed Flint properly for the first time since they'd arrived.

Flint nodded. 'Yeah. I do actually.'

'Well – there you go then. The two of you could come up for a golfing weekend. Stay at the Old Course hotel. It's supposed to be very romantic. I could come out with you. We could hire a buggy, or something and then you could come and have a quick drink with me in the union bar . . .' His face had lit up. 'But only if you want to, obviously.'

'Absolutely,' said Ana, 'I definitely want to stay in touch. Really.'

'Well, then maybe we should all swap phone numbers? Then I can let you know what my number's going to be in St Andrews.'

Ana pulled paper and a pen from her rucksack and they all exchanged numbers and then got into the car. Zander wheeled himself over to the passenger door and gestured at Ana to wind down her window. 'The will,' he said, 'we haven't talked about the will.'

'Oh, well, maybe . . .'

'I can sort it out,' he said eagerly, 'I've got a solicitor. He administers my trust. He'll be able to find out if it's binding or not. And if it is – if I *am* getting everything, then I'd really like to, you know, make sure you get something.'

Ana shook her head. 'Don't be silly,' she said, 'Bee wanted you to have everything. For your future. You know.'

'Ana,' he said, 'I don't need Bee's money. I'm *loaded*.'

'Are you?'

'Uh-huh – I'm worth half a million or something.'

'What!'

'Yeah. One of the advantages of being the only surviving member of a resolutely middle-class, professional family with fully paid-up life insurance policies. It's all in trust till I'm twenty-one, but I really don't need Bee's money.'

'Well,' said Ana, feeling uncomfortable with the nature of this conversation, 'I mean. Whatever you want to do. But really, I don't . . .'

Flint revved the car.

'Sorry,' she said, smiling at Zander.

'Yeah, yeah, yeah,' he said, 'you need to get going. The traffic'll be starting to build up now.'

Ana nodded and smiled and wound up her window. She and Flint waved and smiled at a beaming Zander, who waved them off from his wheelchair, long after they'd disappeared from view.

38

Flint and Ana drove together in a kind of numb silence. Of all the places that the rollercoaster journey of the past few days could have taken them, this was the last one either of them could have possibly expected. Ana's brain boggled at the immensity of Bee's confession, at the size of the secret that she'd been hauling around with her for fifteen years. It was unthinkable.

Flint put a hand on her knee and squeezed it. She looked across at him and smiled tightly. She felt like she was in another country, on another planet, in another *universe*. Poor Bee. Her life in stasis. Never being able to move on. Never being able to develop. Never being able to get close to anyone. What must it have been like? Waking up every morning and knowing that there was no way forward. Sixteen years of hopelessness. And not even being able to indulge her hopelessness. Not being able to get pissed and moan about her life with her friends, not being able to go to counselling or buy a self-help book or watch people on chatshows talking about having the same problem as you. No sympathy, no empathy, no outlet for her guilt. Not being able to share it, with anyone.

It was a wonder she'd lasted as long as she had.

'D'you want to come driving with me? Tonight?'

Ana looked at Flint and felt herself melt inside with gratitude. She nodded. 'Yes, please. I really don't think I could handle being on my own tonight with all this stuff in my head.'

'I know exactly what you mean. You can stay at mine, too. If you want. Nothing *untoward*, you know. Just for the company.'

She nodded again, thinking that it was what she wanted more than anything. The way she was feeling right now, she never wanted to leave Flint's side again. And then another thought occurred to her. It was done. It was over. They'd found out why Bee killed herself. There was no reason for her to be in London any more. And the ties that had bound her to Flint for the past few days had disappeared. What happened now? She felt her heart miss a beat with anxiety. She swallowed and put the thought to the back of her mind. She was with him now. She was with him tonight. That was enough for now.

Flint put on some music and Ana retreated into her own thoughts. She fantasized about a world in which her mother had never gone to Gregor's funeral and Bee had never kicked her out and her own relationship with Bee had developed and they'd eventually become friends. And in her fantasy, she and Bee would get very drunk one night and start talking about life and regrets and the past, and Bee would suddenly start crying and Ana would ask her what was the matter. Bee would refuse to tell her, but after a lot of patient coaxing would finally open up and tell her all about what had happened on that road in France. And the two of them would hold each other and cry together – for Zander, for his family, for Gregor and for Bee. And maybe then Bee could have started to move on. Maybe just knowing that someone knew her secret would have made it easier to bear, even if she never told another soul. Maybe then she'd have gone on with her life, resumed her music career, kept her friends, had relationships, found someone to spend her life with, had children, been happy . . .

And then Ana felt herself deflate as she admitted to herself that her fantasy was a load of old cobblers and that nothing in the world could have helped Bee to deal with the guilt of having wiped out an entire family and crippled a baby. Absolutely nothing.

39

The following day Ana got back to Gill's house early in the morning. Gill was out, as usual, and Ana made herself a cup of tea and installed herself in front of Gill's PC. She clicked a switch and the machine whirred into life, and then she peered underneath the desk to find this 'modem' thingy. There was a sort of black box-thing attached. She felt around for a switch, and lots of little red lights started flashing when she pressed it. She presumed that meant that it was on. Ana had used PCs at college, but really only for typing and research and she hadn't so much as touched one since she left. She had absolutely no idea how they functioned or what else they were capable of. It took her another quarter of an hour to work out how to dial up the modem and get online.

She pressed a bar at the top of the screen, looking for a search box, and a big list of website addresses scrolled down in front of her. She clicked on something, randomly, and the screen changed before her eyes. Loud lurid graphics: 'FULL PENETRATION', 'GIRL ON GIRL', 'ASIAN GIRLS', 'SCHOOLGIRLS', 'WET', 'HARD', 'XXXXXXXXXXXXXXXXXXXX-RATED'. Ana went back to the bar with the addresses on it and dropped it down again: 'Trailertrash.com', 'Chazbaps.com', 'Asian-babe.com', 'Hotsex.com'.

Ana smiled at the predictability of it. The woman was

obsessed. Ana had never met a woman before with such a male attitude towards sex. And not even good male, but bad male. Sex without strings. Sex with strangers. Sex only with people who fitted some preordained idea of physical perfection. Sex only when you're pissed. Sex you can't remember the next morning. Sex on screen. *Virtual* sex. It occurred to Ana that Gill really was a very disturbed individual indeed.

Ana found the search box and typed in the name 'Bee Bearhorn'. A list appeared immediately and she whizzed through it. Good God, she thought, there's *millions* of them. She clicked on a few and found herself in obscure Eighties-music sites which only mentioned Bee in passing. But then finally she found it. The site that Zander had told her about. It was still there. 'The Unofficial Bee Bearhorn Website'.

The site was divided into several pages: biography; discography; trivia; photo gallery; guestbook. She clicked on the photos page and then looked in wonder at pages and pages and pages of pictures of Bee. Amazing, she thought. Bee had only been famous for about five minutes but seemed to have spent the entire time being photographed. She clicked on one thumbnail picture and watched it enlarge on the screen. And as it downloaded she looked into Bee's eyes and tried to imagine what might have happened to her if she hadn't been driving on the wrong side of the road that day in 1986, tried to imagine who she'd be and what she'd have done. But there was a hardness behind those eyes, a glint of steel that reminded Ana of exactly the sort of person Bee'd been all those years ago. A bitch. A hard-nosed bitch who got her own way by manipulating people. A heartless woman who wanted only to be the centre of everybody else's universes. A woman just like her mother. And it occurred to Ana that Bee had been on the path to annihilation, in one way or another, ever since she'd first slipped out of the womb and set eyes on her mother. She was never going to be fulfilled, never going to be happy, never going to be successful. Because she'd been born with a self-destruct button implanted in her soul. And Bee had known it, too, she thought, thinking back to her letter to Zander. Even before she'd driven that family off the road, she'd known that she'd end up alone. And dead. From the minute she came into the world, that flat in Baker Street had already been expecting her. And looking into Bee's eyes now, Ana knew that she'd known it, too.

Ana derived a strange sense of calm from the thought that when Bee went out for her last meal of sushi, when she swallowed those pills and alcohol on 28 July, she'd probably been feeling an inexplicable sense of resignation, a sense of inevitability and a sense of everything falling into its correct place.

She thought of others who'd died young, who'd self-destructed. She thought of River Phoenix, Marilyn Monroe, James Dean, Kurt Cobain, Ian Curtis, Michael Hutchence. And she thought about how, as the shock of these people's deaths receded, one was left with the sense that they'd always been destined to die young. It seemed almost *obvious*, in retrospect. And then she realized that there was one huge difference between Bee's death and the deaths of all those other shiny people: they'd been mourned. Venerated in their deaths. Iconicized. Swollen by their tragic departures to beings twice their original sizes. Whereas Bee had had nothing. An inch or two in the *Times*. A funeral with three people. Her departure from this world had actually *shrunk* her, diminished her status. Looking at the screen now, at this website set up in Bee's honour by someone she'd never even met, it occurred to Ana that this Stuart Crosby, who'd sweated over his computer for hours painstakingly building this site, scanning in photographs, writing the text, probably had no idea whatsoever that his idol was dead. And he *should* know. Bee deserved some grief. She clicked on a line that said 'contact' and an e-mail form popped up. Her fingers hovered over the keyboard for a while as she tried to find the right words to express what she wanted to say. And then she started typing.

Dear Stuart,

My name is Ana Wills and I am Bee's sister. I've just been looking at your website and it's really very impressive, particularly your photo gallery. I don't know if you're aware of this or not, but my sister died recently. On 28 July, to be precise. We've just found out that the official cause of death was suicide. We're all very, very upset. Bee was such a vibrant, exciting person, and I don't think any of us were as close to her as we could have, or should have been. But this was due to circumstance rather than a lack of affection or concern. I'm not sure why I'm telling you all this. I suppose it's just that I remember Bee primarily as a star, as a glamorous, famous popstar. And so do you. I didn't really know her as an adult, just as a child. And it's nice to think that there are still people out there who think fondly of Bee. And in fact, what I've discovered during my time here in London, is that an awful lot of people in the world thought fondly of Bee. Loyal people. People who managed to see the best in her no matter how hard she may sometimes have made it. She was an extraordinary person but she died a rather ordinary death. Her funeral's already been and gone so unfortunately there's no way now to celebrate her life. Which is really quite tragic. Anyway – for some reason I just really thought that you should know since you've obviously taken such an interest in her over the years. Maybe you could post the news on your website so that other fans might find out . . . Please feel free to write back if you'd like.

Yours,

Ana Wills

She read through the e-mail and was about to press Send when another thought occurred to her. She quickly highlighted the last few lines of text, deleted them and then rewrote it:

. . .Her funeral's already been and gone and only three people attended. I wasn't even there. No matter what mistakes a person makes in their life, I truly believe that they deserve a better send-off than that, particularly someone like Bee, who was always so happy to be in the limelight. So I've decided that I'm going to organize a proper wake for Bee. If you can have a wake after someone's been buried for over a week, that is. But anyway – I'm going to organize something worthy of Bee and I'm going to invite all the people who weren't there three weeks ago. And I'd really like it if you came. And anyone else you know who loved Bee. Anyone who wants to celebrate her life. I haven't decided what I'm going to do yet, but watch this space and I'll let you know.

As Ana typed faster and faster her mind started buzzing with thoughts and ideas. She was going to throw a party Bee would have been proud of.

40

Ana covered one ear to block out the deafening racket of a road drill and shouted into the crackly entryphone. 'Hi, Mrs Tilly-Loubelle. This is Ana. Bee's sister.'

'Ana! How marvellous. You came back! Do come in.'

Ana took the lift up to the third floor and felt a shiver of recognition. This is where it had all started on Thursday, just under a week ago. It felt to Ana like she'd been a completely different person then.

It seemed to take about half an hour for Mrs Tilly-Loubelle to undo all the locks and chains on her door. She finally greeted Ana in a fug of talcumy confusion, with the ever present Freddie clutched tightly to her chest. She looked chic in a black polo-neck and blue trousers, and was wearing large gold earrings and a slick of coral lipstick. Radio 3 played in the background.

'Ana,' she beamed with porcelain teeth, 'how wonderful to see you again so soon. Though I presume you're not here to see me?' She smiled at her knowingly.

'Of course I am,' Ana said, wondering what on earth she was talking about.

She held the door open for Ana to enter.

'Gosh,' said Ana, 'what a beautiful flat.' It was exactly the same as Bee's old flat next door, but exquisitely furnished with unusual antiques, expensive curtains, engraved mirrors and gilt-framed paintings.

'Bit crammed I always think. I moved here from a seven-bedroom house in Paris, you see. I sold a lot of things, but couldn't bear to part with most of it. But anyway – you've not come to look at my soft furnishings, have you? Now, where is he?'

Mrs Tilly-Loubelle bent down and began making kissy-kissy noises.

'He's over here,' said Ana, pointing at Freddie, who was now stretched out and snoring gently, where Amy had put him down, on a green-velvet footstool.

'No, no. Not him. The other one. *Here boy.*' She began moving cushions out of the way and peering behind things. 'I don't know,' she said, straightening up and smiling at Ana, 'he's hiding again. I think he's a little bit traumatized. But then who can blame him? Why don't you have a little look for him, and I'll make us some tea?'

'Have a little look for *who*?' Ana was starting to worry slightly about Amy now. And she'd seemed so *sane* last week.

'Why, John, of course.'

'John?'

'Yes.'

'John the cat?'

'Yes, dear.' Now Amy was looking at Ana with concern.

'But, Amy – John doesn't live here.'

'No – not usually. But I didn't know what else to do with him. It's just the most wonderful luck that you found out about him. Who told you? Was it Mr Whitman? He found him, you know. Wandering around out the back, picking titbits out of bins, if you please. Barely recognized the poor mite at first. He was so thin. But . . .'

398

'Sorry? Amy? Are you saying that John is *here*?'

'Why yes, of course. We found him a couple of days ago.'

'John?'

'Yes – John – aaah, there he is.' She beamed and walked towards a door on the far side of the room. 'Hello, my lovely – and look who's here to see you. It's your Auntie Ana.'

Ana put down her rucksack and started walking towards where Amy stood.

'Careful,' she said, 'go gentle. He's very nervous.'

Ana peered round the corner of a shiny round table laden with silver-framed photos. And there, in the corner of the room, crouched down with his front paws tucked tightly in towards his body and his eyes wide open in terror, sat the most beautiful cat Ana had ever seen in her life. He was huge and cobby with a big square face, thick silver-blue fur and bright copper-orange eyes.

'Hello, beautiful,' she said, moving towards him very slowly with one hand outstretched. His ears flattened against his large skull and he backed himself further into the corner.

'It's all right, little one – I'm not going to hurt you.'

'Goodness only knows what the poor mite's been through these last few weeks. He must have run away when Bee went, with the shock of it. I should imagine he's been down there, in amongst the bins, ever since.'

'No,' said Ana, 'Mr Arif made Bee get rid of him. He was staying with a friend of hers and he escaped through a window. About three weeks ago.'

'And this friend was living where?'

'Ladbroke Grove.'

Amy looked startled and put a hand to her polo-necked chest. 'But that's nearly three miles away. You mean to tell me that this little man found his own way all the way from there to here? On his own?'

Ana put her finger a few inches from John's nose. He ignored it at first, but then tentatively stretched his head forward and took a little sniff. 'It certainly looks that way.'

'My goodness,' said Amy, 'that really is quite incredible. What intrepidity. What pluck. What *spunk*! He's a real hero.'

Ana gently moved her finger across the cat's cheek and gave him a little tickle. He closed his eyes and started purring.

'He was in a terrible state when Mr Whitman found him. Filthy and half-starved. I took him to the vet yesterday and they gave him a clean bill of health. He had a few scratches and scrapes, and he's somewhat underweight but apart from that he's in the *pink* of feline health.'

'I can't believe he's here,' said Ana in wonder, stroking his chin. 'He's so beautiful.' And he really was. It wasn't just his physical appearance – there really was something special about him. Ana could immediately understand why her sister had been so devoted to him. And then she felt a tear start to work its way out of her left eye as she thought of Bee's note and her guilt and sadness about losing John, and imagined Bee's face now if she were to walk into the room and see John here, John who squeezed through a four-inch gap in a window and walked three miles across London to find her.

'I'd been trying to get in touch with you, you know. Frantically. I even phoned the obscene Mr Arif but he was supremely unhelpful. How did Mr Whitman manage to track you down?'

Ana looked at her in surprise. 'He didn't.'

'So – how did you know?'

'I didn't.'

'Then what are you doing here?'

'I just came to see you. I didn't have a phone number for you and I wanted to talk to you about something.'

Amy's face pinkened with pleasure. 'Really,' she said, 'you wanted to talk to me?'

'Yes. I've . . .'

Amy put out a hand up to stop her. 'Tea,' she said, 'let me get some tea first. Then we can have a nice chat.'

Ana curled herself up in a ball on the floor and talked to John while Amy rattled around in the kitchen. He was more relaxed now and rolled over on to his back and mewed at her. 'What?' said Ana, 'what d'you want?' She put a hand on to his big fluffy tummy and rubbed it. And then he straightened himself out and gave himself a quick hard scratch behind the ears before climbing up on to Ana's lap and settling himself down for a snooze. Ana picked him up gently and took him to the sofa. She sniffed the top of his head while she carried him. He smelled of fresh air.

'Good Lord,' said Amy, coming back into the room with a tea tray, 'will you look at that? He's barely moved from that corner since I brought him back from the vet and now look at him. He must sense it,' she said, 'sense your relationship to Bee. Milk? Sugar?'

Ana rubbed John's neck and chin as Amy poured tea, and he purred loud and hard. 'So – what can I do for you?' She passed Ana a minuscule tea cup of bone china so thin it felt like fibreglass.

'Well, we've had the coroner's report back, on Bee, and it's official, I'm afraid. Suicide.'

Amy gasped and clutched her chest.

'And, we – me and Bee's friend – well, we've found out why. Something really traumatic happened to her – about fifteen years ago.'

'Traumatic?'

'Yes. I'd rather not say what it was, but it explains everything. And the thing is, now that everything's final, I just really wanted to do something. Something special for Bee. And I know she'd think that she didn't deserve it. But it seems that everyone else – even those she hurt – feels she deserves it. So I wanted to organize a wake. A funeral. For Bee. You know, a proper funeral, with music and people and wine and tears. Because, did you know, there were only three people at her real funeral? Three.'

'How awful.'

'Isn't it? So. Would you come? If I organized it?'

'What a good idea. Of course I'd come. Will there be lots of young men there, d'you think?'

Ana smiled at her. 'Yeah,' she said, 'actually there probably will be.'

'Well then – count me in. What are you planning?'

'I'm not sure really – I was hoping that maybe you could give me some advice? You must have been to loads of funerals. Oh – sorry, I didn't mean . . .'

'Oh, don't be embarrassed. Ana. You're right. I've been

to more funerals than I'd like to consider. And they're all different, you know. Each one unique. But Bee – well, hers would be something *very* special. Very special indeed.'

They chatted until early afternoon, when Ana looked at her watch and realized it was time to go if she was going to get anything done that day. She gently heaved the still-slumbering John from her lap and let him flop on to the sofa where he stretched himself out, made a funny little noise and then slipped back into sleep. 'What are we going to do about him?' Ana asked.

'Well,' said Amy, smiling brightly, 'don't you think that John might be rather happy in Devon? Maybe you could adopt him, take him back home?'

Ana's face fell. The thought of home just made her want to give up living altogether. Made her break out in a cold sweat. Made her – oh my God – made her feel exactly how Bee had always said she felt about going back home after she had come to live in London. She gulped and shook her head. 'Well,' she said, 'I haven't really decided anything, yet. Would it be all right just to leave him with you until the funeral, until I can decide what I'm going to do?'

Amy looked at her playfully. 'You've no intention of going home, have you?'

Ana looked startled. 'Of course I have,' she began, 'I just . . .'

'Oh come on now, you can't fool me. I can tell you've given your heart to this city, haven't you? You're not going home now. You've come too far.'

'What do you mean?'

'I mean, last time I saw you you were on a daytrip. You had that mentality. All dressed up in your sister's clothes. Drinking champagne. Playing out a role. But now you're a person in your own right, aren't you?'

Ana's stomach flipped over and a blush crept up her face. Amy was right. She *was* a person in her own right. For the first time in her life, Ana felt as if she had an identity. Her own identity. Nothing to do with her mum or Bee or Hugh. But to do with her. Ana Wills. She beamed at Amy and got to her feet.

'Well,' said Amy, heading towards the front door, 'I really hope you'll be able to persuade your poor mother to conquer her terrible fears and make it to the funeral. It would be a tragedy if she missed it. And you know, I think it would be more harmful for her in the long term if she didn't make the trip.' She looked poignantly at Ana.

Ana felt her breath catch. She hadn't even *considered* her mother. But Amy was right. She couldn't plan an event like this without trying her hardest to get her mother to attend. It was another chapter in Bee's damaged lifestory that needed closing. She nodded. 'I'm going to see what I can do,' she said.

Amy smiled. 'Good,' she said, 'that's very good. Now. You've got my telephone number. Just call if you need anything. And I have yours and will be in touch. Say goodbye to your Auntie Ana, John.' She turned to address the snoozing cat, who flicked his tail at her. She smiled. 'I must admit, I'm not really much of a one for cats. But he really is a particular delight, isn't he?'

They both turned then and regarded the cat, who studiously ignored them. And then Amy unlocked her many locks and unchained her many chains, and Ana kissed her on her floury cheek, before heading back home to complete the next part of her plans.

41

'I want to come with you.'

'What?'

'To Devon. Let me come with you. I can drive you there. And I'm good with mothers.'

Ana's breath caught. The thought of going back to Devon was worrying enough, but going back with a *man*? It was close to unthinkable. 'Honestly, Flint. I'll be fine.'

'But honestly, Ana – I insist.' He smiled at her and twisted her hand over into an armlock.

'Are you threatening me with physical violence?'

'Yeah,' he said.

'Are you being a big, fat bully?'

'Yeah,' he said.

'Why?'

'Because,' he said, 'I'm really scared that if you go home on your own, your mother will persuade you that you're a pointless piece of pond-scum again and that you'll lock yourself in your bedroom and never come back.'

'And who's to say that I don't *want* to lock myself in my bedroom, eh? Maybe I was *happy* being pond-scum?' She smiled and grabbed hold of his arm and began twisting it.

'Well, if that's the case then you can get the train. But I know it's not the case. And I know you're really scared about going home. And I know that, actually, you'll feel much better about the whole thing if I'm there with you.

And, besides, I've always wanted to have a little chat with your mother . . .'

'But what about work? Surely you'll be too busy . . .'

Flint shrugged and let go of Ana's arm. 'I've got another airport run tomorrow morning, but I'll be finished by midday. We'll be in Devon by teatime. Oooh,' he said, smiling, 'd'you think your mum will do a cream tea for us?'

Ana traced a fingertip over the smooth skin on the underside of Flint's arm and smiled. 'Yes. Without a doubt.'

'Well, then – I'm coming whether you like it or not.'

Ana smiled at him. 'What – *again*?' She got to her knees and straddled him.

He grinned at her lopsidedly and put his hands on her naked hips. 'Yeah,' he said, 'again. And whether you like it or not.'

As they pulled up on the pavement outside Gay's house, Flint felt a shiver go through him. For so many years, ever since he'd first met Bee, the concept of the house on Main Street had had this mythical, almost Amityville quality about it. The house where Bee had been miserable. The house where soft furnishings were treated with more respect than children and husbands. The House Where Gay Lived. In his mind's eye it had yellowish windows, a full moon hanging above it and a wooden gate that creaked back and forth in a perpetual ghostly wind. In his mind's eye it was 25 Cromwell Street meets the House That Bled To Death. In reality, it was a very smart, flat-fronted townhouse with a shiny red door, sash windows framing expensive-looking swagged curtains and windowboxes full of tumbling ivy and tiny topiaries.

'You all right?' He turned to Ana and squeezed her hand.

She exhaled and nodded. 'I can't believe it's only been a week,' she said. 'I feel like I've been away for ever.'

He squeezed her hand again. 'Ready?'

'Uh-huh.'

Flint straightened his tie – he was still wearing his chauffeur's uniform – and helped Ana out of the car. A middle-aged couple strolling past eating chips eyed them up and down with unashamed curiosity. 'Hello, Anabella,' they said.

'Hello Anne, hello Roy,' said Ana, hitting them with an impressively fake smile.

'How's your mother?'

'Oh – she's not too bad. I think.'

They tutted and shook their heads. 'That poor, poor woman,' said Anne.

'She's in our prayers, Anabella. Do tell her,' said Roy.

Ana nodded at them, and they nodded at her and looked at Flint before going on their way, leaving an aroma of chip fat and vinegar in their wake.

'Christians,' Ana whispered in Flint's ear.

Flint nodded.

It took a while for Gay to come for the door, but eventually they heard the sound of locks being opened and then, a few seconds later, Gay's face appeared through a crack in the door.

'Yes.'

'Mum – it's me.'

'Who?'

'Ana. Anabella.'

The crack in the door opened a bit wider. 'Oh.'

Gay looked smaller than Flint remembered, and much older. But she still had all that jet-black hair pinned haphazardly all over her head and those soulful lilac eyes lined with smudged black kohl.

'And who's this?'

'This is Flint, Mum – he's a friend of Bee's.'

Flint prodded her in the waist.

'And of mine,' she smiled.

'Hi, Mrs Wills – we've met, actually, once before . . .'

Gay stared at him intently and interrupted him. 'You're very tall. You remind me of Gregor. Come in.'

She hurried them in and pulled the door closed behind them very loudly and very quickly. Flint noticed that she was having trouble catching her breath. She headed straight for the living room and collapsed on the sofa, with one tiny hand clutching her chest.

'So,' she said, turning to Ana, 'how nice of you to come home, finally. Can you imagine? Can you even *begin* to imagine what I've been going through for the last week? Can you?' Her voice was quavering and weak.

'Yes. I can actually. I can imagine every last horrific second of it.'

Gay looked thrown. 'Well, then – *why*? Why did you do this to me?'

'Because I hate you, that's why. Because I wanted you to *starve* to death.'

'Oh Anabella, you know I don't appreciate your sarcasm.'

'Who said I was being sarcastic?' Ana murmured, under her breath.

Flint still hadn't been invited to sit down so he hovered hopefully in the background, waiting for someone to suggest a cup of tea and maybe a scone or two.

'So – Hugh tells me you've been living with a pair of lesbians?'

Ana laughed out loud and Flint stifled a grin. 'Sorry?' she said, bemusedly.

'He says you're living in a very small house with two lesbians. In a *ghetto*.'

'A ghetto?'

'Yes. He wasn't at all impressed by the locale. He said it was very dirty and very menacing and there were large numbers of *black* people. Everywhere, apparently.'

Ana raised her eyebrows and dropped her rucksack on a sofa. 'Mum,' she said with her hands on her hips, 'you are *horrendous*. And I can absolutely assure you that neither Gill nor Di is even vaguely lesbian. Quite the opposite in fact.'

Gay clutched her heart. 'Please, Ana,' she wheezed, 'my nerves. Please don't exacerbate my nerves.' She pulled herself to her feet. 'I'll make some tea.'

She eyed Flint up and down as she passed him, as if she'd only just realized he was there. She smiled. 'Oh, how rude of me. Sit down, Clint. Please.' She patted a cushion and Flint saw her pull in her stomach and push her shoulders back. She put a hand to her hair before making her way elegantly towards the kitchen. Flint and Ana looked at each other and flopped on to a sofa.

'Isn't she vile?' said Ana.

Flint shrugged. 'She's ill, Ana. Give her some slack.'

Ana shrugged. 'Just because she's already flirting with you. She's a man's woman, you see. Just like Bee.'

'Women don't like men's women, do they?'

Ana shook her head. 'They're the worst.'

'*Do you like Earl Grey, Clint?*' Gay chimed girlishly from the kitchen.

'Yes, please, Mrs Wills. Thank you.'

'Please, call me Gay.'

She emerged a minute later carrying a tray laden with scones, clotted cream, jam, slim mugs, an antique teapot with gold-leaf flowers painted on it, linen napkins, crested silver cutlery and a small saucer of Belgian truffles.

'Where d'you get this lot?' asked Ana, accusingly.

'Well, darling, you didn't expect me just to sit here like Miss Havisham, growing cobwebs and starving to death while you gallivanted around London, did you?'

'Yes – I did actually. The way you carry on . . .'

'Mr Redwood has been his usual indispensable, chivalrous self and has been shopping for me every day.'

Flint threw Ana an 'I Told You So' look.

'But of course, I can't depend on his generosity for ever. It's the responsibility of the family, really, isn't it, when someone is unwell?'

'Yes, Mum, that's right. Like we were there for Bee when she needed us. When she was ill.'

'Ill?' Gay suspended the teapot over a strainer.

'Yes. Ill. Depressed. Suffering from post-traumatic-stress syndrome. For years. And where were we?'

'Oh, for goodness' sake – Bee wasn't *depressed*. What on earth would she have had to be depressed about? She had everything, everything that a woman could possibly dream of.'

'Like what?'

'Talent. Looks. Money. The adoration of strangers.'

'She had looks, Mum. She had money. She had absolutely nothing else. Take it from me. I've seen her life. Why d'you think she *killed* herself?'

Gay flinched.

'Mum – why didn't you tell me the real reason that you fell out with Bee? Why didn't you tell me?'

'I don't know what you're talking about.' Gay slid a scone on to a plate and passed it to Flint.

'Oh, for God's sake. Stop being so obtuse.' Ana pointed at Flint. 'Do you think I haven't been talking to people who were at Gregor's funeral? People who heard the way you spoke to Gregor's friend?'

'A complete overreaction,' she sniffed, 'ridiculous. It was ridiculous. Bloody poofs . . .' She trailed off and turned her mouth down into a sourpuss frown.

'Mum – you accused Gregor's friends of *killing* him. At his funeral. How can you say that they were overreacting?'

'Well. I was grieving. I was in shock. Belinda still had no right to throw me out like that. Humiliate me, in front of everyone.'

'Gay,' began Flint, trepidatiously, 'er – I was there. And I have to say that I don't think that Bee overreacted in the slightest. I think you deserved to be humiliated, quite frankly.'

Gay's face rearranged itself dramatically from browbeaten frown to icy shock before rapidly reassembling itself into a mask of feminine delight. She smiled at him. 'What do you mean, you were there?'

'I mean, I was at Gregor's funeral. I saw everything.'

'But how? Who on earth invited you?'

'Bee did. Bee invited me.'

'Well – I can't think why.'

'I was her friend, Gay.'

'Really,' she beamed, her voice laden with innuendo. 'Well, Clint. I'm sure you were Belinda's friend, but, and please don't think me rude to say so, but this is a family affair, as it were, and if you don't mind . . .'

Flint had long suffered from an innate compulsion to speak the truth when he felt that others were avoiding it. This trait had got him into trouble on more than a few occasions, but it still didn't stop him. Flint attributed half the world's problems to pleasant people pussyfooting around unpleasant people. And looking at Gay now, he saw a woman who'd been spoiled rotten all her life, who'd been refused nothing, who'd been pampered and preened and protected from the truth at all costs. Flint remembered Bee explaining to him why she hadn't gone to Bill's funeral – because she was scared she'd speak the truth. Flint had tried to reason with her at the time, but Bee had told him he was wrong, now wasn't the time – not while her mother was grieving. And meanwhile, Gay had been allowed to spend another year spreading poison, damaging her children and becoming more and more unhappy. He took a deep breath and moved in towards Gay, establishing a firm line of eye contact with her and taking one of her cold bony hands in his own. She looked shocked.

'Gay,' he said, in a measured, soothing voice, 'I knew Bee

for fifteen years. That's longer than I've known anyone I'm not related to. And in a way, she *was* family. So in a way, so is Ana and so are you. And I know there were lots of things that Bee wanted to say to you over the years. But she was too scared to say them. Well – I'm not scared, Gay. So I'm going to say them to you.

'You drove Bee away from home. You cut her off from Ana. And then you made sure that Bee would never contemplate coming anywhere near you again. You treated Gregor appallingly. You treated Bill appallingly. You manipulate people, and if you can't manipulate them you destroy them. I understand that you're not entirely healthy. I know about your agoraphobia and I'm sure life isn't particularly easy for you. But you can't expect everyone else to make all the effort. You can't expect your twenty-five-year-old daughter to give up her life for you. You missed Bee's *funeral*, Gay. Your own daughter. Because you weren't prepared to work through your problems. Now – the reason that Ana and I are here today is that we've learned a lot about Bee's life over the past few days, and actually it was a very bleak, very lonely life, and we've decided to give Bee a proper farewell. We're organizing a party for her and we want you to come. Even if that means you going through hell to get there. Literally. You don't even need to go on public transport. I've got a limousine outside. You can go straight from your front door and into my car. I can take you now. Or I can come back and get you. But you *are* coming. No matter how much it hurts . . . You owe it to Bee.'

Flint stopped and bumped his eye contact with Gay up a notch. Her eyes bored into his. For a second the silence in the room was overpowering. And then Flint yelled out as he felt a searing, burning pain in the palm of his hand. He snatched his hand away from Gay's, and she immediately leaped to her feet and strode into the kitchen. Flint looked down at the palm of his hand. '*Fuck*! Fucking *bitch*!' Blood was seeping from four half-moon cuts in his skin. Gay appeared in the doorway, wiping her hands on a sheet of kitchen towel. 'Get out of my house,' she said in a dead voice.

'Mum!' Ana leapt to her feet.

'And you,' she said, turning to look at Ana. 'Both of you. Get out of my house now.' She screwed the tissue into a ball and brushed a loose wisp of hair out of her eyes. Her hands were shaking. Ana walked towards her. 'Mum, listen to him. *Please*. He's right. You're damaging yourself. If you don't come and say goodbye to Bee you're just going to get iller and iller. I'll help you. I will. I'll do whatever you want. I'll . . .'

'Please. I beg of you. Get out of my house now.' Gay's voice quavered, but she wasn't about to cry.

'No,' said Ana, 'I'm not going anywhere. Not until you've agreed to at least think about coming to London . . .'

'*Get out!*' Gay screamed, and her face fell apart into a mass of ugly, angry lines. '*Get out now!*'

Flint nodded at Ana and got to his feet. Ana stopped and stared at her mother, whose chest was rising and falling. Then Ana picked up her rucksack and she and Flint left the house, letting the door slam loudly behind them.

42

Saturday 2 September 2000

It was a stunningly beautiful day. No cloud around and just the right temperature. Ana adjusted the straps on her new dress and smoothed a crease out of the hem. She'd been shopping last week. In a moment of guilt she'd phoned Zander last week and told him about the £7,000 that she'd found under Bee's bed – that was legally his. And try as she might to persuade him to let her give it to him, he'd refused. He'd insisted that she keep it to set herself up in London. So, last week she'd deposited the cash into her bank account and then spent nearly £500 of it on clothes. She'd never spent more than fifty quid a time on clothes before in her life. But Lol had insisted. And she'd had little choice. She had no clothes and now that it was becoming increasingly obvious that she was never going home again, she needed them. Lol had taken her out shopping in Kensington and Notting Hill, whisking her in and out of quirky boutiques down sideroads, where the staff all knew her by name and welcomed her like an old friend. She'd bought new jeans, three pairs of shoes – one with heels – a few funky T-shirts and this dress. £125. For a dress. Lol had almost had to hit her to get her to part with the cash. But it was so pretty and so *her*. Black silk, straight up and down, a split at the back and sprinkled with black sequins.

That evening she'd gone out with Lol and the famous Keith, who was finally home from his Cornish exile. He was fifty years old. And almost completely bald. With rather a large paunch. And three grown-up daughters. All of which Ana had found quite surprising. When Lol had said he was a Romany, a clichéd image of oily olive skin and thick black hair had immediately come to mind. But he was cool and funny and completely besotted with Lol, and Ana had liked him enormously. Flint had arrived at the bar at eleven o'clock to pick her up after a job and Lol's face had been an absolute picture.

'No,' she'd exclaimed, when Flint had gone to the bar to get some drinks, 'please. Tell me it's not so.'

'What?' Ana said, obtusely.

'You. And Flint. You haven't . . . ?'

'Haven't what?'

'Oh. Jesus. You have, haven't you? You've let him have his wicked way with you?'

Ana flushed and Lol screeched.

'After everything I told you. After all those warnings. And you *still* fell for it.'

'I did not fall for anything,' Ana defended herself, 'I just wanted . . . I just needed . . . I just . . . it just happened. And it's good. It's really good. He's lovely.'

Lol rolled her eyes. 'Yes,' she hissed, 'that's exactly what I told you you'd think.'

'Look. Flint and me. I really think it's . . . different . . .'

Lol covered her eyes with her hands and wailed. 'Oh God. Help me. Help me someone. I can't bear it.'

And then Flint had come back with the drinks and sat next to Ana, and he'd run his hand over her hair and smiled at her and kissed the end of her nose and squeezed her knee, and Lol had made all sorts of extraordinary facial expressions until Ana went to the toilet a few minutes later. When she got back, Flint was checking his car and Lol had grabbed Ana's hand and said, I've never seen anything like it. That man is in *lurve*. And Ana had blushed and said, Don't be so ridiculous, and Lol had shaken her head and said, *Never*, I have never seen that man so excited to be with someone. And he could not stop smiling while you were in the loo. Kept looking over his shoulder. And grinning. What the *hell* have you done to him?

Lol's words had worked their way into her stomach and swished around and made her feel almost faint with joy. Because Lol was just confirming what she already knew. There *was* something special going on here with Flint. Something natural and real and *inevitable*. She felt totally and utterly secure with Flint, never doubted his intentions, never analysed his words for hidden meanings, just accepted him exactly as he seemed. And he did everything right. He didn't come on too strong. And he didn't play it too cool. He did just enough to make her feel loved, protected, respected and admired, without ever making her feel trapped or tricked or vulnerable or cruel.

Ana thought about Lol's words now, as Flint's car pulled up to the entrance of Kensal Rise Cemetery, and a smile played on her lips. She turned to Flint and beamed and he beamed back at her. In the back of the car were Lol and Keith, Gill, Di and Amy, who'd brought Freddie in a specially bought black velvet coat.

Flint brought the car to a halt in the car park and everyone piled out. Father Anthony, the smiley and pink-cheeked vicar who was going to carry out the memorial ceremony, greeted Ana near the entrance to the crematorium with a bone-crushingly firm handshake.

'Well,' he said, 'you've certainly chosen a lovely day for it.' He looked upwards at the sky as if he was half-expecting to see God himself giving him the thumbs-up from a cloud. Ana introduced Anthony to everyone, and then they began the walk towards Bee's grave.

'A lot of the attendees are already here,' he said, rubbing his hands together, 'but we won't start until everyone's arrived. We've still got a few minutes.'

Ana caught her breath. She suddenly felt very responsible. She'd never really organized anything before, not even a house party. Her mother had been the queen of organization when Ana was growing up and then, when she'd left home, Hugh had always looked after all their social arrangements. He'd made all the phonecalls, planned the menus, sent out the invites. All she'd had to worry about was trying to think of something to say to Hugh's intellectual friends that wouldn't make her sound retarded and then doing the washing-up afterwards. But in the space of the last week she'd exchanged e-mails with Stuart Crosby, who'd put a notice up on his website with details. She'd organized for Zander to come to London with Dr Chan. And she'd invited Ed. She'd phoned him at his office, and he'd said no at first. He'd cut off all links with Bee for the sake of his family and he didn't want to take any risks. But then he'd phoned back the next day and said he'd been thinking about it and decided that he owed Bee a last goodbye and that his wife and babies were spending that night with her mother anyway, so he'd be able to come.

Having sorted out the guest list she'd then had to decide on the blessing with Father Anthony and plan for the party afterwards, which, after many hours of heated discussion between her, Flint and Lol, was to be held at Bee's favourite pub in Belsize Park, just next to where her old flat had been. Ana had spent that morning at the pub with Flint and Lol, decorating the function room upstairs with posters of Bee and lots of black and yellow balloons. She'd been in touch with caterers, and Lol had put a band together for her so she'd had to hire sound equipment, too, as well as writing a speech.

The outlines of a small group of people emerged as they neared the grave – men and women of varying ages and appearances. Ana caught her breath when she saw the outline of a small woman with black hair – she'd sent Gay an invitation last week and even though she knew it was highly unlikely, a small part of her was still hoping that she might be here. The woman turned round and Ana felt slightly deflated when it wasn't her mother.

She didn't recognize any of the other people by the grave so presumed they were fans. Bee's fans.

'Hi,' she said, as she approached them, 'I'm Ana. Thank you all so much for coming.' They all turned to smile at her and Ana saw something in their eyes as they looked at her that made her stomach lurch. Awe. They were in awe of her. They thought she was something special because she was Bee's sister and because she was the organizer. They thought she was a proper person. And looking around her now, at Flint and Lol, Ana suddenly remembered that she *was* a real person, a person whose psychological stature finally matched her physical stature. They looked at her expectantly. 'We're just waiting for a couple more people and then we can get started. Did you all get here all right?'

Zander and Dr Chan arrived a minute later, Zander looking very smart in chinos and a black button-down shirt. And then finally Ed arrived, looking flustered and with a small shred of tissue clinging to a shaving nick on his chin. He smiled grimly at Ana and Flint and looked hideously uncomfortable.

Father Anthony cleared his throat and began the blessing.

'Well,' he started, 'I have to say that I have never before performed a memorial service so shortly after a funeral, but I understand that there were those among you who were unaware of Bee's passing, or unable to attend for other reasons. I think that the old cliché of "better late than never" is quite apt in this situation, because it really never is too late to celebrate the life of someone who has touched us, in whatever way. I see amongst you friends and family. Also here are neighbours, business associates and admirers. You are a wide and disparate cross section of people, but you all have one thing in common. The departed touched you in some way during her short life, and in a way that has changed you profoundly and for ever. I understand from Ana that Bee's life was sometimes tragic and often very lonely. That she still managed to exert such positivity on those around her is a testament to her vibrant personality and her love of people. Let us say a prayer now for Bee and ask for God's help in providing her with an afterlife that makes up for the shortcomings of her earthly life. May God bless her soul . . .'

Father Anthony made the sign of the cross. 'Now,' he said, 'Ana has asked to say a few words about her sister, not about her life which, as I have already said, was not always a happy passage through time, but about her. But first, I am sure that there are others who would like the opportunity to say something. Please feel free to say whatever you wish. Anyone?' He looked round the guests encouragingly. 'Ah, good,' he said, as someone moved towards him. It was Stuart, shuffling nervously towards the head of the grave clutching a piece of paper. He cleared his throat.

'I wasn't sure whether I was going to read this or not, after I wrote it. It's very sentimental and it'll make me look a right wimp. But anyway, here goes.' He grinned and cleared his throat again. 'I was fifteen years old the first time I saw Bee. She was performing "Groovin' for London" on *Top of the Pops*. I have to admit that it was love at first sight.' He smiled apologetically at his wife and everyone sniggered a bit. 'She had so much energy and so much bare-faced confidence in front of the camera. I was a shy kid back then. I didn't have many friends and Bee just seemed to me to be everything that I wasn't. And she was also stunningly beautiful and wearing a very short skirt, which didn't hurt.' He grinned again.

'I became a huge fan. Used to follow her wherever she went. And then one day she came over to me at a record-shop signing and she said, "You again?", and I nearly fell over. I started stuttering and shaking and I must have been the colour of a beetroot. "I'm a really big fan," I said. And I thought she'd just shrug it off because she was used to that sort of thing, but I remember she looked really pleased. And then she turned round to her body-guard' – he smiled and turned towards Flint – 'this guy here, in fact. And asked him to take my address so that she could send me some signed photos. So I gave it to him and never thought I'd hear another thing. Then three days later this *huge* parcel turns up at my house. I opened it, and it was just full of stuff. A T-shirt, picture disc, about twenty signed photos, pens, rubbers, stickers. Just – everything. And a handwritten note from Bee saying that she'd look out for me in future and that if I ever wanted anything I should just write to her via her manage-ment company and she'd see what she could do. I mean – can you imagine? There's me, a spotty, unconfident fifteen-year-old, and this beautiful, famous popstar has taken the time and trouble to get in touch.' He shook his head, his face displaying his disbelief, fifteen years later.

'I met Bee quite a few times over the course of that year or so and she was never anything but gracious, charming, warm and generous. And then, of course, her father became ill and she dropped out of the music business. I grew up, too, and my spots went away and I developed other interests. But she was a really important part of my youth. Knowing that I knew her, that I was accepted by her, changed me radically as a person. So when I bought my first PC, a few years ago, I pulled all my old Bee Bearhorn memorabilia from the loft, and for a few weeks I was obsessed again, as I went through all this stuff. And out of all that old paper, all those old memories, came the Bee Bearhorn website. It was really just for me. I didn't think anyone else would have much interest. But here you all are. It's nice to know that I'm not the only sad old loser out there.' He smiled and turned the paper over.

'I hadn't really thought much about Bee over the past few years. But when Ana got in touch last week and told me about Bee – I cried. I can't believe I'm telling you all that. But I did. And it was completely unexpected. And I think it's because when Bee died, a little part of me went with her. Because she was the only person who made me feel like anything when I was an awkward adolescent. And for that, for me, she will for ever be, unforgettable. May her soul rest in peace.' He bowed his head and refolded his paper and shuffled back to his wife, who squeezed his hand reassuringly.

Father Anthony looked round for another volunteer, and smiled when he saw Zander wheeling himself towards him.

He eyed the group confidently and began reading. 'Hi. My name is Zander. And I'm Bee's secret . . .'

Ana put her hand to her face in horror and went to step towards Zander, but Flint held her back. 'It's fine,' he whispered, 'it's fine.'

'I'm Bee's secret friend. My family were killed in a car crash in 1986. The same car crash which injured me and put me in this chair. Bee read about my plight in the papers, and for years she followed my progress. Secretly. When I was ten she started sending me postal orders for large sums of money at Christmas. And I never knew who they were from. And then, one day, in 1997, this woman

424

turned up at the home where I've lived for the last sixteen years. She was very small and very pretty and she told me she was my aunt. I knew she wasn't my aunt, but they're quite strict at my home about people from the outside having access to us. So she made up this stupid story. Apparently, she even managed to come up with some kind of paperwork to prove it. I don't know to this day how she managed it. But I did know that I liked her, instantly. That she was different. That she was refreshing. That she was on my wavelength. And that was a novelty for me because I'd never met anyone on my wavelength before. So eventually I got the truth out of her . . .'

Ana tensed.

'. . . and it emerged that her life had been very empty since she lost her precious father to AIDS in 1988. She'd never quite found the enthusiasm to resume her career. She'd taken a lot of knocks and her confidence had been eroded. She had all this money so she never really needed to test herself, to see what else life could offer her. So I became Bee's project. She came to visit every weekend and we'd go out for walks if it was fine or just sit in my room watching telly together if it was raining. I loved watching telly with Bee. She was such a bitch. We'd just sit there and pick everyone to pieces, talk about their hair or their accents or how stupid they were. I know that's not very Christian,' he looked at Father Anthony, 'but it was fun. And I'd never really had fun before. Not that sort of fun, anyway. I much prefer to talk. And then, after a few months of these visits, Bee did something incredible for me. She bought us a house. A little house, by the sea. And every weekend, she would leave London behind her,

her friends and her social life, and she'd drive down to the coast and hang out with me. Me. An annoying little kid in a wheelchair. And it was great. We'd cook together. And listen to music. I wasn't really that into music before I met Bee, but she really turned me around on that one. She'd bring three videos with her every week – always a comedy, a thriller and an action film. And we'd chat and laugh. Make up names for all the numbskulls in the village. Spy on the neighbours with our binoculars and take the piss out of them. I got her into bird-watching and board games. She got me into trainers and Teenage Fanclub. And she treated me like the most normal person in the universe. That was what was so special about my times with Bee. I felt normal. And special. Abnormally special. But especially normal. She gave me the self-confidence I'd been pretending I already had for the thirteen years before I met her. She broke down all my façades and replaced them with something substantial. And I know that I'll never meet anyone like Bee again as long as I live and that makes me feel very, very sad. I'm just really glad I knew her at all. There was a song on the radio this morning, a Janet Jackson song called "Together Again". It was all about someone being dead and how that person lived on through other people's smiles and in the stars and such. I just have to say at this point and in order to maintain any semblance of cool, that I really don't like Janet Jackson. But to Ms Jackson's credit, it was a truly joyous song and it was really comforting to me, to think of Bee being everywhere, to think of Bee being a star shining down on me. Bee was always more of a force than a person anyway. Thank you.' He smirked and tucked his paper in his pocket and bowed his head before wheeling himself back to Dr Chan, who smiled at him affectionately.

'Er – thank you, too, Zander,' said Father Anthony with a hint of confusion in his voice. 'So. Anyone else?' But no one came forward. He caught Ana's eye and beckoned her. Ana took a deep breath and pulled a tightly folded piece of paper from her bag. She smoothed it out with sweaty fingers.

'Bee,' she began, 'was my sister. But Bee was a stranger. I have only come to know Bee in the past fortnight – through the people here today. Through your stories and your emotions. To me, Bee was a mirage, but to you she was real, and I now know that to all of us she was a mystery. I have experienced every possible emotion getting to know Bee over the past weeks. Joy on finding the same records in her collection as I have in mine. Confusion on finding her life devoid of emotional depth. Deep and instantaneous love on meeting her closest friends. Sadness on learning of the tragedy and pain in her life, which she shared with no one. Pride on encountering the love and loyalty she inspired in others. And shame on finding that she was so much more than I'd allowed myself to imagine her to be.

'Bee was not a straightforward woman. Bee was not an *easy* woman. Bee was a dichotomy. She was sweet and sour. Happy and sad. Good and bad. High and low. Nasty and nice. She could bring the best out of people and inspire them. But she could also intimidate and crush. She was loyal to her friends but indifferent to her family. She could take a huge interest in a person and then forget their birthday. She was private. She was self-sufficient. She was independent. But she was closed. And guarded. And dismissive. She made mistakes. And went far out of her way to pay for them. She was beautiful. But she depended on more than beauty to make her way through life. She was unattainable and she was distant, but she was emotional and giving. She was an inspiration and a disappointment. She was everything and nothing.

'But Bee,' she continued, 'was Bee. And just being Bee was enough, because Bee was special and Bee was unforgettable. Bee was my sister . . . God bless her soul.'

She cleared her throat, refolded the damp piece of paper and edged her way back to Flint, keeping her eyes to the ground. Flint immediately put an arm around her shoulder. She felt another hand squeeze her arm, and when she looked up, she saw Lol, smiling crookedly at her with big tears plopping off the end of her nose. 'That was beautiful,' she mouthed, before launching herself at Ana and hugging the life out of her. Ana hugged her back and then felt tears dampening her own cheeks.

And then she felt Flint stiffen and grab her by the arm. 'Ana,' he whispered urgently, 'look.'

Ana unpeeled herself from Lol and wiped some tears from her cheeks. And as she turned, she jumped. Because, walking towards her, one arm supporting a large bouquet of white longi lilies and the other threaded through the arm of a joyful-looking Mr Redwood, was her mother.

43

She was wearing a grey tweed jacket with enormous silver buttons, a long black pleated skirt and a very smart grey felt hat, with a lily in it. She looked frail and very beautiful – like an old Hollywood movie star.

'Hello, darling,' she said smoothly, as she approached Ana. 'Hello, Clint.'

Ana stared at her in wonder.

'What?' said her mother with pursed lips.

'Nothing,' said Ana, 'nothing. I'm just . . . really glad you came.'

'Yes, well,' she said, fanning herself with a piece of paper, 'I won't be staying long. I really don't think I'll manage more than few minutes. I'm feeling very weak. But I think I will just say what I came to say and then we'll be on our way.'

Ana nodded numbly and made way for her mother to pass by. There was a long pause as Gay looked around her and then down at her paper and then around her again. Her eyes were filled with emotion, but her mouth was immobile. Until eventually she began to talk.

'I've been listening,' she said, 'from just over there.' She indicated the gravel path. 'Listening to you all talking and it's . . . well. It's been humbling. When you give birth to a child, you have so many hopes and ambitions for that child. But generally you're just happy if they follow convention and don't harm themselves or anyone else. For most parents that's the best they can hope for. But when Belinda came into this world, I took one look at her and I knew she was going to be different. I knew she was going to exceed my expectations. And she did. Not in any of the usual ways. She didn't excel at school. She didn't have any particular skills. But she exceeded my expectations just by being her. This vibrant, joyful, rude, noisy, colourful, unmanageable, irritating bundle of raw energy and ambition. And do you know why that pleased me so much? It pleased me because she was turning into the sort of person I'd always wanted to be myself. She was born without inhibitions. I was born with far too many. And I resented her, I'm ashamed to say. I resented the way she just took hold of the world with both hands and shook it and shook it and shook it' — Gay used her hands to demonstrate — 'until something fell out. I resented her independence. Her strength. And I tried to stifle those things. And eventually she had enough and she left home and went to live with her father. I'm afraid I didn't make the transition very easy for her, but then she didn't make it very easy for me either. That was always one of the greatest problems with Bee and I. So different in certain ways and so infuriatingly alike in others. On the rare occasions when we did see each other, we made very hard work out of it. It can't have been very pleasant for my late husband or for our daughter. But it seemed it was the only way we knew how to communicate. It was a terrible time for me. My eldest daughter was living out all my dreams and ambitions. She was famous. I used to watch her on the television and feel like my heart would burst with pride. But I was incapable of communicating that pride to Belinda. I'm not sure she ever really knew how terribly, terribly impressed I was by her. How in awe of her I often felt. I didn't really know how to cope with feelings like that for my daughter. For someone I'd created. So, instead of making her feel good about her success, I tried my hardest to make her feel bad about it.

'And then there was an incident, a long time ago. I'm afraid I behaved rather badly. Bee didn't forgive me. In retrospect, I can see why. And I never saw her again. And it's . . .' Gay stopped suddenly and clenched her face tight, holding in tears. 'And it's the worst feeling in the world knowing that now there's no way of saying sorry. So – here I am. Hoping that somehow my words will make it through that piece of marble and to my darling daughter. Who was always so much better than me. In every way. God bless you, Belinda. And I'm so sorry . . .'

She scrunched up her piece of paper and walked away abruptly towards Mr Redwood. Father Anthony wrapped up the proceedings. People laid their flowers at Bee's grave. Lol gave everyone directions to the pub. People started walking away. But Ana stayed glued to the spot, watching her mother, who was sobbing into Mr Redwood's handkerchief. Ana had never seen her mother cry before. She'd seen her threaten to cry and pretend to cry and sniff dramatically into tissues, but never actually, really cry.

'D'you mind waiting in the car for me?' she said to Flint.

He looked at Gay and then at Ana. 'Course not,' he said. He dropped a kiss on to the end of her nose and walked away. When Ana got to her mother, Amy was already there, chatting away to her.

'You're a very brave woman,' she was saying, clutching Gay's arm and smiling up into her face, 'agoraphobia is a terrible affliction. But I'm so, so glad you managed to overcome it for this occasion. So glad. Your daughter was a wonderful girl, Mrs Wills. So kind to me. So charming. One of the few people in this city I would have counted amongst my friends. And Ana is just a delight. Very different to her sister, but every bit as special. You've every right to be proud. Of both of them. Really . . .' She gave Gay's arm one last squeeze and Ana watched in wonderment as a small smile started to form on Gay's face. Not a smug smile, not a wicked smile, not a sly smile, not a fake smile – not any of the smiles in Gay's usual smile repertoire, in fact. But an embarrassed and slightly pleased smile.

'Thank you,' she heard Gay say, 'that's very kind of you. Now, if you'll excuse me, I'm feeling rather faint. I think I'm going to have to sit down.'

'Of course. Of course.' Amy smiled at Ana and made her way daintily towards the car park, Freddie trotting along behind her.

'Mum,' called Ana, as she started to turn away, 'wait. Just one minute. Hi, Mr Redwood.' She smiled at the slim, dapper man in his blue blazer and tan cords and he grinned at her.

'Hello there, Anabella. You're looking very well.'

Ana thanked him. 'I wondered if I could have a moment alone with my mother, please. If that's all right?'

Mr Redwood nodded effusively and grinned at them

both again before heading back towards his shiny Rover in the car park

Gay turned to Ana. She looked pale and was breathing very heavily. 'You've put on weight,' she said eyeing her up and down.

Ana rolled her eyes.

'It suits you,' she said, 'you look – nice.'

Ana nearly fainted. 'Er – thanks,' she managed.

'I really am going to have to sit down, Anabella. This has been a very traumatic day for me.'

'Well – let's walk then, towards the car. But I wanted to say a prayer first, with you. For Bee.' She indicated the grave with her eyes.

Gay looked at her suspiciously, then nodded imperceptibly. Ana held her arm while she lowered herself to her knees, and for a moment the two women knelt in silence with their heads bowed. A dog barked somewhere in the distance and a breeze ruffled the thick foliage of an elm tree. Ana thought about holding her mother's hand, or putting an arm around her bony shoulders. But every time she went to do it, she remembered her mother's face the day they'd found out about Bee, and the way she'd slapped away her hand. So she didn't, and after a minute or two, they both got to their feet and started heading back towards the car with three feet of space between them.

'I'm glad you came, Mum.'

Gay nodded. 'Yes,' she said brusquely, 'so am I. It's good to close things properly. Isn't it?'

'How did you manage it?'

'Well – I suppose I, er ... *psyched* myself up, as they

433

say. And Mr Redwood's been marvellous. In fact' – she stopped and turned to look Ana in the eye – 'Mr Redwood has proposed to me.'

Ana stared at her mother incredulously. 'What!'

'Mr Redwood. He proposed to me. A few evenings ago.'

'And you said . . . ?'

'Well – being a widow doesn't really suit me, you know. I'm not the type to enjoy being alone. And now that you've finally come out of yourself, started making something of your life – well, I can't expect you to sit around with me for the rest of your life. And Mr Redwood really is a kind and caring man and . . .'

Ana turned to her mother and grinned. 'You said yes, didn't you!'

Her mother pinkened very slightly and nodded. Ana screamed and then put her hand over her mouth when she remembered she was in a graveyard. She almost threw her arms around her mother, too, and then remembered that her mother would probably die of shock if she did. So she just stood there and beamed at her instead. 'I think that's fantastic,' she said. 'Really, really fantastic.'

'Well,' sighed her mother, 'it's not the most romantic of comings-together – more of a collaboration really. But I think it's for the best.'

'You will – you will be *nice* to him, won't you, Mum?'

'What on earth do you mean?'

'I mean – you'll appreciate him. Tell him he's good. Tell him he's kind. Tell him you're glad you married him. Won't you?'

'I have no idea what you're talking about, Anabella. I

shall treat Mr Redwood with every respect. The same respect he shows me.'

Ana beamed at her and Gay allowed a smile to slip across her face.

'So,' she said, 'what of you? What are your plans for the future?'

Ana shrugged. 'D'you know? – I have no idea. None at all. I'm going to have to move out of the house I'm staying in next week. Gill's got a long-term tenant moving in at the weekend. I'll find another flat. Or I might stay with Flint . . . I've really been too busy to think about it.'

Gays pursed her lips. 'This Flint fellow. Was he a lover of Bee's?'

Ana giggled. 'What?'

'You know what I mean.'

'Well – actually, yes. They did sleep together once. A long time ago. But he's *my lover* now,' she said.

She waited for her mother's shocked reaction, but it didn't come. 'Yes,' she said dryly, 'Hugh did tell me he suspected there was something going on with you two. Well. I'm glad. I like the look of him. And he's a big man. I've always liked a big man. They make you feel very protected. And they tend towards gentleness.'

They were approaching Mr Redwood's car now and Ana sped up. 'Mr Redwood,' she gushed, 'Mum's just told me the news and I think it's *wonderful*. I think you're completely insane, but it's still wonderful. Congratulations!'

Mr Redwood's neat face opened up into a massive grin. 'Well – I can't tell you how happy I am to have your approval, Anabella. That really does mean an awful lot to me.' He pulled himself nimbly from the car and gave Ana a strong, very un-English bearhug.

'Welcome to the family, Mr Redwood. And at least I know that you know exactly what you're letting yourself in for.'

He beamed at Gay. 'Oh yes,' he said, 'I most certainly do.'

'Now,' said Gay, ignoring Mr Redwood's affectionate overtures, 'I've brought you some things. Clothes. Books. Records. Etcetera. I thought you'd probably like to have them with you.'

Mr Redwood leapt to attention and unlocked the boot of his car.

'And there's this, too.' Gay handed Ana a large manila envelope. 'It's a letter. To you. From Bee. I'm afraid I, er . . . well – I should have given it to you before. I'm not really very sure why I didn't. It's not something I'm very proud of. Maybe you should save it for later – save it for a quiet moment. Urgh . . .' She put her hand to her forehead and drew a deep breath. 'Now I really, really must be going. I really am feeling rather . . . urgh.'

Mr Redwood dashed from the back of the car to the front and opened the passenger door for Gay, who collapsed daintily on to the seat.

Ana called Flint and Keith over to help Mr Redwood transfer her boxes from the back of his car to Flint's and then Gay said goodbye.

'You will keep in touch, won't you? Things will be much easier now that I've got Mr Redwood. He can answer the phone for me . . .'

'Or you could answer the phone for yourself?'

'Well. One thing at a time, Anabella. One thing at a time. And thank you for this, by the way. For organizing this. I think it's been a very good thing.' She smiled tightly and Ana smiled back at her.

'Me too, Mum, me too.' She kissed Gay lightly on one cheek and closed the door on her.

'Oh, Clint,' said Gay, suddenly winding down the window and beckoning at him. 'I wanted to apologize for last week. For your hand. I'm terribly sorry. It was most unnecessary and really rather vulgar. I'm most embarrassed.'

Flint shrugged it off and waved a nearly healed palm at her, and then Mr Redwood and Gay reversed from their parking space and drove away.

Ana turned to Flint as the car disappeared from view. 'Thank you,' she said.

'What for?'

'For that. For what you did with Mum. She wouldn't have come otherwise.'

'Yeah she would,' he said, enveloping her in a hug.

'She wouldn't,' she insisted, wrapping her arms around his huge torso, 'and you are wonderful.' She tipped her head up towards his and smiled as his lips touched hers.

'Come on, you two – enough of all that,' said Lol, twirling a shawl over her shoulders as the sun started disappearing behind the trees, 'we've got a party to go to!'

44

'Hi there, everybody. Hope you're all enjoying this very special soirée. My name is Lolita Tate and these other guys' — she indicated the musicians behind her — 'are just some weird old blokes who can play instruments. This bloke' — she pointed at Keith — 'is the world's greatest living tambourinist. And also, I am very happy to say, my lover. And we'll be your band for tonight. We're happy to do requests, so feel free to offer suggestions. We're also very happy to accept guest musicians during the course of the evening, so if anyone thinks they can do any better than us, just let us know. OK, boys — take it away.' The drummer tapped his cymbal three times and then the band launched into a fantastic version of 'Born to Run'.

Ana turned to Flint and smiled. 'Can you dance?' she asked.

He grimaced. 'Not even slightly,' he said.

'Good,' she said, 'neither can I.'

They both leaned back against the wall and watched the party. Flint had his arm around her shoulder and she drew his fist towards her and kissed his knuckles. There were about thirty people in the room. A lot of the 'fans' had stuck around, having originally said they were only going to stay for one drink. Amy was still here and was now dancing with one of Keith's friends, who looked as if he was thoroughly enjoying himself. Ed had left immediately after the service at the cemetery, his eyes looking slightly red but with a sense of relief about him that it was finally over. And Dr Chan had told Zander about a dozen times that they had to leave but he was still here, drinking a warm shandy and sneaking puffs on other people's cigarettes when Dr Chan wasn't looking.

Lol's voice was absolutely incredible. Ana had never heard her singing live before, only on tape, and shivers ran down her spine just listening to her. And the band was brilliant. Ana had no idea that Lol was going to put together such a professional outfit for her. Saxophones, trumpets, electric, acoustic and twelve-string guitars. The band was almost bigger than the party.

Flint and Ana held each other tight and watched the band, swaying around a bit, both with matching stupid grins on their faces, chatting every now and then. A still-dancing Amy tottered towards them, grinning from ear to ear.

'Oh Ana,' she said, 'Bee would have loved this, you know. It's been a marvellous day. Absolutely marvellous. Now. There was something I needed to ask you. And I know that now's probably not the best of times, I know how busy you young people are, but I needed to ask you – about John. Not that I'm not thoroughly enjoying his company. I am. But dear Freddie has some, er . . . objections to his presence. And I wondered if you might give some thought to alternative arrangements for the dear creature . . .'

Ana looked at Flint.

He smiled at her. 'I'll have him,' he said, easily.

Amy clapped her hands with delight.

'Really?' said Ana, 'are you sure?'

'Yeah,' he said, why not? I've always wanted a pet. And he can catch spiders for me.'

'You're scared of spiders?'

'Uh-huh. Terrified . . .' He addressed Amy. 'How's about I pop round tomorrow and pick him up?'

But before Amy could answer there was a lull in their conversation, just in time for them to hear Lol say, 'We have a singing virgin in the house, a certain young lady who tells me she thinks she can sing but she's not sure because she's never sung in front of anyone before. Well, singing runs in her family so I'm convinced she'll be great. Ana – where are you?'

And before she could do anything about it, half a dozen pairs of hands, including Flint's, had bundled her up on to the stage, and six seconds later she was standing over the microphone shielding her eyes from the glare of a spotlight that she hadn't even realized was there until that moment.

'Give her a huge round of applause, everyone.'

Ana looked blindly into the crowd. Thirty-odd people suddenly looked like three hundred. A two-foot rostrum suddenly felt like a vast Wembley-esque stage. Expectant faces beamed up at her and she didn't recognize any of them. She tried discreetly to get off the stage, but hands kept appearing from everywhere to push her back on. She turned round to Lol. 'I can't,' she mouthed.

'Yes you bloody well can,' she replied, turning her back towards the microphone.

'But I don't know what to sing.'

'What's your favourite shower song?'

'My what?'

'What do you sing in the shower?'

'God. I dunno. Loads of different things.'

'Well. Pick one. Tell the band what it is. And then sing it. You can sing it backwards if you like.'

'Backwards?'

'Yes. Facing away.'

'Oh God. This is horrible Lol.'

'Yeah. It is. At first. But once you get going, you'll be addicted. I promise you. Now. What d'you want to sing?'

'God. I dunno.' She bit her lip and looked at Lol, desperately. Every fibre of her being was telling her to get off the stage. Now. Every brain cell she possessed was shouting at her to get off immediately before she made a gigantic tit of herself. But then a little voice started talking to her. The little voice who remembered all those nights she'd lain in bed fantasizing about a moment like this, wondering if she'd be up to it, dreaming about having the sort of life where she'd even be asked to do this in the first place. And here she was, finally, at the ripe old age of twenty-five, being given the opportunity to sing anything she liked with a band of professional musicians in front of a friendly crowd at her sister's wake. She took a deep breath and said the first thing that came into her head. 'What about . . . "Time Will Pass You By"?'

'What?'

'Tobi Legend.'

'Who?'

'Northern Soul classic.'

'Never heard of it.' She turned to consult with the band. 'OK,' she said, turning back to Ana, '*they* have. You're on.'

She winked at her and suddenly the drummer was tapping out the rhythm and suddenly the intro was playing and suddenly Ana was facing the crowd and suddenly she was singing. Fuck. How had that happened? She was singing. She was breathless at first, her voice slightly weak and quavery, but within the first few bars she was just . . . singing. In front of people. She didn't look at them as she sang. She looked at the dartboard. She looked at a poster on the wall for a pub quiz. And all the notes came out properly. And she even started dancing a bit. And half-way through the song she actually forgot she was singing in public and just concentrated on getting the full meaning of the song from her soul to her lungs and to her lips. All she was aware of was the lyrics and how apt they were and how much she wished Bee could have been out there listening to them . . . and then suddenly she was bowing and it was over and everyone in the room was going mental. A huge smile split her face in two and Lol grabbed her and hugged her and Flint leapt on to the stage and buried her in a bearhug and held her face in his hands and kissed her on the lips. Her heart raced with adrenaline and her face was flushed with heat and excitement. Oh my God. She'd done it. After all those years of fantasizing. All those years of dreaming. She'd got up on stage in front of people and she'd sung. And it was *brilliant*. One of the best feelings she'd ever experienced. She beamed at the crowd, who all cheered her on. She turned to Lol. 'What about a duet?' she whispered.

Lol nodded and hugged her again. '"Suspicious Minds"?' she said.

Ana nodded enthusiastically.

The band started up again and the two of them launched into the song, Ana providing the harmonies. This time it was even more enjoyable and by the time the song finished and the crowd started shouting again, Ana was ready to spend the rest of the night on the stage. 'Am I all right?' she whispered to Lol.

'Ana, my love, you are much more than all right. You are fucking fantastic. Now sing something else. Quick. The crowd is getting restless.'

Ana turned and faced the audience. She smiled. They cheered. This was fun. And as she looked around the faces in the crowd, she spotted a beaming Zander, his hands held above his head, clapping loudly and whistling, and it suddenly occurred to her that he was probably the bravest person she'd ever met. This party was for Bee, but Zander deserved a moment in the spotlight. Because he was here. At a party to celebrate the life of a woman who'd taken everything away from him. And then she remembered something. 'A Song for Zander'. She'd finally put some music to it, last week. She'd been intending to ask Lol if she'd be able to get it recorded for him and she had been going to send him the tape, in St Andrews. But now . . . well, now was just perfect.

She leaned down and asked Flint to pass her her bag. And then she asked a big guy with a beard if she could borrow his guitar. She looped the guitar around her neck and strummed it quietly, getting used to the feel of it after so many weeks without practising.

'Erm. This is a song. This is a really, really special song. Because Bee wrote it. And no, it's not "Space Girl" and it's not "Honey Bee"' – there was some muted sniggering 'but it's a song I found in her flat when I cleared it out last month. These are Bee's lyrics. I just added a simple tune. And it's called "A Song for Zander".'

Tears started catching at the back of her throat as she sang and for a brief second she felt something powerful entering her – an external force. And for a brief second it was as if it wasn't *her* singing any more, as if it was somebody else, and as her eyes found Zander's again a jolt shot through her and she saw it hit him too, and it felt like Bee.

She handed the guitar back to the beardy guy when she finished and leaned into the microphone.

'It's somebody else's turn now,' she said, and then she clambered down from the rostrum.

'Ana,' said Flint, clasping her immediately, 'that was . . . Jesus . . . that was just fucking brilliant. *You're* just fucking brilliant.' He squeezed her tight and kissed her and then other people came up to her and they all had the same look in their eyes. Respect.

Zander wheeled himself towards Flint and Ana. 'Well,' he said, 'that was officially the best moment of my life. That was beyond and above everything. That was better than getting my A level results, better than Napster, better than anything. Ever. Thank you, Ana.' He clasped her hands in his and she leaned down and kissed him and he whispered in her ear. 'Did Bee *really* write that? Or were you, you know, just saying that for effect? You can tell me. I won't tell anyone.'

'Bee wrote it, Zander. I promise. I'll send you the lyrics, if you like.'

'Bee really wrote that song? About me?'

'Uh-huh.'

'Fuck me.'

Dr Chan appeared at Zander's shoulder. 'OK. You've had an extra hour and now you've had a song written and performed in your honour. It's time for Cinderella to go home.'

Zander sighed and shrugged. 'Looks like my time is up. My carriage awaits. I have to go. Thanks for such a great day. It's been really – well, you know. It's just been brilliant. I know that's a weird thing to say about a funeral, but you know what I mean. I think we all really needed this, Ana. Thank you so much for organizing it.'

'You are incredibly welcome.'

'By the way, I've spoken to my solicitor about that will. Apparently it's kosher. It's legal. Obviously it all needs to be finalized, and I can't help thinking that your mother will have something to say about it. But in the mean time, I'd really like it if you treated the cottage like your own. I'll be living there in the holidays, but it'll be empty most of the time. I'd really like it if you used it. And the bike' – he looked at Ana – 'I really want you to have the bike. I obviously won't have much use for it. And I think it would really suit you . . .' He grinned at her.

As Flint carried Zander down the stairs to the ground level and helped Dr Chan get him into the ambulance, amongst more promises to keep in touch and come up and see him in St Andrews, Zander pulled Ana towards him urgently and whispered in her ear.

'I felt it. When you were singing. I felt Bee.'

She nodded at him knowingly and he kissed her hard

on the cheek. 'Thank you,' he whispered. And then Dr Chan closed the door, climbed into the driver's seat and the ambulance disappeared into the dark.

Flint and Ana ordered a cab at eleven. They wobbled drunkenly down the stairs when it arrived and were about to get in when Ana remembered something.

'Oh,' she said, 'my stuff. That Mum brought. It's still in the back of your car.'

'We can pick it up tomorrow,' said Flint. 'Don't worry about it.'

'No, but Bee's stuff. Mum said there was a letter in there. From Bee. To me. I want to see it.'

'OK,' said Flint and handed her his car keys.

Ana made her way unsteadily towards the car and pulled open the boot. She peered inside and then pulled out the manila envelope. She opened it, but in the muted tangerine streetlights she couldn't see a thing. Just a wodge of paper. She locked the boot and weaved back to the waiting cab where she angled the letter closer to the light.

'What does it say?' said Flint.

'God,' she said, 'I dunno. It's really hard to tell in this light. I'll look at it when we get back to yours.'

She slid the paper back into the envelope, slipped it into her bag and snuggled into Flint's shoulder as the cab bore them homewards through the empty streets of North London.

It was still warm outside when they got back and neither of them was even slightly tired, so they decided to crack another beer and sit in the garden for a while. Flint wedged a CD-player under the back window and put on a Green Day album and Ana draped herself over his lap in the old brown armchair. The moon over the railway line was a perfect half-moon. They sat in silence for a while, breathing in the fading scent of summer and listening to the distant city noises. Someone having a party up the road opened a window and the bangbangbang of the Chemical Brothers ate into their own music.

'God,' said Flint, 'it's never just quiet, is it? Not even at this time of night.'

'Silence isn't all it's cracked up to be,' said Ana. 'That was one of the things I hated most about Torrington. The silence. It was, like, I knew there was this whole world out there, all this life to be lived. But nobody was sending me any smoke signals. D'you see?'

'So, I take it you're not going back then?'

Ana snorted. 'No way,' she said. 'And now I don't even have to think about it, thanks to the lovely Mr Redwood taking my mother off my hands. But I don't think I was ever supposed to have been there in the first place, really. Like Bee. A fish out of water. From the second day I was in London I already knew it was right for me. And then I met you . . .'

'Ye-es . . .'

'And then I met you and suddenly I had the best reason in the world to stay here.' She turned around and kissed him on the cheek and she loved that she didn't have to feel insecure about saying things like that to Flint.

'What are you going to do about your flat? About moving out of Gill's?'

'I dunno,' she took a slurp of beer, 'find a flatshare. Or something.'

'You know you're welcome to stay here? With me?'

'Oh. You don't want me hanging around here. Surely. I'd be cramping your style. Mr Confirmed Bachelor.'

'No. I mean it. Honestly. Just temporary. Obviously. I mean, you're only young, too young to make any lasting decisions just yet. But I'd rather you stayed here for a while than just rushed into the first flatshare you came across. And besides, you've got to get a job first, haven't you?'

She shuddered. 'Urgh, God. Don't remind me.'

'You know you can do anything you like, don't you?'

'Yeah – right.'

'No. Really. Don't just settle for any old thing. Take a leaf out of Bee's book. Follow your dreams. Look how far you've come just in a fortnight. Give yourself some time and I reckon you'll conquer the world. What would you like to do? In an ideal world?'

Ana thought for a moment. In an ideal world. In *this* world. What would she like to do? 'Soundtracks,' she said in a flash of inspiration. 'I'd like to be the person who does the soundtracks for films.'

'You mean a composer?'

'No – the one who chooses the songs to go with the scenes. Like "Stuck in the Middle with You" in *Reservoir Dogs*. Inspired.'

She laughed and nestled her head into Flint's shoulder. They sat for a while in silence and absorbed the atmosphere.

'Did you ever use to think that Bee was destined to die young?' she asked.

Flint thought for a moment. 'Yeah,' he said, 'I suppose in a way, I did. Not consciously and not the way she went, obviously. But she always had this air about her of someone who was just passing through.'

'D'you ever think . . . ?' began Ana.

'What?'

'Well – this might sound a bit *callous*. But d'you ever think that Bee . . . ?'

'Yes,' said Flint, 'all the time.'

'But you don't know what I was going to say.'

'Yes I do.'

'Go on then. What was I going to say?'

'You were going to say – do I ever think that Bee died so that you and I could meet?'

Ana looked at him in shock. 'Fuck,' she said.

'And the answer to that question is that yes, I do. I believe that everything happens for a reason. And I believe that you and I were destined to meet. Now. In these circumstances. Here. Tragic as it is.'

Ana turned slightly and planted a big kiss on Flint's forehead. And then she looked up at the sky. 'No stars,' she said, 'no stars at all.'

Flint looked upwards, too.

'I was thinking of what Zander said in his speech. You know, that Janet Jackson song? I was looking to see if I could see a star for Bee.'

The two of them craned their necks for a moment, scanning the navy sky for stars. And then they saw one. A big fat one. It was all alone. And it was twinkling at them. They both raised their beer cans to the solitary star.

And then they put down their beer cans, unfurled

themselves from the armchair and hand in hand they walked barefoot across the grass and into Flint's flat.

Ana awoke at five that morning, needing to go to the loo. As she passed the kitchen, a shaft of moonlight highlighted her handbag, and she suddenly remembered the manila envelope. She padded across the warm linoleum and pulled the envelope from her bag. It had one word written on it, in her mother's scratchy handwriting. 'Sorry.'

She pulled the letter from the envelope. It was mauve. It was the same paper that Bee had written her letter to Zander on. She looked at the date. It was a year ago, almost to the day. And then she started reading.

'Dearest Ana,' [it began]

'I never expected to have a sister . . .'

Acknowledgements

There were some hairy moments writing this book and I'd particularly like to thank Nic for the tears in Norfolk, Katy for not saying it was crap in Portugal and Yasmin for being extremely brave on the phone from Sydney.

A massive thank-you to everyone at Penguin for being uniformly brilliant, with especial thanks and love to Louise, Harrie and Jess. And of course, thanks as ever to the wonderful Jascha, my husband, best friend, keeper of my sanity and maker of many, many cups of tea. It's been a joy sharing my days with you and I'm going to miss you like hell when you decamp to your posh new offices in the West End. Please can I come and sit under your desk? I promise I'll be quiet . . .

But my greatest debt of gratitude is to two people in particular. To the splendid Sarah Bailey, who spent an entire day going through the manuscript with me when I was about to shred it and brought me back from the edge. Everyone knows that friends should be there for you – but helping you write a book isn't usually in the job description. My gratitude is boundless.

And equal thanks go to my agent, the marvellous Judith Murdoch, who spent a whole brainstorming day with me, inspiring and motivating me and reminding me of just exactly what the hell it was I was actually trying to do. What a completely great agent!